DISARMING DETECTIVE

BY
ELIZABETH HEITER

MILLS &
BOON

Published in Great Britain 2015
by Mills & Boon, an imprint of Harlequin (UK) Limited,
Eton House, 18-24 Paradise Road, Richmond, Surrey, TW9 1SR

© 2015 Elizabeth Heiter

ISBN: 978-0-263-25297-2

46-0215

Elizabeth Heiter likes her suspense to feature strong heroines, chilling villains, psychological twists and a little romance. Her research has taken her into the minds of serial killers, through murder investigations and onto the FBI Academy's shooting range. Elizabeth graduated from the University of Michigan with a degree in English literature. She's a member of International Thriller Writers and Romance Writers of America. Visit Elizabeth at elizabethheiter.com.

For Kathryn and Caroline.
I'm proud and lucky to call you sisters.
I love you!

Chapter One

The instant Isabella Cortez left the safety of the FBI building, goose bumps skittered across her skin and her senses went on high alert. Her instincts and training, like a sudden alarm shrieking inside her head, told her she wasn't alone.

The door slammed shut behind her before she could dart back inside, and Ella cursed the heavy briefcase weighing down one hand and the stack of file folders clenched in the other. Just because she was taking her first real vacation in two years didn't mean killers took time off, so her cases were coming with her. Assuming she made it to her vacation.

Tonight, she was the last one out of the bland office building in Aquia, Virginia. It was set back off the road, nestled deep in the woods, and manned by an armed guard. Entrance to the parking lot was supposed to be reserved for the FBI's Criminal Investigative Analysts who worked there and no one else. If a visitor was arriving, the guard at the gate called ahead. Anyone who could make it past security was a threat.

Pushing back her fear, she blinked, trying to adjust to the darkness outside. Her arms tensed, but she didn't drop the files and reach for her gun. Not yet. Not until she identified the threat. If she acted too soon, she'd probably get shot.

No, all the instincts honed by two years in the Behavioral Analysis Unit told her to let him think she was oblivious. Let him show himself before she brought him down.

Her heart thudded too fast, reminding Ella all too clearly of her first years in the FBI, in the gangs unit in Dallas, when she'd taken a bullet to the leg and her partner had taken two to the chest. At the memory, all the nerves in her leg burst to life, painful and fire-poker hot.

Lock it down, Cortez. Focus.

A tiny movement made her glance left, toward the only two cars in the lot. A bulky figure shifted beside her car, stepping into the dim glow of the overhead light.

He was big, taller than her by half a foot and outweighing her by a good fifty pounds and all of it muscle. But none of that mattered if she didn't let him get close.

Her eyes darted to his hands. Empty. She let out a breath, but it caught when she spotted the telltale bulge at his hip. No way was she giving him a chance to go for the weapon. She dropped her briefcase and files fast, yanking her Glock pistol from its holster. "Hands up!"

"Whoa!" He lifted his hands near his head. "Look, I—"

"Higher. Get on your knees."

"Hey, I didn't—"

"Now!" Ella took a step closer, let him see the dead seriousness in her eyes, the solid, steady aim of her gun. "Pull your weapon out with your left hand. Toss it over here."

"Crap." He complied, getting on his knees and sending his own Glock skidding across the pavement toward her.

"You have any other weapons on you?"

"No. Look, I'm a homicide detective. I flew up here from Florida to talk to a profiler."

She narrowed her eyes, noting the slight Southern drawl in his voice now that she wasn't laser-focused on containing him. "How'd you get in here?"

"The guard let me in. My badge is in my pocket, okay?"

Ella frowned. With the regular guard on maternity leave, maybe the newbie had broken protocol. "Fine. Toss it to me with your wallet."

He let out a breath through his nose, something like amusement in his voice. "Wow, you're thorough."

He was right about that. At the BAU, her job was to create criminal personality profiles of the country's most depraved killers. Every day, her work told her what one inattentive moment, one second of blind trust, could cost.

It was a lesson she'd first learned nearly ten years ago, when her best friend had been violently attacked. It had introduced Ella to a kind of evil she'd never known existed, and completely altered the path of her life. Now, viewing everyone as a potential threat seemed almost normal.

He tossed his wallet and badge over, but even before she picked it up, she knew it was the real thing. Still keeping her weapon leveled on him—mostly for scaring the crap out of her and making her dump her case files all over the ground—she flipped open the wallet to his ID. The face staring back at her, with its hard lines and no-nonsense stare, looked every bit a homicide detective. "Logan Greer. Oakville, Florida."

Reholstering her weapon underneath her blazer, she tossed the wallet back and tried to slow her heart rate to normal speed. "Way to make an impression, Greer."

He gave her a smile full of self-deprecating humor that

made her realize again that the bulky size that had un-
nerved her in the darkness was impressive muscle tone,
that beneath the piercing stare were moss green eyes. She
was a sucker for green eyes. Too bad she hadn't run into
him on the beach next week with a margarita in her hand
instead of on her last day before vacation, toting a gun.

As he gathered his badge and weapon, Logan asked,
"And you are…?"

Ella brushed her bangs out of her eyes and extended
her hand. "Special Agent Ella Cortez, BAU."

"Perfect," Logan said, giving her another hit of that
one-sided grin as he took his time shaking her hand.
"Because I need a profiler to look at my homicide case."

Ella pulled her hand free and collected the files scattered on the pavement. "You're gonna have to go through
channels."

"I did that." When she started to walk past him, he
put a hand on her arm. "Please. Look, they wouldn't assign anyone to it."

Ella sighed, frustration warring with sympathy. He'd
flown here for help and she knew if her boss had already
refused, he would get shut down again. Getting a profiler
assigned meant that the case needed one. The most likely
reason Logan hadn't gotten help was because he had a
case where the killer would logically come up without
resorting to a profile.

She couldn't take this on even if she weren't about to
leave on vacation. Even if she were allowed to pick her
own cases. She already had more files stacked up than
she could possibly handle with the attention they needed
in her regular ten-hour days.

"Sorry." Ella didn't look at him as she dumped her
briefcase and files in the trunk of her car.

"How is your office supposed to know whether I have

a serial killer from a one page form?" There was frustration in Logan's voice, but steel underneath. "I'll wait as long as I have to, but I need help on this."

"I'm the last one out. Everyone else has already gone home."

He stepped around in front of her, leaning against her car between her and the driver's door, his arms crossed loosely over his chest. "I'll wait here until tomorrow if I have to. But wouldn't it be easier for everyone if you took a look? Please, just hear me out. An hour of your time. That's all I'm asking. Just take a look at my case file. Give me *something* I can take home and use, before the bodies start piling up."

When she heaved out a sigh and looked up, he shot her a determined stare, as if he could get her to agree through force of will alone. She stared back into his imploring green eyes, which were close enough that she could see little flecks of gold around the edges of his irises.

She didn't have time for this. And she needed to get away from case file after case file of vicious murders. She needed those two weeks at the beach with her two best friends, while they all tried to distract themselves from the anniversary coming up too fast, the one they all wanted to forget.

She needed to have dinner, then pack and make her way to the airport. Of course, three weeks of late nights trying to get ahead of work before taking time off meant her refrigerator was stocked only with condiments. She looked into Logan Greer's green eyes and heard herself say, "Tell you what. You can buy me dinner and while we eat, I'll look at your case."

The genuinely grateful smile he flashed her sent unexpected shivers of awareness over her skin that reminded her she hadn't had a date in months. Another casualty of the job.

Wow, she *really* needed this vacation.

"Ten o'clock is a little late for dinner. Is the FBI opposed to meal breaks?" Logan asked, one eyebrow quirked, as she scarfed down French fries as if she hadn't seen food in weeks.

In the light of the little diner, which Ella frequented because it reminded her of something she'd find back home in Indiana, Logan looked a lot less like a potential threat and a lot more like the kind of guy she'd try to flirt with in the grocery store. The kind of guy she'd be tempted to chase after, no matter how it would inevitably end.

Wearing jeans and a faded gray T-shirt, with a five-o'clock shadow heavy on his chin, he looked exactly like her type. Laid-back attitude, but intensity in his eyes. Masculine, but judging by the easy way he was teasing her half an hour after she pulled her gun on him, secure enough not to find her intimidating.

Of course, that was her initial read on him. Given that her longest relationship in the past had lasted a whole five months, she'd decided she was far better at profiling murderers than potential dates. Not that Logan Greer was a potential for anything except being easy on the eyes while she helped him with his case.

"You're the one who showed up late at night expecting someone to be there."

"I came straight from the airport. And you weren't the first profiler I harassed in the parking lot. You're just the first one who succumbed to my charm."

Ella snorted. The agent out the door before her had been Jack Reid, perpetually in a foul mood and perpetually using a foul mouth. "You mean Jack didn't invite you out to dinner?"

"Well, he invited me to do something. But it sounded anatomically impossible."

"Probably a come-on," Ella joked, then feigned hurt as she stuffed another fry, heavily coated with ketchup, in her mouth. "So, you're telling me I wasn't your first choice?"

Logan's gaze shifted appreciatively over her, lingering on her mouth. Then he gave her steady eye contact, let her see an interest that went beyond the case. "Believe me, if I'd known *you* were coming, I would have waited."

Ella rolled her eyes, even as she willed her cheeks not to heat. This never happened to her, this instant, powerful lure to a man she'd just met, let alone to one she'd just pulled a gun on. "I was trying to get caught up on some work before I left town." She held out a hand, palm up. Back to business. "You have a case file?"

He set a thin manila folder in her palm, his big calloused hand brushing hers. "Where are you going?"

"Vacation with some friends. I plan to sit on the beach and do nothing more strenuous than put on sunscreen." Of course, that would last about a day and then she'd be searching for kayak rentals or somewhere to take surfing lessons. Sitting still wasn't her strong suit.

"I don't suppose you're coming to Florida? Because I'm willing to help you out with the sunscreen."

One of the cases in the trunk of her car—the only one she hadn't actually been assigned—was from Florida. No, she and her two best friends were heading as far from Florida as possible. "California, actually."

"Too bad. Other than the recent murder, Oakville is a pretty nice place to visit."

Ella blinked, so surprised to hear real disappointment

in his tone that she almost missed the part about the case. "Wait a minute. Murder? Not murders?" No wonder her boss hadn't assigned an agent to create a profile. Well, this was going to be a quick dinner. At least she'd be able to put Logan's mind at ease and hopefully point him in the right direction. One kill probably meant the perpetrator had been in the victim's life.

"Yeah, I know. One murder doesn't make a serial killer. I get it." He leaned forward. "But look at the file, okay? This isn't a first kill. We got lucky, finding this body. There are more. I'm sure of it."

"Why?"

"The kill was too perfect. I don't think it was someone she knew, and the evidence is so slim. The fact that we even have a body—that we even know she's dead— is a fluke. We don't have a lot of murders in Oakville, but a killer just doesn't get that good without practice."

Logan frowned. The attraction he'd been broadcasting since they'd arrived at the diner was still in his eyes, but now it was tempered, pushed behind a sudden seriousness telling her he'd do whatever it took to find this killer.

Ella didn't need to see him work to believe it. She knew he was a good detective. It was there in the doggedness of his stare, in the trust he put in his instincts, in the way he was chasing this lead with all he had.

But she also saw this was more than just another case to him. He'd flown all this way for help, probably on his own dime. "You knew the victim, didn't you?"

"Jeez, you're good. I didn't know her well. But she was a friend of my sister's. Visiting from out of state. She'd actually left for the airport and we assumed she was back home." His lips tightened into a hard, thin line. "When all along, she was in Oakville. We found her in the marsh. Well, what was left of her anyway. We've got gators in the marshes, which is why I say we got lucky. Why I think there are more victims—because that's a pretty genius way to destroy evidence."

Ella nodded, flipping open the file folder next to her sandwich. The sight that greeted her should have made her lose her appetite, but she'd long ago learned to eat while reviewing case files. "Doesn't look like you had much to work with at the autopsy."

When she glanced up at Logan, he was carefully not looking at the photo and she reminded herself he knew the woman. She flipped past the autopsy photos, folded her hands under her chin and leaned toward him. "Why don't you give me the highlights?"

Logan raked a hand through his dark, close-cropped hair and she noticed the shadows under his eyes, the weariness lurking underneath those quick smiles.

"The victim was Theresa Crowley. My sister's age—twenty-five."

She must have looked surprised, because he said, "Yeah, Becky's ten years younger than I am. My parents didn't think they could have any more kids after me. Anyway, Theresa was a friend of Becky's from college. She lived in Arkansas. Flew in to visit for a week. She left as scheduled and my sister assumed she was already home until we identified the body."

"Who found her?"

"Local fisherman. He pulled out the remains and brought her in by boat."

Ella realized she was gaping as Logan continued, "Yeah, I know. Not great for evidence, but better than not having a body at all because the alligators finished her off."

"How long was she missing?"

"She left for the airport early Sunday morning and her body was found Monday afternoon."

"Short window to run into a killer."

"Unless he'd already been stalking her," Logan argued.

"What makes you think it wasn't someone she knew? Statistically, that's much more likely."

"Yeah, believe me, I don't run to the FBI every time we get a murder, whether or not I know the victim. But who did she know in Oakville? My sister and some of our family. That's it. Her rental car turned up the next day, abandoned in a mall parking lot a few towns over, in the opposite direction from the airport."

Ella sighed and set down her milkshake. "Are you sure you should be on this case?"

"Why? Because my family are obvious suspects?"

Instead of agreeing, Ella said, "Because you knew her."

"Another detective on the force already cleared my family. It was pretty easy. We were at a town function at her time of death."

Ella stared at him, looking for any tiny twitch that would tell her he knew—or suspected—his family could be involved. All she saw was his determination to get her to help. And that heavy dose of attraction. Her heart rate picked up and she glanced down at her food before she gave anything away. "She have any obvious enemies?"

"Stalker exes, that kind of thing? No."

"Sexual assault?"

Logan shrugged. "My guess would be yes, but too much postmortem damage to tell for sure. She died from lack of oxygen, but there was no water in her lungs. She didn't drown in that marsh. She was killed somewhere else."

"Okay—"

"And she had burns on her body."

Ella felt her hands tense into fists. Hiding them under the table, she forced them to loosen. "What kind of burns?"

"What were they made with? I don't know. But she had several. On her arm, her back…" Fury pulsated in his voice. "Someone burned her on purpose."

Ella held back a string of curses. Burns were close enough to branding that those cases hit her hardest. She always wanted them and her boss, knowing why she'd joined the FBI six years ago, always passed them on to another agent.

As much as she hated it, she understood that he was right. She made them too personal, and getting too close to a case meant making mistakes. Like Logan was in danger of doing right now.

She gave him her best profiler stare, the one she'd learned from her boss—a legend in the Bureau. "I'm going to read this case file and give you my best insight. But I'm going to tell you something you already know. You're too close to this case. You shouldn't be on it."

It was hypocritical advice, given the very, very personal case file sitting in the trunk of her Bureau-issued car right now, and judging by his scowl, Logan didn't seem any more inclined to follow it than she was.

"I'm not handing this over to someone else, not when everyone seems to think it was a fluke. I'm not going to sit around and wait for the next body to show up before I investigate this. This was my sister's friend and someone murdered her and tossed her in the marsh like garbage. I'm going to find this guy and make sure he pays."

Realization struck Ella. "You're not supposed to be here, are you?"

Logan let out a sound that was half laugh, half exasperation, but his face told her he was impressed. "Tell
you what, profiler. Check out the file and tell me I'm
wrong." He gave her a smug look that said, "I dare you."

Ella nodded slowly. "Okay." She skipped over the autopsy photos and started reading. The further she got
in the file, the more she felt her mouth tug downward.

When she looked back up at him, Logan raised his
eyebrows. "Well?"

"You've got good instincts, Greer."

Logan tapped his fingers heavily on the table. "I
thought so."

She had just flipped the file back to the beginning
when he suggested, this time sounding completely serious, "Maybe you and your friends could vacation on
some Florida beaches instead."

"No." The word came out more harshly than she'd
intended, so she covered up her instant reaction by tilt-
ing her head and offering him an exaggerated coy smile.
"Are you trying to solve a case here or get into my pants,
Greer?"

He blinked and leaned back, but just as quickly sat forward with a full-wattage version of the smile he'd been
laying on her all night. "Is it too much to hope for both?"

A short burst of laughter escaped her lips as desire
zinged through her body. "Probably." She turned back
to the file and all humor and lust instantly fled.

She lifted the page closer, squinting at one of the close-
ups underneath the main autopsy photo, and her entire
body suddenly felt as though it had been submerged in
ice. The blood left her head so fast she actually swayed
in her seat.

From a great distance, she heard Logan saying,
"Whoa. Are you okay?" and before she knew it, he was

squeezed in next to her in the booth, his hand on her back like fire against the frost that had come over her. "Ella?"

"What is this?"

Logan studied her face with concern before looking down. "The burn on her neck?"

"Yeah." She thought of marshes and fishermen. And images of hooks, burned into human flesh. "Could it be a brand?"

His forehead creased and he was staring into her eyes again, searching.

This close, he'd be able to see too much. Fear, maybe. Pain, probably. Recognition, definitely.

She'd seen a mark like this before, way too up close and personal. Her friend had covered it with a tattoo, but Ella would never forget how it had looked the day Maggie stumbled home to their dorm room. An angry red permanent reminder of a man the media had dubbed the Fishhook Rapist. He'd started with Maggie nearly a decade ago, then claimed a new victim every year since in a different part of the country. His last victim had been in Florida.

Ella had joined the FBI to catch him. She'd never even come close before. But maybe—just maybe—that was about to change.

"I don't know," Logan answered. "It's possible. Why?"

Ella released her breath, tried to regain control as she slapped the file shut. "I'm coming to Florida."

Chapter Two

There was definitely something about this case Ella Cortez wasn't telling him.

The bustle of Dulles Airport seemed to fade into the background as Logan watched her walk toward him, carrying two cups of coffee. A Bureau blue duffel bag was slung easily over one shoulder and it bounced against her hip with every purposeful stride, swinging in a hypnotic arc. More than one man's head swiveled as she passed.

Logan had come directly to the airport to change his flight and book hers, while she'd gone home to pack. And apparently to change. Instead of the all-business suit she'd had on earlier, now she wore jeans and a T-shirt that highlighted appealing curves. Dark hair that had been wound into a bun earlier was now in a loose, low ponytail that trailed to midback and made his fingers itch to slide through it.

He sat up straighter as she joined him, taking the scalding cup of coffee she offered. "Thanks."

"Sure." She looked distracted as she dumped her bag on the floor, pulled out her cell phone and hit Redial. It must have gone to voice mail, because she swore and stuck the phone back in her pocket.

"Boyfriend?" When she squinted at him, he added, "That you're calling?"

"No. The friends I was supposed to go on vacation with. I can't get them."

Which didn't exactly answer the subtext of his question. Not that it mattered.

He'd gotten a lot more than he'd hoped for out of his trip, which he'd booked yesterday on a whim and a hope. He'd expected to badger someone from the FBI's profiler unit into giving him something to take home. It was how he got to the bottom of most of his cases—his ability to push until he got what he wanted. And this time wasn't any different. He wanted to close this case. And it didn't matter whose toes he had to step on back home.

He snuck a peek at Ella, who was frowning beside him as she pulled her phone out again. However much he'd like to believe it, she wasn't here because of his persuasive charm. She was in this for her own reasons. And before they landed, he planned to find out what they were.

"Ella!"

The yell jolted Ella to her feet. She hadn't made it two steps before a man and woman reached her. "I tried to call you," the man said.

He was tall, with a sharp, intent look that pegged him as law enforcement or military. He seemed to buzz with energy, and everything about him screamed his readiness for a vacation. Logan could read his type instantly—lady killer. Ella had called him a friend, but was that all?

The woman with him was dark-haired and muscular, with pretty blue eyes. She looked exhausted, frazzled and slightly jumpy.

"You're at the wrong gate." The man's eyes flicked speculatively to him, then back to Ella. "We're at the end of the terminal."

Ella bit her lip. "I can't make it."

"What?" The man's eyebrows shot up. "What do you mean?"

Logan got to his feet, which made her friends glance his way.

Ella's words suddenly doubled in speed. "This is Logan Greer. I have to help him with a case." She slowed down to add, "Logan, these are my friends, Maggie and Scott Delacorte."

Logan smiled. Well, that answered his question about Ella's relationship with Scott, if he was married to her friend Maggie. "Nice to meet you."

Maggie gave him a nod while Scott studied him with narrowed eyes before saying, "You, too."

"The three of us grew up together," Ella continued, still talking fast, as if trying to keep her friends from returning to the previous subject. "Maggie and Scott lived down the street from me. I probably spent as much time at their house as my own."

It took Logan a few seconds too long to deconstruct her words and realize Maggie and Scott weren't married, but brother and sister. By the time he'd figured out a response, Scott had turned to Ella again.

"You have a case?" Scott pushed. "You're supposed to have two weeks of vacation. We planned this months ago."

Ella's whole face twitched as she told them, "I don't have a choice. My boss made me cancel. If I can wrap it up fast, I'll fly out and join you."

Logan tried not to let his surprise at her lie show on his face, but from the way Scott squinted at first Ella, then him, he was pretty sure he'd failed.

Maggie, though, must not have noticed. Bloodshot eyes full of disappointment locked on Ella's. "There has to be someone else who can take the case."

Ella couldn't seem to hold Maggie's gaze as she said, "I'm sorry."

Just as boarding for their flight was announced, Scott's hand closed around Ella's arm, pulling her off to the side. It was probably to keep him from overhearing, but Scott's voice was too loud when he asked, "Can't you get your boss to reassign it? Did you tell him…"

Scott glanced back and Logan figured it was at him until Maggie sighed. "Let it go, Scott. She'll fly out if she can."

The scowl lurking on Scott's face shifted to resignation as he gave Ella a quick hug. "Okay. I guess you can't refuse orders. Good luck with the case. Wrap it up fast and join us, all right?"

Maggie hugged Ella with a barely audible, "Don't worry about it," and then she was shaking Logan's hand with surprising strength. "Which field office are you out of, Logan?"

"I'm—"

Ella jumped in. "Logan's not Bureau. And he's got a case down South I'm going to help him with. Hopefully, it'll be quick and then I'll grab a flight to California."

Her answer brought more questioning looks from Scott, but then final boarding for their flight was called and Ella grabbed her bag, looking relieved.

Logan waited until they were belted into their seats in the last row of the small plane and the doors were closed. "Are you planning to let me in on the big secret?"

"I don't know what you mean."

"Okay. What I mean is, why did you tell your friends you were assigned the case and couldn't get out of it?"

She turned sideways to face him, her knee jabbing his thigh, and raised an eyebrow. "You want me to get out of it?"

Logan grinned as the engines started up. "It's a little late to change your mind now."

Ella leaned back in her seat. "This vacation was kind of a big deal. I didn't want to tell them I'd taken the case unofficially."

She was extremely close to Maggie and Scott, that was easy to see. And from the way she'd twitched and changed the subject as fast as she could in the airport, it was clear she rarely lied to them. Which meant that whatever she'd seen in the case file, whatever had persuaded her to come to Florida, was big. "So, why did you take the case?"

"Why? Because you were right about having a serial killer. Because you need a profile. And because it didn't seem like you were about to get one from anyone else."

"That's why you took the case?"

She shot him a look full of exasperation, color rising high in her cheeks. "Yes."

"You want to try that again?"

She looked sideways at him. "Okay, fine. There's a chance it could be connected to something I've seen before."

She held up a hand to forestall any argument, but he'd been focused more on the movement of her lips than her words, so by the time his brain caught up, she'd moved on.

"If it looks like it really is connected, I'll tell you about it. Until then, we need to focus on this victim."

"If you're here because it might be connected, shouldn't we look at the old case, too, so we don't miss anything?"

"No."

Ella turned to face him, bringing her knee back into contact with his thigh and sending his mind way off track. Jeez, he either really needed a date other than the ones his well-meaning family set up for him, or Ella Cortez was going to be a distraction. One he'd better learn to ignore. And fast.

"If it's not the same perp, we could just go in the wrong direction," Ella said.

"So, what's it going to take for you to decide if these cases are connected and let me in on the secret?"

Her lips tightened but her tone was calm when she replied, "Trust me. I'm good at what I do. I'll tell you if you need to know."

Any answer that included the words *need to know* sounded suspicious to him, but she was the expert. And since her consultation was unofficial and she could leave whenever she wanted, he decided he'd take what he could get. At least for now.

The direction he was taking in the investigation wasn't exactly sanctioned, so he couldn't fault her for having her own motivation. Especially since she'd soon see just how far off the approved path he'd veered.

He leaned back against the headrest and closed his eyes as the plane bounced up and down and then plummeted briefly as if it was aspiring to be a roller coaster. "I guess we all have our secrets."

As soon as Logan walked through the door of the Blue Dolphin, he could tell he'd made a mistake. But Ella had already gone in, so he let the door close behind him and followed through the crush of tourists and locals, through the smell of sunscreen and salt water.

Having lived in Oakville all his life, Logan knew a lot of the locals. If he hadn't, he would have been able to separate them from the tourists by dress alone. The locals all wore layers in deference to the heat outside and the air-conditioning blasting inside. Most of them, acclimatized to much warmer weather come summer, were still in pants. The tourists sported flip-flops, cutoffs and tiny bathing suit tops, their wet hair still dripping from the nearby ocean.

Crammed around a table near the front of the deli were four uniforms who'd set their sandwiches down as soon as they saw him. He watched the smiles quiver at the edges of their lips, the laughter dance in their eyes, and knew what was coming.

Hank O'Connor was senior in the group, nearly as big across as he was tall. He gave his companions a nod, an unspoken "watch this," then called out, "Hey Greer, catch your serial killer yet?"

The rest of the table snickered, and Ella stopped staring at the menu above the counter long enough to glance questioningly from the uniforms to Logan.

"I'm working on it, O'Connor," Logan threw back. "How about you? Catch any speeders today?"

The smile dropped off Hank's face. They'd taken the detective exam at the same time. They'd both passed, but only one job had opened up and since Logan had been there longer, with more experience, procedure dictated that he got it. Hank was about as happy with Logan's position as the chief was.

Hank jerked a little straighter in his seat and Logan knew he should just have let it go. Hank had a bad temper, a long memory and a penchant for petty revenge.

"Not everybody's daddy can buy them a job," Hank spat.

As one, the cops with Hank went for their sandwiches again, their eyes cast downward.

Familiar frustration filled Logan, threatening to overflow, but he clenched his teeth and turned back to the counter. He'd fought this battle too many times to bother.

Yes, his family had a long history in Oakville. Yes, his father, the mayor, had been in office for years. Admittedly, it had given him some advantages in his life. But when it came to his career, it always seemed to be a disadvantage. Because no matter how hard he worked, there was always someone anxious to claim he was just trading on the Greer name.

"Your family were the last ones to see the Crowley girl, right?" Hank pressed. "You spinning your serial killer story so nobody brings *that* up in the next election?"

Logan's fingers curled into his palms as he spun back toward Hank, acid on his tongue.

With a speed he wouldn't have expected from a desk jockey profiler, Ella ducked in front of him and held her hand out toward the table of cops with an overly cheery smile. "Officer O'Connor, is it? I'm Special Agent Ella Cortez, FBI. I'm here because Detective Greer's serial killer theory looks promising."

Hank engulfed Ella's hand in his own bear paw and shook it a few times, a startled expression on his face. His mouth opened and closed, but no words emerged. His companions looked at each other with equal surprise.

Before they could recover, Ella grabbed Logan's arm and steered him back toward the counter, ordering herself a sandwich. Logan fought his laughter until they were both out the door and back in his Chevy Caprice with their food.

But any urge to laugh faded as he drove toward the marsh. Knowing Hank, both the fact that Logan was still pursuing the serial killer angle and the fact that he now had a cute FBI profiler in tow would make it back to his chief before the end of the day. Which would lead to a conversation that he had hoped to avoid a little longer.

Swallowing a sigh, Logan eased his unmarked police vehicle off the side of the road as close to the marsh as they were going to get. "We're hoofing it from here," he told Ella.

She stuffed the last bite of her sandwich in her mouth and got out of the car, drawing a deep breath that told him she wasn't used to the heavy humidity. "I thought we were going to the marsh?"

"We are." They were standing off the side of the road, bracketed by hundred-year-old live oaks. Spanish moss dangled from every branch almost to the tall grass below, like a fuzzy gray curtain obscuring the path behind it. "Follow me. And stay on the trail. Snakes hide in the grass."

Behind the trees, the dirt path was packed down. Locals used it often to bike and walk or to get to the marshes for fishing. Right now, in the midday heat, the path was empty.

It was also narrow, so Ella walked behind him. He could sense her taking in the details, so he wasn't surprised when she asked, "Is the area we're going to pretty populated?"

"We definitely get locals looking for redfish, but not too many tourists wander back here. We won't get out as far as where the body was found. To do that, we'd need a boat. The trail loops back around, which is where most of the runners take it, but there's a split that goes farther out, about to the point the water will come up to at high tide. From there, I can show you where we found Theresa." He glanced over his shoulder at her. "You're wondering if this guy knew the area in order to get back here?"

"That's part of it. Also trying to determine how likely it is he'd run into other people. How much risk he'd take dumping the body where he did. Things like that help me figure out his personality."

"Hmm." Logan dropped back so he could walk beside her and watch her face as she talked. They were a close fit on the narrow trail. Every few steps her arm brushed his and the feel of her skin fired way too many nerve endings to life. "From what I know of profiling, you'll be able to tell me things like he's a white male in his twenties."

From the reaction he'd gotten when he'd suggested bringing in a profiler to his chief, he knew skeptics joked that was all profilers were good for—looking at a crime scene and predicting that the serial killer was a white male in his twenties. Which happened to be the most common age range and race for serial killers.

Ella's mouth quirked, but with annoyance or amusement, he couldn't tell.

"The basic concepts behind profiling are actually pretty simple," she said. "Take you, for example. Things like your upbringing, your intelligence, your personality— all of that contributed to why you became not just a cop, but a homicide detective. Creating a criminal personality profile analyzes that. I look at the evidence—things like the way he dumped the body—and figure out details of his personality. From that, I can say what kind of job that kind of personality would likely pick, what kind of environment he'd live in, if he'd be married, that sort of thing." She shrugged. "Make sense?"

"You make it sound easy."

"No, it's definitely not easy. But it is pretty grounded in psychology." As they reached the end of the trail, she turned to face him, and he instantly became hyperaware of how short the distance between them really was. "If I tell you he's a white male in his twenties, there'll be a reason behind it besides averages."

Turning again, she squinted out over the marsh, her expression slipping back to serious, and after allowing himself another few seconds to watch her, Logan did the same.

He'd been to this spot hundreds of times before, but in the sudden stillness, he saw it as she might. The feeling of intense calm that came from being the only people there, then the slow realization that nature was moving all around. The murky waters, lapping against tall grasses. The curious expression of a wading egret, the distant lump indicating an alligator underneath.

"It's pretty quiet," Ella said.

He could almost hear her thoughts, calculating details about the killer. He'd picked an isolated spot where there wouldn't likely be tourists. The body had been found in the morning, so the killer must have dumped Theresa before dusk, when the alligators would've been feeding. A smart killer. Patient.

Logan felt the blood drain from his face as he realized what else it probably told Ella. The killer knew specific details about the marsh. "He's a local, isn't he?"

Ella turned, and her deep brown eyes seemed to bore holes through him. "He's not a typical tourist passing through for a week or two. He could be a local, either here or in one of the neighboring towns. At the very least, he's been holed up here for a few months, getting familiar with the town and trolling for victims."

A string of curses burst from deep within, a sour, sick feeling that he might actually know the person who had burned and then murdered his sister's friend.

The sick feeling persisted when his cell phone trilled and the display read Chief Patterson. He hadn't even finished "Hello" before the chief was yelling loudly enough that there was no question Ella could hear every word.

"Why am I hearing about you bringing the *FBI* to Oakville for your ridiculous serial killer theory? How often do you need to hear orders before you follow them, Logan? We're investigating *Theresa's* murder. We are *not* inventing more victims and we are *definitely* not scaring the whole town by turning an isolated crime into a huge spree!"

"Chief—"

"I'm going to tell you this one last time, Logan, and you'd better listen. There's only so far that nepotism can protect your job. You drop this serial killer angle *right now.* Send this profiler home and get back to the station."

"Chief, listen—"

The sudden dial tone cut him off. As he tucked his phone back inside his pocket, he prayed he'd made the right decision in bringing Ella here, prayed that one crazy theory wasn't going to bring down the career he'd fought so hard for.

Chapter Three

"Why isn't she on a plane?" Chief Patterson folded his arms on his desk, glaring with an intensity he seemed to save just for Logan.

Chief Patterson was his father's age. He'd headed up the Oakville PD for twenty years and his dislike of anyone with the last name Greer came from way before Logan's time. Part of it had to do with the Greers' long history of prominent positions in Oakville. And part of it had to do with the chief courting his mother before his father won her away.

Logan looked through the glass door of the chief's office to where Ella sat perched on a chair along the wall, attracting attention from far too many members of their all-male police force. Logan scowled. She was here to consult on *his* case.

"Logan," Chief Patterson snapped, making his head whip back around. "What part of my orders was unclear to you?"

"Listen, Chief, Agent Cortez agrees this crime looks serial."

The chief's scowl deepened, intensifying the lines that raked across his forehead and bracketed his mouth. "I don't care *what* she thinks. I don't buy into that profiling hokum. And I am *not* going to scare away all our tourism revenue with some ridiculous theory. If you keep pursuing this angle, I'm taking you off the case. I'll assign it to someone else."

But Logan knew that none of the other detectives in their small police force would want to touch the case, not after he'd had his hands on it. Just like none of them wanted to risk the chief's ire by partnering with a cop named Greer. The uniforms joked that the position of his partner was like a revolving door. Right now, he was the only member of the force without a partner—which was true for most of his tenure as a detective.

But it didn't matter if there was another detective who'd take this case; Logan wasn't handing it over to anyone.

The chief didn't give him a chance to say that, merely held up a hand. "There's nothing your father can do about it. I won't be cowed by political pressure. This is *my* office. I'm your boss and you'd better get used to it."

Logan clamped down hard on his instant response. Not once had he ever used his family's name—or his father's position as mayor of Oakville—to get ahead in his job. If anything, they had held him back.

He fought to keep his voice level. "And this is *my* case. I can't ignore a potential lead because it might hurt tourism."

"Trying to invent a serial killer is *not* a lead," the chief barked. "If you find another body, then it might become a lead, but we don't have any active missing-persons cases, much less any other victims. So, you're *not* spending resources chasing this. Send the profiler home. Get back to work figuring out who had it in for Theresa Crowley."

The chief leaned back in his chair and opened the file in front of him, which meant Logan was being dismissed.

He didn't move. The problem with the chief's plan

was that no one had it in for Theresa, or at least no one in the state of Florida. Theresa had spent her entire trip with his sister and their family, so she hadn't had time to meet anyone unsavory. And it was unlikely she'd run into someone she knew on her drive to the airport.

Every investigative instinct in his body was clamoring that Theresa's killer hadn't known her personally, and that if he wasn't stopped, he was going to strike again. To solve the case, he needed Ella. And he owed it to his sister to make sure Theresa's killer was caught.

The chief looked up from his file, raising his eyebrows as he glanced pointedly from Logan to the door.

Instead, Logan took a deep breath and did something he'd sworn he would never do. Something that might well be career suicide.

"Fine. But if you insist I stop working with Agent Cortez and another body *does* turn up, I'm going to the paper to tell them we had a profiler here and you sent her home." He didn't need to add that because of his last name, the story was guaranteed front-page coverage.

A deep red flush spread across the chief's cheeks all the way to his ears, and when he spoke, his voice was an octave too high. "Fine, Logan. You want to play it this way? Then if you're wrong and no other body turns up, but you're too busy chasing an imaginary serial murderer to catch the real killer, I'll be the one talking to the press. And it'll be to tell them why you've handed in your badge."

WHAT WAS SHE THINKING?

Ella stared up at Logan as he held the car door for her to get out and follow him into his parents' house for dinner. When he'd initially told her he had dinner plans with his family, she'd expected to be eating at the hotel's tiny restaurant by herself. But Logan's Southern-boy manners had him inviting her along, and his Southern-boy charm had her stupidly agreeing.

Now that Logan had told his family she was coming and it was too late to change her mind, she wished she'd gone back to the hotel instead. It had been ages since she'd eaten with her own parents and two younger brothers back in Indiana; joining the family of a homicide detective she barely knew was just strange. She wasn't even inside and she was already uncomfortable.

Logan was still standing with his hand on the car door. "You planning to sit in there all evening?"

"And miss the chance to meet this famous family of yours?" She managed a smile as she climbed out of the car. "Not likely."

"Great," Logan muttered, shutting the door and escorting her to the house.

It was a big white colonial with columns in the front, surrounded by magnolia trees. It looked as if it belonged in the Old South, so Ella wasn't surprised when the door opened to reveal a foyer that resembled a smaller-scale version of something from *Gone with the Wind.*

This was where Logan had grown up? It was a far cry from the blue-collar neighborhood surrounded by wheat fields where she'd spent her childhood. She wondered what path had taken him from this to becoming a homicide detective.

"Logan!"

The woman who opened the door and wrapped Logan in an immediate hug appeared to be in her early sixties. Dark hair streaked with silver was pulled into a twist and when she let Logan go, Ella realized he had his mother's eyes.

"Mom, this is Ella Cortez. She's consulting with me on my case at work. Ella, this is my mom, Diana Greer."

Ella had expected a dainty handshake from the woman in the pressed khakis and green blouse the same shade as her eyes, but what she got was the kind of tight hug usually reserved for long-lost relatives. "Nice to meet you," she choked out.

"Come in, come in." Diana led them through the foyer and a formal living room back to a connected kitchen and family room that looked casual and lived-in.

This was more like the way she might have imagined Logan's childhood home, with the paperbacks stacked on an end table, a big TV on mute against the far wall, and family pictures lining the walls. Ella resisted the urge to take a closer look at Logan as a boy.

"Logan, your father is just finishing up his speech, and then we'll all sit down for dinner. Ella, would you like something to drink? An iced tea?"

"Sure."

"Logan?"

"No thanks, Mom." Logan sank onto a long couch positioned against the wall.

Diana poured an iced tea, then handed it to Ella. "So, Ella, tell me about yourself. What do you do that you're working with Logan?"

Ella settled into the chair across from Logan, and smiled at his mom. "Well, I'm with the FBI's Behavioral Analysis Unit in Virginia. I can't really talk about the case, but basically, I create profiles of unknown offenders."

"Sounds mysterious." She glanced over at her son. "Logan, before I forget, do you remember Laura Jameson? She just moved back to town and she doesn't know a lot of people her age. I was talking to her mother the other night at a function and I told her you'd love to take Laura out for dinner tomorrow. I've got her number in the other room for you."

Logan let out a long sigh, a hint of red visible despite the scruff on his cheeks. "Mom, you've got to stop doing this."

"What? It's one date."

"I'm in the middle of a case. I don't have time for one date."

Diana sat in the chair across from Logan, a frown creasing her forehead. "Honey, I already told Laura's mom you'd pick her up at seven." Diana turned back to Ella, and asked, "So, Ella, what made you join the FBI?"

If she hadn't still been focused on not staring slack-jawed at Logan and his mother during their exchange, Ella might have tensed up at the question. As it was, she'd barely opened her mouth to answer when Logan cut in.

"You're going to have to call her back, Mom."

"You can't work all the time, Logan. A few hours—"

"Logan!" The woman who walked into the room in jeans and a T-shirt, her dark brown hair plaited, and who shared the green Greer eyes, was clearly Logan's younger sister.

Even though they lived in the same town and presumably saw each other all the time, Logan gave his sister a tight hug, then said, "Becky, this is Ella Cortez."

Ella stood, self-consciously tugging her T-shirt down over the gun holstered on her hip as Becky hugged her just like Logan's mom had done, with the kind of easy familiarity her own family could never hope to match. At least not with her. Not since a single event had changed her life plans and she'd left Indiana to join the Bureau all those years ago.

The pang of loneliness caught her off guard. There'd

been a time when she'd expected to stay in Indiana like her brothers. It had been such a tight-knit community where they lived, with her parents, brothers, and grandparents. Growing up, she'd envisioned herself settling down there, too; working at a safe, normal job, getting married, having kids.

But it had been almost a decade since the Fishhook Rapist had made Maggie his very first victim and all those plans had changed. She'd made her choice. If her family hadn't accepted it by now, they never would.

"Did I just hear you getting roped into another date with some lonely woman?" Becky asked Logan as she flopped onto the couch next to him.

Her tone was light. If it hadn't been for the deep shadows under her red-rimmed eyes, Ella might not have known she was grieving.

Logan scowled at her. "Yeah, well, not this time. And don't worry, Becky, Mom will be after you next."

"Ha!" Becky shot back. "Unlike you, big brother, I just say no."

"Logan—" Diana tried again.

"Not this time, Mom."

Becky looked from Ella to Logan to her mom and then laughed. It sounded rough, the laugh of someone who hadn't found anything funny in a while. "So, how come I've never met you before, Ella? It must be pretty serious if Logan's refusing to go out with whoever Mom's set him up with this time."

Heat crawled up Ella's neck at how easy it was to suddenly imagine she was here in a totally different context. How easy it was to imagine having something "pretty serious" with the intense homicide detective.

What was wrong with her? Logan Greer was a colleague and she had to work with him on what might be the most important case of her career. He was off-limits.

"Ella doesn't live here," Diana said, before she'd mustered a reply.

At the same moment, Logan told her, "Ella's not my date. She's consulting from the FBI."

All humor fled Becky's face, leaving behind a strained expression, and Ella saw not Logan's little sister, but a loved one of a victim.

Ella gave herself a mental slap for losing her focus. She was here for a case and she was completely failing to maintain proper boundaries.

"FBI?" Becky said, her voice wobbly. "Are you here about Theresa?"

Ella tried not to fidget. "Unofficially, yes."

Becky looked from her to Logan and back again. "So, Logan is right? Becky was murdered by a *serial killer*?"

Ella glanced questioningly at Logan. He shared case theories with his family?

"Guess you're not used to small towns," Logan said, answering her unspoken question. "Nothing is secret here."

She definitely *was* used to small towns; she was from one herself—an old farming community that had gotten partially enveloped by the surrounding college-town melting pot but somehow still kept its close-knit feel. But she wasn't used to being a cop in one. "We're checking into that possibility," Ella said, uncomfortable.

Before Becky could ask anything else, Logan's father strode into the room. Besides being the only member of the Greer family with blue eyes, he looked like an older version of Logan. He stopped in front of her and offered his hand. "I'm Andrew Greer. You must be Ella Cortez. Nice to have you join us."

And suddenly, Ella understood all the references she'd heard the police chief shout over the phone about Logan's family. Everything about Andrew, from his perfect posture to his instant smile and handshake, screamed *politician*. "Thank you. You must be Mayor Greer. Am I correct?"

Andrew gave her a wink and let go of her hand. "Until I get Logan here to succeed me." Logan rolled his eyes, but Andrew continued. "I have to say, I wasn't sure what to think about Logan bringing in a profiler, but now I'm a believer. What gave me away, Ella?"

Ella smiled back at him. So, this was where Logan got his charm. "Trick of the trade. If I divulge all my secrets, they'll kick me out of the club."

"Well, we can't have that." Andrew turned to his wife. "Should we eat?"

"Not yet." Becky stood, folding her arms as she stared at Ella. "Don't you want to question me about Theresa?" She sounded wrung out, but the strength underneath reminded Ella of Logan.

Ella shifted from one foot to the other. At the FBI, she was generally at a remove from the investigations. Most of the time, she didn't even leave Virginia—she consulted on a case directly from a police file. When she did travel somewhere to give a criminal personality profile, she still didn't do interviews—except on rare occasions with suspects. She was almost never involved in questioning the friends and families of victims. And she didn't want to start with Logan's little sister.

"Becky, we already took your statement," Logan said quietly, getting to his feet and putting a hand on his sister's shoulder.

"What if Ella has different questions?"

"I usually work from the police files," Ella said gently,

forcing herself to look directly into Becky's misery-filled eyes. "If there's something else I need, I'll let your brother know."

"Well—" Andrew started, in his cheery, politician's voice.

Becky cut him off. "Okay. But just answer this for me—how would Theresa have run into a serial killer? It's not like we were out partying with weirdos." Her voice broke, but she composed herself and managed to say, "We hung out at the beach. We went dancing at the club right in town. We went shopping. It was mostly just the two of us. I don't think she talked to a single person I didn't know." She looked from Logan to Ella, tears filling her eyes. Her voice wobbled when she asked, "Did *I* introduce her to the person who killed her?"

"No," Logan insisted. "This isn't your fault."

"There's a good chance that whoever killed her never even spoke to her," Ella said.

Relief broke through the misery in Becky's eyes. "Really?"

"Really."

Becky wiped her hand over her eyes and squared her shoulders. "Okay. Let's go have dinner." She hurried out of the room and after sharing a concerned glance, her parents followed.

Alone in the family room, Logan put his hand on Ella's arm and said softly, "Thank you."

Ella shrugged, trying to ignore how close Logan was standing, how sensitive the skin under his fingers had suddenly become, and trying to distract herself with what she knew. Her job. "There's a very good chance it's true. Yes, the killer had probably been watching Theresa, but it looks like the abduction was an ambush. Someone who does that probably isn't confident. It's unlikely he approached his victims first."

She took a deep breath, aware that she'd been talking too fast, that Logan hadn't taken his hand off her arm. Was it her imagination or had he shifted closer? She could smell his aftershave, something woodsy that made her want to close her eyes and inhale. She tilted her head back a little farther, gazing up into his eyes.

The moss green that had drawn her in from the moment she met him was just a small ring around his pupils now. The desire in his eyes seemed to heat her whole body.

She wasn't sure if she stretched up on her tiptoes or he leaned down, but his lips were inches from hers, his breath on her face. One hand moved from her arm to the back of her head and he slipped his other hand onto her lower back, pulling her closer.

He gave her plenty of time to do the professional thing and back away, but instead she swayed forward and pressed her mouth to his. The stubble on his chin felt abrasive, but his lips were soft as they slowly brushed hers, as though he was determined to memorize every millimeter.

She was the one who insisted on more, who fused her body tightly to his until he slid his tongue between her lips and backed her against the wall. She wove her fingers through his hair and clung tightly to him as his mouth covered hers. Only a loud clink of silverware against china brought her to her senses.

She turned her head away from Logan's and pried her hands off him. Her legs shook and her face burned even hotter as she met his eyes.

He was breathing as heavily as she was. His eyes were hooded, but she could still see passion there, and she got the feeling that if she asked, he'd forget dinner and follow her back to her hotel.

She actually didn't know if she was going to suggest it until she heard herself say instead, "Sorry. That was a mistake."

Logan blinked, shoved his hands in his pockets, and stared at her. Finally, he gave her that sexy, one-sided grin and winked. "Then try to keep your hands off me." He ran a hand over hair she'd mussed, then headed for the dining room. "Let's go to dinner."

Ella followed more slowly, trying to will her pulse back to a normal rate. *Get it together, Cortez.*

She didn't have time to mess around. There was a killer on the loose. And if she was right and it was the same person who'd raped Maggie back in college, he wasn't going to stay in Florida forever. He'd be going somewhere else soon, looking for a new victim to dangle in front of the FBI, and she'd lose her shot at him.

She owed it to Maggie—and Scott and herself—to catch this guy. Especially since, after almost a decade of silence, the Fishhook Rapist had sent Maggie a letter. As a profiler, Ella knew that unexpected contact like that could be a precursor to physical contact. Much as Maggie had tried to play it cool, Ella knew her friend was secretly terrified. And right now, Ella might have the chance to end Maggie's years of silent, buried fear.

It didn't matter what Logan Greer did to her libido. She was going to have to figure out how to resist him.

Chapter Four

"How did Logan get the FBI to give him a profiler?" Hank O'Connor leaned against the door frame, blocking Ella's entrance to the Oakville police station with his sheer bulk.

Ella busied herself hefting her briefcase, avoiding eye contact, hoping a quick answer would satisfy him. "We like to get involved if we think there's a serial case."

Hank snorted. "Really? I thought there was some big, long process to get a profiler. He find a way to cut to the front of the line?"

The innuendo in Hank's tone made Ella glance up to his dark brown eyes. Yep, definite laughter there. Which was better than true suspicion about whether proper Bureau protocol had been followed, but not by much. Especially considering the way she'd plastered herself to Logan at his parents' house last night.

A flush started climbing Ella's neck, so she put on her flat, all-business tone. "Once I have enough to provide a useful profile, I'll be on to my next case." She looked pointedly at where he leaned against the door. "If you don't mind, I'm expected in the conference room."

Hank rolled his eyes, but got out of her way. As she passed, he muttered, "Guess it's true. Feds have no sense of humor."

Ella didn't slow her stride, just marched straight to the conference room at the back of the station that Logan had booked so they could go over Theresa's case. It had been this or Logan's house and after last night's kiss, she'd immediately picked the station. Now she wondered if she'd made the wrong choice.

If it got back to her boss at BAU that she'd agreed to give a profile on her own time, her vacation could be permanent.

A lump the size of her gun formed in her throat. She tried to swallow it down, but it stuck. A pact with Maggie and Scott nearly ten years ago had made her apply to the FBI, but the job had become a huge part of her life. She'd weathered her family's disapproval, the FBI Academy's ruthless selection process, and four years of cutting her teeth on gang cases to get into the BAU.

Her goal all along had been to get to this case. She needed to catch Maggie's rapist, and the hook-shaped burn on the back of Theresa's neck told her this could be her chance, but she really didn't want to sabotage her own career to do it.

"Something wrong?" Logan asked.

Ella stumbled, catching herself on the door frame. She'd been so caught up in her thoughts she hadn't realized she'd arrived at the conference room. "N-no, nothing."

She turned her back to him, pouring a cup of coffee as a cover for calming herself. She'd never crossed the line with a colleague before. Seeing Logan today was awkward and uncomfortable—despite knowing that after two weeks, she'd never see him again.

That thought made the lump in her throat sink to her gut and settle there uncomfortably as if she'd drunk a pot of coffee on an empty stomach.

You've known him for two days, Ella reminded herself. *You can't be this attached to him already.*

But when she turned around, Logan was perched on the edge of the table, his perfectly groomed dark hair begging her to muss it up again, his green eyes studying her with concern, and she knew she was in trouble.

"You sure you're okay?"

"Fine." Ella set her coffee on the table, then pulled a legal pad and a pen out of her briefcase. "Let's get to work."

Logan settled into the chair next to her, a respectable distance that somehow still felt too intimate.

"You're the expert," he said, his tone normal, as if he hadn't had his tongue in her mouth last night. "Where should we start?"

She fiddled with her pen, then managed to look up at him. "Let's just…" Ella glanced at the door, making sure it was closed, before she continued, "I just want to be clear that what happened yesterday was an anomaly."

"An *anomaly*?" Laughter curved Logan's lips, but it quickly faded, his tone immediately becoming stiff. "You were pretty clear yesterday that it was a mistake. I got it. It won't happen again."

She nodded. "I know this case is important to you. I'm staying. But if it gets out that I'm not supposed to be here…" She stared into those unreadable green eyes. "I could lose my job."

His hand closed over the top of hers, igniting all the sparks she was trying to ignore. "I'm not going to do anything to put your job in jeopardy."

She pulled her hand away. "Thanks. Okay, let's get to work. Tell me about the car."

"The car?"

"Theresa's rental car. Was it processed?"

"They're still working it, but prints are a bust. The front of the car had been totally wiped down. Nothing there. We found some prints in the trunk, but those were ruled out. One set we've identified as Theresa's and one was my dad's, probably from when he took her luggage out of the trunk."

"Hmm."

Frustration rang in Logan's voice as he said, "My dad was cleared. My whole family was cleared. The coroner narrowed her time of death down to a pretty small window and we were at a town function. Practically the whole town can alibi us."

"That's not what I was thinking. I was thinking it's too bad he wiped down the whole front of the car instead of just one side."

"Because now we don't know if the killer was in the driver's side or the passenger side?"

"Right. Although possibly he was in both. She could have picked him up voluntarily, placing him in the passenger side, and then later, he drove the car to dump it."

"But you don't think so?"

Ella studied the table, considering, then gazed back up at Logan, working it out aloud. "Well, since Theresa wasn't meeting anyone and was headed for the airport when she disappeared, it looks like an ambush. So, either he stalked her beforehand and waited for his opportunity or he picked her at random because he was looking for a victim and she came along at the right time. Either way, why would she pick him up? Given his knowledge of the dumping spot, he's probably been here a while, so it seems unlikely he'd be hitchhiking."

"Theresa wouldn't pick up a hitchhiker."

"Are you sure?"

Logan gave a tired nod, leaning back in his seat. "She

roomed with the sister of a homicide detective in college. Trust me, I drilled that kind of thing into Becky. Call me an overprotective brother, but I asked her about Theresa's safety habits. If anything, I think Becky's stories made Theresa overcautious."

"Okay, well—"

"The spare was on the car." Logan swore. "It didn't really occur to me before, but maybe this guy caught up to her when she was changing her tire. Although obviously, she put the spare on, so he didn't grab her then."

"Maybe that was just the way to meet her. He caused her tire to blow, helped her fix it, then grabbed her."

"He caused the flat? How?"

"Maybe a tack board in some deserted stretch of road he knew she'd take to the airport." An ambush. The way Maggie had been ambushed ten years ago.

Ella pushed back familiar anger and kept going. "That's assuming he was stalking her. Can you think of a spot along the route to the airport that would fit?" To her embarrassment, she'd fallen asleep on the drive from the airport near Fort Meyers to Oakville. Logan had needed to wake her when he'd arrived at her hotel.

Logan clenched his fists and Ella understood every ounce of his frustration. His sister's friend was dead and there wasn't a thing he could do to change that. He could only stop it from happening to someone else.

"Well, Theresa was staying with my sister. The fastest route to the airport would be directly through town to the highway. Once you get on the highway, there are some pretty deserted stretches, just marshland on one side and empty land on the other. It doesn't get busier for a good ten or so miles, once you get closer to Naples."

"Maybe we should have some patrol officers drive it," Ella suggested. "Not the whole route, but the stretch you're talking about. See if they locate any evidence of a blowout, or if we get lucky, maybe something of Theresa's, since none of her personal items have turned up."

Logan sighed, rubbing his temple. "I'll go talk to the chief. Hang on."

While he was gone, Ella unfolded the map she'd grabbed at the airport and studied the distance from Oakville to Cape Coral, Florida. That was where the Fishhook Rapist—who'd started with Maggie in DC almost ten years ago—had assaulted his most recent known victim. It was only forty miles up the coast. The woman had started her first job after college when she'd been grabbed. Like Maggie, she'd been given Rohypnol before she was raped and branded on the back of her neck with the image of a hook.

Then, just like Maggie, just like every other victim over the past ten years, he'd released her on September first and disappeared. Until the next year, when he would reappear somewhere else in the country to do it again.

Ella had always assumed he'd gone to ground between abductions. She'd never considered that he was claiming victims between each September first. But maybe the ones he released were simply his way of getting attention. Maybe the rest he killed and dumped in marshes so their bodies—branded with his signature—were never found.

And maybe he'd finally made his first mistake.

"THAT'S NOT HOW he abducted Theresa," Logan announced when he returned to the conference room, tucking his cell phone in his pocket. Luckily, he'd called Becky before asking his chief to send a bunch of officers to follow a bad lead. He didn't need any more trouble with Chief Patterson.

"What?" Ella quickly folded a map and tucked it in

the briefcase by her feet, drawing his attention to her bare legs.

In deference to the Florida heat, she was wearing a skirt that didn't make it any easier to keep his distance. It figured that the first woman he'd been this attracted to in years lived in another state and was determined to keep things professional while she was here.

She'd acted flustered during dinner last night, and his mom had definitely guessed something was up. Ella's inability to hide her feelings was such an odd contrast with her ability to quickly dissect the personalities of killers that he was tempted to probe the inconsistency. Preferably with more kissing.

A smile pulled on his lips, and he fought to contain it.

Ella's eyes narrowed. "What?"

"I called my sister." Logan rejoined her at the table. "Theresa's tire went flat when they were together, not when she was on her way to the airport. Becky says it blew close to her house the day before Theresa left and the two of them changed it. That's not how the killer grabbed Theresa."

"So, we still don't know how he targeted Theresa or how he grabbed her. Or where. But it still looks like an ambush to me, so he must've gotten her to stop along the way to the airport—maybe to help him if he pretended *he* had a flat tire?"

Logan shrugged, not convinced. "It's possible, but honestly, I don't see Theresa stopping in a deserted area by herself. Calling the cops to tell them someone was stranded seems more likely."

"Well, let's assume he got her to stop somehow. Maybe he blocked the road."

Logan felt his back teeth grind together as he imagined Theresa punching down on the brakes, relieved not to have hit someone, only to be abducted. As he'd done over and over again during the past few days, he tried not to think about what his sister's friend had endured after that.

When he didn't say anything, Ella suggested, "The other option is that he met Theresa sometime earlier in the week and set up a meeting with her, but from everything we know, that seems unlikely."

"Yeah, I think you're right about the ambush."

"Well, like I told your sister yesterday, an ambush abduction—instead of some kind of charm approach—suggests the killer isn't likely to have talked to Theresa beforehand. Followed her, yes, but not gotten too close." Her words picked up speed, and he could tell she was in her zone now. "He's probably socially awkward, unmarried, a loner."

Logan grabbed his pen, started jotting notes. This was what he'd been waiting for—the profiling magic that would help him stop this killer. "Okay. So, I'm not going to find him trolling for victims in the local bar?"

"Probably not. If he is, he's the guy sitting in the corner by himself watching everyone."

"Well, that sounds creepy."

"Which is why I don't think he'd do it. People might remember him. Plus, he'd be uncomfortable."

Logan readied his pen. "Okay, so if I'm not going to find him by hitting the clubs Theresa and Becky went to, then what?"

"You should still retrace their steps. He might be trolling in the same places. And if he's worried about the fact that we have a body—which he probably is—he might try to talk to the cops to find out what they know."

Logan raised an eyebrow. "Really? That doesn't seem very inconspicuous."

"Well, he'd either try to play it casual—act like a concerned citizen who's shocked at the murder and wants to know how we're keeping everyone else safe. Or, if there's reason to talk to him in the course of the investigation—say, he's working at one of the places Theresa went—he might use that opening to try and find out what we know. Your patrol officers should get the name of anyone they talk to about the case."

Logan frowned, but jotted down the suggestion anyway. "That could be a long list. We don't get many murders in Oakville. We're questioning everyone. What else can you tell me about this guy?"

"He's intelligent. He knew to wipe the car down for prints *and* he dropped it in a spot seemingly unconnected to Theresa's abduction. He disposed of the body in a way that meant we almost didn't have one. Plus, he abducted her once everyone here thought she was already home and apparently no one in Arkansas had noticed she wasn't back yet."

"You think that's important?"

"It would be quite a lucky coincidence. And I don't believe in those. So, yes, I think it's important. I think it means he stalked her first. And I think once the thrill wears off, he'll be trolling for his next victim."

Theresa had been stalked. Logan had gone to dinner one evening with Becky and Theresa, and had joined them for ice cream another day. And all his police training had failed him. He hadn't noticed the man who was watching and would ultimately kill Theresa. And that man was still out there, still a threat.

The guilt gnawed at his insides, making his throat constrict. He looked away from Ella, but it was too late.

Her hand on his wrist was light, but it affected him

more than a stack of case files dropped on his head. He sucked in a deep breath. "Sorry."

"I understand. I have a case like this, too."

He whipped his head back, his guilt morphing into frustration. Since Theresa had died, too many people had told him they understood. Too many people had pretended to know how he felt investigating the person who'd killed his sister's friend, in the town where he was supposed to have kept her safe. He was tired, and he was tired of the placating. His words came out rough and angry and staccato before he could rein them in. "You have a case where you didn't protect someone and that person was murdered?"

He knew he'd crossed the line even before her dark brown eyes shifted to near-black, before her jaw jutted out, and she replied, "Well, that's not what I was talking about, but actually, I do."

She didn't give him time to apologize, just grabbed his hand and placed it just underneath the hem of her skirt.

His brain instantly shut down. When it started working again, he realized the skin on her thigh was puckered and rough. A scar.

"I got one bullet to the leg. Just missed my femoral artery or I wouldn't be here. My partner got two bullets, both to the chest. He didn't make it."

She jumped to her feet and turned her back to him, but he heard her shaky, indrawn breath. "I was a newbie in the gangs unit. My partner had been there for years. We got a tip and it went bad. Intellectually, I know there was nothing I could have done, but that doesn't really stop me from feeling it was at least partly my fault."

She spun back around, and her anger was palpable. "Let's take a break."

She had already left the conference room before he'd finished saying sorry.

Almost instantly, she ran back in. "Logan, get out here."

"What?" He jumped to his feet and followed her.

At the front of the station, through the glass separating the area open to the public from the secure area, he could see a group of cops gathered around someone. Even Chief Patterson was there, his body hunched forward. Logan didn't need to be able to hear what they were saying to read their tone, and it was grim.

He hurried past the station's bullpen out through the key-card doors to the front desk area, with Ella right behind him. They pushed their way around the crowd until they could see the focus of the cops' attention.

It was a woman in her twenties, wearing a T-shirt she'd put on backward and jeans. Her long blond hair fell in a tangled mess. Thin streaks of mascara bled down her face, tears still falling, and even from a distance, the smell of alcohol seeped from her.

"I'm telling you, this isn't like her," the woman cried. "She should have been back at the hotel by now!"

"How long has she been missing, ma'am?" the chief asked. His calm tone didn't match the anxiety radiating from him.

"My name is Kelly. And she went missing yesterday. We were planning to drive home this morning, but we decided to stay a few more days, so we went to the club last night."

"Did your friend leave with anyone, Kelly?" the chief pressed.

"No. Look, I lost track of her at the club, so I went back to the hotel and fell asleep. When I woke up this morning, she still wasn't back."

"Have you tried calling her? Is it possible she went home with someone?"

"Yes, I tried calling her! It goes straight to voice mail. And Laurie's not like that. She likes to party, sure, but she doesn't go home with random guys."

"Do you have a picture?" Ella spoke up.

Kelly turned toward Ella. Maybe because she was the only other woman in the room, Kelly rushed over, digging around in the purse dangling from her shoulder until she pulled out a camera. "Here." She held it out to Ella, an image on the screen.

Logan leaned over Ella's shoulder to see it and an anvil seemed to punch through his chest, leaving behind a deep fear of just what evil Oakville was facing.

The woman in the picture had long, dark hair, just like Theresa. She looked like a college student, just like Theresa. And right before she was supposed to leave town, she'd gone missing. Just like Theresa.

Oakville's serial killer had found his next victim.

Elizabeth Heiter

Chapter Five

"Let's go over it one more time."

Logan's expression was mild, but even through the one-way glass, Ella could see the strain lurking below the surface. Across from him, Kelly slumped in her seat, her hands trembling around her third cup of coffee. It was hard to tell if the coffee had sobered her up or just made her jittery, along with hungover.

"I've told you everything," Kelly groaned. "Why are we still talking? Go out and find her." Her voice shook when she added, "Look in the marsh where that other girl was found."

Logan leaned closer, his face softening. "We have officers searching for Laurie right now. I'm asking you to tell me again because sometimes the smallest detail—the thing you think is unimportant—is what matters."

He was good at this. Ella had listened to a lot of police interviews in the past two years and she'd learned that the best detectives were patient. Kelly had already told the story twice, but certain little details had been off just enough that Ella knew she was hiding something. Whatever it was, it might be the key to finding Laurie—and maybe to finding their perp.

"So far the marsh is clear."

Ella spun to face the officer who'd come into the observation room as he dragged a chair toward the glass and slumped into it.

"What about the bars?" It had been four hours since Kelly had shown up at the station and officers had been sent out to talk to everyone who worked at the bars she and Laurie had hit before Laurie disappeared.

The officer blinked bloodshot eyes, and Ella realized he was one of the second shift officers who'd been called back in to join in the search. "So far, we've got a number of people who remember Laurie. Apparently, she was drinking a lot and being pretty loud. And dancing with half the local boys."

"Does anyone remember her leaving with someone?"

"Not yet. But we have two reports of her mentioning that she was driving home first thing in the morning."

Ella frowned. "Kelly says they changed their mind about leaving this morning, that they were going to stay a few more days."

The officer shrugged. "That's all I know."

"Huh."

"What?"

Ella glanced down at him. "Maybe that's what Kelly's lying about. Maybe they really did plan to leave today."

"Why would she lie about that?"

"I have no idea."

"Why do you think she's lying about anything?"

Ella gestured through the one-way glass to where Logan had gotten Kelly back to the point in her story where she said she'd lost track of Laurie.

Kelly fidgeted, staring down at her coffee cup. "I just turned around and realized she wasn't there anymore. I couldn't find her, so I figured I'd see her back at the hotel."

"And you were on the dance floor when you realized this?"

"Yeah."

Logan didn't say anything for a long moment, and Kelly looked back up at him. "When you talked about this earlier," he said, "you told me you were up at the bar."

Kelly scowled, turning the coffee cup around and around. "Whatever. Why does it matter?"

"You did talk to her before you went back to the hotel, didn't you, Kelly?"

Kelly's shoulders dropped just as the chief walked into the observation room behind Ella. "Yeah, okay. I was afraid you wouldn't look for her if I told you…"

The chief crowded between Ella and the officer, leaning toward the glass. "I knew there was more to this," he muttered.

"She was talking to a couple of guys, okay? She wanted to stay at the bar longer, but I was tired."

"We need a description of these guys, Kelly," Logan said, only a hint of frustration in his voice.

Kelly waved a hand in front of her. "Okay, yes, she was trying to pick one of them up, but it wasn't going to happen!"

"We still need those descriptions."

"She texted me an hour later. Said the guy had a girlfriend, and she was going to have another drink and then come back."

Ella glanced at the chief, who was standing so close to her she could see the individual strands of silver weaving through his dark blond hair. "I knew it," he mumbled, but he sounded relieved.

The officer straightened in his chair. "Maybe she wasn't grabbed on her way back to the hotel. Maybe she went home with someone."

Ella frowned. "Maybe."

The chief looked at Ella as Logan had Kelly describe the men Laurie had talked to at the bar. "I thought you said the killer was socially awkward?" the chief pressed.

"Well—"

"The profile you gave Logan said he wasn't charming these women, that he wouldn't troll at bars."

"That's true—"

"So, either Laurie went home with someone she picked up at a bar who *isn't* the killer or your profile is wrong. Which one is it?"

"Profiling isn't an exact science," Ella said as the door opened again and Hank O'Connor ran in. "I don't think this killer would be picking up women at bars, but—"

The chief gestured to the interrogation room. "It sure sounds like she didn't leave that bar alone."

"That's true," Hank said. "We've got reports from a couple of tourists at the last bar they hit that Laurie left with another spring breaker. Tall blond kid who was hitting on every girl in the room."

The chief looked pointedly at Ella, his tone mocking. "That sound like your serial killer?"

AFTER SPENDING A long day trying—and failing—to track down Laurie, Ella fell into a deep sleep. If she dreamed of bodies surfacing in marshes and women with burns on their necks, she didn't remember it. She woke to the sound of a door slamming.

"Let's *go!*" a man's voice, full of panic, called.

Ella blinked the sleep from her eyes and threw off the covers. When she peeked into the hotel hallway, she saw a pair of women hurrying toward the front lobby, lugging suitcases behind them. Across the hall, a man pushed open his door, holding it for a woman who was still jamming clothes in a duffel bag as she walked.

"Excuse me," Ella said, "What's going on?"

The man gave her an incredulous look. "You didn't hear? There's a killer in Oakville. Some sicko targeting women on spring break. If you're alone, I'd get out of here now. I'm taking my girlfriend home."

The woman, a tiny brunette in her early twenties, rolled her eyes as she passed her boyfriend. "We're heading up the coast. We're going to find a beach that doesn't have a serial killer feeding people to the alligators."

Apparently the news was out. The locals at least had already known about Theresa, but the serial killer angle hadn't seemed to catch on. Until now.

"Thanks," Ella managed, closing the door to change out of her pajamas and into another skirt and T-shirt that would be sticking to her by midday.

She grabbed her phone, but instead of calling Logan, walked to the hotel lobby. Near the check-in desk was a stack of newspapers. Weaving through the crowd of tanned and hungover spring breakers standing in line to check out early, Ella opened a paper.

The headline for the lead story screamed out, Serial Killer Stalks Coeds in Oakville.

Dropping some change for the paper, she carried it back to her room, reading as she walked. The reporter had led with a quote from Kelly about Laurie's disappearance. After a few paragraphs theorizing on the serial killer angle, he'd shifted into summarizing Theresa's murder—including details of the burns she'd sustained.

Ella cursed as she let herself back into her room. If Theresa's killer had murdered before, he'd managed to destroy all evidence in the marsh. Now, between Theresa's body showing up, Laurie's disappearance and the sudden media flurry, he was either going to go to ground or he was going to forget about being careful and troll for as many victims as he could, as fast as he could.

Which meant she needed to get to the Oakville police station and help them find him before either of those things happened.

She picked up her briefcase and crammed her notes back inside. She was locking the hotel room behind her when her cell phone rang. "Logan," she answered without looking. "I'm on my way."

"Good to know. But this isn't Logan," Scott drawled.

"Scott." Ella forced herself to keep moving. The police station was two blocks over; usually Logan called and picked her up, but today she was glad to have the time to herself. "I'm sorry I haven't called." She tried to put a cheery note in her voice. "How's California?"

"Well, I'd rather you were the one hitting the spa with Maggie, but otherwise, not bad."

Ella couldn't help feeling guilty. Normally when the three of them went on trips together, she and Maggie spent a certain amount of time pampering themselves while Scott took off on his own, usually chasing skirts. "You're not letting her out of your sight, are you?"

"Are you kidding me?" There was nothing funny in Scott's tone. "Maggie may be the SWAT agent, but I'm still her big brother. I'm sticking close."

Not that Maggie should be in any immediate danger, even if Ella wrong and the Fishhook Rapist wasn't still in Florida. He had never gone back for any of his victims. But they'd planned the vacation a few months ago, when Maggie had gotten a letter, in which the writer claimed to be him.

The letter hadn't made any threats. If the sender hadn't made reference to an evening in September nearly a decade ago, you might have thought it was a love letter. It made Ella feel nauseated just thinking about it.

Follow-up by a case agent had revealed that he hadn't communicated with any of his other victims. The FBI lab hadn't been able to get anything useful off of Maggie's letter. And none of them were really sure how the Fishhook Rapist had tracked down Maggie's address. Follow-up on the postbox in Georgia from which the letter had been sent hadn't given them anything useful. Without any real leads, that had seemed to be the end of it.

But ever since the letter had arrived, she and Scott had made a vow to watch out for Maggie. Between the three of them, Scott and Maggie were the most trained and skilled in a fight. Maggie had been with the Washington Field Office's SWAT team for the past four years and Scott had joined the FBI's Hostage Rescue Team as a sniper a year ago.

Ella knew she could help best by being here, and now that she had just Scott on the phone… She opened her mouth to tell him why she'd bailed on their vacation, but he spoke first.

"Maggie got another letter."

Anger flooded her system, mixed with a heavy hit of fear. Sudden contact like this wasn't good. Especially if it was escalating. "When?"

"The day we left for California."

Which explained why Maggie had looked so uneasy at the airport. The guilt Ella had been holding back burst like a broken dam. "Where was it postmarked from?"

"Some town in Florida."

"Not Cape Coral?"

"No. Somewhere north of there."

So not Oakville, either. "What did the letter say?"

"Same old crap," Scott said, fury simmering in his voice. "No overt threats, just…his sick fantasy."

"I'm so sorry I'm not there."

She'd spoken so quietly she wasn't even sure Scott had heard her until he replied, "Are you going to tell me why you're not?"

"I got a case—"

"I've known you all your life, kiddo." Beneath the anger over what was happening to Maggie, there was a hint of annoyance in his tone. "Give it to me straight."

"Really. Logan came to me with a case. I was planning to read the file, give him a quick analysis, and get to the airport. But when I read it…" Ella let out a heavy breath. "Scott, I'm in Florida. A place called Oakville, south of Cape Coral. The victim here was murdered and dumped in the marsh, but first she was burned on the back of her neck. Too much decomp to tell for sure, but it could be a hook."

There was a long pause before Scott said, "You took the case on your own."

It wasn't a question, but Ella answered anyway. "Yes. I still don't know if they're connected, but this girl looks a lot like Maggie did ten years ago. And if it is the same person… Scott, I might be able to catch him before another September first comes around."

There was a strong protective note in Scott's voice when he warned her, "Be careful, Ella. And call me. I want updates. Every day, okay?"

"Yeah, okay. You're not going to say anything to Maggie, are you? Not until I know for sure?"

"No, I'll wait. She actually bought your story. And she's relaxed for the first time in months. The beach is doing her good."

"That's great." Ella raised her head and realized she'd

reached the police station. She didn't even remember walking there, didn't remember leaving the long dirt trail behind the hotel and arriving in the main part of town, where the station was located. "I've got to go."

"Be careful, Ella. Hurry and get this guy and join us in California, okay?"

"Believe me, I'm trying. I'll talk to you soon."

Hanging up, Ella walked into the station, which was brimming with cops, but not as many as yesterday. One of them let her into the locked back area and she spotted Logan almost immediately, pouring himself a cup of coffee from one of the station's carafes that seemed to be everywhere. His hair was sticking up on top, she could tell even from a distance that there were circles under his eyes, and he was still wearing the jeans and green T-shirt he'd had on the day before.

Ella hurried over to him. "Did you come straight back here after you dropped me off last night?"

Logan looked up with surprise, apparently so tired he hadn't even heard her approach. "I hadn't planned on it, but I got a call that they found the guy Laurie left the bar with."

Ella grabbed his arm, her eyes widening. "And?"

Logan shifted his coffee mug to his other hand. "We still haven't found Laurie. I spent a lot of the night questioning Jeff, the kid who was with her. Local, twenty-one, lived here all his life. He's got a reputation with the women, but nothing violent, no record. He says she went back to his apartment with him, but that she left around three a.m. and he figured she was home by now. He claims he didn't take her number, that she didn't ask for his."

"You could have called me last night. I would have come back."

"No need." Logan rubbed the back of his hand over his eyes, took a long swallow of coffee. "Jeff shares an apartment with a friend, who came home around two, when the bars closed. His friend alibis him, says the girl left and that Jeff was home until we came to question him."

Ella frowned. Her gut told her Laurie's disappearance was connected to Theresa's and that the killer wouldn't have picked her up at a bar. But whenever someone went missing after going someplace alone with a stranger, you had to consider that stranger suspect number one. "You believe the alibi?"

"Yeah. And, honestly, I've met this kid on occasion. He's a surfer and he's got a reputation there, too."

"So?"

"His reputation is that he surfs because he thinks it's a good way to pick up women, but he's a wimp. Apparently he's afraid of just about everything in the ocean. He runs to shore a lot, afraid he's seen a shark fin, only to have his friends make fun of his fear of dolphins. I don't see him going to the marshes when the alligators are feeding."

"Oh." Ella sighed. "So, we've still got nothing?"

"Pretty much. At this point, most of the station believes Laurie is sleeping it off somewhere and that she'll show up soon."

"But not you, right?"

"No. Laurie's picture looked too much like Theresa for me to accept that this is a coincidence."

"About that—" Ella looked around, then realized she still had her hand on Logan's arm. Flushing, she quickly dropped it to her side. "Can we grab the conference room? I want to talk to you about something."

Logan grinned and even with his bloodshot eyes and

rumpled, day-old clothes, it shot Ella's heart rate up. "I hope it's about going to dinner at my parents' house again."

His parents' house. Where she'd thrown herself at him. She felt her cheeks color and turned away from him before he could notice, heading for the conference room where they'd worked yesterday. "It's about why I'm really here."

"I WAS WONDERING when you were going to spill your big secret." Logan perched on the edge of the conference table as Ella closed the door behind them.

When she turned to face him, she looked nervous, making him wonder just how bad her news was. "If you're telling me, you must be pretty sure Theresa's murder is connected to the old case you had, right?"

Ella ran a hand through her long hair, pushing it out of her face. "It's not..." She closed her eyes briefly. "It's not exactly an old case, Logan."

He sat a little straighter, praying she wasn't about to tell him she'd personally known the murder victim she thought was connected to his case.

She let out a heavy sigh, and then, to his surprise, she walked over and lifted herself up onto the table beside him. "When I was in my senior year of college, one of my best friends was abducted."

Sympathy and dread mingled, and a wave of sorrow rushed over him at the thought of Ella having to endure that. "Oh, man, Ella, I'm so sorry."

He didn't even realize he'd threaded his fingers through hers until she looked down at their entwined hands and then back up at him. The expression in her eyes—a mixture of sadness, determination, and something that looked an awful lot like affection—made him want to wrap his arm around her shoulder and haul her close. Instead, he tightened his hold on her hand, trying to tell her without words that there was nothing she couldn't share with him.

Her lips trembled, as though she was trying to smile at him but couldn't manage it, and then she continued, "We shared a dorm room. Honestly, I was worried when she didn't come home that night, but I thought she..." Ella's shoulders jerked and she shook her head. "I knew she and her boyfriend had been talking about taking things to the next level. I thought she was with him and she'd forgotten to tell me."

And she'd probably carried around the guilt of not going to the police sooner ever since. "It's not your fault, Ella."

Her dark brown eyes were more serious than he'd ever seen them as she replied, "Yeah, I know that. But it doesn't mean I'll ever forget how wrong I was."

And when she finished college, she'd picked a job that required her to be right about that kind of predator pretty much one hundred percent of the time. So, apparently, she'd never really forgiven herself, either.

From the few days he'd known her, Ella had shown a quick wit, an easy smile, so much personable confidence. He'd never for a second have guessed she had tragedy in her past.

"Then, the next morning, when she stumbled back to the room—"

"Whoa. She's alive?" Logan interrupted.

Ella's face twisted. "Yes. It was Maggie. My friend you met at the airport."

The woman with the pretty, but haunted, blue eyes. "What happened to her?"

The emotion left Ella's voice and Logan recognized her clinical, detached profiler mode instantly. "She was raped. And he branded her on the back of her neck with the image of a hook."

A heavy weight sank to the bottom of Logan's stomach. "The Fishhook Rapist?" Every fall, Logan hoped not to see that name in the national news, but each year, it was there again. And this past September, he'd come to Florida. "You think the Fishhook Rapist is now a killer?"

"I think maybe he was always killing in between and we just never knew it."

Logan let out a string of curses. "The burns on Theresa's body," he said. "That's why you asked me if they could've been brands."

"Yes." Ella pulled her hand from his, turning to face him. "Logan, back in college, Maggie had long dark hair. She looked a lot like Theresa."

Logan felt his shoulders slump. Could this get any worse?

"Logan—"

From Ella's tone, Logan knew it was about to. "What?"

"The Fishhook Rapist seems to pick girls in their late teens or early twenties, girls with long dark hair and slender builds."

"Like Theresa," Logan agreed. "It makes sense. The women he lets go are his way of bragging, and in between, the others feed his twisted need for violence."

"Logan, what I was going to say is that there's someone else who fits that description."

The room seemed to close in around Logan. He felt Ella grab his arm as he realized. "My sister."

Chapter Six

"How sure are you that Theresa's killer is the Fishhook Rapist?" Logan paced back and forth in front of her, running his hands through already messy hair, which made Ella's fingers itch to slide through it, too.

"I'm *not* sure. It's a theory. Based primarily on the hook-shaped burn on Theresa's neck. It looks a heck of a lot like the Fishhook Rapist's signature. But if it is the same person, then we're not looking at a killer who's been getting away with this for a few weeks or months. We're talking about a perpetrator who has eluded the FBI for a decade."

Logan stopped pacing. "Well, that's a cheery thought."

Ella hopped off the table and found herself standing closer to Logan than she'd expected. Close enough to see the scruff on his chin, the sexy curve of his lips. Close enough to imagine how easy it would be to reach her hand up and around the back of his neck, then pull him close and fuse her mouth to his.

Focus, Cortez.

She scooted quickly sideways to create a little distance. He inhaled sharply, as if he knew what she'd been thinking.

"Well, if it is the same person, do you think he's sticking around here? The rapes happen once a year, in a different part of the country each time. Is he picking one location in between and killing? Or is he traveling the whole time like those highway serial killers the FBI is always after?"

Ella shrugged, frustrated. "I don't know, Logan. I've studied the Fishhook Rapist for years and I never even considered that he might be killing in between until you brought me your case. But my gut tells me that if it is him, he's not in our HSK database." Because of the number of killers who picked up transient victims, often along highways, the FBI had created a database specifically to track those murders.

"The Fishhook Rapist is a planner in every single detail. And the evidence here suggests careful planning, too. Remember how we talked about his choice of drop site?"

"Knowing the kind of details about the marsh that a local would," Logan agreed.

"Right. So, whether or not this is the same person, I think he's been here a while, planning the details of the murder. And I don't think he intended to leave anytime soon. But with the recent media coverage..." She sank into a conference chair.

"So, what do I tell my sister? Leave town? Stay here and move in with my parents?"

"Honestly, she's probably safer here, with you looking out for her. But moving in with your parents until we catch this guy is a good idea. Also not going anywhere alone, since this guy is probably ambushing his victims. He most likely stalked Theresa before he killed her. And if Theresa was with Becky the whole time she was here..."

Logan cursed. "Great. Because I wasn't feeling paranoid enough already."

He grabbed the chair next to her, dragging it close so their knees were almost touching. His eyes locked on hers as if she had all the answers. "What else do I tell her to keep her safe, Ella?"

Panic fluttered in Ella's chest. It was part of her job not just to advise on the behavioral makeup of killers, but also how to catch them, and how to keep the population safe until that happened. But the pressure of trying to keep Logan's little sister out of harm—especially if she'd already been targeted—felt too intense, too personal. It felt way too much like her desire to protect Maggie.

A queasy, nervous feeling swam around in her stomach. She'd only known Logan a few days. Of course she wanted to keep his sister safe, but it couldn't be as personal as Maggie. She couldn't let it. Because as soon as she helped Logan catch this killer, she had to leave town. And she'd never see Logan again.

That thought made the queasiness dart upward, tension clamping her chest. She liked this guy, genuinely liked him, way too much.

Even if he didn't live in a different state, her relationships were destined to be short-term. It didn't matter how good her intentions were, how nice the guy was, it always ended after a few months. She'd get one important case after the next, get tunnel-visioned until it ended and then discover the guy hadn't waited around.

"Ella?" Logan was still staring at her, but his gaze had turned questioning. "You okay?"

Ignoring the question, Ella said, "The best way to keep Becky safe is to keep her close. Drill it into her not to go anywhere she could find herself alone. This guy is smart, but he isn't charming or confident. He's socially awkward. He's not going to approach her in a group somewhere and try to lure her away with him. He's not going to come after her in your parents' house, either. That's not his style. He'd want her to come to him. He'd be waiting for an opportunity to create an ambush and he'd do it somewhere deserted. Just don't give him that chance."

Logan's big hands wrapped around hers, instantly warming them, and sending a suspicious warmth upward. "Thank you, Ella."

Oh, this was not good.

He stood, pulling his phone from his pocket. "I'm going to give her a call." He started pacing as he talked to Becky, gesturing with his free hand as he went into full-on big brother mode.

Ella tracked him with her eyes as he walked, thinking about all the details she had somehow catalogued without realizing it over the past few days. The way his green eyes darkened when he was worried. The way he looked at her with such compassion when he knew she was hurting. The way he could shift from serious, competent homicide detective to easygoing, teasing colleague to intense, irresistible potential lover in a heartbeat.

Oh, she was in so much trouble.

"How come you don't have a partner?"

Logan glanced at Ella as they sped out of town in his Chevy Caprice, grinning as he purposely misunderstood her. "Interested in my love life, are you?"

She flushed and fidgeted and he tried not to laugh. "I meant, why don't you have a partner in your job?"

His smile faded. "Because my last name is Greer."

"Really? Your chief dislikes your dad so much that he wouldn't assign you a partner? That seems…dangerous."

"Not exactly," Logan said, weaving around traffic as he headed toward the highway that Theresa would have taken to the airport, a stretch of road that was often deserted at night. Where Theresa might have been abducted by a serial killer as she drove to the airport at four in the morning. "But the whole force knows how much the chief resents me, so no one wants any of that coming down on them."

Ella was silent, but one glance at her pensive expression and he knew more questions were coming.

She didn't disappoint. "If it's that bad, there must be easier places to work as a homicide detective. I don't think you'd have trouble getting hired."

"I think you'd better wait until this case is closed before you make predictions like that."

"Oh, come on. You're good at your job. I knew that the second you showed up at Aquia looking for a profiler."

"And yet, you pulled your gun on me," he teased, pleased that she thought he was good at what he did. Getting serious, he added, "I may not be planning to run for mayor or the chief of police like my family wants, but I can't really imagine living anywhere else."

She was silent a little too long, but when he glanced over at her again, she said quickly, "It's nice that you're so close to your family."

"Aren't you?"

"No."

"Really?" How could anyone not be close to Ella? With her determination to help her friend, no matter how it impacted her long-awaited vacation? With her humor and warmth, despite the grisly things she saw in her job every day? With that quick smile that instantly lit her whole face, made her dark eyes sparkle? Man, she was… perfect.

The steering wheel jerked in his hand, and he corrected fast, but not before Ella shot him a quizzical look.

She wasn't perfect, he told himself. She only seemed

that way because he hadn't had enough time to learn her flaws.

"Yes, really," she said. "They don't approve of my job."

"Why? Because they think it's too dangerous?" Logan slowed as they reached the outskirts of Oakville and turned slowly onto the highway. Cars honked and sped around him, since traffic was much heavier in the daytime. But at night, if a predator knew how to set an ambush, it was the ideal spot.

He and Ella were looking for any sign that Theresa had been forced to stop the car unexpectedly, like skid marks.

"I'm the black sheep," Ella said, as she peered carefully out the car windows, checking both sides of the road. "I was going to stay in Indiana and be a teacher like my dad until Maggie was raped. Then, Scott, Maggie, and I—we'd been best friends since we were little— the three of us made a pact. We were going to join the FBI and stop guys like that from hurting anyone else."

Logan slowed even more as he divided his attention between watching for skid marks and concentrating on what made Ella tick. "And your parents didn't understand that?"

"They wanted me to stay close to home. They figured the FBI thing was just a phase. That's what they call it— my 'FBI thing.' They figured I'd get over it and come back home. Live close to them like my younger brothers. Give them more grandkids and come over every weekend for dinner."

Her shoulders jerked up, as if she was shrugging, as if it didn't matter, but even though she was facing away from him, he could tell it bothered her.

"My parents are from Puerto Rico," she explained. "My dad's second generation, my mom's first. My dad's a professor. He got a job at a university in Indiana and we moved there when I was six. My dad's parents came with us, that's how close we all are. It's like a family motto—don't make big decisions without everyone's input, and stick together. They just don't get how I could leave, especially for a job like this. They moved to this little farming town close to the university, instead of the city where my dad works, because they wanted to live in the kind of small community where everyone knows each other."

Logan imagined how hard it had been for her to tell them she was leaving.

"I went through the long application process, studied and trained like crazy to make it through the eighteen weeks at the Academy. I've been in the Bureau for six years now and still, the first thing I hear when I visit is, 'When are you going to give up that FBI thing and come home?'" She blew out a heavy breath and turned to face him. "So, I visit less and less often."

He started to tell her he was sorry, but she gave him a stiff smile and said, "But Maggie and Scott live close and they're basically family, too. So, it's not like I'm all alone in the world." The smile shifted into something more real. "So, don't give me that sad look."

"Believe me, there's nothing sad about you." He frowned as the lights ahead grew brighter and he still saw no sign of foul play. As much as he didn't like picturing someone forcing Theresa to slam her car to a stop, then grabbing her, they needed a lead. And Ella thought identifying how and where she'd been abducted would tell them a lot, help them find the killer. This had seemed the most likely option.

Ella looked discouraged, too. "Maybe he took her at the airport and then just drove out of there with her in the trunk? Some of those long-term lots get pretty empty at night. He could have left in her car and then come back for his own later."

Her tone told him she didn't believe it. "But you don't think so?"

"Not really. It is possible, because I just don't have enough information about what happened to Theresa to form a truly solid profile of her killer. But that's what's bothering me. It's not an accident that I don't have what I need. This guy is smart. He didn't get close enough to make Theresa or Becky suspicious, he dropped Theresa in a place where her body would disappear. And he grabbed her when no one would notice she was missing until a day later. The airport parking lot seems too uncertain. If someone else was there, then he'd lose his chance and she'd be gone."

"I've been thinking about the timing, too," Logan said. "If he was stalking her, then he knew she was leaving that day. He knew we'd all assume she was home. Maybe he'd looked into her life and knew she lived alone and wouldn't be immediately missed by someone waiting for her to come home from the airport either?"

Ella continued to scan the road, but her tone was grim when she said, "The timing is suspicious. Especially if he has Laurie right now. I know Kelly said they'd changed their minds and planned to stay a few more days, but if they'd originally planned to leave yesterday…"

"It's the same MO," Logan agreed.

There were officers looking for Laurie now, still trying to track her down, and Logan had wanted to spend the rest of his day on that, too. But Ella had convinced him that if questioning witnesses was going to lead them to Laurie, it would happen with or without him. But no one else was following leads on the serial killer angle, because although the media had jumped on the story, the rest of the police force still didn't believe it.

So, instead of heading into town to question anyone who might have seen Laurie, he was searching the highway. But as the scenery turned from barren, closed-down factories on one side and marshland on the other to city lights, he knew there was nothing to find. If Theresa had been taken while she was on the highway, she'd stopped willingly. And he just didn't believe she'd do that for a stranger.

He pulled off to the side, then did a U-turn and headed back toward Oakville. "What do we do now?"

Ella shook her head, looking troubled. "I don't know."

ELLA'S SHOULDER BLADES TENSED, and her steps slowed as she walked along the long, solitary trail toward the back of the hotel. She strained to listen, and there it was again. The sound of a vehicle, its tires rolling slowly along the dirt road somewhere behind her. She hadn't imagined it.

She whipped her head around, but she couldn't see anything in the dim light. The sun was barely peeking over the horizon. The path behind her curved around a dense patch of trees, sending the road out of her line of sight. She could hear the car still coming, slowly. Too slowly, as if it didn't want to be seen.

She should have let Logan drive her back to the hotel. Instead, after a long, frustrating day that had gotten them no closer to finding Laurie or figuring out how Theresa had been grabbed, she'd told him to go get some badly needed sleep. She'd wanted the chance to stretch her legs, walk off some of the tension that had been building inside her with every day that passed without getting any closer to knowing if this case was connected to Maggie's.

During the day, the trail from the hotel was packed

with tourists walking into town. Even at night, she'd seen enough people walking it that it hadn't occurred to her it might be empty tonight. But it was late. Apparently late enough that everyone was either out at the bars or back at the hotel.

Ella picked up her pace, resting her palm along the butt of the gun she always wore holstered at her hip. Her pulse jumped as she looked over her shoulder and finally spotted the vehicle, which was rolling along at a walker's pace, clearly trying not to be heard. It was a van, dark blue, and as she squinted, trying to see inside the vehicle, it slowed, easing slightly into the shadows of the trees.

Ella cursed and unholstered her gun. If this guy was planning to run her over, she'd have to shoot accurately and fast. And the only reason anyone in Oakville would be after her was Theresa's case.

She tightened her grip on her weapon, aiming straight at the front windshield.

The van's window rolled down and she darted off the trail where it would be harder for the driver to see or shoot her.

But he just called out, "This isn't the way to Seaside Resort, is it?"

Ella still couldn't really see him, so she kept her weapon raised, but her heart rate evened out. "No, this is the Traveler's Hotel."

"Thanks," he called, obviously unable to tell in the dark that she had a gun. Then he rolled up the window and backed his van down the road and around the corner.

Lowering her weapon, Ella let out a brief burst of laughter. She'd been chasing killers so long she was seeing them everywhere. She definitely needed to finish up this case and go lie on the beach for a week.

Holstering her Glock, Ella walked faster, just a little

too relieved once she'd locked herself into her hotel room. Flipping on the television, she changed into her pajamas and flopped onto the bed, ready for an evening of mindless sitcoms.

Before she could find one, there was a heavy knock at the door. Putting the TV on mute, Ella grabbed her Glock and stood off to the side of the door, peeking through the peephole.

"Logan," she breathed, setting her gun on the table by the door. The fact that she'd automatically assumed it was the guy from the blue van, holding a shotgun, confirmed that she needed a break from rummaging around in the minds of demented killers.

Ella opened the door to find Logan staring at his shoes. "I thought you were going home?"

"Ella, I'm sorry. A reporter—" He looked up and stopped midsentence, blinking at her attire.

Suddenly way too conscious of the fact that she was standing in the doorway in a pair of boxer shorts and a tank top with no bra, Ella crossed her arms over her chest. "A reporter what?"

His gaze travelled slowly down to her bare feet and back up again and Ella felt her pulse quicken at the inspection.

Finally he looked into her eyes, and the intensity there seemed to push her backward until he was standing inside her room, the door shut behind him. Then he leaned against it, just watching her.

There was a foot between them, but Ella imagined she could feel his body heat wafting toward her. Her mouth suddenly went dry.

Then Logan took a step forward and the foot became an inch. If she took a deep breath, they'd be touching.

Ella tilted her head back, expecting his mouth to

come down on hers, wanting it to. But instead, he raised his hand, cupping her cheek. Then he lowered his head slowly, so slowly, until his lips brushed hers.

The first gentle contact sent sparks of desire from her mouth to her fingertips and Ella pushed up on her tiptoes, gripped the front of his shirt with both hands, and leaned into the kiss. Then Logan opened his mouth and gave her exactly what she wanted.

With a low moan, she tugged him backward until her legs hit the bed and they fell onto it, his body covering hers. She jerked as the TV blasted on, then realized she'd landed on the remote.

Ignoring it, she slid her hands down to his waist, then up under the hem of his T-shirt, over the bunching muscles in his back, as his lips found hers again. One-night stands had never been her style, but she was completely lost as his tongue tangled around hers and his fingers dug into her hips.

"…an FBI profiler in Oakville."

"What?" Ella mumbled against Logan's mouth, trying to sit up as the words from the television penetrated her desire-fogged brain.

Logan glanced behind him at the TV, then let out a string of curses and pushed to his feet.

Instantly cold without his body covering hers, Ella shivered and stood, hugging herself. The TV screen cut to an image of a tall, blonde reporter thrusting a microphone toward Logan outside the police station as he walked out the door. "Detective, you suspect a serial killer is in Oakville?"

Logan looked blindsided as he ducked past the reporter with a "No comment." But there was something more in the deep red that rushed up his cheeks as he hurried toward his Chevy Caprice.

Ella looked questioningly at Logan.

"Ella, I—"

On the TV, the reporter yelled after him, "Is it true the FBI sent a profiler to consult on the case?"

Logan didn't answer, but the damage was done.

Ella sank onto the bed. Her secret was out. And if it got back to her boss in Aquia, there went her job.

Chapter Seven

"Theresa's credit card information just came in." Logan waved the pages at Ella as she entered the conference room where he'd just started working.

He'd been listening for his phone all morning, waiting for her to call and have him pick her up, but the call had never come. She'd walked to the station again. Probably because of what had almost happened between them last night.

As he watched her now, she turned away from him to get a cup of coffee from the carafe on the table. He felt amused by how poorly she hid her emotions. For some reason, as a profiler, he'd expected her to be expressionless most of the time. But Ella's feelings were usually stamped across her face.

Any second now she'd turn back and tell him the same thing she had the first time they'd kissed. That it was an *anomaly*. Which was not only stupid, but he definitely hoped it would be as untrue this time as it had been then.

To his surprise, when she squared her shoulders and turned around, she said, "If my boss gets wind of the fact that I'm here without permission, he's going to call me back to Aquia."

She rubbed the back of her neck and he suddenly noticed the deep circles under her eyes. She'd been up worrying about this, he realized. He wished she'd let him stick around and distract her instead.

The thought sent a powerful flash of desire through him. It made full-color images of Ella in her little pajama shorts and tank top blast into his brain. Fantasies of her pulling him down on top of her like she had last night. But then he pictured them continuing instead of being interrupted. He pictured her legs wrapping around his waist, her hands in his hair. Her voice, husky with passion, whispering his name.

Logan sucked in a deep breath and tried to blink the images away. He stepped closer, forcing her to look up at him.

"I'm so sorry, Ella. I swear, I tried to keep any knowledge about your presence totally in-station. I don't know how Lyla got hold of it."

"I know you did." She sighed, then squinted at him. "Lyla?"

Logan felt his face heat. "The reporter at the station."

Her eyes narrowed, filled with suspicion. Served him right for trying to get anything past a profiler.

She opened her mouth, so he preempted her, "Yes, we used to go out."

Something flashed in Ella's eyes. "It was pretty serious, I take it?"

When he didn't immediately answer, she cringed a little and he realized what he'd seen in her eyes. Jealousy.

A smile tugged at his lips, but faded fast as he admitted, "We were engaged."

"Oh." Surprise darted across her features. "Well, that *is* serious."

Before he could tell her it was long over, she hurried on, "Not that it's any of my business. Anyway, I just— I don't know what I'm going to do if my boss calls me back in." She set her coffee down untouched, rolled her shoulders. "I joined the Bureau because of that pact I told you about, the one that Maggie, Scott, and I made. But the job has become more than that. It's become really important to me. It's become...." She trailed off, looking lost and completely torn.

"I understand. If your boss calls, you'd have to leave." He reached out and folded her hand in his as dread and sadness coursed through him in equal measure. He didn't want her to leave. And it was about a heck of a lot more than this case.

She looked down at their entwined hands and tightened her grip. She had small hands, but man, was she strong. It was another one of those incongruities he loved about her.

His hand jerked in hers as he realized what he'd just thought. He felt her curious expression just as he felt himself go a little light-headed. He *did* love her odd little inconsistencies. And that nervous feeling rolling around in the pit of his stomach at the thought of her leaving wasn't simply about the way she looked in that skirt or the way her mouth felt against his.

It was about how she'd gone instantly still and serious when he'd asked her to help him keep his sister safe. It was about how she'd stood up for him in the diner that first day he'd met her. It was about how she made him feel every time he looked at her. Which, even in the middle of a homicide investigation, was freaking *giddy*.

A curse wanted to break out, but he held it in. He didn't believe in love at first sight. And given the short time they'd known each other, that was what it might as well be. Which was completely ridiculous.

This was a complication he hadn't expected. And one he didn't need in the middle of Theresa's case. With a woman who lived too far away, who'd be gone as soon as the case was closed. Or sooner.

"Logan?" Ella's voice sounded remote as she asked, "Are you okay?"

"Not really."

"Look, I know you need my help." She gave a quick nod, as if she'd just made a decision. "I'll work it out. I've got important reasons to stay myself."

He took a deep breath, getting it together, then smiled at her, wishing one of those reasons was him. "Whatever I can do, let me know. I'll talk to your boss if you want."

"Well, thanks, but that's probably not the best idea. I'd rather he didn't find out you put in a request for a profiler that he denied and that I took the case anyway. I'll figure it out if he calls. Until then, let's see what you've got."

It took him a second to realize she was talking about the credit card information. "Right. Okay." He glanced out the conference room door into the station to make sure no one was within sight. Then, he lifted her hand and pressed it to his lips before letting go.

He saw her surprise as he picked up the thin stack of charge information. "These were faxed in from her credit card companies. I was about to get started on them when you arrived."

She settled into a conference chair and yanked her hair back into a ponytail, her serious face on. "Great. I'll take half."

She held out her hand and he gave her the coffee cup she'd set down beside the carafe, then sat next to her. He slid the charges from half of Theresa's cards over to her, keeping the rest for himself. "I figured I'd start from the end of each statement and work my way backward, see if I found anything interesting."

"Makes sense," Ella said, taking a quick sip of coffee, then flipping to the last page in her pile. "Uh, Logan…"

"What?"

"What time did Theresa leave for the airport?"

He gave her a half smile. "Show-off. You already have something?"

"This past Sunday, at seven a.m., she's got a charge at a gas station."

"Seven?" Logan leaned forward, until Ella's bangs brushed his forehead, as he squinted down at the small text. "Her flight left at six thirty. I checked right after we found her body, confirming that she hadn't changed the flight for some reason, and she hadn't. Obviously, she didn't make it, but because time of death wasn't pinpointed that closely, I assumed someone had already grabbed her by then."

He looked up and found Ella's eyes inches from his. The other times he'd been this close to her, his eyes had been closed as he'd sought out her mouth. Now, he realized her deep brown eyes were the shade of really good dark coffee. He'd expected flecks of lighter brown around the edges, or a hint of some other color up close, but they were just pure, deep brown. They were mesmerizing, and he realized he was staring, but he couldn't seem to stop.

Her pupils dilated and he leaned even closer, reached his hand up to touch her face.

"Logan," Ella said, her voice unsteady. She moved away from him, breaking the spell.

"I'll bet the killer *did* grab her before she could make her flight. This charge probably means Theresa wasn't using the card. I think it was her killer."

"WHAT TIME DID you need again?" the kid at the gas station asked Logan.

Despite looking as if he was still in high school, the

pimply-faced kid was the manager on duty. He was sitting in front of a dinosaur-age TV in the back room, rewinding through hours of security footage from last Sunday, which, thank goodness, the gas station hadn't taped over yet.

He also had the attention span of a gnat. He kept glancing over at Ella, who stood beside the kid's chair, hands planted on her hips. The kid couldn't stop staring at her gun. And her legs, which Logan had to admit looked pretty fantastic in the knee-length skirt she wore.

The kid checked out her legs again, and Logan was ready to slap him upside the head. "Ten minutes before seven," he bit out.

"Okay." The kid nodded, still rewinding, and glanced over at Ella again, his eyes practically bugging out of his head. "So, what kind of gun do you carry?"

"One issued by the Federal Bureau of Investigation," she replied dryly, then, "Stop!" as the time stamp on the bottom of the tape reached 6:50 a.m..

On either side of him, she and Logan leaned toward the screen. The kid backed up his chair a little, seeming uncomfortable with their sudden intensity.

On the tiny TV, cars came and went as Logan carefully watched the time stamp. The person who paid at 7:01 a.m. was the one they wanted. That was the guy who had Theresa's credit card. And if he had her card, he was almost certainly the person who'd killed her.

With luck, he'd glance up at the camera, give them a good shot to plaster across every news network. Make it easy to track him down so Logan could slap a pair of cuffs on him.

Maybe the guy would even resist, and Logan would have to use a little force to put him down. The idea made his hands tense hopefully into fists.

Another car pulled out of the gas station, and then a little red compact drew up to a pump. Logan leaned even closer, his jaw locking as the driver's side door opened. And then the driver did look up, right at the camera.

Beside him, Ella did a double take. "Logan, is that…"

His shock was followed by a rush of unease. This wasn't right. This wasn't right at all. Had their investigation been going in completely the wrong direction?

He turned to Ella, and the shock he felt was written all over her face, too. "It's Theresa."

Ella looked at the screen, then at him. Between them, the kid's head swiveled back and forth; a moment later, he ducked his head and pushed his chair backward so he was entirely out of their way.

Logan gestured to the door. "We'll call if we need you."

The kid gave Ella one last longing look, then left them alone.

"Are you sure her flight was at six thirty?" Ella asked.

"Positive."

"So, what's she doing on the opposite side of town half an hour after her flight left?" Ella frowned at the screen, where Theresa held out her key fob, as though she was locking the car doors, then headed inside the building, presumably to pay. "She certainly doesn't look like she's being coerced. It doesn't look like anyone else is in the car, either. I'd thought…"

Ella had thought by 7:00 a.m., Theresa had already been snatched by the killer. That she was already being tortured, that very soon afterward, she would be dead. So had Logan.

"What's she doing here?" Logan mumbled. On the screen, Theresa filled her tank, then got in her car and drove away.

Ella shook her head. "Everything we've been assuming is wrong," she said, glancing quickly at the TV. "This means— Whoa!"

"What?"

"Rewind it!" She scooped up the remote herself.

"What did you see?"

"Hang on." Ella leaned close to the screen as she rewound, then paused. "There!" She pointed to the very edge of the shot, at the front of a blue van that backed out shortly after Theresa's car pulled away.

"What? You think the person in the van is following her? It could be any of the cars here, couldn't it? Or, who knows, she could've been meeting someone after all. I mean, why was she still in town after her flight left?"

"No, Logan." The look on Ella's face was dead serious and slightly apprehensive. "A blue van was following me yesterday."

"What?" Logan grabbed her arm, worry filling him. "When?"

"Last night. Right before you showed up at my hotel. I was walking that trail to the hotel. It was deserted. When the van came up, I actually pulled my gun. But then the guy said something about being confused about directions and took off. I figured I was just getting paranoid."

She let out a string of curses so creative Logan felt his eyebrows rise; they would've made him laugh had this not been so serious. "You think Theresa's killer was following you?"

Ella glanced down at his hand on her arm, and he realized he was squeezing.

He relaxed his hold, trying at the same time to loosen the grip panic had on him. Ella was a trained FBI agent who carried a weapon. And, judging by the surprising strength he'd felt in her arms, she could hold her own in a fight.

"I don't know. I can't actually be sure he was following me. Plus, it was dark. It was a guy in the van, that I know from his voice, but I couldn't see him. And how common are blue vans?" She sighed. "But we'd better check this out, because it seems too coincidental that a blue van shows up on the last image we have of Theresa before she died—and there was one at my hotel last night."

She pulled her arm free from his grip. "We'd better get Theresa's phone records, too, and see if she called someone that day. See if we can figure out why she wasn't on that flight."

"I've been working on that. It's a process. Warrants and all. But they should be on their way now."

Ella looked troubled as she turned to him again, and this time it had nothing to do with her fear of who'd been following her the other night. "Logan, we should push the phone company and get them to do it faster. If she *was* meeting someone that day, we might be going at this all wrong. Maybe she called some old boyfriend who lived around here. Or he called her, convinced her to come see him and catch a later flight. This could be a single murder with a typical motive."

She hustled to the door, opened it and called out to the kid, "We need a copy of this tape."

The kid rushed back in to do her bidding and as Ella sank into a chair to wait, Logan heard her mumble, "Maybe this isn't a serial killer at all."

Chapter Eight

Logan's ex-fiancée was tall, thin and blonde. She had the kind of face that made her an obvious choice for an on-camera reporter and the kind of body that could have modeled underwear. She was absurdly perfect-looking, like a supermodel who'd stepped out of the pages of a magazine, still air-brushed.

Ella would have been happy to go her entire life without knowing that was Logan's type.

When Logan had told her this morning that the reporter she'd seen on the TV last night was his fiancée, she'd tried not to react. And she'd tried not to think about it all afternoon as they ran down leads.

Now she stood in the police station bathroom, staring at herself in the mirror above the sink. Compared to Lyla's blonde perfection, Ella was ordinary—with plain brown eyes and plain brown hair. She was average height, with ropey muscle hiding underneath her curves, a mouth just a little too big for her face and bags under her eyes after a sleepless night.

Get a grip, Cortez.

It didn't matter what Logan's type was, because she wasn't going to stick around long enough for it to matter. And if that thought made her chest feel a little too tight, she was just going to have to deal with it.

She was here to catch a killer. And she needed to get back to it.

Straightening her spine, she pushed open the door and found Logan waiting for her.

"Did you get Theresa's phone records yet?" she asked.

"The phone company is faxing them over right now. They should be here soon," Logan said, walking with her toward the conference room they'd staked out earlier in the day. "I just went to the vending machines while you were in the bathroom." He held out a candy bar. "Thought you might want something to hold you over until we grab some real food," he said, peeling back the wrapper on his own candy.

"Thanks." Ella took a big bite, savoring the chocolate, then said, "I know this isn't what you want to hear, but I think you'd better talk to your sister again, Logan."

"I know. I've also got some officers tracking down the license plates from the other cars that were at the gas station, in case any of those people saw Theresa."

"The tech couldn't get a license on the blue van, could he?"

Logan shook his head. "The van never pulled far enough into the station to get a shot of the plate. It was parked right by the pump for air, but if the driver ever got out to fill his tires, he's out of the frame, too." Logan shrugged. "The air is free, so the gas station wasn't worried about having that area covered by the cameras. The guy could very well have been there legitimately. We just can't tell."

Ella put her hand on Logan's arm, stopping him as they reached the conference room. "But someone's running down a list of locals who own blue vans, right?" Just like anyone else, she occasionally got spooked by nothing, but she wasn't the type to pull her gun at every imagined threat. She sensed that she needed to follow up.

"I'm checking on those myself, Ella, in Oakville and the surrounding towns. In the meantime, maybe we should move you to a different hotel."

She smiled. "I'm armed. And the Bureau believes pretty strongly in teaching its agents defensive training. Believe me, I got the bruises to prove it back at the Academy, but I learned. This guy doesn't want to mess with me."

Logan didn't look any less worried. "I'd still feel better if you were somewhere else. You can stay with me if you want. I have an extra bedroom."

Her nerve endings tingled at the idea, but Ella forced herself to give him a look of disbelief. "Yeah, because that would really work." If she stayed at his house, she'd end up in his bed, and they both knew it. Appealing as it might sound, that idea had *heartbreak* written all over it. And she didn't have time to mess around.

"I'm fine where I am. If it's the same person, he's not coming after me in a busy hotel. And I'm not using that shortcut to the station anymore. I'm taking the long way around."

Ella moved to go into the conference room, but Logan stepped in front of her, blocking her way, close enough to make her tip her head back to look at him. "That idea may have held when we were talking about a killer who ambushed his victims in deserted areas, but not anymore, Ella."

"Logan—"

"Humor me, okay? Please."

Deep furrows appeared in Logan's forehead, and Ella realized he was dead serious. He was really afraid Theresa's killer was targeting her, too. He was truly, deeply worried about her.

A rush of warmth went through her as she tried not to smile.

Although the idea of someone tracking her did have her concerned, the truth was, she could take care of herself. And even if she was wrong about how the killer was abducting his victims, she wasn't wrong about his intelligence or his desire to keep a low profile. Since the media flurry hadn't sent him on a spree, he was lying low, being that much more careful. As long as she didn't give him an opportunity to get her in a deserted location, she'd be fine. There was no reason to panic.

Ella ignored the doubt pushing through and told Logan, "Okay, I'll switch hotels."

The worry lines on his forehead smoothed out and he gave her a relieved smile that made the inconvenience totally worth it.

"Good," Logan said, heading into the conference room. "Because I'm already driving my sister crazy, calling her every couple of hours. I'm not sure you want me waking you up in the middle of the night, too."

Actually, she kind of did. But not with a phone call.

Clamping her mouth shut, Ella followed him. "Okay. Let's get to work. Maybe we should start by calling your sister? Make sure she doesn't know of anyone around here that Theresa might have unexpectedly decided to meet."

"I'm on it," Logan said, his cell phone already pressed to his ear.

As Ella sat and devoured the rest of her candy bar, she half listened to Logan tell his sister, "No, that's not why I'm calling this time, but I'm glad everything's okay there." He grinned at Ella as if to say, "See, I *am* driving her crazy."

Logan continued to talk to Becky, and Ella knew she should be listening, but her mind kept wandering. If Theresa hadn't been ambushed on a deserted stretch of road like they'd imagined, then her killer—whoever he was— had grabbed her somewhere else. Not only did they have no idea where that was, but they had no clue how he'd done it, either. Had he lured her out there? It seemed unlikely, unless she knew him. Had she been meeting someone else and the killer had taken advantage of the unexpected opportunity? That, too, seemed unlikely.

The problem was, everything in Ella's profile was based on the idea that they knew certain things as fact. That the killer had tortured and burned Theresa before dumping her body in a location it was unlikely to be found. That he had grabbed her when she was heading in a direct route from Becky's house to the airport.

If they were wrong about where she was grabbed, which they clearly were, then too much of Ella's profile could also be wrong.

Anxiety spiked as she glanced over at Logan, talking to his sister. The sister she'd promised would be safe if she didn't go anywhere deserted, if she didn't give the killer a chance to ambush her. But if he wasn't ambushing his victims after all…

Ella stood, started to pace. She felt Logan's speculative look and when he ended the call, she preempted his question by saying, "Logan, maybe you should put your sister in protective custody."

He stared at her, his expression probing, as if he was trying to read her mind. "Believe me, if we had the resources, I would. But we don't." He stood, took her hand in his own. "The abduction style isn't the only reason you think the killer would wait to get his victims alone, right?"

Ella bit her lip as her heart rate started to crescendo with her nerves. The nature of her job meant that lives always hung in the balance of how deeply she could get into the killer's head. But this—this panic she was feeling—was why her boss had always kept her away from cases where branding could be involved. Being too personally invested meant she wasn't seeing things objectively. It meant she could be making mistakes.

Ella brought her free hand to her temple. When had this happened? When had she started to care so much about Logan that she couldn't see the case clearly?

"Ella," Logan said softly. "The way the body was dumped, the way the killer stalked Theresa, the way he's still lying low now, they all tell you he wouldn't risk breaking into the mayor's house in a security-conscious neighborhood to make a grab, right?"

"Yes. But, Logan, I'm not right one hundred percent of the time. And profiling isn't magic. People do uncharacteristic things and I can't predict that."

And she didn't think she'd ever be able to forgive herself if she was wrong this time and Logan's little sister paid the price.

Logan squeezed her fingers. "I trust you, Ella. But, believe me, I'm not taking chances with my sister's life. And neither is my family. My dad has already hired her a bodyguard. Becky isn't thrilled about it, but it keeps me from panicking if she doesn't answer my million calls on the first ring."

Ella let out a long breath. "Okay." She looked up into Logan's eyes, and something about his steady demeanor calmed her. "What did Becky say?"

"She didn't know of any exes in the area. And she

had called Theresa when she was on her way to the airport because Theresa left a necklace behind. But Theresa told Becky to mail it to her, because she didn't want to miss her flight."

"Huh. So either Theresa was lying or something happened after Becky talked to her that made her change her mind."

Logan shrugged, let go of her hand. "I guess so. Becky and Theresa were close. I have a hard time imagining her lying to my sister, but I can't think of anything that would make her decide at the last minute to skip her flight, either. And neither could Becky. Let me go check the fax machine and see if those call records have come in."

"Great," Ella said, lowering herself into a conference chair as he hurried out of the room. It was hard to muster up a lot of enthusiasm.

Nothing about this case was turning out like she'd expected. And despite the burns, she was beginning to wonder if it was connected to Maggie's case at all.

When Logan returned a minute later and dropped a stack of pages on the table, looking dejected, Ella sat straighter and asked, "Nothing?"

"We got the call records." He gestured to the papers he'd scattered. "But the only calls Theresa got after she left for the airport were two from Becky. That's it."

"Well, what about—"

"No other local calls while she was in Oakville, either." Logan sighed. "It's possible someone followed her from Arkansas and made contact. But it'll take time to track down the rest of the calls she got while she was in town."

He rubbed a hand over his eyes and Ella saw the exhaustion he was trying to hide. Not physical exhaustion so much as emotional.

"I'm not sure which route to take here, Ella. Tracking the phone numbers will likely lead us to the killer if he's someone in her life. But a stranger? For that, we'd probably be better off following up on the people who might've seen Theresa at the gas station. We've got officers on that already, but I want to spend our time on the most likely option. I know I'm putting you on the spot, but what's your professional opinion at this point? Do you still believe we're talking about a serial killer here?"

Did she? Ella pushed back her uncertainty. *Think, Cortez. Think like the killer.*

She might not know how the killer had grabbed Theresa, but she did know what he'd done to her afterward. The burns. The strangulation. The dumping of the body.

Someone from Arkansas might think a marsh was an easy place to dispose of the body, because it was simple to access and the body would sink, disappear in the muck. But what about the logistics? Where would he have carried out the murder? A hotel? How would he have gotten the body out into the marsh? Rented a boat? Would a nonlocal have felt comfortable rowing out among the gators?

And the crime itself. Torture and strangulation could be personal, a vendetta against someone. Or it could be the mark of a serial killer.

But those burns. Whether or not they were brands, they were specific. Part of a fantasy. They weren't about the victim, but about the killer.

Ella felt her confidence returning. "It's a serial killer."

"WE HAVE A WITNESS."

"What?" Ella looked up at Logan as he hurried back to their table at the Blue Dolphin where they'd been eating a lunch so late it might as well have been called dinner. He'd gone outside to answer his phone because the Blue Dolphin was packed and loud, just like it had been the first time he'd brought her here.

Logan hurriedly wrapped the sandwich he'd barely started and Ella did the same, pushing her chair backward.

"That call was from one of the officers who was running down the license plates from the gas station. One of the women who was there not only remembered Theresa, she talked to her."

"What?" Ella's eyes widened. Could this be the break they needed? "What did she say?"

"Come on. I'll tell you in the car." Logan picked up his drink and moved through the crowd toward the door.

Ella followed, her mind working overtime, imagining all the possibilities. "Well?" she demanded as they got into Logan's Chevy Caprice and he pulled the car out fast.

"The woman said she talked to Theresa inside as Theresa was paying."

"Wait," Ella interrupted. "Why was she paying inside? She used her credit card. Why not pay at the pump?"

Logan glanced at her as he pointed the car in the opposite direction from where they'd headed to check out the highway. "She also bought gum."

"Okay, so what did the witness say? And where are we going?"

"The woman said she overheard Theresa asking for directions and she looked frustrated. The woman helped her with the directions and asked if everything was okay. Theresa told her she was just annoyed because she was going to miss her flight. She was meeting someone."

A dozen questions formed in Ella's mind, but she couldn't seem to ask any of them. Instead, her mouth fell open as she realized what Logan's words meant. She'd been wrong. Very, very wrong. Theresa had probably known her killer.

"Ella?" Logan glanced at her again. "You okay?"

Ella shook herself out of it. "Yeah. Did she say who she was meeting?"

"No. Just that it was a friend. But she did say where she was going. And this is even weirder. She was meeting the person in Huntsville."

"And? Why is that weird?"

"Well, Huntsville *is* in the same general direction as where we ultimately found Theresa's rental, and the gas station where she stopped is along that route. But there's nothing there. It's an old farming community, but it's pretty much abandoned. There are a few old-timers left, and at some point soon, developers will buy up the land and build a mall or something. But right now, it's mostly open land and falling-down barns."

Ella gave him a questioning look as he finally left the Oakville city limits and got onto a country highway, picking up speed. "Sounds like a pretty good place for an abduction and murder, then. So why is it weird? I mean, yes, it's weird that she was meeting someone in the first place, but if she didn't know the area and he did…"

Logan briefly turned to face her, and Ella saw something simmering under the surface she hadn't noticed before. Anger. "Ella, my mom's parents owned a farm out here. It's long been deserted, but we still own the land. And the reason Theresa started talking to this woman is that she was trying to get directions and the woman overheard her. Apparently, she knew my grandparents, so she remembered where they'd lived. And according to her, that's where Theresa was going. She remembers—and thought it was odd—because my grandparents have been dead for ten years."

This case just got stranger and stranger. Ella tried to digest the new development. "Logan, you said your family were the last people to see Theresa in town before she died, right?"

"Yeah."

"And now this. Maybe this isn't about Theresa at all. Maybe someone's trying to frame you."

Logan pounded a fist against the steering wheel. "You think someone kidnapped—and *tortured*—Theresa to hurt my family?"

Ella rested her head against the seat, clutching the food she'd barely touched. She wasn't hungry anymore, as dread burrowed inside her. "You're right. It doesn't quite fit. It's not a very good frame-up if it was this much of a stretch for us to even find the information. Plus, the burns are personal to him. I know they are. That's not about your family, or even about the victim, really. It's about *him*."

"So, what? This can't be coincidence," Logan said, his knuckles bone white as he squeezed the steering wheel.

"I don't know. Maybe it was part of a lure? Maybe Theresa thought she was meeting someone from your family there?" Even as she said it, the words sounded far-fetched.

"How? And why? We haven't gone there in years. And Becky was the last person to talk to Theresa, so who would have told her to meet us there? And since she talked to Becky on her way to the airport, why would she go? Why wouldn't she have said something to Becky? And why would she miss her flight to meet us at a deserted farm?"

Ella shook her head, feeling as frustrated as Logan sounded. "I don't know," she said again.

They both fell silent as Logan's Chevy Caprice sped

toward the farm. It took a while for the lights of busy neighboring towns to fade, for the land to shift into something that might have once supported farms.

By then, Ella felt the need to admit what they both had to be thinking. "I was wrong, Logan. Whatever the purpose, however this guy got her here, this wasn't a quick ambush. This was a complicated lure. He wasn't waiting for Theresa to take the usual route and then picking out the most suitable place for an ambush."

She shook her head. "Either he knew Theresa personally, or..." A heavy weight seemed to settle on her chest. "This guy is a baiter."

Logan must have caught her change in tone, because as he pulled the car to a stop outside an obviously deserted house, he turned toward her, waiting.

Ella shifted, looking into the green eyes that had tempted her into a supposedly quick dinner and review of a case file only a few days ago. It felt like so much longer. So much had changed in that short time.

And yet, the one thing she'd ultimately come to Oakville for wasn't going to change. This killer *was* a baiter. And Maggie's rapist liked to ambush his victims. They were very different methods, used by different personality types.

She felt an old pain swell up, and her voice trembled as she told him, "This isn't my shot to catch Maggie's rapist. This is a totally different killer."

Chapter Nine

Logan felt queasy as he picked the lock on his grandparents' old house. It had sat empty for a decade, but his mom couldn't bring herself to sell it. He hadn't been to the house in years, but he had so many good memories here. If they went inside and found evidence that Theresa had died here, it would tarnish all of them.

A gag worked its way up his throat and he swallowed it down, focused on fitting the pick into the old lock. When the lock finally clicked and he pushed the door open, he froze, not wanting to go inside.

Growing up, he'd always felt safe here. Greers had lived in this area going back six generations. And on his mom's side, it had been almost as long. They had history here, and even now, most of the family had stuck around. He'd taken the police job to keep the hometown he loved safe. Now, with Theresa's death, it all felt tainted by something dark and ugly.

Ella squeezed past him. "Why don't you wait here, Logan?" She glanced back at him with understanding in her eyes. "I'll call you if I need you."

"No. I'm coming with you." He just hoped if they found something, he didn't contaminate the scene by throwing up.

With a deep breath, he followed Ella inside. Into the

living room where his grandpa's ugly comfortable plaid chair had once sat in the corner, where the doilies his grandma made once covered all the tables. Now it was bare, covered with a thick layer of dust and cobwebs. But no evidence anyone had been through the house recently. At least not in this room.

He followed Ella toward the back of the house, but it was the same there. To his relief, it looked completely deserted, as if no one had been inside for years.

Ella turned to him.

"Are there any outbuildings on the property?"

"No." Logan studied the house again, remembering the way it had once been, filled with the smell of the cigars his grandpa used to smoke, the smell of his grandma's perfume. Filled with laughter as he and Becky had run down the stairs and out into the backyard. He remembered the sound of his grandma's voice calling after them, admonishing them to slow down, trying to hide the smile in her voice.

The memories faded, leaving behind the image of the empty, dusty house as it was now, as Logan unlocked the back door and stepped outside. The property stretched for miles, but it was fairly flat and unobstructed. Although the area was pretty deserted, it seemed unlikely that someone as smart as this killer would have tortured and murdered Theresa outside.

Logan turned back to Ella. "What do you think?"

"It doesn't look like anyone has been here. Maybe she met the killer here and went with him somewhere else? He might have lured her here, then knocked her out. He probably could have left the car here without attracting attention, then come back for it later. It does seem odd, though. Why here? If he was going to grab her, why not do it on the way to the airport, like we originally suspected? And if he was going to lure her somewhere—if he'd charmed her enough to get her to meet up with him—why bring her here? Why not just meet her wherever he killed her?"

Logan shrugged. "I have no idea. None of this makes any sense. But I don't like it. This feels too personal, this guy picking my grandparents' house. How did he know about it?"

He headed back through the house, ready to lock it up and leave. Even though they'd seen no evidence that Theresa had been here, his nerves were twitching, telling him something about the whole scenario was off. It made him want to get out of there fast, as if he could outrun what had happened to Theresa, somehow undo it.

"Maybe you should call Becky," Ella said as they got back in his car for the return trip to Oakville. "See if she ever mentioned this place to Theresa. Maybe Theresa was the one who suggested meeting here, and not her killer."

Logan nodded, stuck his hands-free device in his ear and dialed. After a short conversation, he told Ella, "Yeah, my sister mentioned the house, but just in talking about my grandparents. They never discussed coming here."

Logan pulled out onto the highway, reaching for the drink he hadn't touched on the way up. The coffee was cold now, but he gulped it down anyway, wanting the caffeine hit. "The more answers we find in this case, the more questions we get. I've investigated a couple of homicides since I made detective, but nothing like this."

Frustration built inside him, together with the fear that this killer was going to outwit him. That he'd never be able to bring the guy to justice. That he'd fail Theresa, fail Becky.

Ella's cool hand sliding behind his neck, kneading

the tight muscles there, surprised him. He glanced over at her, and he could tell from the tilt of her head, from the expression in her eyes. She understood exactly how he felt.

He relaxed his shoulders, focused on the road, and let Ella work her magic on his neck. Slowly, he felt himself relax.

He smiled at her. "Thanks."

She removed her hand and unwrapped her sandwich. She took a huge bite, then asked, "Were Becky and Theresa together the whole time she was here?"

"Pretty much. Becky had the week off work, but she did have a few things she had to take care of while Theresa was here. Theresa told her she was going to the beach while Becky was out. It was a couple of hours, tops, both times. I asked Becky about it when I first talked to her after we found Theresa's body."

Ella nodded, looking pensive. "So, it's possible she met someone Becky didn't know about, set up a meeting."

"It's possible," Logan agreed. "But it still seems strange that she wouldn't mention it to Becky. And that she would set up a meeting for *after* her flight was supposed to leave. And if it was arranged at the last minute, how did the guy contact her if he didn't call her? If he ran into her somewhere, then why wouldn't they just drive together?"

"I'm not sure any of this is going to make sense until we figure out why Theresa didn't take that flight."

Logan frowned. "Any ideas on how to do that?"

He felt Ella's eyes on him as she said, "Nothing brilliant, no. We can try to follow up on the beach angle, see if we can find someone who remembers seeing Theresa with a guy. Maybe put out a request to the public for information. You could use your media contact."

"Lyla?" Logan snorted. "We didn't exactly part on the best of terms. I'll talk to her if you think that could work, but I should warn you that she's tenacious. Once she gets hold of something, she doesn't stop chasing it. I can guarantee you that if she has any chance to get back into the police station, she's going straight back to her profiler story."

"Well, that's a risk I'll have to take."

Logan decided he'd talk to Lyla, do his best to convince her to leave Ella out of it, but ultimately, Lyla did whatever Lyla wanted. She always had.

And even trying to leave his personal feelings for Ella aside—which was pretty near impossible—his gut said that if he wanted any chance of nailing this killer, he was going to need her.

As soon as Logan parked at the station, Ella sank low in her seat and he let out a string of curses.

Out front, far enough away from the station that Logan knew Chief Patterson had thrown a fit, but close enough that the station would be in the long shot, was a television crew. Lyla stood by the camera in a fire-engine-red skirt suit, looking as though she'd primped for hours. She had a microphone angled toward Kelly, the woman who'd reported her friend missing a few days ago.

Far from the hungover, terrified mess Kelly had been then, she now looked as if she'd spent all day getting ready to be on TV.

Logan scowled. He'd seen this in other homicide cases, loved ones of victims trying to get media mileage out of their loss, but it always made him feel sick.

As he stepped out of the car, he heard Lyla's voice ringing across the lot, "So, you were led to believe that a serial killer abducted your friend?"

Logan tightened his jaw hard enough that his neck hurt. There was a lot he'd loved about Lyla, but her determination to get the story, which he'd originally found attractive, now grated on his nerves. What she was doing with this case bordered on irresponsible.

Doing his best to ignore it, Logan made a beeline for the station doors, refusing to look over at the spectacle that was the "news."

He felt Ella close on his heels and he held open the door for her to duck inside. But inside the station wasn't much better.

"I thought your fiancée left town when she left you," Hank O'Connor muttered darkly, as he walked past them.

Logan thought Hank was going to keep walking; but instead he stopped, turned around and poked a finger at Logan's chest. "This *serial killer* angle is getting out of control. Is this your idea of how being a detective works?"

Logan looked down at the beefy finger pointing at him and clenched his fists to keep from reaching up and twisting it until it snapped.

Beside him, Ella took a step forward, getting Hank's attention. "I've worked with a lot of detectives over the past few years."

Ella's voice was too even, too sweet. Logan shot a questioning look at her.

"The best ones chase down every lead, no matter where it takes them." She pivoted and walked past Hank, calling over her shoulder, "Even if they're not happy about it. Even if it leads to a serial killer."

Hank watched her walk away, then turned back to Logan with a smirk on his face. "I guess I'd cry serial killer, too, if it got me a cute little piece of—"

Logan got in his face fast. "You don't like me, fine. I don't like you much, either. Leave Ella out of it."

Hank was a big guy. In a brawl, he'd have a definite advantage over Logan. But as Logan stared him down, fury in his eyes, Hank nodded and backed up.

"Sorry," he choked out, not sounding particularly sincere. But then he rolled his massive shoulders and added, "Whoever this killer is, let's just find him, fast." He gestured out the doors to where the camera crew was packing up. "Because the last thing we need is more panic."

Logan held out his hand. He and Hank would probably never be friends, but they did have to work together.

Hank looked at it skeptically for a minute, then locked his beefy hand around it and shook. "So far, we've got nothing on Laurie's whereabouts. I still think she's sleeping it off somewhere, but…" He glanced back in the direction Ella had gone, then added, "We've run out of places to look. If you need help running something down, let me know. I want to find this girl alive."

Logan nodded. "Believe me, so do I."

He sighed as Hank walked away, because as much as he hoped Hank was right about Laurie, he was banking on Ella's expertise and his own gut here. And both told him that Laurie had met the same fate as Theresa. That if they found Laurie at all, it wasn't going to be alive.

Forcing aside that gruesome thought, Logan made his way to the conference room. Inside, he saw Ella hunched over the table, writing frantically.

"What are you working on?"

She looked up, blinking until she seemed to focus on him. "Questions for the officers searching for Laurie. They're still talking to locals and tourists at the bars and anywhere else Laurie might have been, right?"

Logan dropped into the chair next to her. "They are, but it's not going anywhere. They don't have any leads. You have some new ideas on that?"

"Kind of. I think we should have them ask anyone who talked to Laurie while she was here if she ever mentioned meeting someone. And I think the officers should also ask every one of them if they ever saw Theresa with anyone besides Becky."

Her lips pursed, and her expression turned serious, intense. "Given what was going on outside, I'm having second thoughts about involving the media in this. But since the officers are still canvassing on Laurie, let's use what we've learned about Theresa today."

"Okay, that makes sense." Logan reached across her for his laptop, which he'd left in the conference room during their drive out to his grandparents' farm. "While you do that, I'm going to track down blue vans."

"Thanks."

Ella picked up her pen again and got back to work, but not before he saw something spark in her eyes. Logically, she might not have been sure about it, but he knew she felt that the van was connected. And so far, Logan trusted Ella's instincts more than those of any other law enforcement officer he'd ever met.

She was smart. And she was familiar with this kind of killer, far more than he'd ever be, far more than he ever wanted to.

Logan powered up his laptop, intent on locating every blue van within a fifty-mile radius. He'd go door to door if he had to, but he wasn't stopping until he'd checked out every single person who owned one.

ELLA HAD NEVER thought of herself as a jealous person. But as she strode into her new hotel across town and spotted Lyla lounging in the lobby, obviously planning to ambush her, that emotion bubbled up, strong and sour.

It was late and she was exhausted. She didn't have the energy to deal with a typical reporter right now, let alone Logan's supermodel-impersonator ex-fiancée.

Ignoring Lyla, who'd jumped to her feet, Ella tiredly told the man behind the check-in desk, "I need a room. Detective Greer called ahead."

As Lyla crowded up next to her, Ella was suddenly glad she hadn't let Logan come inside with her. That would've been a career-killing story for both of them.

Logan had driven her to her old hotel to get her bag and check out, arranged a room for her here, and then stopped the car in front of the lobby doors. The hopeful look in his green eyes had told her that, with the slightest encouragement, he'd park and come in with her.

A shiver of desire raced through her veins. She'd almost done it. Almost thrown caution aside and invited him to her room. Almost told him to forget the hotel entirely and take her back to his house. But a tiny thread of sanity had prevailed and she'd gotten out of the car, fast. And alone.

Because as good as she knew they'd be together, with every day in his company, Ella was becoming increasingly certain that this was about more than lust for her. Certain that after one night of passion with Logan, she'd spend the rest of her life looking for anything that could possibly compare. And coming up short.

"Here you go, ma'am," the hotel employee told her, handing her a key card. "Room—"

"I got it," Ella said, looking at the number on the key card. She didn't want Lyla knowing her room number and harassing her there.

As she turned away from the desk, stupidly hoping

that if she just ignored Lyla, the woman would go away, Lyla stepped into stride beside her.

"I'm Lyla Evans. I've been reporting on the serial killer case." She held out a manicured hand that Ella ignored.

"O-kay," Lyla said in response to the snub. "Look, I know you probably don't want to talk to a reporter, but—"

"No, I don't." Ella cut her off, stabbing the Up button on the hotel elevator.

But when the elevator arrived, Lyla got in with her.

Ella threw her an exasperated look, aware that she was being rude, but not able to help herself. "Are you planning to camp out outside my hotel room? I have no comment on the investigation."

"You're the profiler, right?" Lyla pressed anyway. "From the FBI?"

"I have no comment."

Lyla gave her a camera-ready, practiced smile and stepped in front of her so Ella couldn't ignore her. "Don't you think the residents of Oakville have a right to know if they're being stalked by a serial killer?"

Ella raised an eyebrow. "Oh, I've seen the press. I think they're plenty scared. If you were really interested in safety, you'd be coordinating with the police, not chasing headlines."

Lyla blinked, took a step back. "The police aren't all that interested in cooperating."

The sigh that had been building in Ella's chest broke free. "They might have been, if you'd approached this differently. I'm sorry, I just don't have any comment."

As the elevator reached her floor, Ella got off, half expecting Lyla to follow. But she heard the door shut again, and when she glanced behind her, Lyla wasn't there.

Her relief was short-lived, though. Her cell phone rang, and when she looked at the readout, she saw the call was from her boss.

She quickly let herself into her room, dropped her bag on the floor, then took a deep breath and picked up. "Isabella Cortez."

"Where are you, Ella?" From the pissed-off tone of her boss's voice, she could tell he already knew the answer.

Dread sank hard and fast to the pit of her stomach and Ella sat on the edge of the bed. She might be about to lose her job. At least by sitting down she'd do less damage if she fainted.

"I'm in Florida, sir. I'm consulting on a case unofficially, as a civilian."

Her boss released a succinct string of curses that told her that answer wasn't acceptable. "You work for the FBI, Ella. You can't consult unofficially."

"Sir, I thought this might have been connected to my friend's case. Now I'm pretty sure it's not, but—"

"You thought it was about the Fishhook Rapist?"

"Yes." Her boss knew how important solving that case was to her, how it had led her to the Bureau in the first place.

"Ella, you're a good agent. I like having you on my team. Don't screw around with your career by taking side jobs."

"Sir—"

"You're scheduled to be on vacation through next week?"

"Yes, sir."

He sighed. "Fine. I'm probably too busy to be watching every little piece of Florida news anyway."

"Thank—" Ella started, but he cut her off.

"Just get the TV stations to stop talking about FBI

involvement. You're there as a civilian, which is non-sense, but the Bureau isn't taking any responsibility for this. And I don't care where the investigation stands at the end of next week. You get back here, or there won't be a position for you to return to. Understand?"

"Yes, sir," Ella said meekly.

After he hung up, she closed her eyes and dropped backward so she was lying across the bed.

She had just over a week to find Theresa's killer. And she had a very bad feeling it wouldn't be nearly enough time.

Chapter Ten

"I don't think this case is connected to Maggie's."

In response to her announcement, there was a long pause on the other end of the phone.

Ella leaned back against her hotel headboard. California was three hours earlier, and knowing Scott, he hadn't been sleeping at 10:00 p.m. He was either out looking for a woman to charm, or more likely, he'd already found one.

"Hang on a sec," Scott said finally. She could hear him moving around, then a minute later, he asked, "Are you sure?"

"I'm not positive yet. I'm going to try to talk to the medical examiner in the morning, but I think this killer is a baiter."

"Different MO," Scott agreed.

He didn't sound disappointed, just resigned, because a decade was a long time to keep hoping the Fishhook Rapist would finally be caught. Every year, that horrible anniversary rolled around and she, Maggie and Scott gathered together and tried to distract each other, dreading the news the next morning.

"I'm sorry," Ella choked out, mortified to hear the tears in her voice. "I really thought it was him. I really thought I had a chance to get this guy."

"It's not your fault, kiddo," Scott said, and Ella smiled at the nickname he'd had for her since she'd first moved to town and met him and Maggie.

Scott was only a year older, but he had two younger sisters and even before Maggie's rape, he'd taken that role very seriously. He'd quickly extended his big brother protective role to her, too.

Most of the time, these days, she found it funny. After all, she was an armed FBI agent. She was long past needing a big brother to look after her. But once in a while, it was comforting, reminding her of everything that was good about growing up in their small town.

"I know." Ella sighed wearily. "But I just wanted to end this."

"I know you did," Scott said. "I did, too. But sooner or later, he's going to mess up and he'll get caught."

"I hope so."

"What else is going on?" Scott asked.

"What do you mean?"

"Come on, I hear it in your voice. Something else is upsetting you."

In spite of everything, Ella felt herself smile. Her family might have pulled away since she'd joined the Bureau, but Scott and Maggie never let her down. "My boss heard about me coming down here. I'm getting some heat for it."

"Well, I wouldn't worry too much about that. Your boss knows how good you are—he'll get over it. And if the case isn't connected, then you can come join us in California, lie on the beach for a week and relax before you have to go back and deal with him."

Even knowing Scott couldn't see her, Ella fidgeted. "I can't."

"Why not?"

"Well, the police...they need my help on this."

Scott snorted with laughter. "You are such a bad liar."

"I *can* help with this case."

"That's not what I mean and you know it, Ella. What else is going on?"

"Uh..."

"It's that guy I saw you with at the airport, isn't it?" Even over the phone, Ella could sense Scott's grin. "Don't tell me you finally found someone who's actually worth your time?"

"Yeah, and he happens to live about a thousand miles from me."

"So what?"

"Well, that's a long way to travel for a dinner date," Ella tried to joke, but it ended up sounding dejected instead of funny.

"Ella. People have long-distance relationships all the time."

"Yeah, well, I can't even make them work when the guy lives down the hall from me."

"Maybe that's because you never wanted to badly enough before," Scott suggested with a seriousness in his voice that told Ella he and Maggie had talked about this.

Was he right? Was it really that simple?

Ella glanced in the mirror across from her bed, at the tired eyes staring back. Her job was important to her, but it wasn't her whole life. Had she never made time for her relationships before because she hadn't found the right person?

"Hey, kiddo, don't let me upset you," Scott said, making her realize she'd gone silent for too long. "Just think about it."

"You're right," Ella agreed. "And I will."

Hanging up the phone, Ella slid under the covers and

closed her eyes, an image of Logan grinning at her, those green eyes sparkling, instantly filling her mind. Maybe she was foolish to keep resisting the pull between them. Maybe they *could* make something work.

She smiled as she drifted off to sleep.

"WHAT HAPPENED WITH you and Lyla?"

Ella cringed as she finished buckling herself into the passenger seat in Logan's car. Had she really just asked that? She'd been thinking it, but she'd intended to ask about talking to the medical examiner regarding Theresa. She couldn't believe that had come out instead.

Before she could backtrack, laugh lines appeared beside Logan's eyes and he said, "Good morning to you, too, Ella."

"Sorry." Ella felt herself redden. "She was waiting at the hotel last night and I—"

Logan twisted in his seat to face her. "She was *what*?"

"She wanted an interview."

Logan swore under his breath. "I'm sorry about that, Ella."

"Yeah, and about what was on the news... My boss called last night."

Logan actually looked a little queasy as he asked, "Do you have to leave?"

"No, my boss is a good guy. He's giving me some leeway on this."

Logan's shoulders dropped, and he seemed relieved as he nodded and pulled away from the hotel.

"But he's going to be pissed if he keeps seeing mention of the FBI in the news, because my involvement is definitely not sanctioned. Is there anything you can do?"

"I'll take care of it."

Ella willed herself not to get any more flushed than

she probably was as she admitted, "I was kind of rude to Lyla yesterday. She's probably not going to want to do me any favors."

Logan's eyes narrowed as he headed in the direction of the police station. "I'd have been rude to her, too, if she'd been waiting to ambush me for a story."

"Yeah, but I'm usually more professional. I think just knowing about your history with her sort of…" Ella threw her hands up. "I don't know. Sorry."

Logan glanced at her quickly before returning his attention to the road, but that look told her he was surprised. And maybe a little pleased.

"That's been over for years. Believe me, right now, there's no one else." He added softly, "You don't have any competition."

The heat in Ella's cheeks turned to fire. What did he mean by "right now"? It was the perfect opening for what she'd considered asking him all last night—whether there was a chance for them beyond her time in Florida. But her mouth didn't seem to work.

Logan glanced at her again, probably waiting for a response, and still, Ella felt frozen.

She'd never thought of herself as a coward. When it came to the job, back in the gangs unit, she had a reputation for always wanting to be on the first team through the door.

Even on her worst day in the unit, when she'd been shot and was bleeding out on the street, she hadn't done the sensible thing and played dead. Instead, she'd dragged herself farther into the line of fire, trying to get to her partner, not knowing it was already too late. She'd gotten her partner's killer before he'd gotten her, and then she'd put a tourniquet around her own leg while she waited for backup. The FBI had given her a letter of commendation for her actions that day. She hadn't thought of herself as a coward then.

But apparently, when it came to matters of the heart, she was a big wimp.

Buck up, Cortez.

She took a deep breath, but then Logan was saying in his back-to-business tone, "Last night I finished putting together a list of locals who own blue vans. I thought we could run them down today."

"Oh. Okay. Great." Ella felt a mingling of relief and disappointment at her missed opportunity.

"I included anyone from surrounding towns with blue vans, too. The list isn't very long."

"Well, file that in the good news department."

"No kidding," Logan said. "I figured we could run down the names together and interview anyone who looks like they could fit your profile."

"Sounds good. I'd also like to talk to the ME who did Theresa's autopsy."

"Sure. I can call him. Why?"

"I want to ask him about the burns." She wanted to confirm, once and for all, whether there was any chance this was connected to Maggie's rapist. She didn't think so anymore, but until she had a definitive expert opinion, she was going to wonder. And if it wasn't connected, she could stop thinking about Maggie's case every time she tried to analyze this perp's possible next move.

"Okay." Logan shifted, took his cell phone from his pocket, and handed it to her. "He's in there. Just pull up ME in the Contacts."

Ella raised an eyebrow. "You have the ME on speed dial? That's just sad."

Logan let out a short bark of laughter. "It's easier than

having to look it up whenever I get a homicide case. My Contacts list is a Who's Who of Oakville law enforcement." He gave her a goofy grin. "I even have the mayor on speed dial."

Ella rolled her eyes, then called the ME. When he picked up, she told him, "This is Isabella Cortez. I'm consulting—"

"From the FBI," he interrupted. "I watch the news. What do you need?"

Ella grimaced. She definitely had to get Logan to talk to Lyla for her. "I wanted to ask about the burns on Theresa's body. Is there any possibility that they could have been branding?"

The ME went silent and Ella realized she was holding her breath. All her profiling instincts told her the new development in Theresa's case meant it wasn't connected to Maggie, but she found herself actually hoping she was wrong.

Finally, the ME said, "The body sustained significant damage when it was in the marsh. But my professional judgment is no, the burns weren't made from a brand. I suspect they were made by literally holding a flame to the skin."

Ella's lips curled in distaste, but she had to ask, "Are you positive it's not a brand? Even the one on her neck? The shape kind of reminded me of a hook."

"Hmm. It does look a bit that way, doesn't it? If I had to make a guess, I'd say the shape is because the flame caught her hair before it was put out. The burns looked controlled, as if this woman's killer was trying to inflict specific damage, burn specific areas. If that's the case, it probably wasn't intentional, but I suspect the fire got away from him briefly, which would explain the way that particular burn hooks upward, toward the skull. It's definitely not a brand, though. I can tell you that."

Ella slumped, as disappointment gathered in her chest. "Thanks."

As she hung up, Logan asked, "It's not connected to your friend's case?"

"No."

The word came out slightly strangled, and Logan reached out his hand, folding it tightly around hers.

She gave him a half smile. "Because we now suspect baiting, I didn't believe it was connected anymore, but…"

"You wanted the chance to bring him to justice. I understand, Ella."

"But the fact that it's not a brand tells us something, too." Ella considered what the ME had told her, thinking out loud. "The burns were localized, specific. Were they just a means of torture or something more?"

She looked over at Logan as he parked the Chevy Caprice in the station lot. "Do you know anyone around here who's badly burned?"

Logan shook his head. "No. Why? Do you think the killer is burning his victims because he's scarred from burns himself?"

Ella thought about the autopsy photos she'd studied the day Logan had come to see her in Virginia. "Maybe. A brand is a sign of ownership. But a burn is different. It could be a way for the killer to torture his victims, especially if that's his end goal. But it's possible he picked fire because of a connection to his own life."

She stepped out of the car and followed Logan into the station. "It's really hard to say for sure at this point."

With only one body, only one victim conclusively tied to this killer, it was difficult to form a complete profile.

And without more to go on, and with a killer this careful and controlled, it was going to be nearly impossible to find him.

EVERY OFFICER IN the station looked weary, frustrated and dejected.

As Logan and Ella walked through the bullpen, Logan's colleagues looked back at him with bloodshot eyes. Most of them were running on caffeine now, and were well past the point of being fueled by the hope of finding Laurie hungover and apologetic. At this point, she'd been missing too long.

Still, Logan knew most of them didn't believe she'd been grabbed by a serial killer. Some theorized she was hitchhiking home without Kelly, since she'd told people at the bars she was leaving. A few thought she'd shacked up with some local. Others thought she'd gone to the beach after the bar and drowned. It wouldn't be the first time something like that happened to a spring breaker, and the ocean could take a body as easily as the gators in the marsh.

By now, most of the force was resigned to the idea that something bad had happened to her, but none were willing to make the jump to serial killer. They just didn't want to believe serial killings could happen in Oakville.

As Logan bypassed the bullpen for the conference room, with Ella in tow, he wondered if it was time to give up on trying to track Theresa's movements. Maybe they'd have better luck tracking Laurie.

Before he could suggest it to Ella, she asked, "Where's that list of blue van owners?"

Logan booted up his laptop. "I've got it on here."

"Great. Are rentals on there, too? From the closest airports?"

Logan sent her a disbelieving look. "I'm not a miracle worker, Ella. We can get those, but it'll take longer. And I figured locals were our best bet."

"They are."

Ella settled into the chair next to him, making him want to scoot even closer. Making him want to resume the conversation they'd been having in the car, the one that started with her basically admitting she was jealous of his ex-fiancée and ended with him looking like a fool by trying to get her to admit to more.

But he was all too happy to look like a fool if it meant Ella would let him back into her hotel room, pull him down on her bed again.

"But even if Theresa's murder isn't connected to Maggie's case," she continued, "it could still be someone who's been in the area long enough to scout it out for killing, someone who plans to move on. It could be why you don't have any other bodies or reports of missing persons."

Logan frowned. He'd assumed they'd found no other bodies because the gators had taken care of the evidence for the killer, but Ella was right about missing persons. The only missing person report they'd had in the past year was Laurie.

Was he as crazy as his chief and the rest of the force seemed to think? Was he imagining a serial killer here?

Logan forced back his doubt. If he was imagining it, Ella wouldn't have come here in the first place.

"If we're talking about tracking down rental vans from several months back, that would be a big project. And if we're talking about someone who drove here in his own vehicle, we'll never find it. If this guy isn't a local, I think the van angle is a dead end."

"Well, let's see who we've got," Ella said, but he could

hear in her voice that she'd begun to feel as dejected as his fellow officers.

"Okay." Logan pulled up the list he'd run, reminding himself to be impartial. He was probably going to know everyone on it. And he couldn't think of anyone in Oakville he'd peg as a murderer.

"The first name on the list is Jane Franklin." He tried not to snort as he showed Ella the DMV picture of Jane. "She's fifty-seven years old, married, with two kids and one grandchild."

"Does either kid still live at home? Would one of them have access to the van?"

"No."

"Okay. Who's next? We're looking for a man."

"Most of the list is women," Logan told her.

"Okay." He could hear the frustration in her voice as she asked, "Do any of them have men in their lives who might be driving the vans?"

"Besides one widow, they're all married—"

"What about sons? Our killer isn't married."

Logan read over the names again, thinking. "All except one of these women have kids who are too young to drive." He tapped his finger against one name, even as he shook his head. "Marissa Evans."

"Evans?"

"Yeah, Lyla's mom. Lyla moved up north a few years back, but her family lives one town over. And her brother still lives at home. He's in his late twenties, but he's autistic."

"Is he high-functioning? Does he drive?"

"Yes. And yes. But—"

"Is he socially awkward?"

"Yes. But I've known Joe a long time. He's not a killer."

Ella's lips pursed and he could tell she was trying to

be diplomatic when she told him, "In my job, I see a lot of cases where killers hid their impulses so well that no one close to them suspected."

"I get that, Ella, but trust me on this one. Joe isn't a killer. There's no way."

She didn't look convinced, and for a minute she seemed about to argue, but finally she nodded and said, "Who else do you have?"

"Two single men on the list of blue van owners." He held up the first picture. "Adam Pawlter. Sixty-six years old. Unmarried."

Ella studied the picture a minute, then shook her head. "The guy we're looking for would be younger. Does Adam have kids?"

"No, but he took in his sister's son after she died."

"Does he still live at home?"

"I don't know. I think Marshall was his name, but I barely remember him. He works for Adam in his shrimping business, but I doubt he still lives with Adam."

"How old is he? Can you check his information?"

"Hang on." Logan pulled up the station's database, looking for anyone named Marshall, then shook his head. "No criminal record." He stood and stuck his head out the door, calling into the bullpen, "Hey, Hank, you know Adam Pawlter, right?"

Hank ambled over, scarfing down a burger on his lunch break. "Yeah, he lives next door to my aunt. Why?"

"Does his nephew still live at home?"

"Marshall? The guy's in his thirties. He has his own place."

"Okay. Thanks."

Hank's eyes narrowed. "Why?"

"Just running down a lead."

"On Adam and Marshall? They're both nice guys. And hard workers. You ever tried shrimping?"

Logan sighed, not wanting to get into an argument. "No. Look, it's not on them specifically. We're running down anyone who owns a blue van."

"Oh." Hank frowned. "This something the rest of us should be on, too?"

Logan lowered his voice. "It's a long shot."

He absolutely believed Ella when she said there was a problem with the blue van that had followed her. But the truth was, Ella was a beautiful woman in a town still filled to capacity with drunken spring breakers, even after the exodus that happened when news of a potential serial killer hit. Whoever had killed Theresa probably wasn't the only creep in town.

Seeing a blue van in the surveillance footage was suspicious, but it didn't explain why Theresa was there in the first place. Because something had sent her toward Huntsville instead of to the airport that day, and whatever it was, it happened before she showed up at the gas station.

"Okay," Hank said into the silence. "Let me know if you get anything you want help on."

"Thanks." He was surprised that the truce between him and Hank had lasted so long.

It must have shown in his voice, because Hank said, "Look, man, I've been thinking. I know I always hassle you about how you got the job, like a lot of the other guys do. But I realized it doesn't matter. Because you do the work." Hank shrugged. "Truth is, the chief shouldn't have one detective working by himself anyway. I'm lobbying for him to add a new detective position."

Hank grinned and added, "So, put in a good word,

would you?" Then he shoved the other half of his sandwich in his mouth and wandered back into the bullpen.

Logan shook his head as he returned to the conference room. Hank O'Connor wanted to be his partner. If today was a day for miracles, maybe they'd find something useful in the van lead, after all.

"Who else do we have?" Ella asked as he sat back down.

The look in her eyes told him she'd overheard him call this a long shot, but apparently she wasn't going to make an issue of it. Maybe she even agreed.

"One more name. Sean Fink. Thirty-six. Unmarried, no kids. Lives here in Oakville."

"Tell me about him. Is he socially awkward?"

Logan laughed. "Sean? No. That guy tries to be the life of every party. He's not married because he thinks he's still in college, on perpetual spring break."

"Hmm." Ella frowned at his computer, then glanced at him, frustration all over her face. "It doesn't sound like anyone fits."

"Maybe the guy who followed you wasn't connected," Logan suggested, his instincts telling him it might have been Sean following her, hoping to pick her up.

"Maybe not." Ella looked up at the ceiling, as though she might find the answer there, then back at him. "I'm not sure where to search next."

Chapter Eleven

Logan rubbed the back of his neck as he stood on the stoop of the Evans family home. He hadn't been here in two years, since he'd taken the promotion to detective and Lyla had moved away from Oakville, ending their engagement.

Beside him, Ella kept shooting quick glances his way, as if he wouldn't notice. She looked almost as uncomfortable as he felt.

But he'd promised her they would interview any man who fit the basic criteria of her profile who also had access to a blue van. And Joe Evans was on that list.

When the door opened, Lyla's mom looked surprised, then pleased, to see him. Then she noticed Ella and confusion flitted across her face.

Finally, she recovered and gave him a hug that made him feel like a jerk for being here at all.

"Logan. It's nice to see you again. How's your family?"

"They're doing okay, Mrs. Evans." He gestured to Ella. "This is Ella Cortez. She's working with me on a case."

Lyla's mom nodded at her. "Ella, nice to meet you." Then, her attention returned to Logan, her features hardening. "You're here about a case?"

"I'm sorry, but we'd like to talk to Joe."

Mrs. Evans instantly stiffened. "Why?"

"I can't get into details, but we need to ask him a couple of questions."

Her jaw was tight, and he could see all her motherly instincts to protect coming to life. Lyla and her mother looked nothing alike—Lyla was fair like her father while her mom and brother had olive-toned skin and dark hair. But Lyla had gotten her fierce drive as well as her softer side from her mother.

"He's not in any trouble," Logan said quietly. He knew Joe, and he would've bet his badge that Lyla's brother wasn't involved. But he couldn't taint his investigation by ignoring leads simply because he knew the people.

Mrs. Evans narrowed her eyes, obviously trying to read his real intentions, but finally agreed, "Okay. I'm staying while you talk to him, though. And if I don't like the questions, you're leaving, Logan."

"I understand, Mrs. Evans."

She frowned, then stood back and let him and Ella inside. They followed her through the familiar house where he'd come with Lyla countless times during their three-year relationship and into the den, where Joe was sitting.

Joe didn't look up when they entered the room, but Logan hadn't expected him to. He sat down next to Lyla's brother and said, "Hi, Joe."

Joe looked at him, blinked a few times. "Hi, Logan."

He didn't seem either happy or upset to see him, but Logan didn't allow that lack of response to bother him despite the three years he'd tried to befriend Lyla's brother. He knew Joe's autism meant he didn't process the world in the same way as others, didn't feel or show emotions in the same way. But that didn't mean he didn't have them. And it definitely didn't mean he could have killed Theresa or anyone else. Joe might have been different, but once you got to know him, got past his social awkwardness, he was a sweet guy.

Ella sat quietly on the chair across from them, letting him take the lead, while Lyla's mom stood in the doorway, watching carefully.

"Joe, I know we haven't seen each other in a while, but I just wanted to ask you a few questions, okay?"

"Two years, four months, one day," Joe said. "Two years, four months and one day since Lyla moved away."

Logan nodded, knowing without calculating the time himself that Joe was right. "That is a long time."

Joe shrugged, staring ahead of him at some spot on the carpet. "What are your questions?"

"I wanted to ask about your mom's van. You drive it sometimes, don't you?"

"Yes. I drive it to work some days. Some days, Mom drives me and sometimes I take myself to work."

"Have you driven the van anywhere else in the past few weeks?" Logan glanced at Lyla's mom as he asked the question, but she didn't react to it. She just crossed her arms over her chest.

"I took it for ice cream Thursday of last week at eight p.m. And I drove to the movies on Saturday, two weeks ago, for a six o' clock movie. *Indiana Jones* was playing at the Retro."

Logan smiled. The Retro was the theater in town that played old movies, usually classics. It was decked out to look like a theater from decades ago, with red velvet curtains across the screen and everything. He and Lyla had gone with Joe a handful of times when they were dating.

"Did you take the van anywhere else in the last few weeks?"

Joe shook his head, still not looking at Logan.

"Okay, Joe." Logan stood. "That's all I needed to ask you about. It was nice to see you."

"Wait," Ella interrupted, leaning forward in her seat. "Joe, have you been watching the news?"

Lyla's mom took a step closer, and Logan watched her, telling her with his eyes that it was okay.

Joe looked at Ella, then back at the floor. "Sometimes I watch the news. If Mom or Dad has it on."

"Have you heard about the woman in the marsh?"

Joe's mouth turned downward, making him look sad and childlike. "Somebody hurt her."

"Yes," Ella said, "Somebody did."

Lyla's mom opened her mouth, probably to stop the questioning, but Ella stood and said, "That's all we needed."

"Okay," Joe said. "Bye."

"Bye, Joe." Logan briefly felt nostalgic. He and Lyla hadn't been able to make it work, but underneath the career-minded reporter had been a good person, with a great family. He wouldn't have gone back and made a different decision, but he wished things had ended better.

Across from him, Ella—the woman who had recently taken hold of his heart and refused to let go—said, "Thanks for helping us out, Joe."

Joe nodded at Ella, then picked up the remote and turned on the TV.

As Lyla's mom led them back to the door, she said, "Good luck with your case, Logan."

"Thanks, Mrs. Evans."

She glanced over at Ella, who was making her way to his Chevy Caprice, then back to him. "I guess I'd hoped, when you showed up…" She shrugged. "Lyla is happy up north, with her new job. She's dating someone nice." She paused and finally added, "Your girl seems nice, too."

Logan felt himself flush. "She's not—"

"You can't fool an old lady," Mrs. Evans interrupted. "Goodbye, Logan." She closed the door before he could reply.

When he got into the car, Ella said softly, "They're nice people."

Logan nodded. "Yeah, they are." He started the car. "Let's go talk to Sean Fink and Adam Pawlter's nephew."

Ella was silent as they drove toward the Pawlter house, but Logan could practically hear her thinking.

"What's on your mind?"

She turned to face him, but didn't hold his gaze. "Nothing. Just that Joe doesn't fit the profile, I guess."

He could tell there was more, but since he suspected it had to do with Lyla, he didn't ask.

Instead, he maneuvered up to a small weathered house nestled among brand-new condos. The city of Newton was being developed fast, so fast sometimes it barely looked familiar to Logan, even though he'd spent his entire life nearby. "This is Adam Pawlter's place," he said as he parked.

Ella looked surprised. "I thought we were talking to his nephew."

"We can, but Adam's the one with the van. And I don't know Marshall's last name—he's Adam's sister's kid—so we'd have to get his address from Adam anyway." Logan hopped out and headed to the door, hoping this interview would go better than the last one. If nothing else, at least it would be easier.

Ella followed more slowly, gazing around curiously.

"Hank told me developers tried to buy up this whole area. I guess Adam was the only one who wouldn't sell."

He knocked sharply on the door, and had almost given up when it finally opened. Logan had a vague recollection of Adam Pawlter, but the man standing in front of him didn't match his memory.

Once, he'd been tall and sturdy, as if he belonged on a ship, out shrimping. Now, he was frail and hunched over, and he looked years older than he actually was.

"Sir, I'm Detective Logan Greer, Oakville PD. I wanted to ask you a few questions."

Adam turned to Ella and she held out her hand. "Ella Cortez. I'm consulting with the Oakville Police Department."

Adam leaned against the door frame. "And you want to talk to me?" he rasped. "About what?"

"We just need to ask you a few questions about your van," Logan replied.

Adam's eyes narrowed and his mouth twisted in a scowl. "Way to sidestep the real question, son." He produced a hacking cough, then stepped back. "And I remember you, Logan. You kids used to come out to our beaches."

Logan smiled. "A long time ago."

"Come on in. I need to sit down anyway." He turned, leading them into his house, which was dimly lit and cluttered with boxes.

"I figured I'd do some of the work myself," Adam said, gesturing to the boxes as he sat down on his couch, by an oxygen tank. "I've got lung cancer. Aggressive. Figured there was no need to leave Marshall to deal with all my stuff when I was gone." He heaved a sigh. "That boy's already been through all of this once, losing his parents when he was just twelve. Happened on vacation, too, poor kid. He had to wait there while I drove up to North Carolina to get him. Took years to get him out of his shell afterward. And now, he's watching me go, too."

"I'm so sorry—" Logan started.

Adam waved his hand in the air. "I smoked for too many years. Let's not dwell on it. What do you need to know about my van?"

Beside him, Ella spoke up. "Where's the van now?"

"Marshall took it to the docks."

"Marshall...?" Ella prompted.

Adam's eyes narrowed, but he replied, "My nephew. Marshall Jennings. He's always worked for me, but now he'll take over the company. He picked up the van early this morning, left his car here. The pink shrimp season just started."

Logan nodded. Being local, he knew about the fishing industries. "Does he borrow it often?"

Something flashed in Adam's eyes. "Well, now he'll have to, won't he? Since I can't work anymore."

There was an uncomfortable pause, then Ella asked, "Does anyone else drive it?"

"Sure. Everyone on my crew has driven that thing at one point or another."

"Your crew?" Ella asked.

"For my shrimping company. I've got a crew of seven. I bought the van for work, so that's what we use it for."

"Does anyone drive it outside work hours?"

Adam's jaw jutted out and he stared down at Ella's shoes. "Nope. It's for transporting our haul. Doesn't even have seats in the back, and it smells like shrimp, so I don't think anyone would want to."

"Are you sure?"

He looked up at her, anger flashing in his eyes. "Of course I'm sure."

"And what time do your men go out in the morning? Do they all stick together?" Ella asked.

Logan knew exactly what she was wondering—whether one of them could have snuck off before work started and used the shrimping boat to dump a body. But Logan knew Adam's boat was too big to go into the marsh. If one of his crew was responsible, he hadn't used the shrimping boat.

"What do you mean, *stick together*?" Adam scowled at Logan, raising his eyebrows as if the question was stupid. "They go out on the ocean together, of course."

"Can we get a list of people who work for you, sir?" Logan asked.

Adam let out another long, hacking cough. "I don't think so."

"Why not?"

"Because you still haven't told me what this is about, and I don't like the implication that one of my guys is doing something wrong. They're all solid workers. Every one of them has worked for me forever." Adam coughed again, violently, then reached for his oxygen tank. "Please show yourself out."

"Sir—" Logan started.

"I want you out! Go!" Adam fumbled with his oxygen, pressing the mask over his nose and mouth.

Logan waited until Adam was breathing without it before he said, "Okay. Sorry to bother you, sir."

He followed Ella out the door and as soon as they were back in his car, Ella said, "Well, *someone* is using that van."

Logan frowned back at her. "Maybe. I don't remember Adam all that well, but I do know he was always ornery. Plus, everyone in three counties probably knows what case I'm investigating by now, so I'm sure he's not happy with what my questions implied." He started the car. "Ready to talk to Sean Fink?"

"Well, we're on such a roll. Why not?"

Logan grinned as he pulled back onto the street for the short drive to Oakville and Sean's house. "You're a good partner, Ella." Logan winked at her. "And a lot prettier than Hank O'Connor."

He'd expected a laugh—or at least an eye roll—but when he glanced over at her, she looked pensive. "What did I say?"

"Nothing. You're a good partner, too."

Her tone was serious, and just when he realized she might be talking about something other than the case, she added, "But I'm not sure you ever want to let Hulking Hank hear you say his name in the same sentence as the word *pretty.*"

Logan snorted. "I bet he'd like that nickname, though. Hulking Hank."

"Probably."

Logan glanced over at her, trying to read her, but for once, he genuinely couldn't tell what she was thinking. Before he could ask, he spotted someone leaving a house up ahead, and he hit the brakes, jerked the gearshift into park and hopped out. "Sean!"

The thirty-six-year-old spun toward them, surprise flashing across his features. He strolled over and well before Ella stepped out of the car and Sean reached them, Logan could tell he was drunk. He checked his watch. It was barely noon.

"Logan," Sean said. "How's it hanging?"

Sean had been a year ahead of him, but they'd gone to school together, played high school football together. They'd never really been friends, though, and Logan's dislike of the man ratcheted up a notch as Sean grinned at Ella and actually licked his lips.

"Hi, there," Sean said, sticking out his hand in Ella's direction. "I'm Sean Fink."

Ella shook his hand briskly. "Ella Cortez."

Sean nodded, holding on to Ella's hand too long. "You're

the FBI girl, aren't you?" He grinned at her again, the kind of smile that had probably worked for him in his twenties, picking up women in bars, but Logan couldn't believe he still used it. "I like a woman who knows her way around a gun."

Ella's eyebrows jumped, and her mouth flattened, as though she was barely holding in her disgust.

"Sean," Logan said sharply, and the man dropped Ella's hand. Finally. "We have a few questions for you."

Sean nodded, smoothed a hand over his wrinkled shirt. "Sure. You're wondering about the girl who went missing a few days ago, right? The one whose friend was on the news last night? You want to know if I saw anyone sniffing around her at the bars?"

"Well—" Logan began.

"Yes," Ella cut him off. "What can you tell us about that?"

Sean stepped a little closer. "I saw her at one of the bars. She was dancing with every guy in the room."

"Did she dance with you?"

Sean's head jerked back, then he looked Ella up and down. "No way. I like them a little older."

"What about Theresa Crowley? Did you see her anywhere?"

"The one who was found in the marsh?" Sean glanced at Logan, then back at Ella, and his tone was cooler as he answered, "Sure, I saw her around town with Logan's sister. Never talked to her, though. Like I said, I like my women a little older than that. Is that all? I've got places to be."

Probably another bar, Logan thought. "Just one more question. It's about your van." He paused, watching Sean's reaction carefully.

Sean looked at Ella, then down at the ground, then back at Logan. "What about it?"

"You let anyone else drive it?"

"No. Not really."

"Which one?"

Sean seemed confused. "Which one what?"

Logan held in a sigh. "No or not really?"

"Usually not. But sometimes, if I have too many beers, I'll let one of my friends drive."

"You ever let anyone borrow the van?"

"Nah."

Logan stepped closer, invaded Sean's space. "Have you been to the Traveler's Hotel recently?" It was the hotel where Ella had been followed by a blue van.

Sean backed up. "No."

"Are you sure?"

"Yeah, I'm sure," Sean barked. "You got anything else you want to ask me? 'Cause I'm getting sick of this."

Logan locked a steady glare on Sean until he took another step back. "Nope, that's it."

As Sean spun and headed back the way he'd come, Logan called, "Stay away from the hotels, Sean."

"What was that about?" Ella asked as they got back into his car.

"You don't think he could have been the one following you at your hotel?"

Ella studied Sean, watching him out the window. "Maybe."

Logan shifted into drive, going back to the station, frustrated. He was glad Ella was at a different hotel from the one where she'd been followed, but he didn't like that she was now across town from the police station. If he thought there was any chance of talking her into staying with him, he would have tried. But he knew she'd refuse, so instead he said, "I know Sean's not socially awkward, but how do you like him for a killer?"

Ella was silent for so long that Logan glanced over at her.

"Well, I guess *socially awkward* isn't the word for what he is. I was just going to call him *creepy*. Do women fall for that?"

Logan shrugged. "Spring breakers at the bars? I think they do."

"Ew."

A smile hitched his lips, then faded. "Well? What do you think?"

"I'm not sure, Logan. Sean is predatory, but he doesn't really fit the profile. *I* may find him awkward." There was irritation in her tone as she added, "I mean, why did he keep talking about liking older women as though that was supposed to be charming? Women don't like anyone to talk about their age."

"Yeah, well, all his talk about liking women out of college is nonsense anyway. Why do you think he's not working during spring break?"

"You're kidding me. He takes off work to hit on college students?"

"Yep."

Ella's nose wrinkled with distaste. "Well, he definitely came off as slimy. And I'm not crazy about the fact that he specifically mentioned seeing Theresa around with Becky."

Logan's head whipped toward her, then back to the road, his hands tightening around the wheel. "You think he was watching them?"

"I think he noticed them. Enough that he knew exactly who you meant. But like I said, he doesn't fit the profile. He may be creepy, but *he* doesn't think he's awkward at all. He wouldn't feel compelled to lure anyone out to a secluded location to grab them. He's more sure of himself than that. He'd take them right home from the bar." She compressed her lips, as if she was considering, then shook her head. "We should keep an eye on him, but I don't think he's the killer."

Logan's hands relaxed. "Okay. What about the other interviews?"

"Well, Joe definitely doesn't fit. His social skills aren't there, but he was pretty forthcoming about everything. And he showed no interest in the investigation or concern about the questioning. As for Adam's nephew or his shrimping crew? I don't know. Adam was lying about the van, but I kind of doubt he knows whether someone who works for him is a killer and he's covering for that person."

Logan's frustration grew, the frustration he'd been feeling ever since Theresa's body had turned up and he'd had no idea where to look. All along, his gut had told him it was a serial killer who was so good at it that he'd managed to avoid detection until now.

Maybe the killer was so good he was never going to be caught.

Chapter Twelve

When Logan pulled his Chevy Caprice into the station lot, the first thing Ella noticed was Lyla Evans sitting on the front steps, no camera crew in sight.

As soon as Lyla spotted them, she stood and crossed her arms over her chest. She walked toward them like a woman on a mission. Even from a distance, she looked royally pissed off.

"Uh-oh," Ella said.

Logan cursed. "She probably heard that I questioned Joe."

"I guess now isn't a good time to ask her to lay off the FBI references in her newscasts." Ella said, only half-joking.

Logan's eyes darted upward and he made a noise somewhere between amusement and frustration. "Somebody save me from strong-willed women."

Ella gave him a look of disbelief, and he mumbled, "Or from myself."

As Lyla neared Logan's car, he said, "Why don't you go inside? I'll meet you in there." He took the keys from the ignition. "I have a feeling this might get ugly."

"Are you sure—"

"Yes. If I don't join you in ten minutes, send out a rescue party, okay?"

Ella laughed. "You need rescuing from the supermodel?"

Logan's forehead furrowed and Ella instantly regretted her smart-aleck response—and letting him know Lyla's looks intimidated her. "I'll meet you inside," she blurted, then hopped out of the car.

Outside, Lyla glared at her, pretty features twisted in an ugly snarl, but she quickly redirected her anger at Logan when he stepped out of the Chevy Caprice, too.

Ella considered saying something, but figured she'd only make it worse. So, instead, she speed-walked toward the station.

Behind her, she heard Lyla demand, "You questioned my brother about a *serial killer* case like he was some kind of suspect? How dare you!"

"Lyla," Logan said, "Just because I know Joe doesn't mean I can—"

"Was this *her* idea?" Lyla spat.

"Look, we were running down a lead," Logan said calmly. "If I only question people I don't know, it would compromise the investigation."

"A lead," Lyla replied, then her voice faded as Ella got farther away. But she got loud again. "Just because you have a crush on the profiler and want to impress her—"

Ella stumbled. She quickly righted herself, hoping Logan hadn't noticed, especially as he cut Lyla off loudly enough for Ella to hear.

"She's in town for the case, Lyla. And she lives in Virginia." There was such finality in his voice, as though there was no real chance for a relationship between them, and it should have been obvious.

Ella wrenched open the door to the station. Before it closed behind her, she heard Lyla say, "Yeah, believe me, I know that no one's an option unless she lives right here in Oakville."

The venom in Lyla's voice surprised Ella. Why had Logan and Lyla broken up? She knew Lyla had moved somewhere else in Florida, but it couldn't have been that far if she was here now, reporting on the serial killer story. Had Logan really been unwilling to compromise even that much?

If he hadn't, then Scott was wrong. Long-distance with Logan wasn't an option.

An ache formed in Ella's chest and she pressed a hand to it, trying to will it away. Sure, she'd had strong hopes for starting something with Logan, something real. But she'd only known him for...

Ella's steps faltered. She'd only known him for six days. It felt like so much longer. In some ways, it felt as if she had known him all her life, which made no sense.

As much as she'd hoped to jump into a serious relationship with Logan, maybe she'd been fooling herself. People didn't form attachments this fast. Not attachments that lasted anyway. It wasn't logical.

"How's the case going?"

Ella blinked and looked up, realizing she'd stopped just inside the station. Hank was standing in front of her, holding open the door into the locked area.

"Uh, thanks." Ella stepped into the part of the station reserved for police officers, where she'd been working with Logan over the past week. "The case is going slowly." She frowned, thinking about all the contradictory evidence they had. "This killer is smart. Very smart."

Hank nodded. He actually patted her on the back with his enormous hand as he said, "I have faith. Logan said you're the key. He said that if we really do have a serial killer, you'll be the one to figure out who it is."

He had? A new tension tightened her chest—the pressure to figure out something she was starting to worry she no longer knew how to do. "I hope so," she said faintly.

Hank looked at her oddly, maybe because he was used to her being a lot more aggressive and confident. "Well, let me know if I can help." He headed out the door.

"Thanks," she called after him belatedly, then took a fortifying breath and hurried into the conference room. Now was not the time to be having doubts.

Every killer left behind clues, no matter how hard he tried to disguise them. This one was no different. And with Logan's help, she *knew* they could find him. She refused to accept any other possibility.

That decided, she got a coffee and settled at the conference table to wait for Logan.

She didn't have to wait long. He pushed open the door and told her, "Lyla's going to stop mentioning the FBI."

"Really?" That was the last thing she'd expected him to say. "Wow, you must be persuasive."

Logan poured himself a cup of coffee, downed half of it, then sat next to her. "Hardly. Apparently whatever you said to her the other night made an impression. She wants to coordinate with the station on future stories to help us catch this guy. She wasn't happy about us questioning her brother, but she seems sincere about this."

"Seriously?"

"Yeah, seriously. She yelled at me for five minutes about us talking to Joe, and then she calmed down and said she wants to work with us." He gave her a half grin. "So, apparently, *you're* the persuasive one."

He took another sip of coffee, then added, "Which doesn't surprise me. You could persuade me into just about anything."

If only that were true.

Ella forced a brief smile, then got down to business.

"I feel we're missing something that should be obvious. I think we should analyze what we've got again, see if it sparks any new ideas."

Logan was looking at her quizzically, as if he knew she was considering some thought she hadn't divulged, so she picked up the pad on the table and started jotting notes. "We know Theresa stayed in town past her scheduled departure. We *think* she told the woman at the gas station that she was meeting someone at your grandparents' house, but it's possible either the woman or Theresa was lying."

Logan leaned in close as he braced his arms on the table, looking over her notes. "Why would the witness lie?"

"I have no idea. The killer works alone, so unless this woman knows who it is and is trying to protect him—"

"I doubt it," Logan said. "She's in her late seventies and she was my grandma's friend. I mean, she does have grandkids in their twenties, but I have a hard time believing she'd make up this story to cover for one of them. Besides, if she was going to lie, why lie about my grandparents' house? It's not like I was the one questioning her. And even if I was, how would that help?"

Ella agreed with him, but she wanted to separate what they knew for sure from what they only believed. "What about Theresa? Maybe she was lying, either about where she was going, or why."

Logan nodded slowly. "Well, we didn't see any evidence she was at the house, so maybe that's not where she was going. But that doesn't explain why she was still in town."

"I know." Ella frowned at her meager notes. "And that has to be the key. Why was she still here?"

"Her cell phone records seemed like a bust," Logan

reminded her. "There were no calls besides Becky's after Theresa left for the airport. Maybe this guy really did run into her along the way and then convinced her to stay, but to drive separately to meet him somewhere." Logan shrugged. "Maybe he told her he needed to make a stop first and he'd meet her there? And I still have no clue *who* she'd possibly stay for."

"Okay. What about Laurie? Were the officers able to track down where she went after she left that guy's house? The one who picked her up at the bar?"

Logan shook his head. "Jeff told us that when she left, she planned to go back to wherever her friend Kelly was. And Kelly says she was at the hotel, so we can assume Laurie was heading there. Probably she ran into this guy along the way. But we haven't come up with any witnesses who saw her after she left Jeff's place."

Logan lifted his coffee, but then set it back down. "What about the killer? I know we've been assuming all along it was a man. I thought that from the beginning, because I suspected sexual assault, but the autopsy didn't come up with anything. The damage from the marsh and the alligator was too extreme to say for sure. Could I have been wrong? Could we be looking for a woman?"

This time Ella shook her head. "It's unlikely. Even without sexual assault—and I actually wouldn't be surprised to learn there was none—the behavioral details suggest a man. Is it within the realm of possibility that it's a woman? Yes. But my professional opinion is that we're looking for a man, and I suspect he's somewhere between twenty and forty."

Logan nodded and gulped down the rest of his coffee.

"Actually, maybe we need to think more about the burns." She knew Logan wasn't going to like this, given that he'd known the victim, but the burns were important. "Even though we've determined Theresa's injuries weren't branding, the burns could still tell us something about the killer."

"Okay. You mentioned before that it could be how he tortures, right? If he's a sadist?" Logan's words were a little strangled, but he wasn't backing away from the topic.

Ella put a hand over his, knowing this had to be a hard subject, and Logan turned his hand over and fit his fingers between hers.

Ella stared down at their linked hands, holding on a little tighter as if it would keep Logan connected to her. *Focus, Cortez.*

"Yes. And serial arsonists and serial killers often share a desire to control, so that could be part of the appeal of fire for this guy. If inflicting pain to get a response from the victim is his end goal, then fire could simply be his means. But there's a very good chance that fire has some special significance to him."

"Right. You said maybe the killer had burns himself?"

"Yes, and if he does, they would be severe."

Logan frowned. "I don't know anyone like that. And I'm not sure how we'd get that information, other than maybe just asking around."

"Maybe we should call the fire stations, here and in the neighboring towns, see if they can give us any insight."

"Sure, let's try," Logan said, but he sounded as discouraged as she felt.

Who was this killer? Usually, by this point, Ella would have been firmly in his head. She would've been able to anticipate his next move, and she'd have a much clearer picture of what kind of person he was, and why he killed.

Usually, she also had more to go on. More victims, more crime scenes, just more. But still, her instincts were humming, persistently telling her that she was missing something important.

Ella knew if she didn't figure out what that was, the killer was going to get away with murdering Theresa. And right now, he was probably already targeting someone else, maybe even Logan's little sister.

She couldn't let that happen.

"I COULD REALLY use a few rounds with a punching bag right about now," Ella told Logan as she buckled up.

They'd spent the rest of the day talking to the different fire stations, tracking down information on burn victims in Oakville and the neighboring towns. But all of the leads had fizzled fast.

They were one day closer to Ella needing to leave, and she felt no closer to the killer's identity. Frustration boiled inside of her, with no ready outlet.

"Me, too," Logan said as he started up the car. "I've got one in my basement. You're welcome to come over and work out your aggression there."

Ella studied his profile as he pulled away from the station to drive her back to her hotel. She stared at the hard lines of his face, which looked formidable, until he smiled. And then he'd flash those green eyes at her and all her brain cells would cease to function until the only thing left was a powerful yearning.

Wanting to be with someone had never been so complicated for her before. Usually, if she was interested, she gave it a shot. Usually, everything was light and easy and simple until it was over. And she might be sad for a while, might be perplexed about what had gone wrong, but she'd never felt this much angst over anyone. Never felt this soul-deep certainty that to lose this man might be more than she could bear.

Every time she looked at Logan, she was tempted to take what she could get, while she was here, but then her brain would shout a warning that it wouldn't be enough. And if she wanted anything more, she was going to have to take a risk.

So she swallowed her fear, took a deep breath, and asked the question she'd been wondering for days. "Why did you and Lyla break up?"

At her quiet, serious tone, Logan glanced at her. The car slowed before he seemed to realize what he was doing and he put his foot back down on the gas. "I thought we might get onto this topic again."

Her immediate instinct was to backtrack, to tell him he didn't have to answer if he didn't want to, but instead she kept her mouth shut and waited. Her heart pounded as she hoped he'd tell her it was about more than just the distance. Because if he wouldn't leave Oakville for a fiancée, what chance was there for some woman who'd known him less than a week?

And for her, there was no option besides Aquia. She couldn't be an FBI profiler anywhere else. And she'd changed the entire course of her life, become estranged from her family, worked way too many hours, to get there. Now she was finally in a job where she might actually be able to bring down the Fishhook Rapist, fulfill the unspoken part of her pact with Scott and Maggie from a decade ago.

"Around the time my promotion to detective came through, Lyla got the offer for the position as an on-camera reporter. I knew that's what she wanted to do and Oakville doesn't have a local news affiliate."

Logan watched the road, his forehead creased as he continued. "In the end, that's what did it. She wanted to go and I wanted to stay. Finally, we agreed it wasn't going to work. My whole family is here, and you can probably tell we're really close. I never planned to leave Oakville. I thought she'd be happy here, too."

He lifted his shoulders. "I guess it's probably good she got the offer when she did and not after we were married, because our relationship wasn't strong enough to make it through that."

Ella nodded, as though she understood, but she really didn't. How could they not work through something like that? It wasn't as though Lyla had left Florida, so Logan would still have been close to his family. And he could have been a detective anywhere.

But then again, she'd never been in a relationship where she'd even considered something as serious as marriage, so who was she to say? Because if it came right down to it, she didn't know if she could ever leave Aquia, leave BAU, even after they found the Fishhook Rapist. Not for any guy. Not even someone she wanted as desperately as she wanted Logan.

Logan glanced at her, as though waiting for her to comment, but what was there to say? If another city in Florida was too far from his family, Virginia was out of the question. Yeah, maybe short-term they could make long-distance work, but where would that ultimately leave them? If they didn't have a shot at a real future, why set herself up for heartbreak? So, she just nodded again, looking out the window even though it was too dark to see anything but the headlights from other cars.

When he pulled up in front of her hotel and put the car in park, she turned toward him. She couldn't seem to smile, couldn't seem to bring herself to say anything at all, so she just unhooked her seatbelt, leaned into him and pressed her lips to his.

Whenever she'd kissed him in the past, it had been almost instantaneous combustion. But this time, his hand slid around to the back of her head, and he kissed her slowly, thoroughly. The scruff on his chin scratched as his lips caressed hers softly, over and over. It was as if he was giving her a chance to memorize the feel of him. As if he knew it would be the last time.

When he finally pulled back, Ella blinked rapidly, trying to keep the moisture in her eyes at bay, then got out of his car before she could change her mind and beg him to come with her. Beg him never to leave.

Knowing she'd made the right choice didn't stop the tears from spilling over as she went into the hotel alone. And it didn't stop a heavy weight from pressing on her chest, as though she'd just lost something very, very important.

"LOGAN?"

Ella sat up in bed, his name on her lips before she was fully conscious, before she even realized what had awakened her. She blinked at the alarm clock next to her bed. 6:00 a.m.

Then she stretched across the bed to grab her ringing phone. "Isabella Cortez," she said, her voice still husky with sleep.

"Ella, it's Logan."

Come over. The words were already forming on her lips when Logan spoke.

"We found Laurie Donaldson."

Dread rushed through Ella at Logan's dire tone, and she was instantly wide-awake.

"She was in the marsh. There's no question now, Ella. We were right. We've got a serial killer."

And if he'd dumped Laurie's body, he would soon be trolling for a new victim.

Ella pushed back the covers. "I'm on my way."

Chapter Thirteen

Everyone in Oakville was frantic and afraid. Locals and tourists alike were crammed into every available space in the front area of the police station, demanding answers.

Logan kept his head down and pushed through them to the locked door and into the back room. But everyone in town knew he was lead on the case, and the questions followed him.

How close were the police to finding the killer? How were they supposed to keep themselves safe? How could this happen in Oakville, of all places?

Logan didn't have any good answers, so he didn't even try to respond. He just pulled the door closed behind him and rubbed a hand over his eyes, which felt like sandpaper after only five hours of sleep.

As soon as the call had come in, he'd thrown on the first clothes he'd found in his closet and raced to the morgue, where Laurie's body had just been taken. He'd stayed for the autopsy, then called Ella on his way to the station.

He'd wanted to call her as soon as he got the news. He'd had his cell phone in hand, her number already dialed, when he'd changed his mind. As a detective, he'd stood through autopsies before. Every single time, he'd puked his guts out as soon as he left. This time had been no different.

But Logan knew Ella, as a profiler, wouldn't normally go to the autopsies. She dealt with the aftermath, and that was bad enough.

He knew she'd insist on being there if he called her, so he'd waited, hoping to spare her from having those images burned into her brain.

Logan pressed a hand to his mouth, trying not to gag as one of the images he'd had imprinted in his mind rushed forward. He didn't think anything was going to be as bad as witnessing Theresa's autopsy, since he'd known her when she was alive. But the knowledge that he'd been chasing this killer when Laurie was grabbed, the knowledge that he could have prevented it if he'd found the killer, had made this autopsy just as difficult.

Logan entered the conference room, and the smell of burnt coffee wafting up from the carafe made his stomach churn, even though there couldn't possibly have been anything left in there.

"Logan." Hank clapped a hand on his arm. "You were right." There was newfound respect in Hank's voice as he shook his head and said, "It really is a serial killer."

Logan looked up from the T-shirt he just noticed he'd put on backward in his haste to get moving when he'd gotten the call. "I wish I hadn't been."

"I hear you."

"Wait. Where's Ella?" He'd sent Hank to pick her up, not wanting Ella to walk all the way to the station from the other side of Oakville. Not alone. Not with a serial killer loose. He didn't care how many people were around at this time of day. "She was waiting at the hotel for you, wasn't she?"

Logan heard the panic in his voice and Hank must have, too, because he said, "Relax. She's right behind me."

And when Hank moved aside, there was Ella.

Relief rushed through Logan.

Instead of her usual knee-length skirt and T-shirt loose enough to hide her holster, Ella was wearing a pair of capris and a tank top, her gun on display on her hip. Her hair was tied back in a messy ponytail and dark circles showed below her eyes. But she was unhurt, and so, to him, she looked perfect.

Her expression was grim. "Who found Laurie's body?"

Logan gave himself a second to absorb the fact that Ella really was okay, then said, "A couple of tourists who decided they wanted to kayak deep into the marsh and watch the sunrise from there. Luckily, one of them took a cell phone and they called us when they spotted her. Officers on duty borrowed a boat and went out to get her. I just got back from the autopsy."

Ella paused midway to the table, blinking at him. She sounded a little hurt when she asked, "Why didn't you call me earlier?"

Hank took that as his cue to leave, backing out of the room quickly.

"I didn't think there was any reason for both of us to have to watch that," Logan said. Trying to lighten the mood, he added, "Plus, I figured you might think less of me if I threw up on your shoes."

"Thanks. I've never had to watch an autopsy." She crossed her arms, as if the very idea gave her chills. "The photos are hard enough."

He nodded at the folder he'd put on the table as he sat down. "I'm afraid I brought some of those. I thought you might want to see them, in case it tells you something about the killer."

Ella was still for a moment, then her shoulders stiffened and she marched to the table and sat beside him, fast, as if she didn't want to give herself time to change her mind. Whether it was about seeing the photos or getting close to him, he wasn't entirely sure.

When she was next to him, he wanted to wrap his hand around hers—to comfort himself as much as her. If it had been yesterday, he would have. But that kiss she'd given him last night...

It had felt like goodbye.

He'd known she wouldn't like hearing the reason his last serious relationship hadn't worked. That he'd thought enough of someone to propose marriage, but hadn't stuck by his promise. But at least he and Lyla had both realized it would be a mistake before going through with it. And he'd told Ella the truth. He wasn't going to lie to her.

But where did that leave them? With her returning home in a week at the very most? Especially now, when she'd obviously made the decision to resist this pull between them. How was he going to breach her defenses? *Could* he breach them?

He was an idiot. He was an idiot for getting drawn into the discussion about Lyla. He was an idiot for falling for Ella in the first place. Because what he'd told Lyla was true—Ella lived too far away.

And both of them had jobs that demanded all their time. It wasn't as if the investigations would stop coming just because it was a weekend. Ella's job was probably worse. Even if they *did* try to make something long-distance happen, how long before visits started getting cancelled because of cases? Too much of that and a relationship would fizzle, no matter how much he wanted it.

What chance did they have, really?

But as he looked at her now, her dark brown eyes so

serious and wary as she stared back at him, he knew he had to try. Because as much of an idiot as it made him, he loved her.

It was ridiculous. He knew that. He'd met her fewer than two weeks ago; genuine love shouldn't have been able to develop that fast. But he didn't doubt that was what he felt. It was too intense, too tied up in things that went way beyond simple lust.

So, instead of denying himself what he could have in their short time together, he took her hand tightly in his. He locked his eyes on hers, wondering if her intuitive profiler mind could read exactly what he was feeling.

Her lips parted and he thought she was going to say something, but then she ducked her head and pulled her hand free. "We'd better get started," she said, but her voice was barely above a whisper.

Dismay filled him, but he forced himself to focus. Laurie might have been past saving, but she deserved justice. And she deserved his full attention.

He pulled the folder closer for Ella. "We only recovered a partial body, because of the alligators, but Laurie's body was dumped a few days ago. And she was burned, same as Theresa." His voice caught and he cleared his throat. Was this ever going to get any easier?

"A few days ago? I thought officers checked the marsh when she originally went missing."

"They did. But she wasn't found in the same area as Theresa and we have a large system of marshes here."

Ella nodded and opened the folder containing the autopsy photos. "There are a lot more burns this time."

She looked up, staring vacantly ahead of her as she let out a long breath. "It doesn't matter how much of this kind of thing I see, every time, *every time*, it boggles my mind how one person can do this to another."

She clutched the edge of the table and he resisted the urge to reach for her hand again, knowing she'd pull away.

"I mean, I can get into the killers' heads, deconstruct them on a psychological level. Abusive home life, lack of empathy, need for control, whatever." Her voice picked up speed, picked up fury. "But at the end of the day, I'm just left wondering *why.*"

She closed her eyes and he could see her trying to regain composure. He expected her to open them again and go back to the folder, go back to her clinical profiler voice and tell him whatever else she could about this killer.

Instead, when she opened her eyes and turned to look directly into his, he saw tears brimming there. "After we made that pact—Maggie, Scott and I—I wanted this job with the FBI, this particular role at BAU, because I wanted to understand. Like maybe that would, I don't know, make some kind of sense of it all. Make some kind of sense of what had happened to Maggie."

A tear rolled down her cheek and Logan felt her hurt as an ache in his own chest. Not caring if she rebuffed him again, he took her hand in one of his and wiped the tear away with the other.

This time, she didn't pull away. She squeezed his hand tighter as she told him, "It doesn't. None of it makes any sense." He could feel her shaking as she said, "But usually, I'm good at this. And being able to get into the killer's head means fewer victims. That's why I stay. Because I feel like it matters."

She looked at the folder again, then shook her head. "Days like these, though, and I wonder what I'm doing."

She released a loud breath that sounded almost like a laugh. "Sorry. That was morose." She turned on her tough profiler voice. "I can do this. Let's go over the details and catch this guy."

Logan kept hold of her hand, rubbed his thumb over her knuckles. "I know you can. And I admire you even more because it's hard for you and you do it anyway."

Ella turned to him, her eyes unreadable as she studied him for a long moment. "You always know the right thing to say to make me feel better," she finally said softly. "No wonder you're so hard to resist."

"THERE'S NO QUESTION we have a serial killer in Oakville."

Police Chief Patterson made that announcement from a podium at the front of the briefing room, which was filled with officers from every shift. Most of them looked exhausted from pulling relentless overtime, and grim from the recent discovery of Laurie's body.

"Until now, the serial killer angle was considered a remote possibility," the chief continued and Ella glanced at Logan, sitting next to her.

Weariness showed in every line of his face, in the droop of his eyelids, and the longer-than-usual stubble on his chin. But beneath it, Ella still saw the simmering anger over what had been done to the victims, and the relentless determination that had driven him to fight his chief every step of the way to let him chase his serial killer theory.

"But Detective Greer was convinced enough about this to bring in an FBI profiler. And he was right."

Surprise flashed briefly across Logan's features. He'd probably never expected the chief to say those words.

Ella's hand twitched, wanting to reach for Logan's. He deserved the recognition. He was a dedicated and talented detective, and it was about time Oakville realized how lucky they were to have him.

She was biased. She knew it. But the truth was, she'd coordinated with a lot of detectives in her work at the BAU, and Logan *was* exceptionally good. How many other detectives would have seen Theresa's case and recognized a potential serial killer? Heck, even her boss had turned the case down, which meant he hadn't seen it. And he'd been dealing with serial killers his entire career.

"The FBI profiler is going to talk to us now, tell us new details about this killer to help us nail him," Chief Patterson continued, refocusing Ella's attention.

She wished he'd remembered to remind everyone that her consultation was unofficial, that the officers were supposed to keep any discussion of her involvement entirely in-station.

Her boss at the BAU knew she was here, but he'd told her in no uncertain terms that the trip hadn't been approved. She might be sure they had a serial killer on their hands, but it still wasn't an FBI case because it hadn't been through the proper channels.

But hopefully they'd find the killer soon and it wouldn't become an issue. Ella stood and took her place behind the podium, wishing she'd taken the time to put on something more businesslike. "Most of you know me by now. But for those of you who don't, I'm Ella Cortez. I work for the FBI's Behavioral Analysis Unit, creating profiles of killers like this one. I'm here on my own time, but I've been working with Lo—Detective Greer over the past week and we have some points we'd like to go over today."

She looked down at the list she'd jotted, which was still pitifully short. But it was better than nothing.

Scanning the room, she said, "This killer has a type. If you haven't already, look at the pictures of the victims. They're both college age with long, dark hair. And when they were abducted, they were both supposedly leaving town. We're working now to coordinate a piece with the local news warning women to be particularly careful as they leave town to head home."

Lyla was going to do the story on tonight's eleven o'clock news. They'd talked to her earlier in the day. It had been awkward, but when it was over, Ella'd had to admit that maybe she'd misjudged Lyla. And from the way Lyla had been looking at Logan during most of the meeting, she had a feeling Lyla was having second thoughts about their breakup.

A sour feeling climbed up Ella's throat, but she tried to ignore it. As much as she might want a claim on Logan, she didn't have one.

She continued, "The killer is a loner, unmarried, between the ages of twenty and forty. He's socially awkward. We still don't know how he's luring his victims, but before he kills them, he's burning them. And there's a very good chance that the killer has scars from burns himself. If you know of anyone like that in the area, talk to Detective Greer right away. Otherwise, we need to look for someone who has these kinds of scars. But we need to do it quietly and carefully. Because if the killer thinks we're getting too close, he might take drastic measures, including grabbing more victims."

The officers in the room all stared back at her, listening intently.

"There's one final thing. It's possible the killer is using a dark blue van in the commission of these crimes. Any potential suspect with access to that type of vehicle should be approached with particular care."

When Ella stepped away from the podium, the officers looked around, as if they'd been expecting more. As if they'd been expecting her to hand them a miracle. She could only regret her inability to do it.

"That's all," Chief Patterson said. "For everyone who's not on shift right now, thanks for coming in. For those of you who are, get back out there."

As the officers slowly filed out of the room, Ella looked at Logan. Finding Laurie's body had confirmed the things they'd suspected. But it hadn't really told them anything new about this killer.

On Logan's face, she saw reflected the same thing she was thinking—did they know enough? Could they find him before he claimed another victim?

ELLA HAD JUST turned on the TV to watch the live segment on the news when her cell phone rang. She glanced at it across the room and debated ignoring it. It wasn't Logan calling, because he and Chief Patterson were about to be interviewed live by Lyla. But it could still be about the case, so she hit mute and stood up.

Hopefully, it was one of Adam Pawlter's shrimping crew returning her calls. She and Logan had tried to catch them after she'd given her profile at the station, but they'd gone back out on the boat. She would have rather talked to them in person, but over the phone was better than nothing.

She answered the phone just as it was about to go to voice mail. "Isabella Cortez."

"Hi, there. Ella's short for Isabella, is it? I like that."

The voice was a man's and it instantly gave her the creeps, but Ella didn't recognize it. She tried to focus as an image of Lyla inside the police station appeared on the TV screen. "Who's speaking?"

"This is Sean. Sean Fink. We met yesterday near my house, remember?"

Ah, that explained the slime practically oozing through the phone. "Mr. Fink. How did you get my number?"

Sean sounded proud of himself as he replied, "I got it from someone at the station. I told them I had some information you wanted."

Unbelievable. Ella tried to keep her tone neutral as she watched Logan and Chief Patterson come on-screen for the interview. "What information is that?"

"Well, I was thinking some more about what you asked me the other day. About seeing Theresa and Laurie around town before they went missing? I realized I had some more details that could help you."

As soon as Sean mentioned the victims by name, Ella's attention was entirely on the phone call. When they'd talked to him yesterday, he'd referred to Laurie as simply the girl who'd gone missing. He would likely have seen her name in the news, but the casual way he'd just thrown out their names, as if he'd known them all along, had the hair on the back of Ella's neck standing at attention.

She wanted to talk to Adam's nephew and the others in the shrimping crew primarily because of the blue van that had seemed to set Adam on edge. But Sean Fink had a blue van, too.

She clicked the TV off and asked, "What can you tell me?"

"I thought we should meet," Sean said. "I'm at your hotel now."

Chills danced down Ella's spine and she fought to keep the suspicion out of her voice. "I wasn't aware that you knew where I was staying."

Sean laughed and Ella realized he was at least a little bit drunk. "It was pretty obvious from what Logan said yesterday. I'm at the Traveler's Hotel."

The nerves clutching Ella's stomach relaxed. At least he wasn't here. But the Traveler's Hotel was where she'd been followed by the blue van.

She'd dismissed Sean from her suspect list, thinking he was too sure of himself to be the killer, but she might have been wrong. Maybe the persona of confident, smarmy flirt was brought on by alcohol. Maybe when he wasn't drinking, he was awkward and socially inept. Maybe he was a killer.

Ella reached for her gun. "Sure, I'll meet you. But how about we do it at the coffee shop near the police station? Say twenty minutes?"

The coffee shop was open twenty-four hours and catered mostly to cops and tourists. It was closer to the Traveler's Hotel than where she was staying now. Without a car, it would take her fifteen minutes to get there. That gave her five to change out of her pajamas and call Logan.

There was a pause. "Yeah, okay, I guess that'll work. I'll see you soon."

As Sean hung up, Ella tried not to imagine anything ominous in his last words. There was a chance he was the killer, yes, but more likely he was just clueless, intoxicated and trying to use the case to hit on her again.

But as Ella threw on a pair of jeans and a T-shirt, she had to wonder. What if he trolled for victims and set up meetings with them when he was drunk and full of liquid courage? Sober, and back to feeling awkward and shy, he might want the women somewhere isolated to grab them. And he certainly knew the area well enough to use the marshes as disposal sites.

As Ella left her hotel room, she called Logan. But her call went directly to voice mail, and when she looked at her watch, she realized he was probably still on air. She left him a message as she ran down the stairs instead of bothering with the elevator.

Outside, the air was crisp and just cool enough that she wished she had a jacket. And dark enough that she wished she'd brought her flashlight. But once she jogged down the long entryway to the hotel, she'd be on the main street through town, which was usually lit up until the bars closed.

Could Sean actually have legitimate information? Or was she letting her nerves get the better of her?

Shaking her head at herself, Ella jogged around the corner. If nothing else, this was a good excuse to work off some extra energy. She had plenty, between the frustrating hours of investigating and the tension of another sort that buzzed through her whenever she came within five feet of Logan.

Ella increased her pace, her pulse spiking after a week of having her butt planted in a chair or driving around with Logan running down leads. In the distance, she heard cars and people on the main strip.

And what was that rumbling? Ella wondered as she rounded another corner.

As soon as she did, a dark blue van picked up speed, veering quickly toward her.

Ella reached instantly for her gun, but the car was coming too fast, its headlights blinding her. Panic rose in her chest as Ella saw that there was nowhere to go. Into the street was a bad option and there was a steep embankment on her other side. She whipped her gun free of its holster, squeezed off two shots and jumped to the left anyway.

She flew through the air, momentarily weightless and suspended, then gravity took hold and she slammed into the packed dirt, landing hard on her shoulder and hip. Her head bounced off the ground, and then she was rolling, faster and faster, down the side of the embankment.

Branches tore at her arms, something whacked her forehead, and Ella tried to grab at anything to stop her fall. When she finally hit the rise on the bottom, her whole body felt bruised. She blinked and tried to push herself up, but the world spun and she dropped back down.

Above her, a car revved its engine and Ella reached for her gun once more. But she'd lost it during her fall.

She sucked in a deep breath, and grasped the nearest sturdy stick she might be able to use as a weapon. Then she crawled farther into the shadows, still trying to get her equilibrium and her vision back.

Above her, a light suddenly shone down and then someone came pounding down the embankment.

Ella raised the stick over her head.

Chapter Fourteen

"Shots fired at the Oceanview Lodge."

The call came over dispatch as Logan was walking out of the conference room at the station, Chief Patterson on his heels.

Next to him, Lyla was saying something about how well the story had gone, about how maybe they should go get some coffee and talk.

Fear instantly rose up and Logan grabbed Hank's sleeve as he hurried past. "Did I hear that right?"

"Oceanview Lodge," Hank said. "Shots fired." He paused and glanced back at Logan, realization on his face. "Ella's hotel. Come on. You can hitch a ride with us."

Ignoring whatever Lyla was saying, Logan started to run.

What had he been thinking, simply moving Ella to another hotel after the blue van had followed her? It wasn't as if Oakville had dozens of hotels. It wouldn't have been hard for a motivated killer to track her down. He should have insisted she stay with him, insisted on having eyes on her at all times.

Instead, she was on the other side of town. It would only take a few minutes to get there, the way Hank drove, but with a gun in the mix, that was way too long.

He jumped into the transport section of Hank's police cruiser and slapped the back of Hank's seat. "Go!"

As soon as Hank's partner got into the passenger seat, Hank peeled out fast enough to make Logan's head slam back against the headrest. *Faster*, Logan wanted to say, but there was traffic and, even at nearly midnight, pedestrians. The drive to the hotel took fewer than five minutes, but by the time they got there, Logan was shaky with fear.

The drive leading up to the hotel was lit up with the headlights of two police cruisers that had gotten there before them. Sitting in the glow of the lights, just inside an open ambulance, was Ella.

Relief hit hard and fast, but the fear didn't go away entirely. Ella was holding a compress to her head while an EMT bent over her arm.

Hank jerked to a stop and Logan tried to get out, but couldn't, since he was behind the cage. It only took a few seconds for Hank to open the door and let him out, but it was long enough for Logan to realize just how unnaturally fast his heart was going.

He'd been to a lot of crime scenes in his career as a police officer. He'd never felt this terrified.

He jumped out of the cruiser. "Ella!"

"Logan." She sounded relieved that he'd arrived. Or maybe that was just his wishful thinking.

He hurried to her side and by the time he got there, he'd already noted every scrape and bruise along her bare arms, the nasty bump on her head, and the angry, jagged slash in her T-shirt. "Is she okay?" he asked the EMT.

"She'll be fine." The EMT frowned at Ella as he told Logan, "I'd prefer she go to the hospital and get this one stitched up." He gestured to the gash on her arm that he was working on. "But she says she didn't lose consciousness, and it doesn't look like she has a concussion. It can't feel good, but she'll be okay."

Logan's heart rate slowed down a notch. His arms were tensed with the need to hold her, but he forced himself to stay still and let the EMT fix her up. "What happened? We got a call of shots fired."

Ella looked up at him, and in her eyes he could see pain and residual fear.

The desire to wrap his arms around her intensified until he didn't care that he was going to annoy the EMT, didn't care who was watching. He climbed up into the ambulance on the other side of Ella and carefully placed an arm around her waist. "Are you okay?"

"She was okay enough to nearly beat the crap out of me with a stick when I went to help her," their rookie officer piped up.

Next to him, Ella grimaced. "Sorry about that. You were shining your flashlight into my eyes. I couldn't tell you were police."

The rookie's partner laughed as he trudged up next to them. "We heard the shots and put the call out over the radio," he told Logan. "We identified ourselves, but I guess not loud enough." He handed Ella a weapon. "We found your gun down there."

"Thanks."

As the officer walked away, he added, amusement in his voice, "We've learned our lesson. Do not piss off an FBI agent, even if she's unarmed."

Logan felt a smile fight through his worry. That was his Ella: tough as nails.

He turned back to her. "Are you really okay?"

She nodded and then, despite all the people watching, she leaned her head on his shoulder and he felt some of the tension seep out of her. "I'm fine. Nothing some aspirin and a bubble bath won't cure."

He got ready to tell her she'd be taking that bubble bath at his place, when he realized that would probably give the officers standing around the wrong impression. Well, at least about his intentions at this particular moment. When she was feeling better, Ella in a bubble bath… Yeah, that did sound like a good idea.

Ella's head lifted and she squinted at him. "What are you thinking?"

Rather than tell her, he got back to the important issue. "What happened?"

"I was in my room when I got a call from Sean Fink."

"Fink?" Logan spat.

"Yeah. He said he was at my hotel, said he had information about the case and wanted to meet. But when I pressed, he claimed he was at the old hotel, not this one. So, I said I'd meet him at the coffee shop by the station. I was on my way over there when the blue van showed up and tried to turn me into roadkill."

Fury flared up. Logan looked around the crowd of officers until he found Hank; because of his size, citizens generally didn't want to mess with him. "Bring Sean Fink in."

"I am definitely on that," Hank said, with enough malice in his tone that Logan knew he was secretly fond of Ella.

"Then what happened?" he asked Ella as Hank and his partner took off.

"I shot at the van, hoping to stop it, and then I jumped." She gestured to the steep embankment on one side of the road. It was dotted with shrubs and small trees and would have been a painful place to land.

"But you're okay?" he asked, needing to hear her confirm it one more time.

She smiled up at him, let him see her clear, focused expression. "I'm really okay, Logan."

"All set," the EMT said, stepping back so Logan could see her arm was taped up.

"Great." Logan helped Ella out of the ambulance. "Then let's move you out of this hotel."

Ella put a hand to her head.

From the slightly unsteady way she was walking, he could tell she was hurting worse than she wanted to admit, making him wish he was the one bringing Sean Fink in. But Ella needed him right now, and that was more important.

"I'm tired." She sighed.

"I know." Logan took her uninjured arm and led her over to one of the cruisers for a ride up to the hotel. "I'm going to get you that aspirin. And then I'm taking you to my place."

So this was Logan's house.

Ella looked around curiously as Logan led her inside, his arm around her waist as if he was afraid she was going to do something embarrassing like faint. She did feel a little woozy from the bump to her head, but if it had been anyone else, she would have straightened and insisted she was fine. But she liked the feel of Logan's arm around her too much.

So instead, she leaned closer and took in the dark leather furniture filling the living room. There was a large-screen TV in one corner and a bookcase in another. The room was uncluttered, with the exception of photographs on the bookshelf featuring family and friends.

As Logan shut the door behind them, his phone started

beeping. He set her bag on the floor and, keeping a firm grip on her waist, pulled the phone out of his pocket.

He looked at it, then tucked it away again. "That was Hank. He texted me to say Fink is in custody."

"Good." Ella twisted her head to look up at him. "You're not going, are you?" She didn't have the energy to deal with guiding an interrogation right now.

"No. Hank knows not to let him leave. We're going to arrest him and hang on to him until at least tomorrow. I'll deal with him then. Right now, I want to make sure you're okay."

Ella smiled at his concern. One of the other cops had brought Logan's car from the station out to the hotel and it had been waiting when she'd finished grabbing her belongings and checking out. And now she was here, in Logan's house, nervous and filled with a strong sense of anticipation.

As they stepped farther inside, Ella noticed the green plaid chair on the far side of the room, completely at odds with the rest of the furniture. Logan led her to it and helped her sit down.

She smiled up at him, trying not to laugh. "This is the ugliest chair I've ever seen."

Crinkles formed at the corners of Logan's eyes as he crouched low beside her. "It was my grandfather's."

"Oh." Her smile fled. "Sorry."

He grinned. "It's okay. It's the ugliest chair I've ever seen, too, but after my grandparents passed, I couldn't bear to see it go to Goodwill. I look at it and I always think of him sitting in it. So, I had to bring it home." He pushed her bangs gently out of her eyes. "Besides, it's the most comfortable thing you'll ever sit on."

She went lightheaded at his touch, and it had nothing to do with her injuries. Staring into his green eyes, she suddenly didn't care about the cuts and bruises covering her body. She suddenly didn't care that she would have to leave soon and that once she did, she'd probably never see him again. "Can you get me that aspirin?" she asked, and even to her ears, her voice sounded funny.

Worry filled his eyes as he hurried into the other room.

Ella let out a shaky breath as she stared after him, needing the minute alone to untangle her thoughts. When had this happened? *How* had this happened?

She was in love with Logan Greer.

Of all the crazy things she'd done, falling in love with a homicide detective who lived in a different state, who hadn't even been willing to leave Oakville for a fiancée, was at the top of the list.

Tonight's brush with the blue van had been scary, but she'd been in worse situations before. Lying in the street with a bullet to the leg and a gang member coming for her all those years ago, she'd fully accepted the likelihood that she was going to die. She hadn't wanted to go, had been determined to fight until the end, but she hadn't had the same panicked feeling that had rushed over her today. The feeling that she was leaving something unfinished.

She looked up as Logan hurried back into the room, handing her an aspirin and a glass of water.

"Thanks." She took the aspirin, swallowed it dry, and then pushed herself to her feet.

"Will you give me a tour? Maybe we can start with your bedroom."

LOGAN'S MIND WENT completely and utterly blank.

He tried to get some of his blood flow redirected north as he stared at Ella. Had she just said what he thought she had?

She stood close, staring up at him with hope and anxiety in her eyes.

Just last night, she'd been so determined to resist the attraction between them. Had she hit her head harder than he'd realized? Logan took a small step backward, trying to be a gentleman. "I thought you wanted to get some medicine and get cleaned up?" His words came out choked and too high-pitched.

She must have realized how badly he wanted to grab her hand and run down the hall, because she smiled.

He'd seen a lot of her smiles over the past week. Her teasing grin. Her sad-but-trying-to-hide-it smile. Her full-blown, teeth-showing, happy smile. But he'd never seen this sexy, come-hither grin. It made him want to sink to his knees and do whatever she asked.

She held out her hand. "Okay. I hope your shower is big enough for two."

Logan took her hand, twining their fingers together, and stepped closer, wrapping his other hand around her waist.

"Ella," he whispered. He'd planned to ask her if she was sure, but the way she was looking at him, with need and desire and something else, something that looked a lot like deep, deep affection made him shut up and kiss her. He pressed his lips to hers a little harder than he'd intended, with all the built-up emotion he'd been trying to suppress.

She wound her free hand around his neck and leaned into him, kissing him until his head felt as if it was going to explode.

He pulled back just enough to wrap one arm more securely under her arms and hook the other under her knees. Then, he was carrying her as fast as he could down the hall.

She laughed and the sound rung in his ears as she kept kissing him—his chin, his cheek, his neck, whatever she could reach—as he pushed open the door to his bedroom and carried her to his bed. He lay her down gently and then just stared at her, wanting to freeze this perfect moment.

She belonged here. She belonged with him.

He lowered himself carefully down on top of her, trying not to bump any of her bruises. Then, he brushed her hair back, letting his fingers slide through it, wanting to memorize every single detail of the night. He hooked his fingers through hers and found her neck with his mouth.

"I wish we had more time," he whispered as he licked his way up to her earlobe. "I'd like to take you out to my family's cabin, on the ocean, and do nothing but make love to you for a week straight."

Ella made a sound that could have been agreement or desire, as her fingers broke free of his and sank into his hair, pulling his lips back to hers. Then her tongue was in his mouth and he couldn't speak at all, could barely think.

Her hands slid around his back and he could feel them up under his T-shirt. He helped her pull it over his head and then reached for hers, letting his hands glide over her smooth skin on the way up.

When he tossed the T-shirt aside, he discovered she was wearing a black lace bra. For some reason, he'd expected something more basic, like a sports bra. He made a noise of appreciation in the back of his throat, the only sound he was still capable of making, and she laughed at him again.

Until he lowered his head and pressed his mouth between her breasts. Then, her laughter turned into a moan as she arched up toward him. He slid his hands down over her rib cage, careful of the cut slicing her left side, as he circled his hands around her tiny waist. Then he felt her strong hands gripping him, trying to pull his mouth back to hers. He smiled against her skin and kissed his way slowly downward instead as his fingers found the button on her jeans.

She lifted her hips as he slipped her jeans down her long legs and tossed them aside. Then he slid his hand up one leg as his mouth traveled the same path on the other leg until she was squirming beneath him and his lips hit her hip. And, oh jeez, her panties were the same black lace as her bra.

His eyes must have rolled back in his head, because she gave him that sexy smile again and whispered, "I have a pair in every color."

Logan started at her belly button and licked a fast line up to her lips. Then, with his mouth locked on hers, and her hands on his hips, fitting him against her just right, his whole body started throbbing with need.

"Logan," she moaned. She was reaching between them, trying to get his pants off, when they both flinched as his phone started beeping from his pocket.

"Ignore it," he mumbled against her mouth, kicking his pants free and rocking against her until she arched toward him again. Until her fingers dug into his back and she was making encouraging little sounds as her tongue found his.

He slid the straps of her bra down her shoulders and slipped his tongue under the lace. Ella's legs wrapped around his waist, squeezing tight. He was reaching under her back, fumbling for the hook, when his phone buzzed again.

Cursing, Logan forced himself to disentangle his body from Ella's and grabbed his pants, fishing his phone out of his pocket. Two calls so close together probably meant a break in the case.

He had to blink repeatedly to get his eyes to focus on the phone and then he saw it was Becky.

He let out a frustrated groan, looking over at Ella, her lips swollen and moist from his kisses, her pupils dilated with desire.

"One second," he croaked, pulling up the text in case it was important. They'd worried all along Becky could be a target of the killer's, so he couldn't ignore two frantic texts now, not even with the likely killer in custody.

Logan, can you please come over right away? I'm back at my house and I think someone is here, the first text read.

Logan grabbed his pants with one hand, swearing as he moved on to the second text. Bodyguard sleeping, but I keep hearing noises outside. Probably nothing, but can you please come and check, Lo? *Lo* was the name she'd called him as a kid, back before she could say Logan.

He yanked his pants up his legs and put his T-shirt on inside-out, the way Ella had pulled it off of him. "I'm sorry, Ella. I need to go check on Becky."

She sat up, worry replacing the desire in her eyes. "Is everything okay?"

"Probably." He leaned over and kissed her hard on the mouth, a promise that they'd pick up where they'd left off as soon as he could get back. "I'll hurry. If this really is a problem and I don't get back and you need to go somewhere, my car is in the garage. Keys are by the door, okay?"

"Sure. You want me to come with you?"

Man, did he. "No, it's okay. Get some sleep. I'll put the alarm on when I go."

Shoving his feet back into his shoes, he couldn't keep

himself from pressing another kiss to her lips. "I love you," filled his mouth, but he held it back. Now wasn't the time to tell her, when he was leaving. He'd wait until he returned.

And then, screw the challenges of her living in another state. He was going to fight for her.

MAN, HIS SISTER had bad timing.

Logan tried to calm the blood raging through his veins as he dialed Becky and sped toward her house.

Why was she even there? She had been staying with their parents, she and the bodyguard both, and he didn't like that she'd moved back home without telling him. Still, everything had been fine when he'd checked in with her earlier today. Hopefully, she was just nervous about being back home and hearing things. Hopefully, he could check it out quickly and get back to Ella.

Ella, who was waiting for him in his bed.

That thought sent another shot of lust spiking through his system and he turned the air-conditioning as high as it would go as he reached Becky's neighborhood, not all that far from his own. His call went to voice mail, making him frown and unhook the snap on his holster.

When he pulled into her drive, the house was dark. Even the porch light was off. Something wasn't right.

Logan squinted as he put the car in Park, his law enforcement instincts kicking into high gear. Her front door was open.

He grabbed the cell phone off his passenger seat to call for backup and opened his car door. He didn't see anyone, but that didn't mean no one was there. Dread felt like a steel ball in his stomach as he raced for the doorway, slipping his phone in his pocket and pulling his gun instead.

Where was his sister?

Even as he was rushing through the door, he knew he should have called for backup first, but this was Becky. And sometimes, every second mattered.

He realized someone was behind him a second before cold metal prongs touched his neck, before electricity shot through his body at way too many volts. Pain instantly darted along his nerve endings. He felt all his limbs stiffen and then shake uncontrollably, his gun slip from his hands, no matter how hard he tried to hang on to it. He felt himself falling before the Taser pressed against his neck a second time. He felt himself hit the floor before it hit him a third.

Then, he blacked out.

Chapter Fifteen

Something was beeping.

Ella groaned and rolled over. She blinked, confused, and then realized where she was. Logan's bedroom. In his bed.

She sat up and looked around. She was alone.

The alarm clock next to Logan's bed read 8:00 a.m. She listened for sounds in the other room, wondering if Logan had come home and she'd slept through it. Disappointment filled her at the idea. But she didn't hear anything. The house was silent.

And then there was the beeping again.

Realizing it was her phone, Ella climbed off the bed, and all the bruises swelling on her body from her roll down the embankment last night protested. She grabbed her jeans off the floor and pulled her phone out, squinting at the readout. She'd missed a text from Logan.

Becky is fine, it read. Fink confessed.

Sean Fink was the killer. Ella sank back on the bed, mad at herself for ruling him out when they'd first talked to him. Even now, after he'd tried to run her off the road last night, she was still slightly surprised, her gut insisting he didn't quite fit the profile.

But at least it was finally over. Oakville was safe.

They wouldn't need her anymore. She could go home,

or fly to California and spend a few days on the beach before heading back to work. Neither option sounded appealing.

She wanted Logan. And not just for a night.

Ella blinked back sudden tears and lifted her phone again to read the rest of the text. Fink lawyered up, so we're in a holding pattern. Let's get away. Meet me at my family's cabin.

He'd texted her the address. Ella smiled as she thought of Logan's whispered words from last night: *I'd like to take you out to my family's cabin, on the ocean, and do nothing but make love to you for a week straight.*

Desire and anticipation mingled as Ella grabbed her clothes, ready to get dressed and rush over there. Then, she remembered she hadn't showered since yesterday and she realized she smelled like dirt.

Hurrying into Logan's bathroom, Ella shed her undergarments and got into the shower. It felt intimate to use the soap that smelled like him and made her even more anxious to get to the cabin. To make good on all the promises he'd made last night with his lips and his hands and the look in his eyes.

She'd never gone into any relationship knowing it had an expiration date before. But she'd never fallen in love with anyone like this before, either. This crazy, irresistible pull that kept intensifying with every new detail she learned about him, every strength and even every weakness. Love wasn't supposed to be like this. Lust, maybe, but simple lust didn't come with this much desire to know everything about a person, to spend every minute with them, even if it was talking about a serial killer.

Ella laughed at herself as she realized she'd been smiling since she'd stepped into the shower, preparing to see Logan. Wow, she had it bad.

Drying off fast, Ella wrapped the towel around herself and ran into Logan's living room to grab her bag. She dug through it until she found a pair of panties and a bra in red lace. A rush of lust filled her system as she imagined how Logan would react to seeing them, and she quickly slipped them on, topping them with a skirt and tank top. She left her gun in her bag and took it with her as she turned off Logan's alarm, grabbed his keys and got into his convertible.

As she raced through the streets, following his navigation system to the address he'd sent her, she felt downright euphoric at the prospect of seeing Logan. Downright euphoric at the idea of wrapping her arms and legs around him until they both passed out from pleasure. And just downright euphoric at her intense love for him, no matter what happened in the future.

She'd take short-term with Logan over the rest of her life with someone else.

Winding down streets that took her out of Oakville, Ella kept pressing her foot harder on the gas. Forget checking out the cabin, forget looking out at the undoubtedly amazing view together. As soon as she saw Logan, she was going to tell him with her body all the things she was too scared to say out loud.

Way to play it cool, Cortez, her mind screamed, while another part of her brain whispered, *Coward.*

Ella bit her lip as she turned down a long, private road. Could she bring herself to tell him how she felt? Would it make any difference?

The navigation system led her to the last house on the road, a little two-story all-wood cabin with a wraparound porch. It was pretty, nestled in the woods and raised up off the ground, but it wasn't at all what she'd expected his family to own. She'd assumed it would be another fancy Southern-style home that was more mansion that true cabin. But this did remind her a little of the lived-in part of his parents' house, cozy and comfortable and meant for spending time together.

Ella stepped out of the convertible and took the steps up to the cabin two at a time. She was smiling so hard her face actually hurt.

The door was unlocked and when Ella pushed it open, there were rose petals leading into the darkened house, lit by candles scattered on the tabletops and sunlight streaming in the windows, filtered through the woods.

The woods. Ella faltered, ice racing up her spine. Logan had said his family's cabin was on the ocean.

She spun around, ready to race back to the car, back to her bag, which held her gun. But a man was standing there, just far enough from the light that he was bathed in shadows. She didn't know who he was, but he wasn't Logan.

Ella shifted her stance and lifted her fists. If her options were fight or run, today she picked fight. She didn't know this house, didn't know where another exit was, or if it would be blocked.

Fear shot through her, and not just for herself. It hadn't been Logan who'd texted her.

She had a sudden realization of how the killer was targeting his victims, how he was getting them to meet him in a deserted location: hacking their phones and pretending to be someone else.

It would explain how he'd crafted the perfect message to her, too. He'd probably seen the real message from Hank, telling Logan that Fink was in custody.

But right now, the only thing that mattered was that it hadn't been Logan texting her.

So where was Logan? Was he hurt? Was he dead?

A sob welled up and Ella pushed it back as the figure got closer, stepping into the light. She didn't recognize him.

She readied herself to fight, calling on all the training the FBI had drilled into her during her eighteen weeks at the Academy.

Then he pulled his hand from behind his back and fast, too fast, something was swinging toward her head.

Ella ducked and spun, trying to dart around the killer, to get out the door.

But he was quick for his size and he blocked her way and swung again. The block of wood flew past her as she darted backward, throwing herself off balance. And then he was swinging again, before she got her equilibrium back.

His next swing caught her on the arm and sent her flying. She crashed to the floor, sliding into the staircase.

Immediately, she flipped over, tried to push herself to her feet, and then the wood was coming at her again. It struck her temple and pain exploded in her head.

Bile filled Ella's throat and the room dimmed around her. As she felt herself losing the battle for consciousness, the killer stepped over her and raised the wood again.

She tried to lift her hands to block the blow, but they wouldn't move.

And then everything went dark.

CONSCIOUSNESS RETURNED SLOWLY, PAINFULLY.

When Ella forced her eyes open, the ceiling was blurry, moving with every beat of her heart. Her head throbbed so badly she was nauseated.

She was sitting on a chair, her head lolling over the back. When Ella tried to move her head, tried to shift so she could see where she was, she realized her arms and legs wouldn't move. She was tied to the chair.

Fear skittered along her nerve endings. How long had she been out? Was she still in the cabin? Where was Logan? Where was the killer?

She heard a low, pained moan and wondered who else was in the room until she realized it was her making the noise. Sucking in a deep breath, Ella used all her strength to move her head, so she could look around. Another groan ripped from her throat as her forehead throbbed harder and a stream of blood slid down her cheek.

She was hurt worse than she'd realized. She probably had a concussion. The right side of her forehead felt swollen to the size of a grapefruit and there was a haze over her eyes.

Ella blinked and squinted, trying to get her bearings. She was in a room, probably a bedroom, though the chair she was sitting on was the only furniture. The shades were down on the sole window, but she was pretty sure she was still in the cabin, probably upstairs now.

She listened hard, trying to determine whether the killer had left, but all she could hear was a buzzing in her ears that she suspected was connected to her head injury.

Then a form filled the doorway and Ella swallowed back a scream. He was blurry through her clouded vision, but he was big. Not quite Hank O'Connor big, but close.

"You're awake," he snarled, stepping closer.

Ella blinked and blinked until her vision started to clear, until she could make out his face. Light blue eyes, sandy blond hair, average features. She didn't recognize him. But the look in his eyes told her all she needed to know: he was planning to kill her.

Why hadn't he done it yet? Why had he bothered to

knock her out and tie her up? Bile rose up her throat. Did he plan to burn and torture her like he had his victims?

The idea made tears rush forward, but Ella held them in, staring him dead in the eyes. If he was a sadist, he wanted her afraid, and she refused to give it to him. Not that easily.

As if he could read her mind, as if he was anticipating her taking the hard way, he smiled. A slow, calculating curve of his mouth that made her want to shrink backward.

But there was nowhere to go.

Ella tugged at the bonds tying her hands behind her back, but they were tight, digging into her wrists. Her ankles were latched to the legs of the chair equally tightly.

He watched her test them, then laughed, a deep, guttural sound. "Believe me, I know how to tie a knot. Don't bother."

Ella forced words through her dry mouth. "Who are you?"

He scowled at her and the average, unmemorable features became a dark mask of fury. "You should know. You came looking for me."

Ella ran through the options in her head, the people she had specifically questioned. "You work for Adam Pawlter, don't you?"

"And it's a waste of my time," he spat, his scowl deepening.

Ella squinted at him, trying to read him. "But it works for you. It's physical work, but it doesn't take too much mental energy. It gives you time with your fantasies. You've had them a long time, haven't you? Probably most of your life."

"Trying to profile me?" he asked darkly, pulling off

his long-sleeved T-shirt and tossing it aside as if he was about to get physical.

"Burns," Ella murmured. His face was untouched, but the burn marks covered his arms completely down to his elbow, disappearing up under the sleeves of his undershirt. She'd been right. And the fact that he had burn scars meant he burned his victims for a personal reason, maybe not to torture them, but for some other gratification. Maybe to make them look like him.

He stepped close, bracing his hands on her arms, making her twitch with the desire to break away from his touch. Then he leaned down so his eyes were inches from hers. He smelled like ocean brine and smoke.

Ella tried not to flinch.

"Yes, I have burns. You planning to analyze me, profiler? Maybe we should talk about why I burn them." His voice dropped low, almost to a growl. "You want me to show you? You want to see how it feels?"

"No," Ella croaked, panic erupting. Was this where Theresa and Laurie had died? Tied to this chair, begging for their lives?

She needed to get him on a new subject, fast. But what would distract him?

"How did you lure them to you? That's what I couldn't figure out," she said quickly, even though she already knew. She was betting that he'd want to brag about how clever he was. She could tell by the sick smile spreading across his face when she asked that he loved feeling the power he gained from tricking his victims.

Then his eyes narrowed, as though he knew what she was doing. He pushed himself away from the chair and said, "They thought they were meeting someone else. Just like you did."

"You hacked their phones."

"Yes." Amusement flickered in his eyes. "I got the idea a few years ago. It took me a while to figure it out. I had to make a rather unsavory friend, get him to teach me. Then he hooked me up with his spoofing service, made that part real simple for me. And the connection turned out to be mutually beneficial."

"Why?" Ella asked, not sure she wanted to know the answer. Had he killed for someone else, too? It wouldn't fit his self-centered needs, but maybe it had given him a chance to practice.

"It's not what you're thinking. I just gave him an alibi. He doesn't know what I do. And now I've got something to hold over his head. Just in case."

"What about Theresa and Laurie? Tell me about them."

"They were so stupid. They got the texts and neither of them bothered to call and verify. I didn't think they would. I was very, very careful with the wording, to make it sound like the person they expected." He smiled, baring his teeth, and the light that came into his eyes was unnatural and evil. "They came right to me. And then it was too late for them."

"It was you who texted Logan," she realized.

"Of course. Becky is still at her parents' house, safe and sound. At least for now. But I knew he'd go running to save her. He made it so easy. I actually thought he might have been more of a challenge, being a *detective* and all. And you." He shook his head. "You were pitiful. Running up the stairs like that, the look on your face when you saw the rose petals I put out for you."

Shivers inched up Ella's skin. Where was Logan now? The need to ask was overwhelming, but she was terrified of the answer. And terrified that if by some miracle he was still alive, she shouldn't remind the killer.

How had he known Logan had told her about the

cabin? Hacking Logan's phone might have told him Sean Fink was in custody, but it wouldn't have told him about the cabin. Had he been listening at Logan's house last night? The thought made her time with Logan feel tainted.

She desperately wanted to ask if Logan was okay, but she forced herself not to, forced herself to ask instead, "How did you know to mention a cabin?"

He smiled, that creepy, self-satisfied smile that made Ella want to knock it off his face. "I followed Theresa all week. I knew as soon as I saw her that I wanted her. I thought she was going to be perfect." His smile fell off. "But she wasn't. She wasn't perfect at all."

"You overheard her talk about the cabin?"

"I overheard Becky telling her all kinds of things. About her grandparents' house in Huntsville, about the family cabin on the ocean, about her nickname for her brother." He leaned close to her again, so close that she could feel his breath on her face. "Becky could be perfect, too. I don't know yet."

A new sort of fear rushed through her. She couldn't let anything happen to Logan's little sister. Even if he was gone, he would want her to try to protect Becky.

The thought that Logan could already be dead, that she'd never see his green eyes sparkling with laughter or desire again, that she'd never have the chance to tell him she loved him, made her feel as if she was choking. As if all the air had been sucked out of the room and her heart was compensating by beating faster and faster.

She was having a panic attack, she realized as her head dropped to her chest. She'd never had one in her life, but that had to be what this was.

Get it together, Cortez.

She focused on slowing her heart rate, on evening out

her breathing, and tried not to think about anything beyond getting out of this chair. She'd worry about everything else afterward.

But how could she get free?

She knew her best chance was to keep him talking, learn as much as she could about how he thought, and then try to use it against him, use it to get him to make a mistake. From the BAU office, she did that all the time. Analyzed killers and told the police how to make them slip up. But the stakes had never been her own life, the lives of people she loved.

Ella jerked her head back up and the room spun. When it straightened out, the killer was staring at her, studying her.

"You don't want anything to happen to Becky," he said in flat tone. "Or to Logan."

Ella felt tears rush to her eyes with relief. Logan was still alive.

"But you should have thought of that before you talked to Adam. Before you stopped by the dock and called me. You're way too persistent. The other guys never ask why I keep my shirt on out on the ocean. They just figure I'm out of shape and embarrassed. But if the cops started asking about burns, it might have come out that I stay covered up. It might have made you suspect me specifically. I can't have you digging around anymore." He walked around behind her and she felt his hand slide underneath her head to grab the back of the chair.

Then the chair tilted backward and he was dragging her through the doorway as the whole world spun. He pulled the chair down the hall and then kicked open the door to another room, yanking her inside and setting the chair straight again.

When she had her equilibrium back, she saw she wasn't alone.

Tied to the chair next to her was Logan. She didn't see any immediate injuries, but his head lolled to the side, his eyes closed. It was only by staring intently that she could see his chest faintly rising and falling, and confirm that he really was alive.

"Logan," she breathed.

But he remained silent and still.

"He had no idea until you showed up in town," the killer spat at her. "I would have left him alone. It's your fault. Remember that."

"No." Ella shook her head frantically and pain burst behind her eyes. "We have someone else in custody. You know that." She sounded desperate, even to her own ears.

"It was only a matter of time before you realized Sean Fink wasn't smart enough to do this." A half smile formed on his lips. "You're quick." The smile dropped off and was replaced by a dark scowl. "You shot the van. That's going to be a problem. But if you'd just been easier to kill, we wouldn't be in this situation right now."

"No," Ella protested. "It's not—"

He shrugged. "It's too late now, profiler. You're going to have to disappear. Both of you."

Chapter Sixteen

He heard Ella's voice. It was coming from a great, great distance, and Logan struggled to reach it, fighting the blackness that threatened to pull him under again.

As his mind cleared, he started to remember. Going to Becky's house and being ambushed. He'd woken again, trussed up in the back of a van that smelled like shrimp, bouncing along the road, not knowing where he was headed. As soon as the van had opened and the killer had realized he was awake, Logan had gotten stunned with the Taser again, then hit in the head with something.

It had happened a fifth time when he'd come to in the bedroom of a cabin. And then he'd stayed under. For how long, he had no idea.

But if he could hear Ella… He prayed it was just his unconscious mind wishing for her, that she wasn't really here, but even before he pried his eyes open, he knew she was. He could sense her beside him.

And as his eyes focused, there she was. Tied to the chair next to him, the right side of her forehead swollen, blood streaking over her cheek. "Ella," he rasped.

"Logan." She sounded so relieved, and more clear-headed than he was, despite her injury.

Logan forced his head to lift, and his spine creaked in protest after too long with his head hanging sideways.

194   *Disarming Detective*

He drew in a deep breath, trying to get his mind to focus. The air felt thick and noxious, and he tried to identify why, but all he could focus on was Ella. "Are you okay?"

It wasn't Ella who answered. "Neither of you are going to be okay for much longer."

Logan turned his head to face forward. Fury rushed through him that the killer had hurt Ella, and it helped clear the cobwebs in his brain. "Marshall."

Adam's nephew nodded. "So, you know me. I wasn't sure if you would."

"Why? Why would you do this?"

Marshall tilted his head, his lips stretching into something that might be called a smile if it wasn't so filled with malice. "Why would I abduct and murder young women? Or why would I kidnap you and your profiler girlfriend?"

Marshall sounded so calm, as though this was a normal conversation.

How had no one around him noticed he was totally nuts?

Logan cursed himself for not following up more aggressively on Marshall and the rest of Adam's shrimping crew. If he had, maybe he and Ella wouldn't be here right now. Maybe they'd still be back at his place, tangled together in his sheets, making plans for the future.

Now would they even have a future?

Logan tugged at the knots around his wrists, trying to be subtle about it. "Why would you do any of it?"

And what was Marshall planning to do with them now? Why were they here, tied up in some cabin in the woods instead of already gator food?

Marshall sighed, looking bored with the question, with him. "The profiler over there already wanted to know about the burns." A light came into his eyes. "You want to talk about the burns?"

Logan studied the dark brown, raised scars on Marshall's arms, remembering what Ella had said about the killer having burns himself. Judging from the too-excited expression on Marshall's face, burns were a topic to stay far away from. "Not really."

Man, the knots around his wrists were tight. Trying to stretch them was just slicing into his skin. But of course, Marshall was a sailor. He would know how to tie a proper knot.

Logan glanced around for anything to work with in case Marshall left them alone, but the room was mostly empty. It just held the chairs he and Ella were sitting on and old newspapers, crumpled up on the floor around them. And his ankles seemed to be tied as tightly as his wrists.

"Don't bother," Marshall said. "You think I'd leave anything nearby that you could use to get yourself out of those knots?" He shook his head. "I'm not stupid. Even though I took your gun from you at your sister's house, I'm not taking chances."

Becky. A new worry filled him. "Where is she?"

"Your sister?" Marshall smiled again, this one an anticipatory smile that made Logan's skin crawl. "She's still at your parents' house, I assume. She never really went back home."

Insight flashed through him. "It was you on the phone." It had been Marshall all along. That was why Theresa had gone to meet him. She'd thought she was meeting Becky. The second number on Theresa's cell phone records that had looked as if it came from Becky had actually been Marshall. Logan swore, a string of offensive names that just made Marshall shake his head.

"That's not nice," Marshall said, taking a step toward him, pulling the Taser from his pocket.

"I want to know about the burns," Ella suddenly spoke up.

Logan's head whipped toward her. What was she doing?

Her eyes darted fast to his and then back to Marshall, her face never turning, and he realized. She wasn't just trying to prevent Marshall from hitting him with the Taser again. She was profiling Marshall, trying to talk their way out of this. Or at least trying to distract Marshall long enough for Logan to make a move.

As Marshall's attention turned entirely, disturbingly, to Ella, Logan wrenched at his bonds again, but he'd been right before. They were tight, too tight, and all he succeeded in doing was slicing through the skin at his wrists and wetting the rope with his blood.

But as he twisted his hands, he realized they weren't tied to the chair; they were only tied together behind his back. If he lifted his shoulders and shifted forward, he could yank them over the top of the chair. He'd still have his hands tied behind his back, but if he could just get his ankles free…

He'd been a linebacker when he'd played high school and college football. If he could get his ankles free, he wouldn't need his hands. He could rush Marshall. Just use brute strength, go low and twist a shoulder up under his rib cage and then run him straight into the wall as fast and as hard as he could.

He just needed to wait for an opening.

Because Ella was as smart and resourceful as she was gorgeous. If he gave her the chance, if he could hold Marshall down long enough, she could get out. Even tied to her own chair, even with a set of stairs to somehow get down, he knew she could do it.

And as long as she was safe, it didn't really matter what happened to him.

But watching her now as he shifted his legs, trying to see how sturdy the chair was, he realized she'd never leave him there. That just wasn't her style. And although it was one of the things he loved about her, right now he wished she were just a little bit less courageous.

She was staring at Marshall with her chin tipped up and such a challenging expression in her eyes, as if she was daring him to take her on, that it scared him. Because right now, Marshall held all the cards. Not to mention the Taser and Logan's gun.

Marshall ran a finger across Ella's arm with such blatant ownership it made Logan want to shove his chair sideways and slam it into the man as hard as he could. Especially when Ella shivered in disgust. It took all his self-control to remain still, to let Ella use her profiling talent.

"You want to know why I burn them?" His voice dropped to a near whisper. "Or you want to know how?"

"Neither," Ella said, her voice surprisingly strong and even. "I want to know about *your* burns."

Darkness fell over Marshall's face, and Logan watched him carefully, holding his breath as he turned his feet sideways, trying to hook his heels on the sides of the chair legs. But the knots were tight and his heels kept slipping off. Finally, they caught hold, and he pushed outward, testing the strength of the chair legs. They shifted slightly at the pressure.

Marshall took a small step backward. His mouth moved, as though he was having some kind of silent debate, then he said, "Why not? It's not like you'll be telling anyone."

His forehead furrowed, and he looked down at the

floor. "There was a fire, back when I was twelve. We were away on vacation. My parents didn't make it. And I got caught in it, too. But all anyone here knows is that my parents died when I was young. Adam made sure no one knew the details, that no one knew about the fire at all. I told him it was too hard to talk about."

Ella's eyes narrowed. "You set the fire, didn't you?"

His lips stretched a tiny bit as he looked back at Ella. "Not even Adam suspected that."

"But he's always wondered about you, hasn't he? He always knew something wasn't right."

Marshall threw his hands up, made an ugly noise in the back of his throat. "Sure, Adam knows I'm…different, but he doesn't think I killed his sister."

"You did it on purpose, didn't you? Were your parents your first murders?"

Logan glanced over at Marshall, whose mouth darted in and out of a smile as if the memory was a mix of good and bad. Which it probably was.

"They deserved it." His voice rose. "You know what they did to me?" He took a ragged breath, quieted down to tell her. "My father saw things in me. Things he didn't like. He figured if he beat me enough, I'd stop. I didn't stop. And after they were gone, it was easier. Adam had no idea what I thought about. He never looked on my computer, never wondered what I liked to look at. He doesn't know what I'm doing now."

"But he started to suspect after we talked to him, didn't he?"

Marshall's smile slipped and his tone hardened. "Yes. He hasn't said anything, but I can tell. He knows I've taken the van out at night. He wonders if it might be me."

Ella nodded. "And you found out recently that he's dying."

"You profiling me again? Yeah, now he's dying. And he expects me to take over his stupid business."

"And you don't have time for that," Ella said as Logan worked his feet up and down, frantically trying to fray the rope against the legs of the chair.

He could hear the rope sawing, and it sounded much too loud, but Marshall hadn't looked at him at all since Ella had asked about his burns.

"I only took the job in the first place because it gave me plenty of time to do other things, plenty of time to plan. To imagine what would happen when I took them. But it never goes quite how I picture it." He shrugged, visibly trying to calm down. "But it doesn't matter that Adam wants me to take over the business. It's not happening."

Ella must have figured the conversation was heading in a bad direction, because she asked quickly, "Theresa wasn't the first girl, was she, Marshall?"

Marshall folded his arms over his chest and Logan realized the man had more muscle than he'd originally suspected. Sure, Marshall was big, but big didn't always mean strength. But he should have realized Marshall would be strong, given what he did for a living.

Logan pulled his feet harder inward, making the ropes dig painfully into his ankles, sliding them against the chair faster. He needed his feet free.

"No, Theresa wasn't the first," Marshall said slowly. "Two years ago, I picked up this hitchhiker. She started telling me about her past, and it was like mine. A lonely childhood, parents who didn't understand her. I thought…" He scowled. "But when I showed her the burns, she looked at me like I was disgusting. And when I burned her, she still didn't get it. So, I got rid of her. Dumped her in the marsh. I worried about it for a long time, thinking the police were going to show up, but they never did."

He laughed and looked over at Logan, who went instantly still.

"You never even knew she was missing, because she wasn't supposed to be here in the first place. And that's how I figured out what I should do. How I could get away with it. Just wait until they were getting ready to leave before I grabbed them. I thought the second one might work out, but when she didn't…" He shrugged, turned his attention back to Ella. "No one even knew she was missing. Not here anyway. And I waited, took my time, to be sure. I waited months and months. And then I saw Theresa."

Praying Marshall wasn't going to share details about Theresa's death, Logan started slicing his bonds against the chair leg again. It was working. The bonds were fraying. Just not fast enough.

Suspicion filled Marshall's face and he started to look Logan's way again when Ella asked, loudly, "What did you mean, about her working out?"

Marshall looked down at the floor and Logan froze, thinking he might have seen the frayed rope, but then he turned his attention back to Ella and there was something new in his eyes. Something dark and dangerous that made fear rise up, stronger than ever.

Even Marshall's voice was different when he replied, "When they first come to me, they're happy and smiling and I think they might understand. But then when they see me, really see *me*, they change. They don't want me anymore."

Logan felt disgust curl his lips at Marshall's fantasy that the women he abducted had in any way gone to him voluntarily. Even when they'd first shown up, they'd thought they were meeting someone else and he knew it. Of course he knew it. That was his plan.

Marshall reached into his pocket and pulled something out. He stared at his closed hand as if it had all the answers. "And so I try to show them what it feels like to look this way. I figure if we're the same, they might understand, they might feel for me how I feel about them. So, I give them burns like mine."

His eyes lifted to Ella's, suddenly dead and empty. "But they still don't understand. They're supposed to want me the way I want them. But they don't." He lifted his shoulders. "And so they have to die."

When Marshall opened his palm, Logan saw the lighter there.

Then Marshall flicked the switch on the lighter, firing up a flame. He took a step closer to Ella, and panic took flight in Logan's chest.

No, no, no. His feet weren't free yet. Tears stung the backs of his eyes.

Next to him, Ella's jaw clamped and he could tell she planned to endure it, keep talking, keep giving him time to get free.

But he couldn't do it. He couldn't watch Ella get burned. "Don't touch her!"

Marshall froze, then slowly, very slowly, turned toward Logan. And then, just as slowly, he looked down at Logan's feet, then back up at his face, and smiled. It was a sick, disturbed smile. He'd known all along what Logan was doing.

Anger tensed Logan's arms. Forget distraction. There was no way this pathetic excuse for a man was burning Ella. Not while Logan had breath left in his body.

He put every ounce of disgust and contempt he was

feeling into his voice. "What kind of coward burns women?"

Next to him, Ella made a noise of distress at his tactic, but he kept his attention focused on Marshall, silently willed Ella to start working on her own ropes.

Rage flickered in Marshall's eyes, but he was still eerily calm as he took a step toward Logan. "You think you can distract me better than she could?" He snorted. "You think you're better than me? Smarter than me?" His voice picked up volume, then quieted down again as he said, "No."

He took another step toward Logan, flicking the lighter on and off.

Keep coming, Logan willed Marshall, as he heard Ella frantically using her chair to saw at the ropes on her ankles.

Marshall glanced briefly at Ella. "There's no time for that," he said, monotone, but Ella kept working on her ropes.

He looked at Logan and flicked the lighter back on. "I never wanted her, you know. Your profiler. If she hadn't come looking for me, I wouldn't have come for either of you. But you don't have to worry. I'm not going to burn her."

He took a step back, away from Logan. "Not like that. No, you both need to disappear. And the marsh isn't going to work. Not for what I have in mind for you two. That would be too easy, too quick a death." He scowled, directing a dark glare at Ella. "You ruined everything and I'm going to punish you for that."

Then he looked pointedly up at the ceiling and Logan's gaze followed to the wood beams up there. "No, this isn't like Theresa at all. This is like my parents."

Dread settled low in Logan's stomach as he finally

identified the scent he'd noticed when he'd first regained consciousness. Gasoline—it was probably on the newspapers. It wasn't strong, so there couldn't have been a lot, but that wouldn't matter. He glanced quickly down at Ella's feet. She had too far to go on the ropes.

And Marshall planned to set the cabin on fire. The wooden cabin that would burn fast, with them trapped inside.

Chapter Seventeen

"You really think you can get away with that?" Logan demanded, yanking his feet inward hard, not caring anymore that Marshall knew what he was doing. "You kill us in your cabin and there'll be no question it was you."

Marshall laughed, a deep, booming sound that suggested he'd come totally unhinged. He kept flicking the lighter—on, off, on, off. "This isn't my cabin."

"Whose is it?" Ella demanded, frantically working on her own ropes.

But neither of them was going to get free. Not in time. And they all knew it.

Panic and regret mingled as Logan wished he'd taken more care going into Becky's house. That he'd just ignored his beeping phone in the first place, and kept focusing on learning the curves of Ella's body. That he'd told Ella how he felt, before they ran out of time.

"It's Fink's cabin," Marshall said, flipping the lighter up in the air and catching it. "I don't think he'll mind us using it, since he's in custody and all."

"That kind of ruins the frame-up, doesn't it?" Logan asked desperately, still tugging hard at the ropes on his feet. But they weren't breaking. "Sean's not going to be a suspect."

"No." Marshall shrugged. "But maybe the cops will

think he's got a partner. I know you're the only ones who suspected me. Besides Adam, but he's dying anyway. And if it looks like the other cops are getting too close, I'll disappear, too. I'll figure it out if I have to."

He glanced down at Logan's feet and then his eyebrows jerked up. "You're better than I expected. I almost got distracted with all this talking." He sighed. "But it's time to go."

"No!" Ella screamed, lurching to her feet. She was still tethered to the chair and she was hunched over awkwardly, barely maintaining her balance as she inched closer to Marshall.

Surprise flashed across Marshall's face and he took a quick step back. Then he seemed to realize what he was doing and he strode forward, got in Ella's face, and flicked the flame on the lighter way too close to her cheek, madness in his eyes. "You want me to start the burns early? Once I set this place on fire, the smoke might get you before the flames. But I can make sure you feel the fire."

Logan looked down at his ankles. The right one was closer to being free, so he shifted his weight left, then pulled his right foot in and kicked it out again as hard as he could.

Agony ripped up from his ankle and something definitely tore, but the chair leg came loose from the seat. Then his weight shifted and the chair crashed down on the right side. The back of the chair slammed into his upper arms as he hit the floor at an awkward angle.

Panic flashed in Marshall's eyes as Logan thrust himself to his feet, still attached to the broken chair by both ankles.

Marshall jerked away, but not before Ella head-butted him, sending him stumbling backward across the room.

But he got his balance back fast, not going down, lighter still in hand. He flicked it on as Logan hobbled toward him as fast as he could.

He picked up speed, ignoring the pain shooting up his leg from his ankle. Instead of tackling Marshall low like he'd planned, he hit him full-on, just slammed into him and kept going.

The lighter flew out of Marshall's hand and Logan heard a whoosh behind him as the flame caught something.

Logan kept shoving. With his hands behind his back and his ankles still attached to the chair, he didn't have the momentum to do any real damage if he slammed Marshall into the wall, so Logan twisted his shoulders and angled the other way.

Marshall got his hands up and tried to push Logan off. But Marshall's massive upper body strength wasn't enough to overcome the desperation and fury fueling Logan, with the image of Marshall holding a lighter up to Ella's face imprinted on his brain.

With an inch of space suddenly between them, Marshall smiled, probably thinking he had the upper hand again. But it gave Logan the perfect amount of room to put one last burst of power into his final hit.

He slammed into Marshall as hard as he could and Marshall flew backward, right into the window. Glass shattered, showering Logan as Marshall fell, his scream tearing through the air.

For a second, Logan thought he was going to fall out headfirst, too, but he regained his balance as the oxygen rushed in.

And then there was another, bigger whooshing sound behind him and heat rushed up his back. When he spun around, he saw that the entire room was on fire.

The newspapers that had been scattered across the floor had gone up fast, then jumped to the curtains, and now flames were licking the ceiling. Ella was still near the center of the room, surrounded by flames, slamming her chair up and down against the floor, trying to break it. But it wasn't happening.

Logan lurched toward her, desperately trying to yank his hands free, but they were tied too tightly behind his back. He sucked in a breath full of smoke that made his lungs burn and his eyes water.

"Go!" she screamed at him, then started coughing violently. Tears were streaking down her face and he knew she was struggling to get enough oxygen. "The whole place is going to go up," she gasped as he finally reached her side.

Smoke swirled in the air around them, and Logan could feel the fire singeing his skin even though it wasn't touching him yet. He was moving too slowly with the chair broken and dragging behind him, attached to his legs. He wasn't sure he'd make it out at his speed and Ella was going to be much, much slower.

"Logan," she hacked as he looked around for another option.

But the door was the only way out. When Marshall had gone through the window, he'd hit the branches of a tree before landing a story below directly on the concrete patio. It was possible he'd survived the fall, but it seemed unlikely.

"Get out of here," Ella insisted, moving painfully slowly toward the door. She pressed her chin down near her chest to suck in a breath, then said, "Now! Go!"

"I'm sorry, Ella," Logan choked out. Then he hobbled past her, reaching back to grab her chair with his bound hands, and pulled her with him.

His shoulders ached as he yanked her out the door as fast as his feet could go, but slowly, too slowly. Their chairs slapped together, tripping him up, and he nearly fell over and over as he lurched down the hallway toward the stairs. He could feel his throat closing up as it clogged with smoke. The stairwell looked far away through vision that was blurring and shifting.

His lungs felt as though they were on fire, and his face felt swollen around his eyes. His mind was starting to go fuzzy from lack of oxygen. If it had just been him, he might have given up, given in to the intense desire to stop, close his eyes and rest.

But Ella was behind him. He could feel her head loll against his hands and he thought she'd lost consciousness, but he couldn't stop to check.

Finally, he reached the stairs. Carefully, he lowered one foot onto the top stair, stretching the ropes, trying to get balanced. But it was no use.

He toppled forward, and pitched face-first down the stairs.

He turned his head in time to avoid doing a face-plant on the edge of the stair, but the side of his head slammed into a step, and then he was lying at the bottom of the stairs, his legs twisted awkwardly behind him, Ella's chair on top of him squeezing out what little oxygen he had left.

Logan's vision blurred and blackened.

Move, his mind demanded. But he felt paralyzed, not enough oxygen getting into his lungs to power his muscles. When he tried to push off the stairs with his feet, nothing happened.

He sucked in a deep breath, but got mostly smoke. He couldn't even seem to cough anymore. His body wasn't working right. His lungs screamed, shooting such intense pain through him that he thought he was going to pass out.

But his vision came back just enough to see the door. It was so close. Only a few feet away.

But it seemed way too far. He could barely think, let alone move.

Then a weight shifted on his hands, a lock of hair falling across his arm. *Ella.*

Logan willed all his energy to his feet and pushed. This time, he and Ella scooted forward, tumbling the rest of the way off the stairs. Her chair shifted sideways, off him, and Logan fumbled for a hold on it again.

He managed to get to his knees, his shoulders and head pressed against the floor, and then he pulled and pulled, but nothing happened. He tried again, and this time, they inched toward the door.

He'd have to stand to open it. On his knees, Logan stared up at the doorknob, his throat and lungs burning, his eyes swollen nearly shut and his vision dotted with black. Despair filled him. Had he come this close not to be able to open the door?

Letting go of Ella's chair, he inched forward on his knees, but he couldn't get to his feet. So, he pressed his shoulder over the doorknob, which was a lever-style. It moved down, then bounced back up, not catching.

He didn't have much time left. He could feel his whole body starting to shut down as every breath he took contained less and less oxygen, more and more smoke.

He shoved down with his shoulder again, hard. He knew he didn't have the strength to get to his feet, so he turned, bent low and raised his hands as high as he could behind his back, pulling the door open.

Fresh air should have come in, but upstairs, the fire was spreading, and smoke swirled down toward them, darker and darker. Logan still couldn't get any air into his lungs.

He leaned back to grab Ella and he fell, the back of his head hitting the floor and his knees aching. Beneath him, more of the chair broke, making it easier to get purchase on the floor. He twisted to put his feet down flat and dragged himself along, pulling Ella with him.

Somehow, he got them out the door, and they rolled down the steps together, landing in a tangled heap at the bottom.

Ella's eyes were closed and he couldn't see well enough to tell if she was breathing.

He knew he needed to move them farther away, knew the whole cabin was going to go up soon, but as he tried to suck in fresh air, it felt as though he was choking. As though his lungs were so filled with smoke, there was no room for oxygen.

He kept gasping for breath anyway. And then he lost his battle for consciousness and slipped into the darkness.

Epilogue

"He's awake."

Relief rushed through Ella so strongly that tears streaked down her cheeks as she nodded her thanks to the nurse who'd come out to the waiting room to tell her.

It had been three days since she and Logan had been caught in the fire. She didn't remember much after Logan had grabbed her chair, tipped her backward and started hauling her through the house. She recalled watching the flames get closer, thinking they'd never make it. She recalled feeling an overwhelming sadness that she wouldn't get the chance to tell Logan she loved him. And she recalled gasping in a deep breath to tell him while she still could, then choking on the smoke, and fighting the blackness that had come over her.

Apparently, the blackness had won. The next thing she knew, she'd been lying on the ground outside the burning house, an EMT leaning over her.

They'd told her she'd stopped breathing, that they'd revived her on scene as they fought to contain the fire. They'd finally put out the flames, but not before the second story collapsed.

They'd found Marshall's body out back, dead from his fall out the second-story window. Since then, Adam had been making a lot of noise about a frame-up, claiming his nephew couldn't possibly be the killer, but Ella had let Chief Patterson deal with that. She'd gone straight to the hospital and stayed there.

Ella pushed herself to her feet, and standing after so many hours in the plastic hospital chair made her sway. She'd been praying for three days straight that Logan would make it.

Around the room, cops from the Oakville PD who had been taking turns waiting at the hospital stood, too, and started walking toward the nurse.

Beside her, Maggie clutched her elbow. On her other side, Scott wrapped a steadying arm around her shoulder. They'd both flown out as soon as she'd called them, frantic and nearly hysterical with fear.

"He's okay," Maggie reminded her, blue eyes clear and strong despite what she was dealing with, the continuing contact from her rapist and the upcoming anniversary Ella had hoped to cancel by coming here. Two weeks ago, she'd been so certain she'd get a shot at bringing down the Fishhook Rapist. But he was still out there, and September first was coming fast.

As Ella looked at Maggie, even after telling her the truth about why she'd originally come to Florida, she knew her friend wasn't thinking about that right now.

Maggie grinned at her. "Let's go meet your detective."

"Come on," Scott said, a smile in his voice as he helped propel her behind the nurse, toward the patient area. "I've got to meet the man who finally made you fall in love."

But the nurse held up a hand as the three of them reached the doorway and the cops crowded behind her. "Sorry. Just family."

Ella shook her head, ready to wage a huge protest when the nurse added, "Come on, Ella."

Maggie pressed a kiss to the side of her head and Scott

patted her back. She even felt Hank's massive paw rest briefly on her shoulder as she moved forward. She looked back at them as she followed the nurse out of the waiting room, and they were all smiling, all so happy for her.

But Logan had been in bad shape. The fact that she'd stopped breathing, which meant she hadn't inhaled as much smoke, had actually worked to her advantage. Once they'd revived her, she'd had her head patched up and stayed overnight for observation.

But Logan had required intubation and he'd been in ICU, so she couldn't even sit in the room with him. They'd told her they didn't know if he was going to wake up again.

She couldn't help sobbing as she remembered, and the nurse gave her an understanding smile. "He's looking good. He's breathing on his own, and next to that, the broken ankle and torn shoulder and the minor burns are nothing. He'll be fine."

Ella drew in a calming breath and wiped away her tears. "Does his family know?"

They'd spent most of the past three days waiting with her, but they'd decided to take a break about half an hour ago, and left to get dinner. They'd wanted her to come along, but she hadn't been able to bear leaving. She'd been afraid that if she did, it would be like breaking some kind of fragile connection and Logan would be gone. It was ridiculous, but her friends had understood and stayed with her.

"We just called them. They're on their way back now."

"Thank you." His family had been so optimistic, so certain Logan would pull through. They'd spent the days talking about all the things they wanted to tell him when he woke up, making plans for Ella to come back and visit him as though it was a given that she would. And the whole time Ella had been paralyzed with fear.

A new sort of fear inched forward now, a fear of losing him from her life. But at least he was alive. And she wasn't giving up without a fight. She was putting everything on the line and seeing where it got her.

She'd never been so terrified.

"Go ahead," the nurse said, holding open the door to Logan's room.

"Ella," Logan rasped as soon as she stepped through the door. He looked pale and exhausted in the hospital bed, an IV running into his arm and hooked up to all kinds of monitors.

But he was finally awake. A smile broke across her face and the tears fell again, racing down her cheeks until she was gasping.

"Hey," he said, holding out his hand. "Come here."

She stepped forward, put her hand carefully in his, and he laced their fingers together, holding tightly enough that she knew he was really going to be okay. She brushed her tears away, embarrassed. "I was so worried."

He smiled at her, and she had to lean down and place a kiss on his forehead, then another and another.

"Come here." He shifted on the bed, obviously trying to suppress a noise of discomfort as he made room for her.

"Be careful," she said as he insisted, "Get in."

"I don't know if—"

"Ella." He locked those green eyes on hers, steady and clear and full of...

Her breath caught. Could it be love she saw there?

He tugged on her hand. "Get in."

She climbed cautiously into the bed beside him, trying not to jostle him, and he laughed, a raw, raspy laugh, and pulled her close.

Wow, she loved this man. It was crazy and unexpected and so, so right. And it was time to tell him.

"Logan…" She cut herself off, realizing she couldn't do this with her head against his chest. She needed to look him in the eyes.

So she propped herself up on her elbow and, her heart beating a frantic staccato, said, "Logan, I don't know how or when this happened, but I…" Nerves flared up and she smiled at him, stared directly into those eyes that had pulled her like a magnet from the day she'd met him. "I love you."

He smiled back at her, a great big grin that told her she hadn't made a fool of herself.

"Ella." He slid his hand from her shoulder up to her head, pulled her down to press a soft kiss to her lips. Then he continued to hold her close, her face millimeters from his as he told her, "I love you, too."

Joy seemed to burst inside her. She gave a laugh full of happiness, then got serious. "Logan, I want to make this work. I know long-distance isn't easy, but—"

He was already shaking his head. "I don't want to do this halfway, Ella. I want to give us a real chance. With our jobs, long-distance… We'd both get pulled into cases and have to cancel flights and miss visits all the time. I don't want to see you on random weekends. I want you next to me every day."

Ella let out a heavy breath. "Logan, maybe down the line, but…" Her shoulders sank, weighted down by the realities of trying to make this work. "I can't just up and move. I'd have to put in a request to go to a different office and the FBI would have to approve it. That can take months, waiting for a spot to open. I can't be a profiler anywhere else, either. BAU is in Virginia. And I can't leave Maggie. Not right now."

She stared into his eyes, willing him to understand.

He lifted her hand to his lips and pressed a kiss to it. "Ella, I meant that I was thinking of moving to Virginia. Your job may not move, but I *can* be a homicide detective anywhere. Yeah, I might have to take a downgrade initially, but I'll work my way back up fast. I got a detective slot once, even with a chief who can't stand me. I'll get it again." He grinned. "Heck, I'll even let you tell Hank he gets my spot here. If you ever need a favor in this state again, he'll make sure it happens."

Her eyes widened. He was willing to leave Oakville? For her? "Really?" she whispered.

He smiled at her, a soft smile full of love. "Really."

Tears welled up in her eyes again, tears of joy, and she blinked them back. "Your family is going to hate me," she joked.

"I kind of think they saw this coming. Trust me, they'll be happy for us." His tone turned teasing. "And besides, Mom will just call you every week and ask about grandkids."

Kids with Logan. The thought made anticipation and happiness fill her until she knew she was grinning like an idiot. "Okay. Let's do it." She felt a laugh bubble up. "I've even got room in my den for your ugly old chair."

He tilted his head, his expression serious. "You want to live together?"

Oh, no. She'd misunderstood him. Moving to Virginia was a big enough step, especially considering the short time they'd known each other. Moving in together was a huge deal.

Ella frantically tried to figure out how to backtrack just as the door to Logan's room burst open and his family filed in, hurrying over to the bedside, demanding to know how he was feeling.

Embarrassed, Ella tried to disentangle herself from Logan's grip to get out of his bed, but he just held her tighter.

"Ella."

She looked back at him, and knew he could see her fear that she'd screwed everything up.

Amusement twinkled in his eyes. "I'll move in with you."

Ella sensed his family sharing glances behind her, but she couldn't turn her gaze from Logan's sparkling green eyes as he added, "And since we're diving right into serious, Ella, will you marry me?"

Ella could feel her mouth opening and closing silently, but she couldn't seem to say anything.

"I'm sorry I don't have a ring," Logan added, sounding nervous. "But as soon as I get out of this bed...if you say yes..."

Someone nudged her from behind. "Say yes," Becky whispered.

"Yes," she breathed.

And then Logan was kissing her and his family was laughing and crying and congratulating them. And she knew, she just knew, that coming to Oakville to find a serial killer had been the best decision she'd ever made in her life.

* * * * *

"Okay, what's going on?"

"Nothing I can talk about."

"Why not?" Her gaze moved from his eyes to his lips, where it lingered, and then continued down his body.

That was the sexiest thing to happen to him in the past year. "I need a shower."

"Want some help?" she teased.

"Normally I'd take you up on that." He stalked across the room, pausing at the door to the bathroom.

"I was kidding. No man on earth would want to shower with me the way I must look."

He moved to the bed and leaned over her, stopping a fraction of an inch before their lips touched. "Why not? Most men I know appreciate a beautiful woman."

Those stunning hazel eyes of hers darkened. Being this close was probably a bad idea. Even if she wasn't his witness, she was injured. No way could they do anything in her condition.

But then autopilot kicked in, and Reed couldn't stop himself.

HARD TARGET

BY
BARB HAN

Published in Great Britain 2015
by Mills & Boon, an imprint of Harlequin (UK) Limited,
Eton House, 18-24 Paradise Road, Richmond, Surrey, TW9 1SR

© 2015 Barb Han

ISBN: 978-0-263-25297-2

46-0215

Harlequin (UK) Limited's policy is to use papers that are natural, renewable and recyclable products and made from wood grown in sustainable forests. The logging and manufacturing processes conform to the legal environmental regulations of the country of origin.

Printed and bound in Spain
by CPI, Barcelona

Barb Han lives in North Texas with her very own hero-worthy husband, three beautiful children, a spunky golden retriever/standard poodle mix and too many books in her to-read pile. In her downtime, she plays video games and spends much of her time on or around a basketball court. She loves interacting with readers and is grateful for their support. You can reach her at barbhan.com.

This book is dedicated to the amazing and strong people in my life. Allison Lyons, you continue to amaze me with your insight and passion. Jill Marsal, you are brilliant and I'm grateful to work with you.

Brandon, Jacob and Tori, you bring out the best in me every day—I love all three of you more than you can know. John, none of this would be *this* amazing and fun without you—my best friend and the great love of my life.

Liz Lipperman, a huge thank-you for answering my many medical questions and offering brainstorming support. You really are the bomb!

Chapter One

Emily Baker pulled her legs into her chest and hugged her knees. Waves of fear and anger rolled through her.

A hammer pounded the inside of her head, a residual effect from the beatings. Her busted bottom lip was dry and cracked from dehydration.

"Move," one of the men commanded, forcing her to her feet.

A crack across her back nearly caused her to fall again.

The whole experience of the past few days had been surreal. One minute she'd been kayaking in a tropical paradise, enjoying all the rich sounds of the dense forest. The next she was being dragged through the jungle by guerrillas. She'd been blindfolded for what had to be hours, although she'd completely lost track of time, and had been led through pure hell.

Vegetation thickened the longer she'd walked. Thorns pierced her feet. The sun had blistered her skin. Ant bites covered her ankles.

A man they called Dueño had ordered the men to change her appearance. They'd chopped her hair and poured something on it that smelled like bleach. She assumed they did it to ensure she no longer matched the description of the woman the resort would report as missing. Oh, God, the word *missing* roiled her stomach.

She'd read about American tourists being snatched while on vacation, but didn't those things happen to other people? Rich people?

Not data entry clerks with no family who'd scrimped and saved for three years to take the trip in the first place.

Men in front of her fanned out, and she saw the small encampment ahead. The instant a calloused hand made contact with her shoulder, she shuddered.

"Get down!" He pushed her down on all fours.

The leader, Dueño, stood over her. He was slightly taller than the others and well dressed. His face was covered, so she couldn't pick him out of a lineup if she'd wanted to. "You want to go home, Ms. Baker?"

"Yes." How'd he know her name?

"Then tell me what I want to know. Give me the password to SourceCon." Anger laced his words.

How did he know where she worked? All thoughts of this being a random kidnapping fizzled and died.

"I can't. I don't have them." The night before she'd left for vacation, she changed them as a precaution. Her new passwords were taped to the underside of her desk at home.

"Fine. Have it your way." He turned his back. "Starve her until she talks."

Twenty-four hours tied up with no food or water had left her weak, but she couldn't give him what she didn't know.

He returned the next morning. "Do you remember them now?"

"No. I already told you I don't have them." Anger and fear engulfed her like a raging forest fire.

He backhanded her and repeated the question. When another blow didn't produce his desired result, he ordered one of the men to beat her, and another to dig a hole.

Fear gripped her as she was shoved inside the dark cramped space.

After dark, there were only three guards keeping watch. One drank until he passed out. She'd been working on loosening her bindings all day and had made progress. Maybe she could make a move to escape.

"I need to go to the bathroom."

One of the guards hauled her out of the hole, removed the rope from her ankles and then shoved her into a thicket. He looked at her with black eyes. "Two minutes."

He hadn't noticed the ropes on her arms were loose. Hope filled her chest for the first time since her capture. Immediately, she shucked the bindings from her arms, and then took off.

For two days, she'd carved her way through the dense vegetation, fearful. Any minute she'd expected the men to catch up, to stick her in another hole. Her punishment this time surely would be death.

Exhausted, feet bleeding, she made it to the edge of the jungle. In the clearing ahead, she spotted ships. Her heartbeat amplified as her excitement grew. She'd rummage around for something to eat, and then wait until dark.

Time stilled and the hours ticked by. The few berries she'd eaten kept her stomach from cramping.

When all commotion on the dock stopped, she checked manifests until she located one in English. The ship was heading to Galveston, Texas. She buried herself inside a small compartment in one of the crates. No matter how weak she was, she didn't dare sleep.

By sunrise, voices drew closer and the ship moved. The boat swayed, and she battled waves of nausea. Her stomach rumbled and churned, protesting the amount of time that had gone by without a meal.

How long had it been since she'd eaten real food? Five days? Six?

Hours had gone by and the air was becoming thicker. Her breathing labored. She swiped away a stray tear, praying she was nearing shore. All she had to do was survive a little while longer. The panels of the wooden freight box she'd jammed herself into seconds before the ship had left the dock were closing in on her, making it hard to move, or breathe. She couldn't afford another panic attack, or allow her mind to go to the place where she was in that dark hole being starved and beaten. A sob escaped before she could suppress it.

The ship had to be closing in on its destination by now. She was so close to the States she could almost taste her freedom.

Or was she?

All her hopes were riding on a journey across the Gulf of Mexico, but the truth was she could be anywhere. She reminded herself that she'd read the manifest, and prayed she'd understood it correctly.

Emily bit out a curse at the men who'd made her feel helpless and kicked at the walls of the crate, withdrawing her foot when she blistered it with another splinter. Her soles were already raw. She'd need to make sure she cleaned them up and found antibiotic ointment when she got off this horrible boat.

She'd already collected splinters in her elbows and thighs. Escaping the compound in a swimsuit wouldn't have been her first choice, but she'd grasped her first opportunity to run. There'd been no time for debate. Her chance had presented itself and she'd seized it, not stopping until long after the men's voices had faded.

She repositioned herself in the crate, grateful she could almost stretch her legs. She'd survived so far by doing mental math calculations, flexing and releasing her stomach muscles, and tightening her abs.

No food left her weak.

The minutes seemed to drip by, and her body cramped from being in such a small space. She had no watch, no cell phone and no purse.

None of which she cared about as much as her freedom.

She could get the rest once she got out of the crate and off this boat.

The resort area had been paradise when she'd first arrived, but nothing sounded better to Emily than home, a hot bath and her own bed.

Holy hell. She couldn't go home. If they knew her name and where she worked, they had to know where she lived, too. A ripple of fear skittered across already taut nerves.

She pressed her face against a crack in the crate. Darkness. Nothing but darkness behind her and darkness in front of her.

The man who'd helped her onto her kayak had told her to stay close to the ocean side and not the jungle because of the risk of running into alligators. Now she wondered if maybe they'd known about the rebel groups scouring the edges all along. They hadn't warned her about men with massive guns, and bandannas covering their faces, leaving only black eyes staring at her, coming to take her. She would've listened to that. She wouldn't have ventured off, following a monkey in the canopy. And where had the monkey gone?

Onto one of her kidnappers' shoulders.

She'd initially hoped the resort would send security once it discovered she hadn't returned to her room. She'd held on to the hope for two days in the jungle. With no shoes, her feet had been bitten, cut and aching after the daylong walks and nights of camping. And hope had retreated faster than the sun before a thunderstorm.

There'd been shouting, too. It had scared her nearly to death. At first she feared they would rape her, but no one had touched her.

Extortion? Drugs? Ransom?

Nope. None.

He'd asked for her passwords.

A sense of relief had washed over her. If she'd had to rely on her family, she'd be dead for sure. Her family wasn't exactly reliable, and they were broke. Even skilled trackers like these would have trouble locating her mother. The Bakers had split faster than an atom, and left similar devastation in their wake. At least the ones she knew.

Emily had always been the black sheep. She'd moved away, worked hard and put herself through college. Her mom had refused to allow her to take the SAT, saying it would only train her to be some corporation's slave, so she'd researched a grandfather clause in a North Texas school, did two years at a community college, and after another three years, graduated from the small university.

She'd come to North Texas solely on the promise of affordable living and an abundant job market, figuring she could build the rest of her life from there. And she had. She'd gotten a job as a data entry clerk at a computer company and was working her way up. Her boss was due a promotion and she'd been promised his job.

There were rare occasions when she heard from her mother, although it was mostly when she needed money. Turns out free love didn't pay all that much. Watching her mom wither away after her dad walked out, Emily had made a vow. No one would take away her power. Ever.

Being resourceful had gotten her through college, and landed her first real job. She'd pulled on every bit of her quick wit to escape her captors. Once back in the States, she could locate a church or soup kitchen, and get help. No way could she find a police station. Not after over-hearing her abductors talk about bribing American border police. Her body trembled. They'd hand her right back to Dueño. She'd be dead in five minutes. Not happening.

Once she was on dry land, she could figure out a way to sneak into her town house. She needed ID and clothes. There was a little money in her bank account. She could use it to disappear for a year or two. Wait it out until this whole thing blew over. Dread settled over her at the thought of leaving the only place that felt like home.

She thought about the threat Dueño had made, the underlying promise in his tone that he had every intention of delivering on his word. The way he'd said her name had caused an icy chill to grip her spine.

The ship pitched forward then stopped. Had it docked?

Emily repeated a silent protection prayer she'd learned when she was a little girl as her pulse kicked up a notch. She had no idea what she'd find on the other side of the crate.

Her skin was clammy and salty. She was starving and dehydrating. But she was alive, dammit, and she could build from there.

There were male voices. Please, let them be American.
She listened intently.

At least two men shouted orders. Feet shuffled. She couldn't tell how many others there were, but at least they spoke English. Her first thought was to beat on the walls of the crate, let them find her and beg to be taken home. But then, she was in a shipment, beaten and bruised, illegally entering the country with no ID.

Would the men call police? Immigration?

There were other, worse things they could do to her when they found her, too. A full-body shiver roared through her.

She couldn't afford to risk her safety.

Besides, the man who'd had her kidnapped had been clear. She'd been his target. If she surfaced now, she'd most likely be recaptured or killed. Neither was an acceptable prospect.

Could she figure out a way to slip off the boat while the deckhands unloaded the other boxes?

If she wriggled out of the crate now, she might be seen. The only choice was to wait it out, be patient until the right opportunity presented itself. This shipment had to be loaded onto something, right? A semi? Please, not another boat.

Painful heartbeats stabbed her ribs. She tensed, coiled and prepared to spring at whatever came next.

A voice cut through the noise, and everything else went dead silent.

The rich timbre shot straight through her, causing her body to shiver in the most inappropriate way under the circumstances.

She listened more closely. There were other sounds. Feet padding and heavy breathing.

Oh, no.

Police dogs.

Their agitated barks shot through the crate like rapid gunfire, inches from Emily's face. In the small compartment, she had nowhere to hide. The dogs' heated breaths blasted through the cracks. If her odor wasn't bad enough, this certainly wouldn't help matters. Now she'd smell like dirt, sweat and bad animal breath.

Emily's heart palpitated. She prayed an officer would stop the dogs. From the sounds of them, they'd rip her to shreds.

"Hier. Komm!" another voice commanded.

Emily made out the fact the officer spoke in another language. Dutch? German?

Damn.

She was about to be exposed. Her heart clutched. She had no idea how powerful the man who'd kidnapped her was. One thing was certain. He had enough money to buy off American border police. Was she about to come face-to-face with men he had in his pocket?

She shuddered at the thought of being sent back to Dueño, to that hell.

Her left eye still burned from the crack he'd fired across her cheek when she'd told him she didn't know the codes.

Maybe she could tell the officers the truth, beg them to let her go.

If they were for real, maybe she had a chance.

Voices surrounded her. Male. Stern.

She coiled tighter, praying she'd have enough energy to fight back or run. She'd have about a half second to decide if they would send her back to that hellhole, but she wouldn't go willingly.

A side panel burst open and Emily rolled out. She popped to her feet.

The officer in front of her was tall, had to be at least six-two. His hair was almost dark enough to be black. He had intense brown eyes, and he wore a white cowboy hat. He was built long and lean with ripples of muscles. Under normal circumstances, she'd be attracted to him. But now, all she could think about was her freedom.

He had a strong jawline, and when he smiled, his cheeks were dimpled. His eyes might be intense, but they were honest, too.

She held her hands up in the universal sign of surrender. "Help me. Please. I'm American."

"YOU'RE A US CITIZEN?" Reed Campbell had taken one look at the curled-up little ball when he opened the crate and felt an unfamiliar tug at his heart. He pushed it aside as she shot to her feet. Her face was bruised. She had a busted lip. Even though her hair was overly bleached and tangled, and she could use a shower, her hazel eyes had immense depth—the kind that drew him in, which was ridiculous under the circumstances. It had to be her vulnerability that stirred the kind of emotions that had no place at work.

"Yes." She spoke in perfect English, but American citizens didn't normally travel home in a crate from Mexico. It looked as if standing took effort. "You can sit down if you'd like."

She nodded and he helped her to a smaller crate where she eased down. He asked an agent to grab a bottled water out of his Jeep. A few seconds later, one of his colleagues produced one.

The cap was on too tight, and she seemed too weak to fight with it.

"I can do that for you." He easily twisted off the lid.

She thanked him, downed three-quarters of the bottle and then poured the rest over her face.

"What's your name?"

She stalled as though debating her answer. "Emily Baker."

"I need to see ID, ma'am. Driver's license. Passport." He looked her up and down. No way did she have a wallet tucked into her two-piece swimsuit. The material fit like an extra layer of skin, highlighting full breasts and round hips. Neither of which needed to go in his report. He forced his gaze away from the soft curves on an otherwise firm body.

He cleared his throat. Damn, dry weather.

"I don't have any with me." The words came out sharp, but the tone sounded weary and drained. The crate she was in was huge and there were several compartments. More illegals? Human trafficking? Reed had seen it all in the past six years as a Border Patrol agent.

"Let's see what else we find in here," Agent Pete Sanders said.

She seemed to realize she stood in front of them wearing next to nothing when she crossed her arms over her chest and her cheeks flushed pink. She suddenly looked even more vulnerable and small. Her embarrassment tugged at his heart. More descriptions that wouldn't go in his Homeland Security report.

She shivered, glanced down and to the right. She was about to lie. "Look. I can explain everything."

"I'm all ears."

Agents hauled over two crew members and told them to stay put.

She looked up at Reed again, and her hazel eyes were wide and fearful. Her hands shook. The men seemed to make her want to jump out of her skin even more. She was frightened, but not a flight risk. Cuffing her would most likely scare her even more. Besides, pulling her sunburned and blistered arms behind her back would hurt more than her pride. She also looked starved and dehydrated. One bottle of water would barely scratch the surface.

Getting her to talk under these circumstances might prove even more difficult. As it was, she looked too frightened to speak. Reed needed to thin her audience. He glanced at the K-9 officer. "I got this one under control. The other agents will see if there are more stashed in there. She's a quick run up to immigration."

The officer nodded before giving the command for his dog to keep searching. As soon as the two disappeared around the corner, the blonde dropped to her knees. Tears filled her eyes, a perfect combination of brown, gray and blue.

"I know how this must look. I'm not stupid. But I can explain."

"You already said that."

"Okay. Let's see. Where do I start?" Even through her fear, she radiated a sense of inner strength and independence.

Hell, he could respect that. Even admired her for it. But allowing a suspected illegal alien, or whatever she was, entry into the country wasn't his call. "At the beginning. How'd you end up in the crate?"

"I, uh, I…"

This was going nowhere. He wanted to reach out to her, help her, but she had to be willing to save herself. "We have some folks you can talk to. They can help."

"No. Please don't take me anywhere else. Just let me go. I'll show up to whatever court date. I won't disappear. I promise. I have a good job. One that I can't afford to lose."

Reed knew desperation. Hell, most drug runners were just as desperate. They'd offer bribes, their women, pretty much anything to manipulate the system.

His sixth sense told him this was different. There was an innocence and purity to her eyes that drew him in. Victim?

He pressed his lips into a frown. "Let's not get ahead of ourselves."

"Am I under arrest?"

"No."

"Then I'm free to go?" The flash of hope in her eyes seared his heart.

"I didn't say that." With her perfect English, he knew she wasn't illegal. But what else would she be doing tucked in a crate headed for the States, looking like a punching bag? Human trafficking? She was battered and bruised. If someone was trying to sell her, she'd fought back. But that explanation didn't exactly add up. Most traffickers didn't risk damaging the "product."

The officers moved to another wall on the other side of the crate. Twenty people could've been stuffed in there. He hoped like hell they weren't about to open up the other side and find more in the same shape as her. Seeing a woman beaten up didn't do good things to Reed. He fisted his hands.

"What happened to you?" Even bruised and dirty,

she was pretty damn hot. The tan two-piece she wore stretched taut against full breasts. Reed refocused on her heart-shaped face. Was someone trying to sell her into the sex trade? One look at her curves and long silky legs told him men would pay serious money for her. His protective instincts flared at the thought.

"I was on vacation and was robbed. They stole my passport. Said if I told authorities, they'd find me and kill me. I spent a night in the jungle trying to find my way back to the resort. I walked for an eternity, saw this ship and hopped on board praying no one would follow, find or catch me."

The bruises on her face and body outlined the fact she wasn't being honest. He shot her a sideways glance. "What happened to your face?"

"One of the men hit me?" Yeah, she was digging—digging a hole she might not be able to climb out of. It would take more than that to cause the bruising she had.

"I hope I don't have to remind you it's not in your best interest to lie to the law."

Her gaze darted around before settling on him.

"So, the story you're sticking with is that they jumped you on the beach?"

"No. I went into town."

"In just your swimsuit?"

A red rash crawled up her neck. Hell, he hadn't meant to embarrass her. She already seemed uncomfortable as hell in his presence. He had an extra shirt in his vehicle he could give her.

"Oh, right. I, uh, I already said I got lost."

"Enough to jump inside a random cargo ship and go wherever it took you? Sounds like someone trying to get away from something." Or someone. Yet another truth that hit him like a sucker punch.

She fixed her gaze on the cement. Was she about to lie again?

"You want to explain what really happened?" he preempted, pulling a notebook and pen from his pocket. She was beautiful. An inappropriate attraction surged through him. He shouldn't have passed on the offer of sex from Deanna the other night. And yet, the thrill of sex for sex's sake had never appealed to Reed.

"I've been through a lot in the past couple of days. Like I said, I got disoriented or something." She blinked against the bright sun. "Where am I?"

"Galveston, Texas."

Relief washed over her desperate expression. "Oh, thank God. That's perfect. I'm from Plano, a Dallas suburb."

"I'm familiar with the area. Have family there." He looked up from his pad. "What are you really doing here?"

"I work for a company called SourceCon. You can call and check. They'll tell you I'm on vacation. My boss has my itinerary."

Finally, he was getting somewhere. She was still lying about getting lost in Mexico, and she was a bad liar, too. That was a good sign. Meant she didn't normally lie her way out of situations. She didn't have the convictions of a pathological liar. But now he had something to work with. It wouldn't take much to make a quick call to verify her employment. He could do that for her, at least.

The sound of one of the crate's other walls smacking the pavement split the air.

"Hey, Campbell," Pete said.

"Yeah. Right here."

"You're gonna want to see this." He rounded the corner, hoisting an AR-15 in the air. "Looks like your friend here is involved in running guns."

Reed deadpanned her. "You just bought yourself a ride to Homeland Security."

Chapter Two

The trouble Emily was in hit with the force of a tsunami. "I'm broke. I'm exhausted. And they promised to hunt me down and kill me if I crossed them."

A strong hand pulled her to her feet.

"You can lean on me," he said before turning his head and shouting for someone to bring water.

The agent's gaze skimmed her face one more time, pausing at her busted lip. His brilliant brown eyes searched for the truth. A thousand butterflies released in her stomach with him so close.

Emily hadn't seen a mirror, but based on her amount of pain she had to be a total mess. The only good news was that he seemed to be considering what she was saying. *Please. Please. Please. Believe me.*

Another bottle of water arrived. The agent twisted off the cap and handed it to her. His broad cheekbones and rich timbre set off a sparkler inside her.

The glorious water cooled her still-parched throat. She downed most of the contents, using the leftovers to splash more water on her face. "Thank you."

Her stomach growled. "Any chance you have a hamburger hidden somewhere?"

He shot her a look full of pity. Something else flashed

behind his brown eyes when he said, "We can stop and pick something up on the way."

"Please don't turn me in. I can prove I'm American if I can get to my belongings." She took a step forward, and her knees buckled.

The agent caught her before she hit the ground. "Let's get something in your stomach first."

He helped her across the loading dock to his Jeep parked in the lot.

She eased onto the passenger seat.

"You're welcome to my extra shirt." He produced a white button-down from the back. "And I have a couple extra bottles of water and a towel."

A spark of hope lit inside her. Was he going to help? She thanked him for the supplies, pouring the opened bottle of water onto the towel first. The wet cloth felt cool on her skin. She dabbed her face before wiping her neck, chest and arms.

Pulling on the shirt required a little more finesse. She winced as she stretched out her arms. The agent immediately made a move to help. He eased one of her hands in the sleeve, and then the other. She managed the buttons on her own. Taking in a breath, the smell of his shirt reminded her of campfires lit outdoors and clean spring air.

"I have a power bar. Keep a few in a cooler in back for those long stretches of nothingness when I'm patrolling fence." He held out the wrapped bar and another water.

She took both, placed the water in her lap and tried to steady her hands enough to open the wrapper.

The protein bar tasted better than steak. She drained the water bottle in less than a minute. "I've already thanked you, but I'd like to repay you somehow."

His gaze locked onto hers. "Tell me the truth about

what happened to you. I can't stop these men from hurting other women without information."

Was he saying what she thought? The men who'd abducted her belonged to a kidnapping ring? Of course they did. She hadn't even considered it before, she'd been too concerned about her own life, but they seemed practiced and professional. If she could stop them, she had to try.

She nodded.

He climbed into the driver's side, put the key in the ignition and then waited.

"At first, I couldn't believe what was happening to me. I just kept thinking this couldn't be real." She looked over at him, hating that she was trembling with fear. "I was dragged through the jungle for hours, starved and then stuck in a hole with no food or water." Tears welled. She would hold back the information about knowing she'd been a target until she was certain she could trust him. As it was, maybe he'd let her go.

"Do you know how long you were there?"

"What day is it?"

He glanced at his watch. "Monday."

"My flight arrived in Mexico last Monday."

"A week ago."

"The sky was clear blue, the most beautiful shade I've ever seen. I'd stayed up late at a welcome party, so I didn't get outside until noon or so the next day. Took a kayak out, and that's when they grabbed me."

Compassion warmed his stern features. "Now we're getting somewhere. How many men were there?"

"Half a dozen."

"Can you give a description?"

"They wore bandannas to cover their faces. Other than that, they were a little taller than me." She was five foot seven. "They had to be five-eight or five-nine. Black hair and eyes."

His face muscles tensed.

"I just described half of the country, didn't I?"

He nodded, his expression radiating a sense of calm. "Dark skin or light?"

"Dark. Definitely dark."

"Can you describe their clothing?"

"Most of them wore old jeans and faded T-shirts. Looked like secondhand stuff. They were dirty."

"Some guerrilla groups live in the jungle," he agreed.

Did he believe her? He'd stopped looking at her as if she belonged in the mental ward, so that had to be a good sign.

"If they abducted you for extortion, they would've contacted your family. Can I call someone? A spouse?"

"I'm not married." An emotion she couldn't identify flashed behind the agent's brown eyes. "As for the rest of my family… There's not really… It's complicated."

"Mother? Father?"

"I don't know where he is. My mom isn't reachable. She's sick." Why was she suddenly embarrassed by her dysfunctional family?

The better question might be when had she not been?

Emily remembered being scared to death she wouldn't pass the background check required to work in her job for a major computer company. She'd had to get clearance since she entered data for various banks, some of which came from foreign interests. With a mom living in basically a cult and a dad who was MIA, Emily had feared she wouldn't get through the first round with her prospective employer. Emily had always been responsible. She hadn't even sampled marijuana in college as so many of her friends had. While all her classmates were "experimenting" and partying, she'd been working two jobs to pay tuition and make rent. Not that she was a saint. She just didn't have spare time or energy to do anything besides work, study and sleep.

She had to keep a decent GPA, which didn't leave a lot of time for anything else.

Heck, her college boyfriend had left her because she'd been too serious. He'd walked out, saying he wanted to be with someone more fun.

What was that?

Life hadn't handed Emily "fun." It had given her a deserter for a dad and a mom who was as sweet as she was lost.

Fun?

Emily clamped down a bitter laugh.

She'd had fun about as often as she'd had sex in the past year. And that really was a sad statement. Getting away, going to the beach, was supposed to represent a big step toward claiming her future and starting a new life.

"There's no one we can call?" The agent's voice brought her back to the present.

She shook her head. There was one name she could give him, her boss. She hated to do it. The last thing she wanted to do was jeopardize her job, but Jared could corroborate her story and then the agent would believe her. Possibly even let her go?

With the information she'd given the agent so far, she had a feeling she was going to need all the help she could get. "My boss."

Agent Campbell pulled his cell from his pocket.

She gave him Jared's number and took a deep breath.

REED PUNCHED IN the number the witness had given while he kept one eye on her.

She was still desperate, and there was an off chance she'd do something stupid, like run. He didn't feel like chasing after her. He'd catch her. And then they'd be having a whole different conversation about her immediate future.

As it was, he figured a quick trip to Homeland Security would be all that was required. Minimal paperwork. Let them sort out the rest.

His years on the job told him she wasn't a hard-core criminal. There was something about her situation, her, that ate at his insides. God help him.

"This is Jared," came through the cell. His voice was crisp, and he sounded young. Early thirties.

Reed identified himself as a Border Patrol agent. "I'm calling to verify employment."

"Then you'll want to speak to HR."

"I'd rather talk to you if it's possible," Reed interjected.

"That's against policy—"

"I wouldn't ask if it wasn't a matter of national security. You can clear something up for me. Save me a lot of time going through rigmarole, sir." Reed listened for the telltale signs he'd convinced Jared.

A deep sigh came across the line.

Bingo. "Does Emily Baker work for you?"

"Yes, she does. Why? Is she all right?"

Reed picked up on the uncomfortable note in Jared's voice. Was it curiosity or something more? "Is she there today?"

"No. She's on vacation. Mexico, I think."

Part of her story matched up. The woman sitting beside him could be anyone, though. He'd already caught her glimpsing his gun. Logic told him she was debating whether or not to make a run for it.

"Can you give me a description of Miss Baker?"

"Why? Did something happen to her?" Panic raised his tone an octave. Something told Reed the guy on the phone was interested in more than her work performance. Wasn't he the caring boss? A twinge of jealousy shot through him. What was that all about?

She was vulnerable. Reed's protective instincts jumped into overdrive. He was reacting as he would if this was one of his sisters, he told himself.

"No. Nothing to worry about, sir. Routine questions." Reed hadn't exactly lied. She was a witness.

"Okay. Good. Um, let's see. She's medium height, thin, light brown hair. She's a runner, so, um, she has the build for it, if you know what I mean."

"Yeah. I get the reference." How nice that her boss paid attention to her workout routine. Clearly, there was more to this story. An office affair? Disappointment settled over Reed for reasons he couldn't explain. Why did he care whom she dated?

He reminded himself to focus on the case. This woman fit two-thirds of the description. It was obvious her hair had been bleached. The dye job was bad, and so was the cut. Her hair had been chopped off. Even so, she was beautiful.

And her legs were long and toned. She could be a runner. He made a mental note of the fact, in case she decided to bolt. It was easy to see she was in good physical condition, aside from events of the past few days.

She glanced around, antsy. Her expression set, determined, as she skimmed the docks. Was she working with someone? For someone?

Or was she just a few grains of sand short of a castle?

The tougher job was to assess her mental fitness. If she wasn't involved in bringing guns into the country, and, really and truly, she would've been smart enough to have one loaded at the ready if she was, he had to consider the possibility she might be a danger to herself or others.

He'd witnessed all kinds of crazy.

In fact, in six years with Border Patrol, he'd seen just about everything. And a whole lot of nothing, too, especially when he was a rookie.

"Eye color?"

"Green, I think."

They were hazel, but lots of people confused hazel with green or blue. The description was close enough. "Thank you, sir. That clears everything up."

"She'll be back to work next Monday, right?"

Reed figured the boss wanted the answer to his question more for personal reasons than anything else. "I don't see why not."

"And she's okay? You're sure?"

Another sprig of jealousy sprouted. "She is. That's all the information I need. Have a nice—"

"I don't want to ask anything inappropriate, but our job requires a certain level of security clearance. She hasn't gone and done anything that might jeopardize her position at work, has she?"

"Why would she do that?" Reed knew she wasn't telling him something, but he doubted she was involved in criminal activity. Couldn't rule it out yet. Even though his instincts never lied, he preferred logic and evidence.

Did this whole episode have to do with her job? What would she have to gain?

A relieved sigh came across the line. "She wouldn't. At least, I don't think she would. I guess you can never really tell about people, but I don't have to tell you that. Not in your line of work."

The man finally said something smart. "Desperate people can do all kinds of interesting things."

"I'm sure. I already asked, but she's okay, right?"

"Yeah. She'll be back to work next week, and I'm sure she'll explain everything then." Reed ended the call.

"I lost my job, didn't I?" She sounded defeated. "It doesn't matter."

"You didn't tell me everything," he hedged.

She repositioned in her seat.

"You're tired and hungry, so I'm afraid you're going to make a bad choice. Whatever you're running from, I can help you."

She deadpanned him. "No. You can't."

"Not if you don't tell me what it is."

"I won't run. Please don't take me in." Her wide hazel eyes pleaded.

"There's protocol for situations like these. You came into the country in a shipment full of guns. Who do they belong to?"

"I'd tell you if I knew." Tears welled in her eyes.

"I need a name. They'll take it easy on you if you co-operate."

"Are you arresting me?" She glanced toward the field to her right.

Was she getting ready to make her move?

He started the engine, determined to keep her from

making another mistake she'd regret. "Buckle up. We can finish this conversation over a burger."

"You didn't answer my question. Are you going to arrest me?" she repeated slowly, as if he was dim.

"No. Why? Do you plan on giving me a reason to?"

The drive to the nearest fast-food burger place was quiet. His passenger closed her eyes and laid her head back.

She didn't open them when he pulled into the drive-through lane and ordered two burgers, two fries and two milkshakes at the speaker box.

Reed gripped the steering wheel tighter, thinking about what she'd been through in the past few days. He also realized she was keeping secrets. Professional curiosity had him wanting to find out what they were. Or was it something else?

He dismissed the idea as standing in the sun too long back at the docks. His interest in Emily Baker was purely professional.

At this point, he'd classify her as a witness. However, she was walking a fine line of being moved into another category—suspect—and she didn't want to be there. He should probably haul her up to Homeland Security and be done.

But he couldn't.

Something in those hazel eyes told him there was a bigger story, one that frightened her to the point of almost becoming mute.

If she talked, he might be able to track down gun runners, or get the connection he needed to stop another coyote from dumping illegals across the border. Heck, most died of dehydration before they ever reached their desired location. She was weak. No way was she illegal, but they used the same paths for everything from human trafficking to gun running. Besides, maybe she had information that could help him make a bust. The innocence and desperation in her voice had drawn him in. He needed to make sure she'd be okay.

He couldn't turn his back on her any more than he could walk away from one of his sisters. Something about Emily brought out a similar protective instinct, but that's where the similarities ended. Nothing else about her reminded him of his siblings.

After paying at the window, he accepted the food. There was a shady spot in the parking lot across the street. He pulled into it and parked.

She blinked her eyes open when he cut off the engine.

He unwrapped a burger and handed it to her. "It's not steak, but it should help with your hunger."

Her eyes lit up as she took the offering. "That smells nothing short of amazing."

A few bites into her meal, she set her burger down. "I don't understand. I'm famished but I can't finish it."

Poor thing was starving. Another fact in this case that made Reed want to punch something.

It was one thing for traffickers and drug pushers to maim and kill each other, but to drag women and children into their web made his fists clench and his jaw muscle tick. Five minutes alone with any one of them, and he'd leave his badge and gun outside the door.

"That was the best food I've ever had," she said, wiping her mouth with a napkin. "Ouch. Sorry. I'm bleeding again." She searched the empty food bag and seemed to fight back tears. "You've been really nice to me and I don't want to get blood on your clean white shirt."

"Nothing to worry about." Reed handed her his napkin. "It's an old shirt. A little blood won't hurt anything."

Her back was ramrod. He wasn't any closer to getting her to trust him.

Maybe softening his approach would work. "Believe me when I say I've had to clean up worse than that. The shirt's yours. Keep it."

She apologized again. Her bottom lip quivered, indicating she was probably on the brink of losing it. Who could blame her? She'd been amazingly strong so far.

For now, the person of interest in his passenger seat was safe and calm. She'd had a few minutes to think about where she might end up if she didn't give him something to work with. "Why'd they really hit you?"

She searched nearby shrubs and buildings as if expecting the men who'd hurt her to jump out from behind one.

Fear was a powerful tool.

Whoever hurt her did a good job of making her believe he'd come back for more if she gave him up. "I know this is tough. Believe me. But it's the only way I can help you."

She brought her hands up to rub her temples and trained her gaze on the patch of cement in front of the Jeep. She was teetering on the edge.

He was getting close to a breakthrough. "They shouldn't be allowed to get away with this. I don't care what they threatened. The US government is bigger than whoever did this to you."

A few tears fell, streaking her cheeks.

"Whatever they said, don't believe them."

She dropped her hands to her lap, and then turned toward him. Her hazel eyes pierced right through him. "You give me your personal promise to protect me?"

Chapter Three

If Agent Campbell made one wrong blink, Emily had already decided she'd bolt. She'd put it out there and asked him to make a commitment. Now it was his turn to make a move.

"It's my job to—"

"I want to know if you promise to protect me. And not just because of your badge." Even though he was a stranger, everything about the agent next to her said he was a man of his word. If he made a personal pledge, she'd trust him a little.

He finished chewing his bite of hamburger and swallowed before he set his food on the wrapper and used a napkin to clean his hands.

"My name is Reed, and you have my word." He stuck his hand out between them.

She took it, knowing she shouldn't. There was no way he could guarantee her safety. The instant they'd made contact, a spark ran between them. She didn't withdraw her hand. Neither did he.

Their eyes locked, and she felt another jolt. An underlying sexual current simmered between them, which was shocking given what she'd been through. He was the first person in ages who'd expressed interest in helping and protecting her, she reasoned, and it felt nice to have that.

Under different circumstances, she might enjoy the spark. Not now. All she could think about was getting out of this mess and going into hiding.

Another thing was certain. By the set of his jaw, she could tell that Reed Campbell meant what he said. No doubt about it. Could he deliver against a rebel faction that could have law enforcement officers bought and paid for?

He looked like the kind of man who, once he gave his word, would die trying to deliver on his commitments. And something about the depths of his eyes had her wanting to move a little closer toward his strength, his light.

All her danger signals flared.

Getting too close to a man who could have her locked up was a bad idea, no matter how much honesty radiated from his brown eyes.

His cell buzzed, and she pulled her hand back, breaking their grasp.

A half-eaten burger sat on his knee on top of the wrapper. He answered the call, keeping his gaze on her.

Was he afraid she'd take off? He had to know she'd scatter like a squirrel at one loud noise.

At six-two with muscles for days, he must realize he could be physically intimidating. Was that why he seemed to make so much of an effort to keep her calm?

Against her better judgment, it was working. She felt a sense of being protected with him near. A luxury she couldn't afford.

"Uh-huh, I have her right here," he said. His gaze narrowed.

Trouble?

"Thanks, but I've got this one."

Was someone offering to take her off his hands? This seemed out of the blue. No way could it be standard procedure.

A shudder of fear roared through her. She folded her arms to stave off the chill skittering across her skin.

"No, I'm sure." He shook his head as if for emphasis. "We're heading northbound on I-45. Why?"

Emily's chest squeezed, and she knew something was wrong. Agent Campbell gave the person on the phone the wrong location. Why would he do that?

"Will do." Agent Campbell ended his call.

"Who was that?"

He sat looking dumbfounded for a second. "That was odd. Agent Stephen Taylor volunteered to meet me and take you off my hands. Said he was headed in and it wouldn't be any trouble to take you along with him."

"I don't know this area at all, but we're sitting in a parking lot, and you told him we were on the highway. Why?"

Using the paper wrap, he wadded up the few bites of hamburger he had left and tossed it in the bag. "That call doesn't sit right. Something's off."

Emily gasped. "That can't be normal."

"Nope. Never happened to me before in six years of service." He checked his rearview mirror.

The last thing Emily wanted to do was tell the agent more about what had happened to her. In fact, she'd like to be able to forget it altogether. But both of their lives were in danger now, and he deserved to know the risk he was taking. "There was a man back in Mexico. They called him Dueño. He promised to…"

Saying the words out loud proved harder than she expected. Tears pricked the backs of her eyes.

Gray clouds rolled in from the coast as the winds picked up speed.

The agent sat quietly, hands resting on the steering wheel, giving her the space she needed to find the courage to tell him the rest.

"To find me no matter what. I know he has law enforcement on his payroll. I overheard them talking about it."

Agent Campbell started the ignition, and eased the Jeep into traffic. "They give any names?"

His rich timbre was laced with anger. She could imagine how an honest man like him would take it personally if one of his own was on the take. "No. All I knew was that once I got away from him, I had to disappear. I couldn't trust law enforcement or anyone else. That's why I can't let you take me in. I'm begging you to let me go."

Thunder rumbled in the distance.

"Hate to believe agents are on the take." He looked to be searching his memory as he narrowed his gaze onto the stretch of road in front of them. He muttered a string of curse words. "There have been a few articles in the paper hinting at the possibility. The department issued a warning. We'd picked up a few bad eggs during a hiring surge, but we've been assured they were weeded out."

"You take me in and he'll get to me. He has people on the inside. I can identify him and testify. They'll kill me."

"Slow down. I'm not going to let that happen. We can figure this out."

"They won't stop until they find me."

"Which is why it's a bad idea for me to let you go. At least while you're with me, I can protect you."

"Can't you tell your department you let me go?"

"Why would I do that?"

"Because you have to. I know what they wanted when they targeted me. There's a fortune on the line."

"Hold on a sec. You led me to believe this was random," he said. His eyes flashed anger.

"I'm sorry. I lied. I wasn't sure if I could trust you before." She had to now.

His grip on the steering wheel tightened. His gaze intensified. "What else?"

"They wanted my passwords. I work at a computer company. We keep account information secure for big banking institutions. I'm sure they planned on moving money."

"Cybercrime can be harder to track if they know what they're doing. Why didn't you just give them the passwords and save yourself?"

She deadpanned him. "I figured they'd kill me either way. Even so, I couldn't give them passwords if I'd wanted to. I always change them before I leave for vacation. I didn't have my new ones memorized."

"He beat you because he didn't believe you."

"Not for a second."

"I'm assuming you have your codes written down somewhere?"

She nodded. A thought struck her. "What if they get to my place and find them? I'm sure they knew where I lived."

Agent Campbell's cell buzzed again. He put on his turn signal, moved into the left turn lane and then shot a glance at her before answering. He turned on his hazard lights, even though there were no cars coming.

Thunder rumbled louder. A storm was coming.

"Yes, sir, I heard from the agent."

There was a long pause.

"No, I didn't turn over the witness. I can run her in to make a statement."

Emily slipped her hand as close to the seat belt release button as she could without drawing attention. Her pulse kicked up a notch.

A light rain started, nothing more than a spring shower. The glorious liquid spotted the windshield.

She had enough sustenance in her to manage a good sprint. Would it be enough to get away? Her feet still ached and her head pounded. A good night of sleep, some medicine, and she'd recover. But would her body give her what she needed to get away now?

Possibilities clicked through her mind.

If she made a run for it, could she disappear in the neighboring subdivision? Maybe hide in a parked car?

The capable agent in the seat next to her would catch her. His muscled thighs said he could outrun her if he needed to. One look at the ripple of muscles underneath his shirtsleeve said he was much stronger than she.

Might be a risk she'd have to take.

Stay there and she'd be dead in an hour if he followed through with his plans to take her to Homeland Security. One of the men in Dueño's pocket would alert him to her whereabouts, and they'd be ready for her when she walked outside.

The best chance she had would be to make a move right now while Agent Campbell was distracted by his phone call. If she were smart, she'd unbuckle and run like hell.

"I didn't say she was a suspect, sir."

Her heart jackhammered in her chest. Should she bolt?

REED GLANCED OVER at Emily. Her back was stiff, her breathing rapid and shallow. He covered her hand with his, and she relaxed a little. A smile quirked the corner of his lip.

"I can take this one, sir. Not a problem."

Confident he'd convinced his boss, Reed ended the call. A rogue agent was a dangerous thing. Reed could personally attest to that.

This one had involved his boss, who was being played. The agent who'd tried to get his hands on Emily wouldn't be allowed to have his way.

"Your boss wanted you to hand me over to someone else, didn't he?"

Reed nodded.

"Could going against your boss cost your job?"

He wasn't sure why he chuckled. "Yeah."

"You're willing to take that risk to help me?"

"It's my duty." "Honor First" was more than words on a page to Reed.

Emily leaned against the seat and pinched the bridge of her nose. "Then, what do we do next?"

"Good question."

Reed checked the rearview and saw a truck screaming toward them.

He banked a U-turn in time to see a metal shotgun barrel aimed at them.

Emily must've seen it, too, because she yelped.

"Get down on the floorboard. Now."

A *boom* split the air.

Reed gunned the gas pedal, made a U-turn and then hooked a right, blazing through the empty parking lot. For a split second, time warped and the memory of being shot and left for dead blitzed him.

A walk down Memory Lane would have to wait. He battled against the heavy thoughts, blocking them out. If he lived, *correction*, when he got them out of this mess, he'd deal with those. *Yeah, right, like that's going to happen.*

The reality was that he'd had plenty of time since returning to work to rationalize his feelings. Doing that ranked about as high on his list as shoveling cow manure out of the barn at Gran's place. He took that back. Shoveling cow manure was far more appealing.

Reed glanced at Emily, who was not more than a ball in the floorboard. Her face scrunched in pain from being forced to move. The thought of doubling her agony lanced his chest. "Hang tight. I'll get us to safety soon."

She glanced at him through fearful hazel eyes. "Maybe we should break up. I can hide on my own. Might be better now that they know we're together."

Was she still worried he'd run her in? Handing her over to his agency would only put her in more jeopardy. "Not a chance."

Anxiety and fear played across her features.

A need to protect Emily surged, catching Reed off guard, because it ran deeper than his professional oath. He knew exactly what it was like to be in her position— to be the target of someone who had a dirty agent in their pocket. Reed had a bullet hole in his back to prove it.

"I'm your best option right now. And I'm not ready to let you out of my sight."

Chapter Four

Pain rippled through Emily's bruised and battered body as she crouched low and hugged her knees into her chest, making herself as small as possible in the floorboard. One of her ribs had to be cracked. The sharp pain in her chest sliced through her thoughts. Being run through a cheese grater would hurt less than the bruises on her face and body.

The agent, Reed, had said she could trust him. He'd said the magic words—he wasn't hauling her butt in to Homeland Security. And yet, her internal alarm system was still set to red alert. Why? What was it about him that had her wanting to run? Was it the alarming comfort his presence brought?

Sporadic turns and the sound of another shotgun blast said they still had company. Emily didn't dare try to peek even though her tightly coiled nerves might break at any moment if she didn't know what was happening. Even so, she doubted her body would be able to respond to her brain's command to get up.

Reed swerved the car left and then made a hard right. "Wish I'd been alone when I found you. That would make things less complicated."

"Would you have believed me?"

His compressed frown said it all. No, he wouldn't have. "I owe you an apology for that."

"I don't blame you. I'm sure you deal with all kinds of crazy people in your work."

"Most have nothing to lose when they run into me. And I've learned logic is a better resource than instinct."

He was used to being shot at? That revelation shouldn't reassure her. Oddly enough, that's exactly what it did. Maybe because she had no clues how to escape armed men or dodge bullets and there was no way she'd still be alive without his expertise. Her world had been catapulted into a whole new stratosphere of danger. Having a man around who knew how to use a gun and was on her side didn't seem like the worst thing that could happen.

Yet, depending on anyone was foreign to her. Thoughts of too many hours of her childhood spent crouched low in the corner behind her bed while her mother experienced "free love" in the next room assaulted Emily. She'd been old enough to remember what it was like to live in a suburb with a normal family and a father whom she believed loved her. Her fairy-tale world had ended the day he left. Emily squeezed her eyes tighter, trying to block out the memory.

Emily slowly counted to a hundred to keep her mind busy, refusing to let fear seize her when more bullets came at them. They pinged by her head tat-tat-tat style, and she knew by the sound difference that whoever was chasing them had changed weapons.

"I can lose them around this bend or when I get on this highway. This turn is going to get hairy, so hang on."

Chancing a glance at Reed, seeing someone who wasn't afraid, held her nerves a notch below panic. However, the contents of her stomach retaliated at the high rate of speed combined with sharp turns. She'd probably eaten too fast because the burger and milkshake churned. "Are they still back there?"

"Get back in the seat belt. The threat has tripled, and we're going to sustain a hit." The authority in his voice sent a trill of worry through her.

"Okay." She struggled to move, wincing as she planted one hand on the glove compartment and the other on the seat, praying she could gain enough leverage to push herself up from her awkward position on the floorboard. Her arms gave out and she landed hard, racking up another bruise on her hip.

A glance at Reed said they were almost out of time.

"Brace yourself for impact." He tapped the brake and swerved.

Emily lurched forward, her head caught by Reed's right hand moments before it hit the dash. Pushing through the pain, she pressed up to the seat and quickly fastened the belt over her shoulder.

Large SUVs pulled on each side of them as the truck she recognized from earlier roared up from behind.

The quick look Reed shot her next said whatever was about to happen wasn't going to be good. He floored the gas pedal, shooting out front. Temporarily.

On the right, the SUV hit the brakes. The one on the left barreled beside them, keeping pace.

The window of opportunity to hop onto the freeway and lose these guys was closing with the SUV on the left blocking the on-ramp.

A bumper crunched against the back of the Jeep. Emily's head whipped forward.

Dueño's reach had long arms. Just as he had promised. Could Emily envision a life on the run? No. She'd fought too hard to put down roots. She'd found a new city, bought a town house and worked her butt off to be next in line for her boss's job. Dueño was forcing her into a different direction. Anger burned through her.

Another hard jerk of the steering wheel and Emily felt herself tumbling, spinning.

Reed's rich timbre penetrated the out-of-control Ferris wheel. "Relax as much as you can."

Time temporarily suspended. Emily drifted out of her own body as the spinning slowed, and then stopped.

Everything went black, but she still could hear shouting. Someone was yelling at her. A deeply masculine voice called. She coughed and blinked her eyes open.

Smoke was everywhere.

Everything burned. Her nose. Her eyes. Her throat.

Her body might've stopped spinning, but her head hadn't.

"Emily. Stay with me." The voice came from a tunnel filled with light.

Or did it?

There was something comforting about the large physical presence near her.

"Emily. I need you to try to move." A sense of urgency tinged the apologetic tone.

Her response came out as a croak. She tried harder to open her eyes and gain her bearings.

Sirens sounded in the distance a few moments after she heard another pop of gunfire. The men. Oh, no. All at once she remembered being on the run. Their car had been forced off the road, while speeding, and thrown into a dangerous spin. The Jeep had rolled. And that voice calling her belonged to Border Patrol Agent Reed Campbell.

Her eyes shot open.

Heat from a fire blazed toward her. Flames licked at her skin. Thick smoke filled her lungs.

She was trapped in a burning car while men shot at her. It took another few precious seconds for her to realize she was upside down. At least the inferno kept the men at bay, except for Reed. He was right by her side. An unfamiliar feeling stuck in her chest at the thought someone actually had her back for a change. Emily wanted to gravitate toward the pleasant emotion, except she couldn't move. She wiggled her hips, hoping to break free. No luck.

The seat belt must be stuck.

There was no feeling in her legs. She tamped down panic, knowing full well that couldn't be good. Even if she could work the belt free, which she was trying with both hands, how would she run?

She'd have to solve that puzzle when she came to it.

"Take this." A shiny metal object was being thrust at her through the thick wall of smoke separating her from the agent.

Reed's face was covered in ashes and worry lines. Blood dripped down his cheek from a cut on his forehead. There was compassion in his clear brown eyes and what appeared to be fear.

She took the offering, a knife.

"Cut yourself free." His arms cradled her shoulders.

"Okay." She shot him a scared look.

"I'll catch you. I won't let you get hurt."

Her gaze widened at the figure moving toward them. "Behind you."

The agent turned and fired his weapon.

She worked the knife against the fabric, wanting to be ready, knowing they were out of time.

Sirens split the air.

Reed turned his attention back to her as soon as the man disappeared. "I'm ready. Go."

The last patch of thread cut easily. Emily didn't want to think about how good his hands felt on her as he pulled her from the burning Jeep across the hard, unforgiving earth. Or how nice it was to have someone in her corner.

The head of the House believed placing labels on people degraded them, so he simply called her girl. Her mom soon followed his lead.

Growing up in a house full of free love and short on anything meaningful, like her mother's laughter, had made Emily wary and distrustful of people. Watching her mom adopt the long hair and threadbare clothes everyone in the House wore made Emily feel even more distanced from everything familiar.

In the twelve years Emily had lived there, her mom had six children by various housemates. It had been like living in a time warp. Apparently, the label "Father" was also degrading because no one stepped up to help care for the little ones, save for Emily. She'd taken care of the children until one of the men had decided that at seventeen she was old enough to learn about free love. She'd fought back, escaped and then ran.

Emily had learned quickly the outside world could be harsh, too.

With no friends on the streets, she'd had to fight off men who confused her homelessness for prostitution. Her first stroke of luck had come when she found a flier for a shelter that handed out free breakfast. A worker there had told her about the nearby shelter for teens. For the first time since leaving Texas as a child, Emily had her own room.

All her life savings, money she'd made from her job at the local movie theater, was hidden in the House. Emily had saved every penny. Needing a fresh start, she'd slipped into the House, took her life savings and then bought a bus ticket to Dallas, where she could return home and put down roots.

By the time she'd finished a few college courses and gotten a decent job, her half siblings had scattered across the country, and she heard from her mother mostly when she needed something.

No matter how honest and pure the agent looked, Emily knew not to get too comfortable.

Feeling vulnerable out in the open, she searched for the men. Where were they?

She glanced around, half expecting more gunfire. Instead, EMTs ran toward them and all she could hear was the glorious thunder of their footsteps.

But, where was Reed?

Then she saw him. He lay flat on his back and her chest squeezed when she saw how much blood soaked his shirt. One set of EMTs rushed to him, blocking her view. Another went to work on her as firemen put out the blaze.

The cavalry had arrived.

But how long before Dueño's men returned to finish the job?

Emily needed a plan.

Heaven knew she could never rely on her mother. The woman had shattered when Emily's father left. Even then, Emily knew she needed to help her mother. The woman couldn't do much for herself in the broken state she was in. When she'd finally forced herself out of bed, a neighbor introduced her to "a new way of thinking."

It wasn't long before Emily's mom packed the pair of them up and moved to California to live in the House. Emily had been excited about the promise of perpetual sunshine, but her enthusiasm was short-lived when she figured out no one ever left the grounds except in groups to shop for food.

Which was why she couldn't afford to rely on the agent much longer. Especially not the way he stirred confusing feelings inside her that had no business surfacing. She knew where that would end up.

REED STRIPPED OFF the oxygen mask covering his face. "I'm fine."

"Can you tell me what day it is?" the young EMT asked.

"Monday. And I know I've been in an accident. I was forced off the road by another vehicle. I have to call local police to file a report." He reached for his phone, needing an excuse to step away and make eye contact with Emily. He wanted to know she'd be okay. Men were huddled around her, working on her. Reed tamped down the unexpected jolt of anxiety tensing his shoulders. "What's going on with my witness? She'll be okay, right?"

"We'll know in a few minutes."

Not good enough. Reed had to know now. He pushed off the back of the truck.

The EMT stepped in front of Reed. "Sir, that's not a good idea."

"Why not? Is she hurt badly?" The young guy was big, worked out, but Reed had no doubts he could take the guy down if necessary. Reed's hands fisted. His jaw muscle twitched.

"The others are working on her. I'm talking about you. I'd like to finish my exam, if that's okay."

The guy seemed to know Reed could take him down in a heartbeat. He reminded himself to stay cool. The EMT was only doing his job. No point in making it any harder for him.

Reed fished his wallet out of his pocket and produced his identification. "Name's Reed Campbell. I'm a Border Patrol agent. I have two brothers and two sisters. It's Monday at…" He checked his watch. "Four o'clock."

"Good. I think it's safe to say you didn't suffer a concussion. Will you let me patch up your forehead before you go, and let me take a look at what's causing all that blood on your shirt?" the young guy asked, resigned.

"Can't hurt." He sat still long enough for his gashes to be cleaned and bandaged.

"I still think it's a good idea for you to go to the hospital."

"I plan to." His gaze fixed on the team working on Emily.

"As a patient."

"I promise to get checked out if I take a turn for the worse."

"No changing your mind?"

"I appreciate all you're doing for me, but I'm more worried about her."

Reluctantly, the EMT produced papers. "Then I need your autograph on these. They say you received basic treatment at the scene and refused to be taken in for further medical evaluation."

Reed took them and signed off, uneasy that Emily was

still surrounded by a busy team of workers. If someone on the inside of his agency was helping Dueño, Reed couldn't chance his phone being hacked. His best bet was to play it cool with the EMT and pretend his had taken a hit. "Any chance I can borrow your phone? Mine's a casualty of the wreck, and I need to check in with my boss."

The worker nodded, handing over his cell.

They needed transportation, and Reed trusted a handful of people right now—most of whom shared his last name. His brothers were in North Texas, too far to catch a ride. His boss was his best bet. After being shot in the line of duty, Reed knew he could trust Gil. And with any luck, no one would be listening in on his boss's phone, either. Reed would play it cool just in case.

Gil picked up on the second ring.

"It's Reed. I had to borrow a phone. I don't have time to explain, but I need a car." There'd be a mountain of paperwork to deal with when this was settled.

"Where are you?"

"My Jeep's been totaled. I was chased off the road. This is big, Gil. Fingers are reaching out from over the border." Reed kept the name to himself to be on the safe side.

Gil muttered a curse.

"We need to be careful here," Reed warned. "We might have another Cal situation on our hands."

Gil grunted. "I'll have transportation waiting for you… Wait, let me think."

"How about the little place you like to visit on special Thursdays?" The Pelican restaurant in Galveston was Gil's wife's favorite seafood spot. He took her there every anniversary and occasionally on Thursday nights for their catfish special. Gil didn't go out on Fridays. Said it was too crowded. Few people knew Gil's habits the way Reed did. He'd learned a lot about his boss during the man's visits to the hospital after Reed was shot.

"Got it."

"Leave the keys so I can find them. The usual spot."

"Okay."

Keys would be under the sink in the bathroom. Reed glanced at Emily. The EMTs were still surrounding her. They'd want to take her to the hospital. With the amount of smoke she'd inhaled and the possible swelling, it was probably a good idea. "Can you get ahold of the local police chief? I'd like a fresh set of eyes on us at the hospital."

"I'll make the call myself from Vickie's personal cell."

His admin's number should be safe. "Appreciate it."

"You need a place to stay in the meantime?"

"I'll figure it out. Besides, the less I involve the department, the better. Probably best if I branch out on my own for this one." And he had no intention of leaving Emily for a second. These guys were relentless and she was scared. Not a good combination. If she made one mistake it'd be game over. The thought sent a lead fireball swirling down Reed's chest. Didn't need to get inside his head about why his reaction to the thought of anything happening to her was so strong. Reed passed it off as needing to keep his promises.

Gil paused. "Be careful."

"You know it." Reed ended the call. Now all he had to figure out was how to get to the bank and withdraw enough money to get by for a while. Then he'd need transportation from the hospital to The Pelican. No way could Emily walk in her current condition. She'd need time to rest and heal.

They didn't have the luxury of either.

Whoever was after her meant business.

The EMTs loaded her into the ambulance. Reed pushed through and took the step in an easy stride.

He was instantly pulled back.

"Sorry. It's policy. No one rides in back except us," one of the men said. He was older than the guy who'd worked on Reed.

"No exceptions?"

"Afraid not. How about you take a seat up front? We've already called a tow truck for your vehicle."

Reed nodded, not really liking the thought of being separated from Emily. Anything could happen to her in the back if those men were waiting, or worse yet, ambushed the ambulance.

Climbing into the cab, he told himself he cared only for professional reasons. The chance to nab a jerk who would do this to a woman fueled his need to protect her. And that it had nothing at all to do with the fact those hazel eyes of hers would haunt him in his sleep if he walked away.

Now that he knew her story had merit, he wanted to know more about her. It had everything to do with arming himself with knowledge that might just save both of their lives and nothing to do with the place in his heart she stirred, he lied.

Chapter Five

The long stretch of country road ahead provided too many opportunities for ambush. Reed reloaded his weapon, his gaze vacillating between looking ahead, to the sides and behind. "How much longer?"

"Fifteen minutes at the most."

"And the woman in back? How's she doing?" Reed glanced out the side-view mirror.

"My guys don't look as busy as they did on-site. That's a good sign in our line of work." He paused a beat. "They've been treating her for smoke inhalation. All I can tell you so far is that they're giving her oxygen, and she can expect to have a sore throat for a few days. Depending on the swelling in her throat, she might need to be intubated."

Reed didn't realize he'd cursed out loud until he saw the surprised look on the driver's face.

"She must be important to your case to get a reaction like that."

"I don't have one without her." Reed didn't appreciate women being beaten up, and especially not by men. His sister Lucy had received injuries as a teenager from an obsessed boyfriend. Reed chalked his current defensive feelings toward Emily up to bad memories.

"I notified my boss of the situation. He's calling ahead so the hospital will be ready with security."

"Thank you."

"She has a lot of other injuries and those might be of concern. Says she sustained them before the crash?"

Reed nodded.

"She needs a chest X-ray to ensure nothing's broken."

The way she'd been hugging her arms across her chest earlier now made more sense. He hadn't considered the possibility of cracked ribs. Anger bubbled to the surface. Reed muttered a string of curse words.

The EMT paused before continuing. "From the looks of it, she's been through hell and back. Those injuries could be far worse than the ones she sustained in the crash, but my guess is the doctor in charge is going to want to keep her for a while based on her pulse oximetry numbers."

"What's that?"

"Shows the amount of oxygen in the blood. Normal is one hundred and hers are ninety. She's experiencing some difficulty breathing, which leads me to believe her respiratory tract has some swelling."

"But she'll be okay?" In a matter of a few days she'd been beaten, starved and denied water. Reed's training and experience had taught him not to assume an injured person was telling the truth. In fact, most of the time they weren't. It was logic backed by years of experience. So why did he feel so damn awful about his earlier suspicions about her now? Was it the vulnerability in her eyes that hit him faster than a bullet and cut a similar hole in his chest? This case was different. Hell's bells, that statement didn't begin to scratch the surface.

"How long was she trapped in the Jeep?"

"Not more than eight or nine minutes."

"Less than ten minutes is good. That and the Jeep being open is a big help. With her oxygen levels being on the low side, best-case scenario is the damage to her airway and lungs is minimal. If there's no real swelling, she can expect a full recovery. We're almost there, by the way. The hospital is only a few minutes out. The doctor can tell you more after his exam. Her vital signs looked good."

"May I borrow your phone? I need to call work, and my cell didn't make it out of the Jeep," he lied. It was easier than explaining the whole situation.

The EMT glanced down at his cell, which was on the seat between them. "Be my guest."

Reed hoped his brother Luke would pick up.

"Hello?" The word was more accusation than greeting. Being in law enforcement made them suspicious of everything unfamiliar, and Luke wouldn't have recognized this number.

"It's Reed."

"What's up, baby bro?" Luke's stiff voice relaxed. "Leave your phone at a girl's house again?"

Reed ignored the joke. "I need help. I'm headed to ClearPond Regional Medical Hospital southeast of Houston with a hot package. I got a lot of eyes on me and fingers reaching from across the border."

"On my way." Bustling sounds of movement came through the line.

"Thanks." Reed would breathe a little easier when he had backup he could trust.

"I need to get anyone else involved?" Luke asked.

"Nah. I'm good with just you."

"Be there as fast as I can." More shuffling noises indicated Luke was already heading to his truck. "How can I reach you when I get close? I'm guessing your phone is toast."

"Yeah, that reminds me. Can you bring me Mom's old phone?" The saying was code for a burn phone, which couldn't be traced.

"Sure. Anything else?"

"Let Nick know what's going on."

"He's going to want to come." The Campbell boys had learned early in life to count on each other after their father had ditched the family and left their mother to bring up five kids on her own. Nick, the oldest, had taken over as a father figure.

"Tell him to stay put for now. I'll call when I need him."

"He may not listen."

"I can use any information he can dig up about a man they call Dueño. He's most likely running guns, trafficking women, but see if he can find anything else we can use to get to know this guy better."

"That should keep our brother busy. He still might want to come." Sounds of the truck door closing came through the line.

"Understood. I'll figure out what to do if he shows up. For now, try to discourage him." Reed totally understood his brother's need to be there. Reed would do the same thing if he were in Nick's shoes. "Let him know I can use him more on the sidelines right now. Plus, I'll have you to watch my back."

"Will do, baby bro."

Reed ended the call, thanked the driver and set his phone on the seat between them.

As promised, Reed saw the large white building ahead.

He surveyed the parking lot as they pulled inside the Emergency bay.

A Hispanic male stood by the corner of the building, smoking. He wore jeans, boots and a cowboy hat. The loose shirt he wore could easily hide a weapon. His head was tipped down, so Reed couldn't get a clear visual of the man's face.

The hospital was regional, so it was decent in size. There were a few dozen cars scattered around the parking lot, the heaviest concentration located closest to the main hospital entrance.

For a few seconds, Emily would be completely exposed while being wheeled inside. She'd be easy pickings for a trained sniper. Heck, any experienced gunman would be able to take her out faster than Reed could blink.

Luckily, there were no tall buildings nearby to gain a tactical advantage. A local hamburger joint, a taco-based fast-food chain restaurant and a gas station were located across the street. Those buildings weren't tall enough to matter.

Only an idiot would blitz them with a head-on attack. If this guy was smart and powerful enough to have a US presence, he didn't employ stupid people.

Reed's main concern was a bullet fired from in between the cars in the lot.

The gurney rolled through the sliding glass doors, where they were met by an officer. A sigh of relief passed Reed's lips once Emily was safely inside the building, but he wasn't ready to let his guard down.

The gurney was wheeled past an officer, and then disappeared inside a room. Reed paused at the door. "Your help is appreciated."

"I'll keep an officer here at all times and another at the elevator. The stairs are located at the end of the hall, so he'll be able to watch both exits from his vantage point." Reed had already counted the possible entry points and memorized the layout. Having someone centrally located was a good idea. Didn't hurt to have another officer right outside the door, as well.

"Hopefully, whoever is doing this will have enough sense to leave her alone for now. If not, your men should be a good deterrent." Reed couldn't be certain the officers appointed to watch over her could be trusted, but he was short on options.

Even if this one was honest, there was no way to know if the others were.

Cal had seemed honest and as if he was with the department for the right reasons. First impressions could be deceiving. Not only had Reed been ambushed and shot, his fiancée had been sleeping with Cal. The double deception had left him leery of trusting anyone whose last name wasn't Campbell.

Reed had doubted Gil for a while, too. But, his boss's true colors had come through when he'd maintained a bedside vigil next to Reed until he was out of the woods. Neither had stopped searching for Cal.

Letting Reed's guard down wasn't an option. He'd stay alert in Emily's room. He could rest when Luke arrived.

And Reed hoped like hell there wouldn't be any more surprises between now and then.

Stepping inside the bleached-white hospital room caused phantom pain to pierce his left shoulder—the exact spot where he'd taken a bullet. His attempt to take a step forward shut down midstride. *Shake it off.*

Forcing his boot to meet the white tile floor, he

couldn't suppress the shudder that ran through him after he pulled back the curtain and got a good look at Emily. Tubes stuck out of her from seemingly every direction. Monitors beeped.

With an uncomfortable smile on his lips, he moved closer.

As soon as she made eye contact, her face lit up. The tension in Reed's neck dissolved and warmth filled him. What was he supposed to do with that?

She lifted the oxygen mask off her face and quickly reined in her excitement, compressing her lips together instead. She could've been a poker player for the facade she put up now. Her even gaze dropped to the blanket covering her. "Thought maybe I'd scared you off."

"It takes more than a woman in trouble to make me run," he shot back, trying to get another smile from her. She didn't need to see the worry lines on his face. It would only make her panic.

A nurse fussed at Emily for lifting her mask. "I'll help you change into a gown." She turned to Reed. "You, sit. Or you'll have to go even though my boss gave me the rundown of the situation and you are law enforcement."

"Yes, ma'am." He took the chair closest to the bed, ignoring the uncomfortable feeling in his chest at seeing Emily look vulnerable and detached again. For her to have escaped the kind of man who could reach her from across a border, she had to be one tough cookie. Reed admired her for it. Hell, respected her even. Under different circumstances, she was the kind of woman he could see himself spending time getting to know better. Experience had taught him to keep his business and private lives separate.

Reed had no plans to break his rule no matter how

much the scared little thing in the bed next to him tugged at his heart strings. *Scared? Little?* He almost cracked a smile. From what he could tell so far, she wouldn't like being referred to as either.

Compared with his six-foot-two frame, most people would be considered small. Besides, it was normal to feel something for a woman in her circumstances. He wouldn't be human if his protective instincts didn't flare every time he saw the bruising on what would otherwise be considered silky, delicate skin. A woman like her should be cherished, not beaten.

The thought of the men in the parking lot waiting to make sure those hazel eyes closed permanently sobered Reed's thoughts. "How are you really feeling?"

A small woman in a white coat pushed past the nurse and introduced herself to Emily before she answered.

Reed sat patiently by as the doctor performed her exam. Based on how much attention Emily had received on the scene and when she'd first arrived at the hospital, he figured they wouldn't be letting her go tonight.

Reed had mixed feelings about her release. He couldn't be certain they were secure here at the facility—hell, in this town. And yet, she'd been in pretty bad shape when he found her. He couldn't deny her the medical attention she needed. The crash had made her physical condition even worse. Even if he had wanted to run her in for questioning, he doubted she would've made it through the interrogation without collapsing from exhaustion.

Then again, he knew better than to underestimate the power of fear. And *scared* didn't begin to describe the woman he'd found on the docks.

The doctor scribbled notes on the chart as she examined Emily.

He recognized the bag of saline. Good. She needed hydration, and that would be the quickest way. She'd already gone through a bag during the ambulance ride, according to the EMT. Her skin already looked pinker, livelier.

A nurse gently washed Emily's face and then blotted ointment. "Your sunburn is healing. This'll speed up the process."

Keeping her alive wasn't the only problem Reed had. He needed to see if Dueño's men had broken into Emily's town house and found the passwords.

The doctor abruptly turned on Reed. "I understand you were driving the vehicle before it crashed?"

Reed introduced himself, producing his badge. "That's correct, ma'am. How is she?"

"So far, so good. We won't know the extent of the swelling for another couple of hours." The doctor gently pinched the skin on Emily's forearm. "She's severely dehydrated."

"She went without water for several days."

A look of sympathy crossed the doctor's features. "Then we'll want to keep her on the IVs, slowly introduce her to solid food." She turned to the nurse. "Start with a clear liquid diet, advance to full liquids, soft and then regular."

"She managed to eat half a hamburger earlier."

"That's encouraging."

"How soon will she recover?"

"Good question. A lot depends on her. But because of the smoke inhalation, I'm apprehensive. She's been having some difficulty breathing due to a swollen respiratory tract. Since she's getting to the ER so late, I'll want to keep her overnight at a minimum to ensure the swelling subsides. We need to keep a read on her arterial blood gases, too."

Reed's lips compressed in a frown. He leaned closer to the doctor when he said, "Doesn't sound good."

"My inspection of her airway is encouraging. Edema is minimal—"

Reed must've given her a look without realizing it because the doctor stopped midsentence.

"The swelling isn't bad. Of course, with any smoke inhalation I'm concerned about the swelling increasing in twenty-four to forty-eight hours. I'm holding off on intubation for now. I'll be keeping a close eye on her, though. Any movement there and I'll have no choice. I've already given her a dose of steroids, and the nurse will give her a bronchodilator treatment."

The thought she needed help to keep her throat from swelling shut didn't encourage Reed. "What about her other injuries?"

"We won't know until we dig a little deeper. I'll send in a tech to take her for X-rays after her breathing treatment."

"I'm responsible for her safety. Any chance I can tag along?"

"Shouldn't be a problem. I'll make a note on her file." The doctor's gaze intensified on Reed. "How about you? Mind if I take a look while you're here?"

"Me? Nah. I'm fine."

"Looks like your forehead took impact and you have substantial bleeding on your shirt. I'd feel a lot better if you'd let me take a look."

"It's just a scratch."

The doctor held her ground. "Even so, I'd like to examine you while the nurse administers treatment."

Reed focused on Emily, who was being told to inhale medicine from a tube.

The doctor kept her gaze on him. "My brother-in-law is a firefighter. His job is to help everyone else, but he's the last person to ask when he needs it."

"A job hazard," Reed joked, trying to redirect the seriousness of the conversation. "If it'll make you feel better, go ahead."

The doctor examined him, cleaned his cuts and brought in another nurse, instructing her to bandage his wounds.

"I'll check in on you both later," she said before making a move toward the door.

"Can those treatments stop the swelling?" Reed inclined his head toward Emily.

"That's the hope," the doctor said. "Like I said, we'll have to keep her overnight for observation to be sure."

Reed hoped they had that long. He didn't like feeling this exposed, and he couldn't be sure he could trust local police. Aches and pains from the day hit hard and fast. His brother would arrive in a few hours and then Reed could get some rest.

Until then, he didn't plan to take his eyes off Emily.

WHATEVER THE DOCTOR had ordered was working wonders on Emily. Her head had stopped pounding, and her body didn't feel as if she'd been run through a cheese grater any longer. News about the results from the X-rays had been promised.

A glance at the clock said she'd been in the hospital for two hours already. Had she dozed off?

She didn't dare move for fear she'd wake the agent slumped in the chair next to her bed. He needed rest.

Other than a bandage on his forehead and chest, he'd
refused medical treatment. He'd taken the nurse up on
her offer of soap, a washcloth and dental supplies. He'd
washed in the bathroom and stripped down to a basic
white T-shirt he'd borrowed from one of the orderlies
before leaning back in the lounge chair and closing his
eyes. His T was the only thing basic about him. His job
would require a toned body. One glance at the muscled
agent said he took his profession seriously.

His rock-hard abs moved up and down with every
even breath he took. The rest of him was just as solid
and in control.

Emily reached for the water he'd placed near her head
on the cart next to her.

"How was your nap?"

She suppressed a yelp. "You startled me."

"Sorry."

"I thought you were out." She took a sip.

"I'm a light sleeper."

Of course he was. A man who was always prepared
for the worst-case scenario wouldn't zone out completely.
"How long have you been in your job?"

"Six years."

Emily had been in her job half that time. She worried
the only steady thing in her life would be gone by the
time she returned to Plano.

But a man who looked like Reed Campbell must have
a wife waiting for him. "The hours have to be difficult
on your family."

"You might be surprised. One of my brothers is a
US marshal, the other is FBI." He cracked a smile, and
her heart skipped a beat. "My sisters aren't much better.
One's a police officer in Plano and the other's a victims'

rights advocate for the sheriff. Guess you could say law enforcement runs in our blood."

"Wow. That's impressive. I was actually thinking about your wife and kids."

He shook his head. "No wife. No kids."

"A committed bachelor?"

"No time."

She almost believed him, until the corner of his full lip curled. Surely, a tough and strong man who looked like him attracted plenty of women. "Are you teasing?"

"It's been a tough day." He scrubbed a hand over the scruff on his face. Lightness left his expression. "How are you holding up, really?"

"They seem to be patching me up okay." Why couldn't she admit how much pain she was actually in or how scared she was about her future? A part of her wanted to believe the agent cared how she was actually doing, and not just making polite conversation, or ensuring his witness could testify. Besides, she couldn't remember the last time she'd opened up to someone. Heck, she'd made herself a loner at the House when she wasn't feeding or bathing one of her half siblings. She'd skillfully hidden behind attending to them. "I took a few bumps. I'll be good as new by morning."

He shot her a look. "Okay, tough guy. I'm not buying that."

Most likely, he needed to assess her condition to see if she was stable enough to travel or go on the run. Duh. What a dummy. She'd almost convinced herself the hunky agent actually cared about her. Wow, she must've taken more damage to the head than she realized. "He'll come for me here, won't he?"

He eyed her for a long moment without speaking. "Suspicious men are already stationed outside."

Was he trying to figure out if he could trust her? "I know my story sounds crazy."

"I've heard worse."

Of course he had in his line of work. "Maybe it just sounds bizarre in my head."

"It's normal to need a minute to let this sink in. Your world was just turned on its head. It'll take a bit to absorb. Don't be hard on yourself. I've seen grown men buckle under lesser circumstances."

Was that a hint of pride in his brilliant brown eyes? Or was she seeing something she wanted to see instead of reality? This was most likely the speech he gave to all the victims he came across. *Victim?* The word sat bitterly on her tongue. She may have had a rough childhood and she might be in sticky circumstances now, but no way was she a helpless victim. "This might sound weird. I mean, we've only just met. But, I feel like I *know* you."

"We've been through hell and back. It forms a bond." A wide smile broke across white teeth, shattering his serious persona.

Emily forced her gaze from his lips.

Chapter Six

Experience had taught Emily the best way to dispel the mystery of someone was the reality of getting to know them. And the last thing she needed was for the agent to realize she was attracted to him. Heck, she'd wanted to crawl under the bed and hide earlier when he walked in the room and she grinned like an idiot. Hopefully, she'd reined it in before she'd made a complete fool out of herself. "You said earlier that you came from a big family?"

"You'll meet one of my brothers in an hour. Luke's the one who works for the FBI." Reed popped to his feet and walked to the window, his thigh muscles pressing against his jeans as they stretched. He had the power and athletic grace of a predator closing in on its meal. His gaze narrowed as he peered out the window.

"Maybe the doctor will let me go tomorrow." She glanced at the door and back to Reed. "It doesn't seem safe for us here."

"All I need for you to do is rest and get as strong as you can." He didn't say because they might need to bolt at any moment, although the tension radiating from his body told her exactly what he was thinking.

"What about you? You ever sleep?"

"Not much when I'm working on a case. Speaking of

which, we should talk about yours." He moved back to his seat, but positioned himself on the edge and rested his elbows on his knees.

"You already know I work at a computer company. That pretty much sums up my life. I'm in line for a promotion, so I've been working nonstop for months. It's part of why I panicked when you called my boss." Telling the handsome agent work was all she had, made her life sound incredibly small and empty. Speaking of which, what would Jared think when she showed up to work Monday looking as if she'd been the warm-up punching bag for an MMA fighter? Her boss was a climber, and she knew he used her to do much of his own work under the guise of training her. Was there any way to finagle more time off without jeopardizing her position?

A lump of dread sat in her stomach. How could she go back at all now? With a man like Dueño chasing her, would she even be able to pick up her old life where she'd left off? She focused on the agent. "How do we keep me alive?"

"I could talk to my brother Nick about witness protection. He's a US marshal."

And leave behind everything she'd worked for? It was sad that her first thought was dreading having to start all over with a new job, and not that she'd be leaving her friends and family behind. A bitter stab of loneliness pierced the center of Emily's chest.

Her reaction must've been written all over her face because Reed was on his feet, his gaze locked on hers. "It's just an option. I'm not saying we have to go through with it. I wouldn't be able to leave my family behind, either."

At least he couldn't read her mind. A man like him with more family around than he could count wouldn't understand her desperation at leaving behind the only thing she'd ever been able to count on. Work. The sadness in that thought weighted her limbs. Emily refused to give in, crossing her arms.

"It's okay. It's a reasonable option. I should definitely give it some serious consideration." She hoped the agent didn't pick up on the fact there was no emotion in those last words.

"I just thought we should explore every possibility of keeping you safe until we can put this jerk behind bars." Whereas her words might've lacked emotion, the venom in his when he said the word *jerk* was its own presence in the room.

Emily had always believed that she was making the best out of the situation she'd been handed. Being successful at work was so much less complicated than dealing with people and especially family. She'd never minded being alone before. In fact, she'd preferred it. So why did it suddenly feel like a death sentence?

Wasn't getting the chance for a new identity, a fresh start in life, the ideal solution to many of her problems? As much as she didn't want to leave the life she'd built in Plano, the option had to be considered. "How does witness protection work exactly?"

"We could talk to my brother to get all the facts, but you'd be assigned to a US marshal who'd become responsible for giving you a new identity, a place to live and a job somewhere no one would know to look for you."

"And contact with my family?"

His gaze dropped to the floor. "I'm afraid that's not possible."

Even though she spoke to her mother only a few times a year, Emily couldn't imagine cutting off that last little connection to her past, to her. "And what if that's not possible?"

"Do you remember anything about the person who did this to you?"

"No. I didn't see him at all. They were careful about protecting him. All I heard was his voice. I'd know that sound if I heard it again." She paused a beat. "Which isn't much to go on, is it?"

"It's something," he said encouragingly.

"Not enough for an arrest, though, let alone a conviction."

He didn't make eye contact when he said, "No. But maybe you can lead us to his hideout. We've already been able to pinpoint the area of abduction, and these guys tend to be territorial."

She told him the name of the resort where she'd stayed, and everything else she could remember about her abduction, which was precious little since she'd been blindfolded most of the time. "That's where it gets even worse. I mean, I wish I could give you more to work with. I was blindfolded for much of the walk, which felt like it took forever."

"These guys are professionals. It's not your fault. We have the location of your abduction. They didn't take you anywhere by plane, right?"

"No. We walked the entire time."

"That gives us a starting point."

"Except that we could've been walking in circles for all I knew."

"Believe it or not, you've narrowed down the possibilities with what you've told me so far. It's a start." Reed stabbed his fingers through his thick dark hair. "Anyone have a spare key to your town house?"

Like a friend? Emily almost choked on her own laughter—laughter that she held deep inside because if it came out, so would the onslaught of tears. "No."

His dark brow arched. "Not even a neighbor or your landlord?"

"I own it." Emily didn't address the bit about the neighbor. She didn't want to admit she didn't know the people who lived around her. A casualty of working too many long nights and weekends, she decided. Her life had never seemed empty to her before, so why did it now? Without her job, her career, it would be.

She'd worked too hard to let it all be taken away by some crazed criminal. What if she told her boss about the car crash? Maybe she could convince Jared to give her an extended leave of absence and save her job. It wasn't as if she took days off. With her rollover vacation days, she could take off two months. That might give the agent a chance to catch Dueño, and she could restore her life. She might have invested a lot of time in her work, but it was all she had. And if Jared asked too many questions or figured out her half-truth, she might not have that anymore. Maybe she could tell him what had happened. On second thought, there was no gray area with Jared. How many times had he fired someone for a slight infraction? Even though she hadn't broken any company rules, he would assume she'd done something to bring this on herself. He'd start viewing her as a threat to the company and find a reason to get rid of her.

The thought of giving up everything she'd worked for sucked all the air out of her lungs. Hadn't she fought long and hard to put down roots? Her place in Texas was home. "It seems like witness protection is my only option, but what if I don't want it?"

Reed ran a hand over the scruff on his chin. "We catch this guy and you're home free. Otherwise, we wait it out and keep you safe. My experience with men like these is that they have a short memory. If I can get you safely through a few weeks, you should be in the clear."

Was returning to her life in a few weeks really an option? Surely, she could get that much time off. The first real spark of hope in days lit inside her. Maybe she wouldn't have to give up the only life that felt like hers. "What if these people are different and don't mind waiting it out? How will we know for sure?"

The intensity in his brown eyes increased. "My brother Nick is digging deeper to find out their story. He'll be able to tell us what we're facing. My plan is to catch them and put them in jail where they belong."

"I could make up a story for my boss. Take time off."

Reed gave her a look as if he understood. Did he? No way could he get that she wasn't staying because of family or friends. He probably had more of those than he could count, too. How did she tell someone who had so many relationships worth living for the real reason she wanted to keep her life was because of her work? Or maybe she needed to dig in and fight for the small life she had. There wasn't much else she could be sure of right now except that she couldn't bear the thought of losing everything again as she had when she was a little girl and the only life she'd ever known had been stripped away from her. "Things get too intense, can I change my mind?"

"WitSec will always be an option."

"And what about you? What will happen to you if I go in?" She hadn't considered the agent before. Wouldn't her going into the program take him out of the line of fire? "I don't want to put you in any more danger."

"This is my job. Besides, I want to catch this son of a bitch as much as you."

WHETHER EMILY WENT into WitSec or not, Reed had every intention of seeing this case through to the end. A bad agent had infected the agency. Reed needed to find out who before someone else got shot, or worse, killed.

At least Emily's story had checked out with her boss. Reed had almost asked his brother to investigate her background. He was still scratching his head as to why he hadn't. The only people he didn't run background checks on were the women he dated, which put him in unfamiliar territory with his witness. He'd have to gain her trust and actually have a conversation with her to find out what he wanted to know. And then, he'd have to trust she'd told the truth.

Trust? Interesting word. Other than his boss, Reed hadn't trusted anyone who didn't share his last name in the past year. He was bad at it. And yet, gaining hers might be the key to unlocking who in his agency was involved in this. He'd always suspected Cal wasn't the only bad crop in the garden.

Reed could give up a little about himself if it meant advancing his case. There were other reasons compelling him to open up a little to this witness, too. None of which he wanted to explore. The image of her smile—the one like when he'd first walked in—stamped his thoughts. She'd suppressed it faster than a squirrel hides its supper, but for the second it was there, her whole face shone. "Someone in my agency is corrupt. I have every intention of finding out who they are and bringing them to justice."

Her gaze intensified. "That part of your code of honor?"

"It's more than that." Uneasy and unsure if he was about to do the right thing, he pulled up his T-shirt and turned to let her see the scar on his left shoulder.

"Ohmygosh. What happened to you?" The warmth in her voice would melt an iceberg.

It drew him in and made him want to connect with it. He lowered the hem of his shirt and returned to his spot on the edge of the chair, making sure he maintained visual contact with the door in his peripheral. The thought of discussing what had happened to him a year ago parked an RV on his chest.

He took a breath and shoved past the feeling. "While on a case a year ago, I got a hot tip on a kidnapping ring. Young girls were being snatched, shuffled across the border and sold before their parents even knew they were missing. Heard a few were holed up and drugged in a house near the border. I'd been tracking a coyote for two years." He paused when her eyebrow shot up. "Human trafficker. Seemed like he knew every time I got close. He'd up and relocate his business. Goes without saying how badly I wanted to put this guy away and toss the key for what he was doing to those young girls. And yet, I was careful not to make a mistake. I was so close I could almost taste it."

"So what happened?"

"This guy had big connections on both sides of the border. He was under the protection of a rebel leader. And that guy had a border patrol agent on his payroll. He discovered I was about to bust the coyote, so… Let's just say I was set up. Wasn't supposed to walk out of the hot spot they'd sent me to. Thought I was close to this guy. Turns out, he was closer to my fiancée."

"Oh." The flash in her eyes went from sympathy to indignant. "Two people you trusted betrayed you? That must make it hard to believe in anyone else."

She had no idea. Or, did she?

There was a subtle lilt to her tone, an unspoken kinship that said she might know exactly what he was talking about. Had someone she'd trusted turned on her? "I spent a little time in a room just like this one. Gave me a lot of time to think. Figure a man should be left alone with his thoughts for about two minutes before he turns against the world."

She didn't laugh at his joke meant to lighten the mood.

"What happened to the people who did that to you?" There was an all-too-familiar anger in her voice now.

"He disappeared across the border before he could be arrested. Someone has him tucked away nicely because not one of our informants has seen him."

"And the woman?"

"Could be with him for all we know." He paused. "She didn't exactly break the law."

"I'm so sorry. Having people you trust turn on you is one thing, but then never having him brought to justice adds a whole new level of unfairness."

The depths of her eyes said she knew about unfair. What had happened in her life for her to be able to sympathize? More questions he didn't have answers to.

A knock at the door brought Reed to his feet, his weapon drawn and leading the way as he stalked toward the entrance to the room.

"There's someone here to see you, Agent Campbell." Reed recognized the voice as belonging to the officer. "His ID says he's Special Agent Luke Campbell."

The past few hours had soared by. What was it about

talking to Emily that made time disappear and the ache in his chest lighter?

"My brother's here," Luke said to ease the tension he felt coming from Emily. Her compassion had melted a little of the ice encasing his heart. Relieved for the break, Reed wasn't ready to let anyone inside. And yet, talking to her had come easier than he'd expected. Even more surprising was the fact that he wanted to tell her more.

"Send him in." Reed kept his weapon drawn on the off chance someone other than his brother walked through that door, refusing to be caught off guard again. It was unlikely anyone would know he'd called his brother, but taking chances was for gamblers—and Reed didn't bet on odds.

"It's me." His brother seemed to understand Reed's apprehension as he walked through the door with his hands up in the universal sign for surrender.

Reed lowered his weapon and returned it to his holster. He greeted his brother with a bear hug and introduced him to Emily, surprised to see a tear roll down her cheek.

"Nice to meet you," she said quickly. Her unreadable expression returned so fast Reed almost thought he'd imagined her brief show of emotion.

Reed caught a glimpse of his brother's reaction to seeing the bruising on her face as Luke handed over the burn phone he'd brought. No Campbell man would take lightly to a woman being beaten, even though they saw it far too often in their lines of work.

"We have a lot of company outside." Luke leaned against the wall near the big window facing the door, and crossed his ankles. Another habit formed on the job— they never put their backs to the door.

"I saw a couple when we came in."

"There's half a dozen now, covering all entrances. One looked twice at me even though I kept my head down." He wore a ball cap, T-shirt and jeans. "I'm guessing they saw the resemblance."

"You two do look a lot alike," Emily agreed.

Reed couldn't argue. So, the men might just think it was Luke leaving when Reed ducked out later. Now that Luke was there, Reed could risk leaving Emily's side without fearing for her safety. "I have to run out in a bit. Mind if we switch hats?"

Luke shook his head and pulled off his ball cap. "Make sure you pull it down low, over your bandage. Looks like you took a pretty good hit."

"I'm fine."

Emily coughed loudly enough to let everyone know she'd done it on purpose. "Um, he pulled me out of a burning car while fighting off men shooting at us. He has to be exhausted. I don't think he should be going anywhere."

Reed had to fist his hands to stop from wiping the smile off his brother's face.

"What did I say?" Emily's gaze bounced from one to the other.

They stood, staring, daring the other to speak first.

"Nothing," Reed said too quickly. He didn't want to share the fact that both of his brothers had fallen in love with women they were protecting. "My brother just has a twisted sense of humor."

Luke turned to her. "I want the same thing you do for my brother."

"Rest?" she asked, puzzled.

"Peace."

When no one explained what Luke meant, Emily shrugged.

Reed handed over his Stetson.

"I think I'm getting the better deal out of this exchange," Luke joked, replacing his ball cap with the white cowboy hat.

"We'd better trade shirts, too," Reed said.

"Can I see you for a second, Reed?" Emily asked. "Privately?"

Luke's gaze locked onto Reed's. He nodded.

His brother excused himself to the bathroom.

"Everything okay?" The fear Emily's condition was getting worse gripped Reed faster than if he'd walked into an intersection and had been hit by a bus.

"Come closer?"

Reed moved to the side of her bed.

She patted the sheets, and he took her cue to sit down next to her. The nurse had helped her shower, and Emily looked even more beautiful. This close, she smelled clean and flowery.

"I'm scared." The words came out in a whisper.

Those fearful hazel eyes were back, the ones threatening to crack more of the ice encasing his heart, and his pulse raced.

For lack of a better way to offer reassurance, he bent down and gently kissed her forehead. "My brother's the best. You'll be safe."

She shook her head, her gaze locked onto his the whole time. "I know. I'm afraid for you."

The warmth of a thousand campfires flooded his chest. Hell's bells. What was he supposed to do with that?

He opened his mouth to speak, but her hands were

already tunneled into his hair, urging him closer. Last thing he wanted to do was hurt her, so he stopped the second their lips touched, waiting for a sign from her she was still okay.

Her tongue darted inside his mouth, and he had to remind himself not to take control. She knew what she could handle, what hurt, so he momentarily surrendered to her judgment, careful not to apply any more pressure than she could handle.

Those soft pink lips of hers nearly did him in. Every muscle in his body was strung so tight he thought they might snap. He wanted more.

For her, he would hold back.

As her tongue searched inside his mouth, he brought his hands up to cup her face.

A noise from the bathroom caused Reed to pull back first.

Emily brought her hand up to her lips, her nervous "tell." "I'm sorry. I probably shouldn't have done that."

"It's a good thing you did."

She smiled and those thousand campfires burst into flames.

"I know you're going to search down the agent who called before everything went crazy."

He didn't deny it.

"Just be careful. And come back." The sincerity in her eyes nearly knocked him back. Her concern was outlined in the wrinkles in her forehead.

He bent down and kissed them. Then he feathered kisses on the tip of her nose, her eyelids.

Not a lot made sense to him right now except this moment happening between them. Underneath the bruises and the bad bleach job, there was a beautiful woman.

And he was a man.

Their lives had been in danger and they'd both nearly been killed today.

Reed couldn't be sure if this was the beginning of real sparks between the two of them or if the attraction was down to basic primal urges and they both needed proof of life, but for a split second, his defenses lowered and she inched inside his heart.

Chapter Seven

The faucet turned on in the bathroom, and Reed heard the rush of water in the sink. He figured it was Luke's polite way of saying he was done hiding.

Reed needed to get moving, anyway. He stood. "All clear."

Emily blinked up at him. "Remember what I said."

"Try to get some rest." He grazed the soft skin of her arm with the tip of his finger. He needed to catch these guys and give Emily her life back.

She closed her eyes and smiled.

"Here's what you need to know before you head out." Luke quietly reentered the room. "Dueño is believed to be a ghost. No one's seen him. Some people aren't even sure if he exists, but if something's illegal and it touches South America, his name shows up every time."

Emily blinked her eyes open. "I've seen him. He's real."

"Our lowlife owns those distribution channels?" Reed asked.

"The guy can get any product moved for a price." Luke's gaze moved from Emily to Reed. "Makes a lot of money on women and children."

Reed muttered a curse. "What else?"

"Like I mentioned, he stays out of the spotlight. No one's seen him. He's like a damn phantom."

"So he likes to hide. Makes it easier to stay under the radar that way."

"And harder to convict," Luke agreed. "He has several high-ranking lieutenants. Marco Delgado, Julian Escado and Jesus Ramirez are at the top."

"I've heard of Ramirez, but not the others. His name was associated with Cal's, but I thought he worked alone."

"I remember. Dueño set up the teams in supercells, so they'd be harder to trace back to him. This group plays their cards close to their vest. Nick found out they have a meeting once a year at Dueño's compound to discuss business. Other than that, there's no communication."

"Makes it hard to track their activity back to him."

"And that's one of the biggest benefits. Has its risks, too."

Reed rocked his head. "Any one of them could go rogue and Dueño wouldn't know about it for a while."

"The lieutenants know each other, obviously, but the men in the ranks don't know they all work in the same organization. Word on the street is that these three are heads of their own groups. Members view each other as competition."

"A misunderstanding and they could end up killing one of their own without knowing it." Reed rubbed the scruff on his chin.

"True."

"If they think they're turning in a rival, we might get them to talk about each other." Reed pinched the bridge of his nose to stem the dull ache forming. This was bigger than he'd imagined. Emily was in grave danger. "Do the low-ranking guys know about the summit?"

"Some do. They think the guys are meeting next week to agree on territory."

"We might be able to get one of our informants to speak. Any idea where this compound is located?"

"Unfortunately, no. It's impossible to get anyone to talk. They're afraid of repercussion. The organization is well run."

"We might know a link. An agent phoned after I pulled away from the docks, asking if he could take her in for me." Reed stopped long enough to pace. "Besides, men who run things for others get greedy. They end up asking why they should do all the work for someone else's gain. Maybe we can figure out a way to pit them against each other."

"Your guy might be the connection we're looking for." Luke grabbed his keys and tossed them to Reed with a grin. "Bring it back in one piece. You know how I love that truck."

"We'll see." Reed glanced at Emily, again thankful her eyes were closed and her breath even. "Take care of her. She's been through a lot."

"You know I will, baby bro."

Reed hugged his brother, the manly kind of hug with backslaps.

Keeping his head low, he tucked his hands in his front jeans pockets and strolled down the hall. Dueño's men would have all the exits covered. The trick would be getting to Luke's truck without being noticed.

It was long past midnight. The darkness should help. Although, it also meant there'd be fewer people coming in and out of the hospital.

Reed took the stairs to the bottom floor and, by memory, located the ER. There was no one in the long hallway leading to the parking lot where he'd initially entered the building. An eerie quiet settled over him.

The click of his boots was the only sound as he entered the sterile white passage.

Going outside without a cover was a bad idea. Last thing he needed was someone following him. Maybe he could grab some coffee in the waiting room, bide his time until someone left.

An agonizing forty-three minutes later, he got his chance as a family left with their teenager. His arm was heavily bandaged, and his washed-out expression said he'd most likely been drinking and had done something stupid to get hurt. The young man had to be six foot and close to two hundred pounds. He took after his father. The pair should offer plenty of cover.

Reed shadowed the family, breaking off in the parking lot as he ducked in between two cars. He located his brother's truck, which was exactly where he'd said it would be. Reed kept his head down as he climbed in the cab. His thoughts focused on Agent Stephen Taylor—get to him and find the answers.

He located the family's car as they pulled out of the parking lot and followed.

A quick call to his boss on the burn phone Luke had provided and Reed had Gil updated and working on finding Agent Taylor's home address inside of ten minutes. Double that, and Luke was on the expressway, blending in to his surroundings. His tail had given up fifteen minutes ago, figuring, as Reed had hoped, that he was part of the family leaving and not a person of interest. It most likely hadn't hurt that Luke had come in twenty minutes before Reed left.

No matter how quickly he returned to the hospital,

his sense of unease about leaving would still produce a lump in his gut. Even though Luke was capable of handling any situation he encountered, he was one man and these guys had brought an army.

Emily's bruised face and vulnerable eyes pierced his thoughts.

His cell buzzed and he realized how tightly he'd been gripping the steering wheel. The text came. Stephen Taylor's address. Reed pulled off the highway and plugged in the location to Luke's GPS.

Another fifteen minutes and Reed was in the neighborhood.

Taylor's street was dark, save for a streetlight next to his house. Reed crept past the front of the one-story ranch house and then rounded the block. There could be a fortress inside and Taylor could be waiting. No doubt, he'd be on edge if he was close to Dueño.

Reed shut off his lights and parked down the street. He put on the Kevlar vest in the backseat of the cab, and then palmed his weapon.

With his Glock leveled and leading the way, he moved along the shrubbery, saying a little prayer no dogs would bark.

The home was a simple brick ranch. More details about Taylor came through via text. Turned out, Taylor had a wife and a baby. He was the last person Reed would suspect to be dirty but then again he had no idea what the guy's personal situation was, and greed was a powerful motivator. Cases like these had a color. Green.

None of this place fit. This was a nice middle-class neighborhood. Wouldn't a dirty agent live in a nicer house? There was nothing wrong with this one, but it was definitely something Taylor could afford on his own.

He didn't need a side income for this. If an agent was dirty, there were clues. They'd live in a house clearly above their pay grade or have expensive hobbies, such as collecting sports cars.

Maybe the guy was in debt. He could have a sick kid or a gambling problem. If he was really smart, he'd give the appearance of living off his means and sock the money away for the future. Men who planned for the long-term usually had more sense than to get involved with criminals.

Blackmail? There were other possibilities Reed considered as he surveyed the perimeter, allowing his eyes the chance to adjust to the dark. The curtains in the living room had been left open. The slats in the two-inch wood blinds provided enough of a gap to get a clear view into the living room. Nothing stood out. The furnishings were simple and had a woman's touch. A baby swing, playpen and toys crowded the place. Not one thing looked out of the ordinary for a young family of three.

Reed could plainly see through to the back door into the kitchen. No keypad for an alarm system. He changed his vantage point. No sign of one near the front door, either.

No alarm system. No dog. No real security.

He'd expected the guy to be paranoid.

Another piece of the puzzle that didn't fit.

Reed ran his hand along the windowsills, looking for a good place to enter the home. He didn't care how careful this guy was. Reed had every intention of getting answers tonight.

The windows and doors were all locked. Twelve windows and two doors were possible exit points. Reed peeked in each, memorizing the layout before returning to his spot. The front door was made of solid wood, which made it difficult to breach without making too much noise. Reed's best bet would be to enter through the kitchen. The top half of the door was glass. He shucked the vest, and took off his T-shirt and wrapped it around his hand like tape on a boxer's fist.

A dog barked. Reed bit out a curse and worked faster. No way was he leaving without questioning Taylor. This guy was the ticket to putting the puzzle pieces together. Memories of the night Reed was shot flooded him. Reed battled to force them away and stay focused.

He punched through the glass and then unlocked the door. A few seconds later, his T-shirt and Kevlar was on. He wasn't taking another chance with a dirty agent.

The house was quiet save for the ticking clock hanging on the wall in the kitchen. Reed cleared the room and rounded the corner toward the bedrooms, his weapon leading the way, and froze. From three feet away, the business end of a Glock was aimed at his face, most likely right between his eyes.

"What are you doing here, Agent Campbell?" Stephen asked.

"Put your gun down and I'll explain." Reed intentionally kept his voice calm and low.

"Not until you tell me what's going on." Stephen's hands shook and he didn't lower his weapon.

Reed leveled his, aiming for the chest. Stephen wore pajama pants and a T-shirt. He hadn't had time to put on his Kevlar. One shot and his chest would have a hole. Reed said a silent prayer he'd get his shot off first. Kevlar didn't help with a bullet in the head. Both were trained shooters, a requirement of the job. "We need to talk."

"In the middle of the night? What the hell could be this important?"

Neither made a move to put down his weapon.

"It's about the woman." Reed took a step back, inching toward the corner, anything that could be a barrier or slow down a bullet. If this guy was in league with a man like Dueño, he'd have no problem doing away with anyone or anything that got in his way. And yet, nothing about his house said he was on the take. There were signs with Cal. He'd driven a fifty-thousand-dollar car. Lived in a neighborhood a little too pricey for his pay grade. He'd chalked it all up to rich parents and a partial trust fund. If anyone had bothered to take a closer look or check his file, they'd have realized his parents were blue-collar workers from Brownsville. But then, it wasn't as if Cal had invited anyone from the department over to his place for backyard barbecues. And he'd been smart about it. He lived in a nice house but not so expensive it would draw attention.

None of those signs was present here at Stephen's. His place looked as if he lived on the paycheck provided by the agency. Then again, looks could be deceiving. He'd also believed his fiancée when she'd said there was nothing going on between Cal and her.

Stephen stepped forward. "What are you talking about?"

"You called me earlier this afternoon. Asked to run in my witness for me."

"Yeah. So what? Thought I was doing you a favor."

Right. Reed wasn't about to let Stephen off with that pat answer. "Since when would anyone want to take on filling out someone else's paperwork?"

Stephen didn't respond. Reed was pretty certain if he

could peel back the guy's skull Reed would see fireworks going off in there.

"You plan to shoot me?" he hedged.

"Not unless you fire first."

"Then why don't we both put our weapons down and talk?" In a show of good faith, Reed lowered his first. He was close enough to the corner to make a fast break if this didn't go as planned.

Stephen lowered his weapon at the same time a baby wailed in the next room. On edge, he bit out a curse and shot a stern look to Reed. "Wait here. And don't you move."

"I'm not going anywhere until I get answers." Reed tucked his gun in his holster, and then crossed his arms over his chest.

"Good." He moved to the end of the hall where the master bedroom was located. "Kiera, the baby's up. I'm in the kitchen with a work friend, and we need to finish our business."

Reed didn't hear her response, but she must've agreed because Stephen turned his attention back to Reed and urged him into the kitchen.

"What the hell's going on?" Stephen asked. Confusion mixed with the daggers being shot from his glare.

"You tell me."

"Tell you what?" he parroted.

"Why'd you feel the need to relieve me of my passenger?" Reed followed Stephen's gaze to the broken glass on the kitchen floor.

"Great." He moved to the pantry, retrieved a broom and started sweeping up the shards. "My baby plays on this floor. And, my wife is going to be pissed when she sees this. You know, you could've knocked."

Well, hell in a handbasket, Reed really was mixed up now. "Stop sweeping and fill me in."

"My wife'll be in to get a bottle, so I can't stop sweeping. She's going to be pissed enough as it is."

Nothing about Stephen's actions said he was anything but a family man. Reed sighed sharply. "If you didn't want my witness, why'd you call and ask for her?"

The sound of crying intensified. Stephen glanced toward the hall. "Grab a bottle from the fridge, and put it in the microwave for a minute and a half."

Reed did as he was told, sticking the glass bottle in the microwave.

"Take the lid off first. Don't you know anything about babies?" Stephen's pleading look would've been funny under different circumstances. Even a tough guy like him seemed to know better than to anger his wife.

"Okay." When his task was finished, he handed the offering to Stephen. "Done. Now talk."

Stephen's wife walked in, baby on hip, wearing a robe. She'd be all of five foot two if she had heels on. She was pretty, blonde. Her gaze bounced from the floor to Reed, and then to her husband. "What's going on? Why is he here in the middle of the night?"

This was all wrong. The house. The wife. The baby. What in hell's kitchen was going on?

"Here you go, honey." Stephen handed her the bottle. "It involves an active case, so I can't talk about it. But I'll be in bed before you put the baby down."

She took the bottle. The crying baby immediately settled the second he tasted milk. Warmth flooded Reed and his heart stirred.

He shook off the momentary weakness, attributing

it to the fact that yesterday had been the anniversary of his planned wedding with Leslie. Her betrayal had come the month before. Infidelity had a way of changing people's courses.

Kiera eyed her husband for a long moment then, on her tiptoes, kissed his cheek. "Don't be too long."

He bent down and kissed her forehead before planting another on his baby's cheek.

Her gaze narrowed when it landed on Reed. "I suspect you know how to use a door to get out?"

"Yes, ma'am." A moment of embarrassment hit. He'd acted on facts. He refused to wallow in guilt if he'd been wrong. Too many lives were at stake.

When she was safely out of earshot, Stephen continued, "Shane put me up to calling you. Said he needed your help on a case he was working, and that I should call you to see if I could take over for you. Said you were working on a routine immigration case."

"Shane Knox? He sure didn't let me in on it."

"Why would he do that?" Stephen's gaze was full of accusation now.

The weight of the conversation sat heavy on Reed's chest. "Because he's dirty."

"Hold on. That's a serious accusation. What makes you think that's the case?"

"I know."

"Then you need to fill me in."

Reed lifted the ball cap to reveal the bandage on his forehead. "Minutes after you made that call I was shot at before being run off the road. My Jeep caught fire."

More fireworks had to be going off in Stephen's brain based on the intensity of his eyes. "What happened to your witness?"

"She's in the hospital, but she'll be okay. The wreck was bad, but she'd been beaten up pretty badly before then."

"And Knox is connected to the initial incident?"

"As far as I know." Reed studied Stephen. "You called. I was run off the road."

"If they were coming after you, why have me call?" He snaked his fingers through his hair. "Never mind. I know. He was hoping to have her handed over to me. But why? I wouldn't have turned her over to him."

"He must've planned to follow you to the handoff so he could find us. He'd already sent men hunting for me, I'm sure of that."

"We traded vehicles a couple of weeks ago. He still has a few things in there. Must've left something in there he can track. Or he figured I wouldn't be suspicious if he stopped me somewhere along the way. You'd be leery after what you've been through. Or, maybe he planned to run me off the road instead."

"They want her alive. She has passwords to a computer. Or at least they think she does, which no longer matters because whether she produces them or not, they'll kill her." Reed rubbed the scruff on his chin. Dueño had gone to great lengths to hide his identity. Emily was the only person on the outside who'd heard his voice or could prove his existence. There was no doubt in his mind she'd been marked for death. The phone in his pocket vibrated. He fished it out and checked the text. As he made a run for the door, he said, "Something's going down at the hospital."

"Which one?" Stephen opened a drawer and pulled out an AR-15.

"ClearPond Hospital on I-45." Reed bolted out the door.

Stephen followed. "Then you're going to need backup."

"I appreciate it." Luke's message said the lights had gone out on the sixth floor, Emily's floor. Luke was smart enough to see it for what it was. But was Emily strong enough to move?

Without selling his brother short, Reed figured it'd be difficult to haul her away and fight off whoever had decided to breach the building.

He cursed Knox as he hopped into his brother's truck and fired up the engine, grateful for the help loading into the passenger's side.

Reed couldn't allow himself to consider the possibility that he wouldn't make it back to the hospital in time.

Chapter Eight

The door opened to Emily's room. Blackness surrounded her. Even with her hand stuck out flat, directly in front of her face, she couldn't see it.

"I'm to your right," Luke whispered, touching her arm.

An officer identified himself, flashing a light on his face. "Hospital security wants to move her to another room. They've established a safe route for us."

Luke squeezed her arm, but said nothing.

"Okay," she agreed.

"We'll unhook you from these machines to make it easier to transport you, okay?" the nurse said as she brushed against Emily's other side.

The beam of light transferred to her, and Emily saw fearful eyes.

"Sounds good. Do I have time to get dressed?"

"I'm afraid n—"

"She does," Luke interrupted, handing her a folded stack. "I brought fresh clothes."

As the tubes were unhooked, one by one, Emily pulled on a pair of jeans that fit perfectly and a V-neck cotton shirt. Thankfully, they'd let her keep her bra and underwear on earlier, and the dark had shielded her.

"You're good to go. Be careful. Those first few steps can be tricky," the nurse said.

"I will. Thank you."

"I'll try to find you later," the nurse whispered so quietly Emily barely heard.

Something hard, made of metal, was pressed to her hand. It had to be a weapon of some sort from the nurse.

The door opened again and footsteps grew distant.

Standing, Emily leaned against Luke for support and took a few tentative steps.

"I gotcha. Don't worry. I won't let you fall," he said.

She wanted to warn Luke. The nurse wouldn't have given her a weapon unless she'd wanted Emily to be able to defend herself. The hospital had been informed about the need for tight security. This instrument was more than a warning.

"Ready, ma'am?" the officer asked.

"Yes." How could she get the message to Luke without broadcasting it?

"Then, follow me."

An occasional beam of light could be seen in front of them as they followed behind the officer.

Emily tugged at Luke's sleeve. He squeezed her arm in response. Good, he knew she wanted to communicate something to him. She placed the metal object in his hand. He took it, squeezed again.

The floor was calm. Too quiet. Where were the other patients? Nurses? How would Reed know where they'd been moved? She remembered Luke had sent a text to his brother earlier.

Fear of not knowing where Reed was or when he'd return sent icy chills down her back. And where did these guys plan to take her? Hadn't she overhead Reed telling his brother that they couldn't trust anyone?

At least she'd had a chance to rest. Her knees were less wobbly with every step. She was gaining her bearings. She'd be ready to fight. *Might have to be.*

The officer turned right, his flashlight illuminating a long hallway.

Luke urged her to veer left. Almost the second he dropped her hand, she heard a shuffle. Then a quiet thud. She couldn't yell for help or she'd alert everyone. She said a silent protection prayer instead.

When a hand gripped her arm, she bit down a yelp.

"It's me," Luke whispered, guiding her through the hallway in the dark.

Walking proved challenging, let alone navigating through the blackness all around them.

A little piece of her feared she'd never see Reed again. But now, all she could focus on was getting out of the building alive.

What if they didn't make it? Outside had more men, more danger, more risk. Even if they hid, and gave Reed a road map to find them, how would he get through?

A wave of hopelessness washed over her as pain ripped through her thighs. Moving hurt.

Commotion from behind caused her heart to skip a beat. She heard at least three voices firing words in Spanish.

"I don't know what happened. They were behind me one second, the next I was on the floor." The voice was familiar, the police officer.

If Dueño had locals in his pocket, how would she and Luke make it out of this building alive? The irony of being killed in a hospital where people were brought back from the jaws of death on a daily basis hit her hard. Who would take care of her mother when she needed help? What about her other siblings? Would anyone other than her boss even know she'd died? Would anyone care?

Jared would notice only if she didn't show for work Monday. Her mortgage company would figure out she wasn't keeping up with her payments after a month or two. Eventually, they'd foreclose. At least she existed on paper.

But would anyone *really* know she was gone? Would anyone miss her?

Suddenly, for the first time in her life, she felt an overwhelming urge to be with someone who cared, with Reed.

The probability he would be able to find them was low. Sure, they could text their location, but that didn't mean he'd get through the militia waiting in the parking lot or the hallway.

Luke stopped and turned, pausing for a moment. Then a door opened and he guided her inside to a corner where she eased down. Pain shot through her thighs. The room had to be small because she'd taken only a couple of steps. A supply room?

The door closed.

"We can hide here for a little while," Luke said. His phone appeared. He covered the screen with one hand, allowing enough light to figure out where they were and thumbed a text with the other.

"Where are we? Don't they lock these doors?" Her guess of being in a supply room was dead-on.

"Supply closet. The nurse handed me the key. I'm guessing she knew what was going on."

"Explains why she gave me the piece of metal, whatever that was."

"She tipped me off that the officer wasn't there to help. Came in handy when I subdued him."

"How so? I didn't see a thing."

"She whispered when she walked past me."

"I heard the officer's voice back there. I'm guessing he'll live."

"A bullet would've made too much noise." The calm practicality in his voice when talking about killing someone was a stark reminder she wasn't remotely connected to the world she knew or understood anymore.

The snick of a lock cut through the quiet. Luke squeezed her arm and then let go, presumably to ready his weapon.

"Don't shoot. It's me. I was your floor nurse."

"How did you get in? I thought you gave Luke your key," Emily said.

"I'm the floor supervisor. I have a spare. Besides, when I noticed the men talking to the officer, I knew something was suspicious."

"Ever think about changing professions?" Luke asked. "You'd make a great cop."

"I'm addicted to all those crime shows on TV." She snickered quietly then suppressed it. "Figured you might need some help."

"Believe me, it's appreciated. And, believe me, I'm glad you're on my side."

"I hoped I'd find you in here. An officer pulled me away as soon as you left the room. I barely got away. Since I know the floor plan of the hospital, I had an advantage."

"I'm good there, too. Memorized it on the way in." His low voice didn't rumble the way his brother's did. Nor did it have the same effect on Emily.

There was something special about Reed Campbell. Being with him made her feel different in ways she couldn't begin to explain, let alone understand.

Would she live long enough to find out where it might go?

REED GRABBED AN extra Kevlar vest and told Stephen to take it. "My brother has the witness in a supply room on the sixth floor. He thinks they're safe. For now."

"No one knows what I look like. I can go first. Blaze a trail."

"On my last count, there were half a dozen men on the perimeter. That number could be double by now," Reed said flatly.

"How long have you been gone?"

"Hour and a half, max."

"Hopefully, the numbers haven't changed much."

The picture of Stephen's wife holding his baby popped into Reed's thoughts. All he had to worry about was himself. He didn't have a wife and child depending on him to come home every night. If anything happened to Reed, of course his family would miss him, but that wasn't the same thing by a long shot. Leslie had begged him to think about changing professions once they were married. And Reed had been dumb enough to consider it. "On second thought, this might be too dangerous. You stay here. I'll call if I need backup."

Stephen muttered the same curse word Reed had thought a second earlier. "This is my job. I do this for a living. What's the big deal?"

"I can think of two good reasons not to send you into what might be a death trap."

"Kiera knows who I am," he said, indignant.

"I don't know. It's risky. Even if I can breach the building, I have no idea what's waiting for me once I make it to the sixth floor. These guys are no joke, either. They probably have more guns than we do."

"Are you saying this mission is too dangerous for me, but the jobs we go out and do every single day aren't? That working for Border Patrol is a walk in the park?" Stephen issued a disgusted grunt as he shot daggers with his glare.

"It does seem ridiculous when you put it like that. You ever think about quitting? About getting a nine-to-five so you can watch your kid grow up?" Reed ran through a few best-case scenarios in his mind as they talked.

"My son is fine. I have every plan to be right there alongside my wife to see him off to college and beyond, but this is what I do. It's who I am. If my wife doesn't have a problem with it, then you sure as hell shouldn't."

Good point. "She never asks you to quit?"

"Why would she? She knew who I was when she married me." The look of disgust widened with his eyes.

Shock didn't begin to cover Reed's reaction. Everything Stephen had said was absolute truth, but Leslie had seen things very differently. She'd begged Reed to reconsider his line of work. Even said she didn't think they could have children as long as he was an agent. Her internet search hadn't done him any favors, either.

Yes, Border Patrol agents had the most dangerous jobs in law enforcement. Reed had calculated the risk when he took the job and had decided he could live with the odds. If he'd gone into Special Forces operations, the danger would've been greater. He figured most women would react the way Leslie had, so he gave up on getting serious for a while.

Good thing most women weren't like Leslie. They probably didn't cheat, either.

Reed put his hands up in the universal sign of surrender. "Sorry. I got no problem standing behind you, next to you, in front of you, whatever. I just don't want to go to sleep at night for the rest of my life with your kid's face being the last thing I remember."

Stephen issued a grunt. "You have a better chance of getting shot than I do. These ass-hats aren't even looking for me."

"True. If you're good with the risk, then I am, too. Besides, I need your help." Reed pulled into the gas station across the street from the hospital and cut his lights. He studied the building. It was the middle of the night, so it was unlikely there would be a shift change. The cafeteria wouldn't be open, either. No way to slip in unnoticed there. Security would be tight, as well. Then there were corrupt local police to deal with if he and Stephen got inside. The sixth floor would be crawling with Dueño's men. "You got any binoculars in your pack?"

"Yeah. Night vision." He pulled his gym bag from the backseat, dug around in it and produced a pair.

Reed surveyed the parking lot. Dueño's men had to be swarmed inside because there were only two left outside. From the looks of things, getting inside the building wasn't going to be the problem. Once there, Reed figured they'd be up against a wall. Almost all of Dueño's men were most likely on the sixth floor—which was the same place Luke and Emily were.

The need to see Emily, to make sure she was okay, seeded deep in the pit of his stomach. A primal instinct to protect her gripped him. Strange that they'd only just met.

After his relationship with Leslie, Reed Campbell

didn't *do* feelings while working this job. Leslie had taught him not to expect more than a casual relationship. He'd convinced himself that one day the adrenaline would no longer be enough to satisfy him and he'd get tired of the job or burned out on the demands. When that happened, he could change careers and could settle down. Having both at the same time seemed as out of reach as finding Cal and bringing him to justice.

Even more surprising was a woman who got it, who supported her husband and his career. Surely, Kiera was one of a kind.

Either way, Emily's case was about to get a lot more interesting. "You have a pen and paper in the bag?"

"Sure. Hang on." Stephen produced the items.

Reed sketched the hospital's layout. It was shaped like a T, the front doors being at the intersection. "Emily's room is here on the sixth so the supply closet must be nearby." He circled a spot on the map he'd drawn to the left of where the letter T most intersected. "So, there are two out here that we know of. No big deal there. Inside, there are at least four armed men, plus whoever else has joined the party that we don't know about. Another pair of local officers who might be dirty round out the guest list. Did I forget anyone?"

"That about sums it up based on what you've said so far. On our side, we have the two of us and your brother who's in the FBI, and he's with the witness?"

"You good with that?"

"I've worked in worse situations," Stephen said honestly.

Having backup was nice. Different. In their line of work, they didn't get that luxury most of the time. Only problem was they hadn't worked together before. Teams required teamwork, and that required people who knew the ins and outs of how each other worked. "No matter what we find in there, I'll always go right."

"Good. I like taking the left side. It's natural for me." Stephen pulled a Kevlar vest from his pack. "Looks like I'll need this."

"Ready?" Reed looked into Stephen's eyes, really looked, for any signs of hesitation.

The slightest delay in judgment and they'd both be dead. And that was most likely why Reed didn't choose a job in law enforcement working with a partner. He'd stand side by side with either of his brothers any day. But his future in another man's hands? *Not his warm-and-fuzzy.*

The black sky was dotted with tiny bursts of light. Highway noise pierced the otherwise quiet night.

Pitch-black covered the sixth floor. The rest of the hospital had lights.

Head down, gun palmed, Reed stalked toward the white building. He stopped at the edge of the parking lot, near the ER. A distraction would be nice right now, but Reed had never been able to rely on luck. Figured it was the reason he'd learned to work hard instead.

Tightening his grip on the butt of his Glock, he tucked his chin to his chest and quickened his stride toward the entrance. Stephen stayed back until Reed reached the glass doors. He took a position inside the building, and surveyed the lot. His buddy easily made it inside. It was all too easy. Then again, these guys were focused on Emily and they must believe they had her right where they wanted her. Plus, Luke could pass for Reed to the untrained eye.

The fact security was loose in the lot most likely meant

these jerks figured they had who they wanted trapped upstairs. It also indicated the closer Reed got to Emily and Luke, the more men there'd be to get past.

"Which way?" Stephen asked, inclining his chin toward the elevator, then the stairs.

"Both make too much noise. Plus, the light will give us away."

Out of better options, Reed pitched toward the stairs with Stephen close behind.

Reed stopped on the fifth floor. The only distraction he could count on would be one he created himself. The nurses' station was quiet save for the click of fingers on a keyboard. The young nurse glanced up. "Can I help you?"

Reed pointed to the badge clipped to his waistband.

She nodded. "I need to talk to my supervisor."

"Understood." He located a fire extinguisher and slammed it into the glass, sounding the alarm.

"Sir, you can't do that." The nurse burst from her chair, shouting over the wail of alarms.

Reed and Stephen made a play for the stairs. Within two steps of freedom, the door blasted open and two men in security uniforms blocked the entry.

"Step aside. We work for Border Patrol and we need to gain access to the stairwell." He motioned toward his badge.

The sound of feet shuffling in the stairwell broke through the noise as security stepped aside and allowed Reed through.

A gunshot split the air.

Must have come from behind.

"You good?" Reed asked.

"Yeah. You?"

A quick scan revealed Reed had not been hit. "Fine."

He took the stairs three at a clip. The stairwell would be full of people in another few seconds. Doors already opened and closed on lower levels. Panicked voices echoed.

If Reed were lucky, the men would scatter, too. He almost laughed out loud. *Luck?* Right. Go with that, he thought wryly. His best-case scenario? The commotion would give Luke a chance to escape with Emily.

Reed trusted his brother. So, why did he want to be the one to take Emily to safety?

Chapter Nine

Alarms pierced through the supply closet. Emily didn't dare cover her ears for fear she'd miss out on critical instructions.

"We need to move. Can you stand up?" Luke offered a hand.

"I'm good." She wouldn't tell him how much her body ached already.

"She needs to take it easy," the nurse said. "Think you can get us off this floor?"

"I have to," Luke said.

"Then I can get us out of here safely."

"How do we know Reed's okay?" Thirty minutes had passed since Emily had watched Luke text his brother with no response.

"Because of that sound." He motioned toward the air.

Reed had set off the fire alarm? She didn't want to acknowledge the relief flooding her, giving her the extra will to push forward.

"I'll go first. Squeeze my arm if you get in trouble," Luke whispered over the noise.

"Okay."

The door creaked open. Emily's breath caught in her

throat. She eased a few steps forward, one hand on the nurse and the other on Luke.

Even in the dark, she could see the silhouette of two men moving toward them. Her eyes had somewhat adjusted. She squeezed Luke's shoulder.

As the pair neared, she could make out a face. Reed's.

Ignoring the shivers running up her arms, she reached for him.

"We managed to scatter them, but not for long," he said. The rich timbre of his voice settled over her as he wrapped an arm around her waist for support.

He nodded toward his brother and took more of her weight as the nurse led them through a couple of back rooms and into a staff elevator.

"You're bleeding. What happened?" Emily touched the soaked spot on his sleeve.

"It's not from me." Reed double-checked himself as though unsure.

"Then who?" Emily asked.

Reed's gaze shot straight to the friend he'd brought with him. "They got you?"

"It's nothing." He lifted his shirt on his left side. "Just a flesh wound."

"Dammit, it's more than that." In a razor-sharp tone, he muttered the same curse Emily thought.

"Don't worry. I can take care of him. You two need to get out of here." The nurse pulled off her scrubs and handed her top to Emily. "Put this on."

"I can't leave my buddy." The anguish in his voice softened the earlier tension.

"You don't have a choice. Take her with you. I'll stay with him," Luke said.

"I—"

"When that door opens, I want both of you the hell out of here. We'll catch up as soon as…" His gaze searched Reed's friend.

"Stephen—"

"I'll catch up as soon as he's square," Luke finished. "I won't let anything else happen to him, I swear."

Emily eased the scrubs over her head with Reed's help. The tenderness in his touch warmed her. She tried her best to ignore it, considering they were about to face a parking lot full of Dueño's men—men who were trying to kill her.

"They'll be watching for her. All the exits will be covered," Reed said.

"Exactly why I'll pretend to be her. I'll hold on to these two and fake a limp," the nurse said.

Emily didn't want to put others in jeopardy for her sake. She remembered the nurse talking about her younger brother on his freshman spring break trip to Matamoros, Mexico, being ritualistically killed and buried. The emotion had still been raw in her voice after three years. Was that the reason she was intent on helping? "I still don't think this is a good idea."

The statement was met with nods of agreement from the men in the elevator.

"I understand why you have hesitations. I do. Seems like I'm putting myself out there for strangers. But I need to do this for Brian. I don't expect you to understand. Please don't stop me." The determination in her tone caused Emily to cave.

"These aren't the same men," Emily protested, but she already knew she'd lost the battle. Because she did understand the need to make things right for something in the past.

"They are in a sense. Those men are cut from the same cloth. They hurt innocent people and destroy lives." She paused a beat. "It's too late for me to help my brother, but I can help you. Don't take that away from me."

The moment of silence in the elevator said no one would argue.

Reed slipped off his Kevlar vest and placed it on the nurse before turning to Emily. The brilliance in his brown eyes pierced through her. "Think you can walk on your own through the parking lot?"

"I'll make it." She ignored the shivers trailing up her spine.

Reed bear-hugged his brother and then Stephen before turning to the nurse. "I'd be even more in your debt if you'll promise to take good care of this guy once you get out of here."

If the nurse didn't, Emily knew without a doubt that Reed wouldn't be willing to walk away. He'd take Stephen with him.

An emotion Emily couldn't quite pinpoint hit her fast and hard. She'd never known that kind of loyalty before. At the House, people would drop in and out based on their own needs. No one seemed concerned with the children other than making sure they had food and clothing. Schedules made people slaves, the guy in charge had said, so there was no routine.

Homeschooling had been inconsistent, too. In addition to a couple of workbooks, the children had been given homemade pamphlets on the importance of peace and love. Emily appreciated both and yet there was no real love at the House. No one had been there at the end of the day to tuck her into bed and make her feel secure as her father had when she was little. No one had taken her to the playground to be with other kids, since leaving the compound was forbidden. No one had nursed her cuts and bruises or held her while she cried herself to sleep. All of which had happened too often in the House, and especially in the early years when she was trying to adjust to her new life.

Busying herself with the little kids had been a much-needed de-stressor. Work had a way of providing a welcomed distraction. Was she still hiding behind hers?

The elevator dinged, indicating they'd reached the bottom floor. Tension billowed out as the doors opened.

Reed took Emily's hand, palm to palm, as they stepped out of the elevator. "Ready?"

"I hope." Contact with Reed seemed to shrink the world to the two of them. Emily prayed she'd be prepared for whatever waited ahead, in her immediate future and beyond.

SCRUBS MADE QUITE a difference in helping Emily blend in. They did nothing to help her walk faster. She had to be in severe pain to stand straight, let alone move. Frustration nipped at Reed.

He had two choices if he wanted to move faster: leave Emily alone for a few minutes in the parking lot to bring the truck to her, or carry her. Leaving her unguarded even for a second wasn't a real consideration, which left carrying her. There was no doubt he could easily hoist her over his shoulder. But could he pick her up and get her to the truck without drawing attention? At least the false alarm had brought people out of the hospital. Standing around in small groups, they provided a buffer between Emily and him and Dueño's men.

Stephen had a bullet scrape to prove how far they'd go to stop them.

A fresh wave of guilt followed by red-hot anger pulsed through him at letting his buddy get shot. Reed would have to face Kiera and her baby to explain and apologize for what had happed. No way would he sleep at night otherwise.

Worrying about a wife and child, even Stephen's, was a distraction Reed couldn't afford when his mind needed to be sharp. Maybe Leslie had been right. A man in this job had no right to put his wife and child through the pain of not knowing if he'd be coming home. Or, if he did, what kind of shape he'd be in. And yet, a little piece of him wanted to believe things would be different if Emily was the one he'd be coming home to.

Small crowds stood, facing the building. Others walked slowly to their vehicles, checking back often. They'd hide Emily's pace as long as Reed mimicked them. He did.

"Slow and steady. Take your time." The feel of her hand in his warmed him in places he shouldn't allow. And yet, it felt so natural to touch her.

The kiss they'd shared earlier wasn't helping his concentration, either.

Distractions he couldn't afford fired all around him when she was this close. Being away from her was even worse.

They made it to the edge of the lot without drawing attention.

He and Emily were safe for now. Part of him was relieved beyond measure. The other part didn't like putting his friend and brother in harm's way.

Once clear of the lot, he'd check in with his brother

while he located a decent hotel. Emily needed a good night of sleep.

Reed wrapped his arm around her waist and took most of her weight. "I can carry you if it'll help."

"We made it this far. I can go a few more yards. I just hope they're all right."

"As soon as they realize they're after the wrong people, they'll circle back to the hospital." He helped her into the truck.

"I hope we're long gone before that happens," she said through a yawn, the medicine obviously doing its job.

"I plan to be. Try to get some rest." He nodded toward his shoulder.

"I doubt I can after all that." She slid across the seat as he belted himself, and leaned against him.

"Close your eyes. You might be surprised at how tired you are." He started the engine and eased the truck onto the highway.

"How far away is the place we're staying?"

"About twenty minutes up the road."

"Now that you mention it, I could use a bed to stretch out on even if I don't sleep."

Sleep was about the last thing Reed could imagine with Emily curled up next to him. He was in dangerous emotional territory with her because he could imagine sleeping next to her, or better yet not sleeping, for the foreseeable future. "You're brave. I'm proud of what you did back there."

She smiled one of her light-the-sky-with-brilliance smiles.

Not five minutes into the drive she drifted off to sleep, her soft, even breathing not more than a whisper in his ear.

Her being with him was the only thing that made sense.

And yet, what did he really know about her?

They'd barely met, he reminded himself for the twentieth time as he looked out at the long stretch of highway in front of him. And yet, he couldn't deny the familiarity she'd talked about earlier—closeness he felt just as strongly as she did even if he wasn't quite ready to acknowledge it as special.

It was special.

The sign for his exit came up. Reed put on his blinker and changed lanes. The movement caused Emily to stir. He stilled as he took the off-ramp, afraid to move too much so he wouldn't hurt her. She burrowed into his side and mewled softly.

Damn, that sound was the sexiest thing he'd heard in a very long time, which pretty much proved the well had been bone-dry for him. What did it say about him that every time she was near his thoughts were inappropriate?

She sat up straight and rubbed her eyes, blinking against the sudden light from the highway. "Are we there?"

"Yes." He heard how thick and raspy his own voice had become. A ride in a truck shouldn't qualify as the sexiest moment of his year. So far, it did.

Reed vowed to change that once this case was over.

"A bed sounds amazing right now."

"Stay here while I grab a key from the hotel desk."

Within minutes, he returned and helped her inside.

Standing in front of the door, he jammed the keycard inside the slip. His effort was met with a red light. He muttered a curse, and then an apology. A couple of more tries yielded the same result.

"I think you have to pull out faster."

Reed wasn't about to touch that statement. "Would you like to try? I don't seem to have the right touch."

"Sure," she said with a coy smile.

He moved to the side and allowed her access. The damn thing lit green before she slid the card out.

"See how it's done?"

Suppressing a grin, he helped her inside, where a plush king-size bed filled the room.

"What's that smile all about?"

"Not going there." He chuckled about all the other things he'd like her to show him. Joking was his way of easing the tension from what had happened earlier.

He immediately texted Luke to get a read on Stephen's condition.

With Luke behind the wheel, they'd gotten rid of the men who'd chased them. Stephen was doing fine.

Relief flooded Reed. He turned to Emily, who was studying his expression.

"Did you get good news?"

"Stephen's grumbling about not needing a nurse, but he's cooperating. And he'll be fine. He and Luke are going to bunk at the nurse's place tonight."

"She's a good woman. We wouldn't have survived without her."

"Agreed. On both counts." He stopped in front of the bathroom door. "You want me to run a bath for you?"

"The nurse helped me shower at the hospital. I'm all clean."

There was an image Reed didn't need in his head. Plus, the smell of flowery soap was still all over her. He tried to shake it off. Didn't help. He settled her onto the bed, trying to suppress the smirk stuck to his lips.

"Okay, what's going on?"

"Nothing I can talk about."

"Why not?" Her gaze moved from his eyes to his lips, where it lingered, then down his body.

Scratch what he'd thought a little while ago. That was the sexiest thing to happen to him in the past year. "I need a shower."

"Want some help?" she teased.

"Normally I'd take you up on that." He stalked across the room, pausing at the door to the bathroom.

"I was kidding. No man on earth would want to shower with me the way I must look."

He moved to the bed and leaned over her, stopping a fraction of an inch before their lips touched. "Why not? Most men I know appreciate a beautiful woman."

Those stunning hazel eyes of hers darkened. Being this close was probably a bad idea. Even if she wasn't his witness, she was injured. No way could they do anything in her condition.

Autopilot had kicked in, and Reed couldn't stop himself from reaching out to touch her face. He ran his finger gently along the line of her jaw, and then her lips.

Her hands came up around his neck, and her fingers tunneled into his hair.

Kissing her would be another bad idea, but that knowledge didn't stop him, either.

Softly, he pressed his lips to hers, careful not to hurt her. She tasted sweet and hot, and a little like peppermint, most likely a remnant of brushing her teeth at the hospital. But mostly, she tasted forbidden. A random thought breezed through that he shouldn't be doing this. His sense of right and wrong should have him pulling away. Where was his self-discipline?

Tell that to his stiff length.

Better judgment finally won out when he realized this was about as smart as jabbing his hand into a pot of hot oil. Even if she wasn't his witness, they couldn't finish.

Reed pulled back. The look of surprise in her eyes caused his resolve to falter. "I can't keep going. Not comfortably."

"Oh." She sounded confused.

"Believe me. I want to." How should he put this? It wasn't his nature to be delicate.

"Oh?"

"I don't want to risk anything with your injuries."

The look in her eyes, the hurt, almost had him changing his mind. She looked away. "I understand. It's probably for the best."

"Can I take a rain check?"

"You don't have to say that to make me feel better. I kissed you in the hospital. Not the other way around. I understand that you're not attracted to me."

That's what she thought? "Do you want to know what you do to me?"

She didn't respond.

"I'm going in the other room to take a shower and quite possibly take matters into my own hands because I want you so badly right now, it's painful." He glanced down at his straining zipper.

She did, too.

"Oh. Sorry about that." Her cheeks flushed six shades past red, causing his heart to stir and bringing an amber glow to her already bright face.

"Don't be embarrassed. I'm not. One thing you can count on from me is honesty. If we're going to spend time together, I expect the same."

He was rewarded with a warm smile. Emily was outdoors, warmth and open skies with a sexual twist. And as long as she was willing, he had every intention of showing her just how desirable she was when he could be absolutely sure he wouldn't be hurting her in the process.

"Honesty is a good thing," she finally said. She winked, and it made her eyes glitter. "And as long as we're being honest, I can help you with that little problem in the shower."

"One time won't be enough for me." He stood and walked toward the bathroom, stopping at the door. "And it's not little."

Chapter Ten

Reed finished drying himself, brushed his teeth and slipped into a clean pair of boxers. He climbed under the covers on the opposite side of the bed so he wouldn't wake Emily. She'd left one of the bedside table lamps on, and it cast a warm glow over the room. He doubted he'd be able to grab any shut-eye for himself, but she needed her rest.

As he settled in for a night of nonsleep, she shifted and threw her leg over his. His pulse kicked up a notch or two. Heck, it raised more than he wanted to admit.

Yeah, he definitely wouldn't be getting any sleep now. Not with her silky warm skin pressed to his. How could his thigh touching hers be so damn sexy?

She reached across his bare chest, only a thin piece of cotton stopping her firm breast from touching his bare skin. He groaned. It was going to be a long night.

He was aroused. She was fast asleep. Even if she was wide awake, it didn't change the fact that she was badly injured.

That she'd taken off everything but a T-shirt and underwear brought his erection back to life with a vengeance.

His whole body stiffened. He didn't want to move for fear he'd hurt her.

And then he felt her hands moving over his chest.

"You can't break me," she whispered, and her voice slid over him, warming him. Her hands moved across his chest, stopping at the dark patch of hair in the center.

He was afraid he'd do just that. Hurt her. So he wouldn't force anything. Her mouth found his, and her tongue slid inside.

His hands moved, too, with gentle caresses as he smoothed his palm across the silken skin of her stomach.

She moaned as he cupped her breast. She carefully repositioned, a reminder they needed to take it slow, and his sex pressed to her stomach.

Last thing Reed needed to think about just now was her light purple panties. He already knew they were silk. With an image like that and her curled against him, things would end before they even started. She seemed to want this every bit as much as he did. Used to being in charge in bed, he'd have to remember to let her be in control.

Lying side by side, Reed slowly lifted her shirt as he bent down then slicked his tongue over her nipple. It hardened to a peak. The soft mewling sound she made stiffened his length. Much more of this and he'd be done right then and there. Her back arched then the sound she made next stopped him in his tracks.

"Are you okay?"

"Y-es." The way she drew out the word told him she wasn't convinced.

There was a point of no return when it came to foreplay, and a breast in his mouth had always been the line for him. They'd careened sideways and beyond as far as Reed was concerned, so stopping now would prove even more difficult. Except when it came to pain. No way could he feel good about having sex if it hurt his partner in any way. And the painful groan that had just passed her lips had the effect of a bucket of cold water being poured over him.

"We can't do this." He gently extracted himself from in between her thighs because one wriggle of those taut hips and he'd be in trouble again.

She didn't put up an argument this time.

Reed settled onto his back as she curled around his left side. "Tell me where it hurts."

"This position is good. The other way only hurt when I moved." She laughed. It was the kind of laugh that promised bright sunshine and blue skies.

He leaned over and pressed a kiss to her forehead.

"You make me happy," she said in a sexy, sleepy voice.

Reed should be coming up with a strategy for how they were going to catch the guys chasing them instead of feeling perfectly contended to lie in bed with Emily in his arms. But that's exactly what was happening. And he wished they could stay there for a while. Except that wasn't an option. They'd have to leave first thing in the morning. "Me, too, sweetheart. Think you can get some rest? We have a long day ahead tomorrow."

She blinked up at him with those pure, honest hazel eyes. "What will you do if I go to sleep?"

"Come up with a plan."

"I want to help."

"The best thing you can do for either of us is rest."

It didn't take fifteen minutes for the medicine to overtake her willpower and for her to fall asleep again.

Reed wasn't so lucky. He ran through several scenarios, none of which gave him a warm-and-fuzzy feeling. Then there was the thought of visiting Stephen's wife. Why did it weigh so heavily on Reed's conscience?

A text message from Luke had confirmed that Stephen was fine. His injury wasn't more than a big scrape, a flesh wound. The trio had made it out of the parking lot without too much trouble as had Reed and Emily. His assumption that the men who'd followed them would give up after they realized they were following the wrong people had turned out to be true.

Then there was the issue of Emily to think about. Her warmth as she pressed against him while she slept. He could get used to this.

EMILY STRETCHED AND blinked her eyes open to a quiet room and an empty bed. The mattress was cold where Reed used to be.

Where was he?

Climbing out of the bed brought a few aches and stiff muscles to life. Surprisingly, some of her pain had subsided. She moved to the bathroom, brushed her teeth and dressed.

Back in the room, she noticed his keys and cell phone were missing. She prayed nothing had happened in the middle of the night to make him leave, such as getting a hot lead.

The thought of Reed being out there, alone, with Dueño's men surrounding him tightened a coil in her chest. Surely, he wouldn't go anywhere near them without someone to back him up.

Moving to the window to peek outside, she heard the snick of the lock and froze.

Reed shuffled in with company. She recognized his brother, who was following closely behind. He glanced at the bed with a raised eyebrow.

Emily let out the breath she'd been holding.

"I brought breakfast," Reed said with a forced smile. "How are you this morning?"

"Much better." She took the brown bag and inhaled the scent of breakfast tacos. "Smells amazing."

Reed slid his arm around her waist as he moved beside her. With his touch, heat fizzed through her body. Too bad they had company.

He helped her to the desk.

"Is something wrong? What happened?" Emily tried to brace herself for more bad news. "Is Stephen okay?"

"Yeah. He'll be fine. The nurse bandaged him up at her place last night."

"That where you two spent the night?" She picked a breakfast taco out of the bag and unwrapped it, keeping one eye on Reed.

"Yeah. Her house isn't far from here. She gave Stephen a ride home this morning, so I asked Reed to pick me up."

She set her breakfast taco down and turned to Reed. "Then what's going on?"

"Luke has to get back to North Texas for a case he's working on. He'll take us to a car my boss has stashed for us and then you and I will have to take it from there." Reed took a breakfast taco and then handed the bag to his brother.

The thought of leaving the relative safety and comfort of the hotel held little appeal. However, staying meant they couldn't follow leads. Besides, wasn't there a saying about sitting ducks? It was probably better to keep on the move. "When do we head out?"

"After we eat," Reed said, taking a seat next to her.

Emily finished her food and then excused herself to the bathroom, stopping in front of the mirror. Even as a teenager, she'd resisted the urge to go blonde. Now she was living proof it was a bad idea. With her hazel eyes, the lighter shade washed her out. Grateful to have real clothing and a rubber band, she pulled her hair up in a ponytail and washed her face. Some of the swelling had gone down, and her bruises were already yellowing. The sunburn had improved dramatically. The peeling was easing up, too.

Her eyes had seen better days, and she wished she had makeup, but other than that she figured nothing had happened that would leave a permanent mark so far.

Circumstances weren't good. Thinking about being broke and totally dependent on someone else didn't sit well. Even though Reed had proved he could be trusted. He'd kept by her side and put his own life on the line to save her, which wasn't the same as needing him more than she needed air.

If men hadn't started shooting at them, would Reed have hauled her in and walked away, though?

None of that mattered now. Second-guessing the situation wouldn't help. Reed Campbell was a good man who was doing what he believed to be the right thing. She respected him for it.

Even so, Emily wanted her own money, her own car and her own clothes. The only way to get those things was to convince Reed to take her to her town house, which was risky.

Looking at her reflection, it was readily apparent she wouldn't get by on her good looks. She almost laughed out loud. How could anyone get past her current condition? And hadn't Reed seemed to look past all that and see her from the inside?

Hadn't he said that they felt close because they'd survived a near-death experience? And that was most likely true because she'd never believed in love at first sight.

Even if she did, no way would she trust it. Relationships grew by getting to know someone. Sure, what she felt for him was different. Special, even. But real love? Her heart said it was possible, but her mind shut down the thought.

Rather than jump into that sinkhole feetfirst, Emily decided to hold whatever else she felt at bay. Yes, she was physically attracted to Reed. There was no denying it, especially with how right she felt in his arms. Crazier still, he seemed to return the sentiment.

She'd be smart to exercise caution, and not get too caught up in emotions that could change in an instant.

Her mom had loved her dad with everything inside her. Look what had happened there. Emily had trusted her father. Look where that had gotten her. She'd tried to save her mother with similar results.

And the last serious relationship she'd gotten involved in? The jerk turned out to be married with kids. Emily had spent last year's vacation curled in a ball on her bed, crying. She'd pretty much acquiesced to the idea that even though her heart wanted things normal people had—white-picket fence, a husband, children—those "things" most likely weren't in the cards for her. She'd settled into the routine of work, free from distractions. With no real attachments, her weekends were free for overtime.

Even though it had been a year ago, being put in the role of other woman had been like a knife wound to her chest. Jack had said he respected her space and wanted to take it slow, for her sake. He was actually busy at his kids' soccer games and then date nights with his wife on the weekends.

Knowing Emily had done that to another woman, even if unintentionally, had left behind an invisible gash across her chest—a scar that might never heal.

Love hurt. Love was unfair. Love had consequences.

Was she falling in love with Reed? Whatever was happening, she'd never felt such an initial impact when she'd met someone before. It was like reentering the earth's atmosphere from space.

Since her heart wanted to plow full speed ahead, she would force some logic into the situation. When it came to Reed, caution was Emily's new best friend.

"Ready?" Reed called from the other room, forcing her attention out of her heavy thoughts.

"Might as well be." She took a last look in the mirror and followed them out the door.

They walked to the car with Reed in front and Luke behind her.

Luke took the driver's seat. Emily squeezed in the middle. Reed was to her right.

She reached for the seat belt and winced, pain shooting across her chest. Her bruised ribs had something to say about the movement.

"Here. Let me get that for you." Reed made a move to help.

"No, thanks. I can manage by myself." And she had every intention of keeping it that way.

Chapter Eleven

By the time they reached The Pelican, the doors had just opened for lunch. Reed shifted in his seat to get a better view, scanning the surrounding area on the two-lane highway. Palm trees lined the streets. Their relatively thin stalks made it difficult to hide behind, giving Reed a decent view of the scattered buildings next to open fields.

The lot to the restaurant was empty. Reed cracked the truck's window. The air outside had that heavy, middle-of-summer, salty-beach smell. They weren't close enough to the water to benefit from a cool ocean breeze. "The car should be parked around back if it hasn't been towed."

Gravel crunched underneath the tires as the truck eased through the parking lot and toward the twin Dumpsters behind the restaurant where a few cars were parked.

"I'll have to run inside to pick up the keys."

Luke backed the truck into a spot positioned in the corner so that they could see anyone coming from around the building. He shifted gears to Park, leaving the engine idling. "You want us to go in with you?"

"Nah. It's better if I go in alone. Fewer people will notice that way. You keep watch from here." Reed slid out of the truck and secured his cowboy hat. He fished his cell out of his pocket and held it up. "Let me know if anything looks suspicious."

"I'm on it."

Reed stuffed the cell in his front pocket, lowered the tip of his Stetson and tucked his gun in his holster. He took Emily's hand and squeezed. "You've been quiet for most of the ride. Are you hurting?"

"A little. Nothing I can't handle." She smiled but it didn't make her eyes sparkle like before when she'd looked at him.

He made a mental note to ask about that later, and turned to his brother. "I'm not out in two minutes, don't hesitate to come after me."

Luke nodded. "Grab that key and get your butt back here."

Reed's boots kicked up dust as he walked.

The hostess looked young, as if she might be home on summer break from college. She greeted him. "Table for one?"

"Men's room first?" He smiled, not really answering her question.

She pointed to where he already knew it was. He'd been in the restaurant once before with Gil.

This early, there were no other patrons. His boots scuffed along the sawdust-covered floors. Metal buckets filled with peanuts were being placed on the tables. A waiter was hovering next to a waitress as she filled an ice pail from the soda machine. Both were laughing. Judging by the way she flipped her hair and smiled, both were flirting, too.

Not much else was going on other than bottles of salt and pepper being filled and placed on tables. The usual prelunch-crowd preparations were being made.

Reed located the men's room and slipped inside, moving straight to the sink farthest from the urinals. He slid his hand under the porcelain rim and felt around for the key. There was nothing. He bent his knees and leaned back on his heels so he could visually scan underneath. Bingo. There it was. Reed palmed it, and headed out of the bathroom.

As he neared the front door, the hostess smiled. "Your table's ready."

"Change of plans." He smiled, and she blushed. Guess she was doing a little flirting herself. Normally, he'd enjoy the attention. It was barely a blip on his radar now, leaving him wondering if his lack of interest had something to do with his stress meter, or his growing attraction to Emily.

He fished his cell out of his pocket and hit Gil's name in the contacts. The call rolled into voice mail. Reed muttered a curse as he fired off a text, and moved toward his brother. Reed shrugged.

Luke kept visually sweeping the area as Emily slid out of the passenger side.

"Got it," Reed said.

Emily took the arm he offered.

Thoughts about her, how warm she felt curled up next to him last night, had no place distracting him. He helped her lean against the hood of the vehicle. He'd just pressed the unlock button when his phone rang.

Reed gripped the handle at the same time he heard a click from underneath the car. What would they have done? The car was there, so they must've wanted him to get inside.

Dropping to the dirt, he climbed around on all fours

until he saw it. Wires and metal were taped together to the underbelly of the car. A bomb. He'd most likely detonated it by lifting the handle. He needed to get Emily off the hood. "Get back in the truck."

"What's under there?" Her gaze widened.

"It's wired!" he shouted to Luke. Reed was to his feet and by Emily's side in two seconds, urging her forward. Not wanting to hurt her was outweighed by his fear of the bomb going off with both of them right there.

His brother said the same curse word Reed was thinking. As he rounded the side of the truck, time seemed to still. The explosion nearly burst his eardrums. The earth shook underneath his boots. The truck had shielded much of his body from shrapnel. He dropped to his knees, managing to maintain his hold on Emily. Her arms tightened around his neck and her head buried where his neck and shoulder met.

Luke was out of the truck, moving toward them. Reed had dropped his cell and so the connection with Gil had been lost. Without a doubt his boss would do everything in his power to protect Reed, so who the hell figured out where the car and key were? The only other person from the agency Reed had been in contact with was Stephen. No way could this have been Stephen's doing. He was clean. Besides, he didn't even know about the stashed car. Someone else had figured it out. But who?

Between Reed and Luke, they hoisted Emily onto the bench seat of the truck. If they'd been parked any closer to the car, Reed didn't want to think about what would've happened to them. Before he could finish asking Emily if she was okay, Luke had pulled a fire extinguisher from the back of his truck and blasted the cool foam toward the blaze.

"I'm okay. Just a little freaked out," Emily said. Her bravery shouldn't make him proud. It did.

"I've already notified the police. We'll need to stick around long enough to give a statement. Then we'll head back to Dallas." Luke maneuvered his jaw as though he were trying to pop the pressure in his ears, and tossed the empty canister into the Dumpster.

Ringing noises blocked most of Reed's hearing. "Can you set us up with a place to stay?"

"Sure thing. How about Gran's?"

"Thought about Creek Bend. Might be a good option given the circumstances."

"We can use my car if you'll take us to my town house," Emily said. Her vacant expression indicated she was in shock.

Luke glanced from Emily to Reed. He nodded. "Might be a good idea to see if they've already been there."

"I guess we'll find out, won't we?" Reed shrugged.

"Want to send Nick over to check it out while we're on the way?"

"Good idea. I'd hate to lose more time, and these guys seem to be a step ahead so far." The tide needed to turn. Reed was getting a little tired of being on the wrong end of the wave.

"How will he get inside without a key?" Emily asked. The answer seemed to dawn on her when her eyes lit up and she said, "Oh. Right. Guess he doesn't exactly need to use the door. Tell him my alarm code is six-one-five-three. There's a small window in the laundry room toward the back. It'll be easy to break in and slip through it. There's a huge shrub in front of it. That window is the reason I put in an alarm in the first place."

Luke's cell was already out before she finished her sentence.

A squad car roared into the lot, kicking up dust and gravel.

Another cop on Dueño's payroll? The thought crossed Reed's mind. Luke's clenched jaw said he feared the same. But they both knew logic dictated only one or two cops would be dirty on any given police force, so the odds were in Luke and Reed's favor. On the off chance the guy didn't walk on the right side of the law, the crowd that had gathered would deter him from doing anything stupid.

Cell phones were out recording the damage, which could bring on more trouble for him and Emily. Social media would soon light up with the account, and the chances of Dueño's men pinpointing Emily at this location grew by the second. Reed turned to where Emily sat in the truck. "Lie down and stay low until we get out of here."

That was the first thing on his agenda.

Luke instinctively moved in between the gathering crowd and Emily, blocking everyone's line of sight and therefore their ability to snap a picture of her.

Reed, keeping his hands out in the open in plain sight, stopped midway between the truck and the officer. The cops around here didn't see much gunfire, which made them itchy, a threat. They constantly prepared for the one-off chance something could go wrong. The nervous twitch this guy had was his biggest tell.

"My name's Reed Campbell and I work for Homeland Security in the US Border Patrol Division."

"Keep your hands where I can see them." The guy inched forward.

Reed kept his high, visible. "My badge is attached to my belt on my left hip."

"Stay right there. Whoever's in the truck, put your hands up and come out." The high pitch wasn't good.

Emily raised her hands and kept her head low.

"Sir, if you make her come out of that truck, you'll be putting her life in danger." Reed motioned toward the sea of cell phones recording the event.

The officer shouted at the crowd to put their phones away or be arrested.

"Your boss should have gotten a call from mine," Reed said.

The cop's radio squawked. He leaned his chin to the left side and spoke quietly. His tense shoulders relaxed, and he lowered his weapon. "My supervisor confirmed your identity, Agent Campbell. Sorry about before."

Reed shook the outstretched hand in front of him. "Not a problem. The woman in the truck is my witness. This is my brother Luke. He's FBI."

The officer's eyes lit up as he shook Luke's hand. Reed choked down a laugh. He'd be hearing about how the FBI was better than Border Patrol on the way to Plano for sure because of that one.

Firemen had arrived and were checking the scene. Luke had already pulled a fire extinguisher from the truck and put out the fire. Reed finished giving the officer his statement. He shook Luke's hand rather enthusiastically one more time before clearing a path for them so they could leave.

When they settled into the truck, Emily leaned her head on Reed's shoulder and closed her eyes.

They hadn't gone five miles before Luke fired the

first barb. "Told you the FBI is better. Take the cop, for instance. Did you see his reaction—"

"We both know more agents are killed in my line of work than yours," Reed shot back, grateful for a light-hearted distraction to ease the tension in the cab. "And I think we also know the officer had a professional crush on you."

"I can't help it if I'm good-looking, too," Luke said with his usual flicker of a smile. "And you're still there because?"

The circumstances might not be ideal, but Luke cracking jokes and smiling was a good thing. He'd gone far too long after his stint in the military in solitude, refusing to talk to anyone. Since reuniting with his ex-wife, signs of the old Luke were coming back. "We both know Julie's going to make you quit after the wedding."

"Look, baby bro, there's something I've been meaning to tell you." Luke's serious expression jumped Reed's heart rate up a few notches.

"Don't leave me hanging. Get on with it."

"Julie and I, well, since this wasn't our first time, we decided not to wait. We got married last weekend."

"And you didn't tell me?" Reed feigned disgust. In truth, he couldn't be happier for his brother.

"We didn't let anyone in on it. Headed over to the justice of the peace's office after thinking about everything. It's not like it was our first go, so we didn't want to make a big production. Seemed to make more sense to keep it about us."

Reed belted out a laugh.

"What's so funny about me getting married to my wife?"

"Well, that for starters."

Luke shook his head and chuckled. "Okay, you got me. That sounds messed up."

"You think?"

His brother's laugh rolled out a little harder this time. "Yeah, it's a lot screwed up. But we never should've divorced in the first place."

"That's the smartest thing you've said today." Reed thought for a second. Oh, this was about to get really good. "Holy crap. You said you haven't told anyone else yet?"

"No." The problem with that word seemed to occur to Luke a second after it left his mouth. "That's not going to go down well, is it?"

"Gran will not be amused."

"Maybe you should tell her. You know, soften the initial impact."

"Oh, hell no. I'm not risking my ears."

"You think there'll be a lot of yelling?"

"Yeah. There'll be a lot of that. Then, she'll tell you that you're not too old for a butt-whooping. This is going to be dramatic."

"You gotta help me out here. Tell her for me," Luke pleaded.

"I plan to be there when she's told. But I have no plans to step into that fire barefoot. Your best bet is to bring Julie with you."

"Good idea. Surely, Gran won't want to scare her off."

"No, that's a great idea. And you owe me one for that."

"Fine. Then, I'll help you tell everyone about your friend here."

Reed glanced at Emily, thankful she was sound asleep. Besides, how'd this turn into a discussion about her? "What's that supposed to mean?"

"I'm not stupid. I can see you have feelings for her."

"And?" Reed wasn't ready to talk about what he had with Emily, if anything. Hell, he hadn't figured it out for himself, yet.

"I'm only saying she's a sweet person. You could do a lot worse."

"She's my witness. This is an investigation." The finality in his words most likely wouldn't sell Luke on the idea, but Reed had to try.

"You sure that's all?" His brow was arched as he leaned his wrist on top of the steering wheel, relaxing to his casual posture again.

Was it? Hell if Reed knew.

"Whatever is or isn't happening between the two of you, I think you need to have a conversation with her about federal protection."

"What? You think I haven't already?" Reed sounded offended to his own ears. His shoulder muscles bunched up, tense. A weekend-long massage wouldn't untangle that mess.

"Oh. Sorry. I just assumed since she was still here that you hadn't brought it up."

"If it makes you feel any better, it was the first thing I mentioned to her. She doesn't want it."

"And you don't, either."

"Here we go again." This conversation didn't need to happen.

"You may have been the quiet one, but nothing's ever gotten in your way once you set your mind to it."

"I gave her the options. She turned them down. End of story. What else was I supposed to do?"

"Persuade her," Luke said without blinking. "You have

to have considered the fact it may be the only way to guarantee her safety."

"Believe me, I have."

"So, why didn't you convince her of that?"

What was with the riot act? "I did what I could. In case you haven't noticed, she's a grown woman capable of thinking for herself."

"I noticed. Half the men in the country would notice her, too. The other half would be afraid their wives would catch them staring with their mouths open. She's a knockout even in the condition she's in. The fact hasn't been lost on you."

"I'm neither blind nor an idiot. Get to your point." Of course he'd noticed how her full breasts fit perfectly in his hands. Her round hips and soft curves hadn't gotten past him, either. The imprint of her body pressed to his still burned where they'd made contact. He'd become rock-hard when she'd thrown her leg over his last night. Did he want to sleep with her? Yeah. Was it more than that? Had to be since Reed hadn't done casual sex since he'd been old enough to buy a lottery ticket. Didn't mean he had to think with his hormones.

Luke hesitated, as if he was choosing his next words carefully. "I know you're too smart to jeopardize a mission or a witness, so I won't insult you. Deciding to keep her with you might not be in her best interest. It's up to you to make her see that."

"I don't care where she is as long as she's safe," he lied. Reed didn't make a habit of deceiving his brothers, so part of him was surprised to hear the words coming out of his mouth. The truth was he did care. And Luke was right. Probably too much. Reed's agitation had more to do with the fact that his brother was forcing Reed to think about his feelings for Emily, which was not something he wanted to do. Not with cars exploding and danger around every corner. His mind needed to stay sharp, so he wouldn't miss a connection when the other guys made a mistake. Given enough time, they would screw up.

His cell pumped out his ringtone. He glanced at the screen, grateful for the distraction. "It's Nick."

"Hey, baby bro," Nick said.

"What'd you find?"

"The place is in good shape but someone's been here. Thankfully the codes are still taped under her desk, like she said."

"Have you contacted SourceCon's security team?"

"Yeah. They're cooperating. Of course, they want to handle their own investigation, but they've agreed to give us full access to their people."

"Good point. Maybe someone on the inside knows something."

The line beeped. Reed checked the screen. "My boss is calling, so I'll have to catch up with you later. Keep me posted on anything you find."

"Will do. Be safe, baby bro."

Reed said goodbye and switched to his other call. "What's the word, boss?"

"I got a rundown on what happened from the chief of police. I tried to call you earlier when we got cut off but my call went straight to voice mail. Didn't do good things to my blood pressure."

"I must've been out of range for cell service. There are a lot of dead spots out this way."

"At least you're all right."

That was the second time someone said that in the

past two minutes. "So far, so good. Someone wants this witness pretty badly."

"Clearly, they want you, too. I believe this case is also connected to yours."

"I know Stephen Taylor was set up by Shane Knox, but what does he have to do with me?"

"He was in the room when I spoke to you yesterday. He must've decoded our conversation and located the car." Anguish lowered Gil's baritone. "It's my fault this happened. I'm sorry that I trusted him."

"What's the connection, though? I don't remember Knox and Cal working together."

"I have their files right here in my hands. Turns out, they went to the same high school. Grew up in Brownsville, Texas, together. Played football. To say they knew each other well is an understatement. As my teenage daughter would say, 'they were besties.'"

"That town is right on the border. Most people have family on both sides of the fence."

"It's certainly true of Cal Phillips. He has relatives in both countries on his mother's side. Her maiden name is Herrera."

"Any chance she's related to the man they call Dueño?"

"There's no immediate connection that I can find, but it's possible he's a distant relative. I'm still mapping out all the possibilities. All I know about Dueño so far is that he's big over there. And well protected. I'm not just talking about his men. Government officials won't give up any information on him, either. There's no paperwork on him. It's almost as if the guy doesn't exist."

Went without saying the man had help. "Except we both know he does. What are we going to do to stop him?"

"I have guys working round-the-clock to uncover the

location of his compound, but it's risky to mention his name. Just knowing he exists is enough to get a bullet through the skull. My investigators have to move slowly on this one."

Reed didn't have a lot of time. "I'll involve my brothers' agencies. See if we can move any faster that way."

"We need all the help we can get on this. I'll let you know as soon as I hear anything else."

"I appreciate it. What about Knox? Where is he now? Should be easy enough to detain him for questioning. Maybe we can get answers out of him."

"I'd like nothing more than to have that SOB in custody. Only problem is, he's gone missing."

Damn. "You think he's lying low or permanently off the grid?"

"Could be either. Or dead. The minute I started asking questions about him in connection to Dueño put his life in danger. If Dueño's inner circle didn't get to Knox, then government officials might. They'll do anything to cover their tracks."

Reed didn't like any of this new information. It meant that Emily might never be safe. And now that he was knee-deep in mud with her, they could be digging two graves. He informed his boss about the upcoming summit.

"I have a guy who's been able to climb fairly high in Delgado's organization. I'll see if he can get information for us."

"Sounds good. Keep me posted."

"Be careful out there. I don't want to visit you in the hospital again. Or worse."

"I have people I can trust watching my back this time. But I won't take anything for granted."

Reed ended the call.

"Did I hear that right? This is related to what happened to you before?" Luke clenched his back teeth.

"Yeah. It's the same group." Reed had every intention of locating that compound and finding a way in.

"I can take some time off work. The FBI will understand. Nick will want to be involved, too."

Normally, Reed would argue against it. He knew better than to turn down an offer for help when the odds were stacked this high against him. "Okay."

"I know what you're thinking. Don't be stupid," Luke warned.

"No, you don't."

Emily stretched and yawned. "Don't be stupid about what?"

"Nothing," Reed lied. His brother knew Reed had every intention of locating that compound and doing whatever it took to breach it.

Because anger boiled through his veins that the same son of a bitch who'd gotten to him wanted to hurt Emily.

Chapter Twelve

Reed opened his eyes the second the truck door opened. He glanced at the clock on the dashboard. He'd caught an hour of sleep.

"Relax, just filling the tank. You need anything from inside?" Luke asked, motioning toward the building.

"I'm good. Thanks."

Emily was already awake, sitting ramrod straight. The sober look on her face said Luke had filled her in. Reed hoped she hadn't overhead their conversation, especially the part where his brother was pressing about her. Reed might not've come across the right way, and he didn't want to jeopardize whatever was going on between them by a misunderstanding. He almost laughed out loud. What *was* going on between them? If someone could fill him in, then they'd both know.

All he knew was the thought of spending more time with her appealed to him. He actually *wanted* to talk to her, and he wasn't much for long conversations otherwise. And the way her body had fit his when they were lying in bed last night was as close to heaven as this cowboy had ever been.

And yet, there was a lot he didn't know about her, and her family.

He made a mental note to talk to her about what he'd said to Luke when the two of them were alone again, which a part of him hoped would be soon. Based on the look on her face, she'd heard something, and he hated that he'd hurt her.

The chance to bring up the subject came when Luke finally quit fidgeting in the backseat and shut the door to pump gas. Thankfully, the large tank would give Reed a few uninterrupted minutes.

"Did my brother tell you about the conversations I had with our older brother and my boss?"

She nodded, keeping her gaze trained out the opposite window.

He couldn't read her expression from his vantage point but knew it wasn't good that she couldn't look him in the face anymore. Bringing up what he really wanted to talk about was tricky, so he took the easy way out. "Did you get any rest?"

Did he really just ask that? Reed was even worse at this than he'd expected to be. Most of the time, he sat back and observed life. That was his nature. He'd never been much of a "wear his feelings on his sleeve" kind of person. This was hard.

If he'd blinked, he'd have missed her second nod.

This was going well. Like hell.

"Emily, would you mind looking at me?"

Slowly, she brought her face around until he could see the tears brimming in her eyes.

"Did I say something to hurt you?" Stupid question. Of course he had.

"No." A tear got loose and streaked her cheek.

He reached up and thumbed it away, half expecting her to slap his hand. She didn't. So, he took that as a good sign and forged another step ahead. "My brother was asking questions I wasn't prepared to answer about us."

"Is there an 'us,' Reed?" Her lip quivered when she said his name.

"It's too soon to tell. If we met under different circumstances, there's no doubt I'd want to ask you out. We'd take our time and get to know each other. Figure it out as we went, like normal people. Start by dating and see where it went from there."

"But now?"

"Everything feels like it's on steroids. Plus, to be honest, I'm not looking to be in anything serious right now. I'm not ready to make a change in my career."

"Why would you have to change jobs? It's only dating, right?" The bite to her tone said he'd struck a nerve.

Damn. Trying to make things better was only making it worse.

Luke had finished pumping gas and disappeared inside the store. He'd be back any second, and Reed would never be able to dig himself out of this hole in time if he didn't do something drastic. Did she need to know how he felt about her? Since he was no good with words, he figured showing her was his best course of action.

Gently, slowly, he placed his hand around Emily's neck and guided her lips to his. That she didn't resist told him he hadn't completely screwed things up between them. Besides, he'd been wanting—check that—he'd been needing to kiss her again the whole damn day.

And that was confusing until his lips met hers and, for a split second, he felt as if he was right where he belonged. Did she feel the same? A sprig of doubt had him thinking she might slap him or push him away.

Instead, she deepened the kiss. With all the restraint

he had inside, he held steady, ever mindful of not hurting her. Control wasn't normally something he battled. With Emily, he had to fight it on every level, mind and body. Let emotions rule and he'd want to get lost with her. His body craved to bury himself in the sweet vee of her legs. With those runner's thighs wrapped around his midsection, he had no doubt he'd find home.

But that wouldn't be fair to her.

He had nothing to offer. He wasn't ready to leave his profession behind, and a woman like Emily deserved more.

She pulled back first. "Who said I was looking for a serious relationship? I have my career to think about, and that takes up most of my time."

Reed was stunned silent. She'd pulled the "my work comes first" card? Okay. He needed to slow down for a minute and think. "Where do you see yourself in the future?"

"Independent."

What did that mean? From what he'd seen of her so far, she was too stubborn to let men with guns scare her. Reed respected her for it. Did she mean alone? She'd also just turned the tables on him. "Why can't you have a job and a boyfriend?"

"That what you're asking for?"

"What if I was?"

She stared impassively at him. "I don't do relationships, so I'm not asking for one with you if that's the impression you're under."

Wait a damn minute. "Why not? Is there something wrong with me?"

"Not that I can see. I don't have time. I work a lot of hours. If I haven't lost my job, I plan to throw myself back into my work when this whole ordeal is over." Her expression was dead serious.

"And what if I wanted to see you sometime?"

"I live in Plano. You live south…somewhere…I'm not exactly sure where."

"I live in a suburb of Houston. Rapid Rock."

"At least that's one thing I know about you." She paused, and a weary look overtook her once bright eyes. "How far away is that from Plano?"

"Three hours. Four if traffic's bad."

"See. Too far."

"People date long distance, you know. It wouldn't be the end of the world."

"I don't."

Luke opened the door, and reclaimed his seat before shutting the door.

The conversation stalled. No way was he finishing this with his brother in the vehicle. Reed was butchering it all by himself. He didn't need an audience to tell him what he already knew. He was bad at relationships.

"Your brother and I spoke about federal protection," she said stiffly.

That's what this was all about? Had Luke encouraged her to go into WitSec? Why did Reed feel betrayed?

"And? What did you decide?"

"I want to discuss my options with your older brother."

"Fine."

THAT ONE WORD was loaded with so much hurt, an invisible band tightened around Emily's chest. She didn't want to upset Reed, but what else could she say? The truth was that she might need to go into the program, just as Luke had suggested. His thoughts made perfect sense, and she'd be a fool to put herself or Reed in further danger.

Besides, Reed was determined to bring the man who'd shot him to justice. And she couldn't blame him. If the shoe were on the other foot, she wouldn't rest until the person was behind bars, either.

And Dueño? That was a man who needed to be locked up forever along with a pair of former Border Patrol agents.

She'd talked to Reed about work, but the reality was she most likely would have to get a new identity if she wanted to live, let alone have a family of her own some-day, which was what she wanted. Wasn't it?

The idea had held little appeal after her last relation-ship. She'd all but closed herself off to the possibility of a real life, or a family of her own. Being with Reed stirred those feelings again, and she couldn't ignore them with him around. Not that he'd be there for long.

The minute he went after Dueño, she feared Reed would be hurt. If she showed up to visit him in the hos-pital, she'd be dead. From the looks of it so far, she'd be running the rest of her life. And the worst part was she'd almost be willing to risk everything for a man like Reed.

How crazy was that?

Especially when he'd made it seem as if he didn't share the same feelings. She'd overheard his conversation with his brother earlier. Her chest had deflated knowing he didn't feel the same way she did.

Which was what exactly?

Were her feelings for Reed real? Could they last? How could anyone figure out anything with bullets flying and cars exploding?

Maybe it would be best to separate emotions from

logic in the coming days in order to stay alive. They could figure out the rest later.

That she felt Reed's presence next to her, bigger than life, wouldn't make it easy as long as they were around each other. But difficult was something Emily had a lot of experience with. And challenging relationships were her specialty.

"We heading to my place?"

"It seems safe enough to stop in and let you grab a few of your things." Reed looked at her intensely before turning his head to stare out the window. A storm brewed behind those brilliant brown eyes. "We'll have to be careful, though."

"That would be nice. I'd love to wear my own clothes again. Can't even imagine what it would feel like to have my own makeup."

"After we make a pit stop, we'll head to my gran's ranch outside in Creek Bend."

Luke cleared his throat. "It'll be easier to connect with Nick and talk about options there."

The tension between brothers heated the air for the rest of the ride.

Emily was grateful to step outside and stretch her legs when they arrived.

Luke had parked a block away, explaining that he wanted to walk the perimeter before they approached her town house. Seemed like a good idea to her. Not to Reed. He grumbled at pretty much everything his brother had said, and she knew it had to do with him talking to her about federal protection.

She wasn't sure what she wanted to do. The promise of a clean slate offered by the program wasn't the worst thing she could think of at the moment. But then, what about her mother?

The woman barely hung on as it was. What would she do if the only daughter she could depend on disappeared altogether? Emily was the only one holding the family together. And she barely did that. Heck, she didn't even know where a couple of her siblings had disappeared to in the past few years. As soon as they'd reached legal age, they'd bolted and hadn't looked back. Emily most likely would've done the same thing, except that she remembered what her mother had been like before. She'd had the same fragile smile, but it had been filled with love.

And now? Everything in Emily's life was unraveling.

She took a deep breath and stepped out of the truck. The thought of having a few comforts from home gave Emily's somber mood a much-needed lift. It was amazing how the little things became so important in times of disaster. Something such as having her own toothbrush and toothpaste put a smile on her face.

Once Luke gave the all-clear sign, she and Reed moved to her town house. She packed an overnight bag as the men watched the front and back doors.

Reed's oldest brother had done a great job patching the hole he'd put in her window. The board should hold nicely until she could get a glass person out next week. Next week? Those few comforts had relaxed her brain a little too much. Clean pajamas wouldn't take away the dangers lurking or give her back her life.

Just to be sure no one could steal her pass codes, she pulled them out from underneath her desk where they were taped and tucked them inside her spare purse. Luckily, she'd taken only her driver's license, passport and one credit card to Mexico. Everything else had been tucked into an extra handbag she kept in the closet.

She checked her messages. The resort had called concerned that she hadn't been back to her room since Tuesday. She made a mental note to reach out to the manager and have her things shipped back to the States. Everything wasn't a total loss. She'd get her IDs and credit card back.

Except if she took up the offer for federal protection, she wouldn't need any of those things again, would she?

Her pulse kicked up a notch. No amount of deep breathing could halt the panic tightening her chest at the thought of leaving everything behind. She prayed it wouldn't come to that.

For now, she was safe with Reed and Luke. She'd have to cross the other bridge when she came to it. Surely, the right answer would come to her. As it was, she was torn between both options.

A good night of sleep might make it easier to think. No good decision was ever made while she was hungry and tired.

She took one last look around her place—the only place that had felt like home since she was a little girl— and walked downstairs. "I'm ready to go."

Reed stood at the window, transfixed.

"Everything okay?"

"They must've been watching for you. Someone's coming. Go get my brother. Tell him we have company."

Chapter Thirteen

Reed crouched behind the sofa near the window as his brother entered the room. "I saw two men heading this way."

"The back is clear," Luke said, standing at the door.

"Then take her out that way." Reed's weapon was drawn and aimed at the front. Anyone who walked through the door wouldn't make it far. He had no intention of being shot and left for dead again.

"I'm not leaving you." The finality in Luke's tone wasn't a good sign.

Reed needed his brother to get Emily to safety. "They get her and it's game over. And I might never be able to find Phillips. Get her out of here, and I'll meet you at the truck in ten minutes. I need to make these guys talk."

Luke hesitated. "I'm not sure that's a good—"

"Go. I'll be right there. If you don't leave now, it'll be too late."

His brother stared for a moment then helped Emily out the back. Good. Last thing Reed needed was someone getting to her. He had no doubt that he and Luke could handle whatever walked through that door, but Emily was weak from her injuries, and Reed didn't want to take any chances when it came to her. Besides, he'd already hurt her enough for one day.

Crouched low, he leaned forward on the balls of his feet, ready to pounce.

The doorknob turned. Clicked.

A loud crack sounded, and the door flew open. These guys were bold. Didn't mind walking through the front door or making noise to do it. Also meant they were probably armed to the hilt.

"Stop right there, and get those hands in the air where I can see them. I'm a federal agent." Reed paused a beat and peered from the top of the sofa. "I said get those hands in the air where I can see them."

The first bullet pinged past his ear as the men split up.

Reed fired a warning shot and retreated into the kitchen. The sofa wouldn't exactly stop a bullet.

His boot barely hit tile when the next shots fired, *ta-ta-ta-ta*.

Reed leveled his Glock and fired as bullets pinged around him. Hit, the Hispanic male kept coming a few steps until his brain registered he'd been gravely wounded. Blood poured from his chest, and he put his right hand on it, trying to block the sieve.

As Reed wheeled around toward the back door, a second man entered. Reed was close enough to knock the weapon out of the taller Hispanic's hand. Tall Guy caught Reed's hand and twisted his arm.

Instead of resisting, Reed twisted, using the force of a spin to gain momentum until he broke Tall Guy's grasp. Reed pivoted, losing his grip on his gun in the process, and thrust his knee into Tall Guy's crotch. He folded forward with a grunt.

About that time, he must've seen his partner because

he let out a wild scream and threw a thundering punch
at Reed's midsection, then grabbed his shoulders and
pushed until he was pinned against the granite-topped
island.

Reed's first thought was that he prayed these guys
didn't bring reinforcements. His second was that he
hoped like hell Emily and Luke had made it to the truck.
With Emily's injuries, Luke wouldn't be able to take care
of her and fight off several men. It wouldn't be possible.
Not even with his gun, although Reed knew his brother
would do whatever he had to in order to protect Emily.

Another blow followed by blunt force to the gut and
Reed dropped to his knees, the wind knocked out of him.
He battled for oxygen as he pushed up, trying to get back
to his feet. His gun was too far to reach. Tall Guy must
not've seen it slide across the room and under the counter.

Reed, fighting against the hands pushing him down,
reared up and punched Tall Guy so hard his nose split
open. Blood spurted.

That's when he saw the glint of light hitting metal.
The sharp blade of a kitchen knife stabbed down at him.
Reed shoved Tall Guy, ducked and rolled to the left. The
knife missed Reed's head a second before it made contact with the tile.

What Reed needed was to restore the balance of
power. And he could do that only on his feet.

Tall Guy dived at Reed, landing on top of him. Even
though Reed rolled, Tall Guy caught Reed on his side.
The knife came down again, fast.

Reed rolled again, catching Tall Guy's arm. The knife
stopped two inches from Reed's face. Testing every muscle in his arm, Reed held the knife at bay. Another roll
and Reed might be able to reach his Glock. With a heave,

he managed to roll and stretch his hand close enough to get to his gun.

He fired and fought Tall Guy. Problem with shooting a guy was that it still took a few moments for his brain to catch up. Reed struggled against the knife being thrust at him for the third time.

The tip ripped his shirt at his chest. Blood oozed all over Reed.

As if the guy finally realized he was shot, he relaxed his grip on the knife. It dropped, clanking against the tile.

Reed couldn't afford to wait for more men to show. He pushed Tall Guy off and managed to get to his feet. His boot slicked across the bloody floor. He wobbled, and then regained his balance, stepping lightly in the river of blood. Before he left, he fished out his cell and took a picture of each man.

All he could think about was Emily's safety. He broke into a full run as soon as he closed her back door.

Maybe Luke could get the FBI to clean up the mess Reed had left behind. As soon as he knew Emily was safe, he'd blast the pictures of his attackers to all the agencies and see if he got a hit.

His heart hammered his ribs. Not knowing if she was okay twisted his gut in knots.

Rounding the corner, he pushed his burning legs until the outline of the truck came into view. Where was she? Where was Luke?

He didn't slow down until he neared the empty vehicle. Sirens already sounded in the distance. If Luke had made it out safely, surely he would've called one of his contacts. Or had a neighbor heard gunfire and called the police?

His heart pounded at a frantic pitch now as he surveyed the area, looking for any signs of Emily and Luke, or worse yet, indications of a struggle.

Was the truck locked?

He moved to the driver's side and tried the door. It opened. That couldn't be a good sign.

The town house-lined street was quiet, still.

Motion caught the corner of his eye.

"Get in the truck," Luke shouted.

A shotgun blasted.

"Get inside and get down." Luke carried Emily in a dead run. By the time he reached the truck, sweat dripped down his face. He tossed Reed the keys.

Reed hopped into the driver's side and cranked the ignition, thankful the two people who mattered to him most right now were safe. The truck started on the first try.

Luke hauled Emily inside and hopped in behind her. He pulled an AR-15 from the backseat. "Drive."

"Buckle up." Reed stomped the gas pedal. He didn't want to admit how relieved he was to see that Emily was okay. He didn't want to consider the possibility anything could happen to her. Exactly the reason he needed to talk her into WitSec. That might be the only way to keep her safe.

"Bastards brought reinforcements. I couldn't get to you in time," Luke said, in between gasps of air.

"You should've kept Emily in the truck."

"And let them kill you? They had three more on the way."

"I could handle myself." He kept his gaze trained out the front window, but he could see from his peripheral that Emily was assessing his injuries. "I got cut with a knife. Most of this blood belongs to someone else."

"Oh, thank God." She let out a deep breath. "I thought…"

He took her hand—it was shaking—and squeezed. "I'm okay."

"Cut right and we'll lose them," Luke said. "They're on foot."

Reed brought his hand back to the wheel and turned. "They must've been watching to see if she'd show up since they didn't find the pass codes."

Luke picked up his cell phone, studied it and held it out. "We're done dealing with these jerks on our own. I'll call in the guys."

No way would Reed refuse the help. Dueño was closing in and Reed still had no idea who the guy really was or in which region of Mexico he lived. Not to mention he remembered what both of his brothers had gone through in the past couple of years. A determined criminal was a bad thing to have on his radar.

"I have a few pics we need to circulate." He fished out his cell and handed it to his brother.

"Good. We can blast these out to all federal agencies."

"Gil's number is on the log. Make sure he gets copies."

"Will do, baby bro." Luke made a move to set the phone down. It pinged. "Looks like we got a hit already."

Reed tightened his grip on the steering wheel.

Luke studied the screen. "Both of these guys are wanted for trafficking. One's name is Antonio Herrera."

"Looks like we found our family connection. That's Cal's mother's last name."

"Tell me about it." Luke cursed. "We have an ID on the other one, too. Name's Carlos Ruiz."

"Guess I don't know him."

It took a little extra time to reach Gran's place in traffic, but Reed couldn't think of a better sight than Creek Bend as the ranch-style house came into view.

In order to protect them and the ranch, men had been stationed along the road and Luke had been reassured there'd be more in the brush, as well. He'd had to call ahead to let Gran know in case she spotted one and panicked. She'd been prepped on what to expect upon their arrival, too. Mainly, so she wouldn't be surprised when she saw Emily's condition. Even though she was improving, she still had the bumps and bruises to prove she'd been through the ringer. Seeing it was another story altogether.

Potholes had been filled on the gravel road, making for an easy trip up the drive. Good that Emily wouldn't be bounced around. The last time she repositioned in her seat, she'd sucked in a burst of air, and her arm came across her ribs. She'd caught herself and immediately sat up.

The fact she'd been silent for the journey didn't reassure Reed. Eyes forward, she hadn't slighted a glance toward him. He needed to make things right. But first, she needed to heal.

The front door flew open before they'd even made it out of the truck.

Nick and Sadie rushed out first, followed by Gran, their sister Lucy, and Julie.

The tension in Reed's neck eased a notch. There was something about having Emily here at the ranch with his family that made sense in this mixed-up world.

Reed offered his arm for Emily to use as leverage to get out of the truck. She sat there, stone-faced.

Damn that he couldn't tell what she was thinking. Did the whole clan overwhelm her?

He hoped not. He hoped she could get used to them being around.

She took his arm, but as soon as she raised hers, she flinched.

"You're hurting worse than you want to let on, aren't you?"

"I'm sure I'll be better after a little more rest."

Why did she always have to armor up when he got close? Reed had never met someone so strong on the outside. Or someone who'd erected an almost impenetrable fort on the inside.

The pain medication she'd been given at the hospital had worn off. "The nurse gave me a few pills. I'll bring them to you as soon as you get settled."

His sister and sister-in-law took over with Emily, and he was left standing, holding the door open.

Nick waited for the women to take Emily inside before he motioned for Luke and Reed to stay out.

"I've got men everywhere. No way can anyone get through the woods or down that lane unnoticed. Now, I know you want to go after these guys, and we will. All three agencies have men on this."

"Good. We'll need all the help we can get." Reed shuffled his boots on the pavement. Dueño's men were smart. If there was a way inside the ranch, they'd find it. But with all the agencies sending men, it would be a lot harder.

"In the meantime, we wait for good intel," Nick said. "Oh, and Gran lifted the ban on guns in the house. Said she figured rules had to be bent when it made sense. She's still on me for not warning her beforehand when I brought Sadie there to protect her."

Reed thanked his brothers. They bear-hugged before splitting up. "Luke here has some news for her."

"Gran already saw Julie wearing a wedding ring." Nick glanced from Reed to Luke.

"And?" The way his face twisted up Reed would think his brother was waiting to hear about another serial killer on the loose.

"You know Gran. There were hugs and tears."

Luke blew out his breath. "Thank heaven for small miracles."

"You're another story, I'm afraid."

"In the hot seat?"

"Guess you didn't see the way she looked at you when you first pulled up."

"I'm hoping Emily will keep Gran distracted and this one can slide past," Luke joked.

It was nice to laugh with his brothers. Maybe Reed should take Luke up on his offer to start a PI business together when this whole mess cleared up. And it would get straightened out. Reed had the chance to right two wrongs in this case. He had no other thought but to bring justice to the men who'd hurt Emily and put his life in danger. Five minutes alone with the bastard and a shallow grave would suit Reed better at this point, but he'd settle for a life behind bars.

"Good luck with that. She might give Julie a break, but you're a different story," Reed teased.

"Yeah. As long as she doesn't bring out the switch, I'll be okay." Luke cracked a smile.

"We knew she'd never really use it on us, but the threat of it was a powerful tool. Even if she had, it wouldn't have hurt more than letting her down."

"We could be trouble," Nick added.

"And we still are," Reed agreed.

"I better go face the music. Get this over with," Luke conceded.

"Better you than me, dude," Reed gibed.

"Where's my backup when I need it?"

"Nick here is your man. I'm planning to take a look and see what needs to be done in the barn. Been sitting too long and need to stretch my legs." Not ready to go inside, he headed to the barn instead.

There was nothing like hard work to clear his mind— a mind that kept circling back to the woman inside. Because having her at Gran's felt more natural than it should.

Chapter Fourteen

When all the outside chores were done and the sun kissed the horizon, Reed took off his hat and walked inside.

Concentrating on work when Emily was in the house took far more effort than he'd expected. The need to check on her almost won out a dozen times. He wanted to be with her, and especially right now, but that's about as far as he'd allowed his thoughts to wander.

Gran stood in the kitchen. "I fixed biscuits and sausage gravy. Your favorites. You want a plate?"

"No, ma'am. I'm not hungry yet. Thank you, though. I'll make those disappear later," he said with a wink. "How's Luke?"

"He's resting. She is, too. In case you were wondering," Gran said, returning the gesture.

Not her, too. Luke had already read him the riot act about Emily. Reed didn't need to hear it from Gran, too. "If anyone needs me, I'll be out checking the perimeter. I'll ask the men on duty if they want any biscuits."

"Here. Take this with you. I already packed sandwiches for them." She motioned toward a box on the table.

Reed kissed her on top of the head before hoisting the box on his shoulder, and grimaced. "Keep mine warm."

He wouldn't eat before he made sure the men outside had food.

Gran opened the door and Reed nodded as he left for the barn. He pulled out a four-wheeler and loaded the box of food on it, using a spring to hold it on the back.

Riding the fence took another half hour. It was dark by the time Reed returned the four-wheeler to the barn and moved inside again. He showered and ate before heading down the hall to Emily's room.

Standing at the door, he listened for any signs she was awake. He hated to disturb her if she was asleep.

Instead of knocking, he cracked the door open and waited. The need to see her, to make sure she was okay, overrode his caution about entering a sleeping woman's room.

Warning bells sounded off in his head all right. And not the ones he'd expected. These screamed of falling for someone he barely knew. Reed prided himself on his logical approach to life. He'd always been the one to watch and wait. Emily made him want to act on things he shouldn't, against his better judgment. Exactly the reason he didn't get all wound up when it came to feelings. Then again, he'd never met someone who'd made him want to before, not even his fiancée. Had he pushed her away? Not given her a reason to stay? The obvious answer was yes. Reed was realistic. Even so, when it came to Emily, he needed to force caution to the surface.

"Hi." Her voice was sleepy and soft.

Reed was in trouble all right. He sat on the edge of the bed and touched her flushed cheek with the backs of his fingers. "How are you, sweetheart?"

"Ibuprofen does a world of good." She moved back to give him more room, froze and flinched.

"Don't hurt yourself."

"I'm okay." She inched over and patted the bed.

"Can I ask you a question?" he asked softly.

"Sure." There was plenty of light in the room. Enough to see her beautiful hazel eyes.

"Why do you always have to put up such a brave front?"

"I don't."

"Honesty. Remember? We promised not to lie to each other."

Her lips pressed together and her face was unreadable. "I just don't know how to be another way."

What did she mean by that?

Tears welled in her eyes.

"Why not?"

"Because it's always been me being the strong one. I don't expect you to understand. You have all this family around, helping, ready to lay their lives on the line for you." She paused and her shoulders racked as she released a sob. "I have me."

Reed couldn't begin to imagine how lonely that must feel. "Can I ask what happened to your parents?"

"Doesn't matter. It was a long time ago."

"It does to me."

"Why?"

"I want to know more about you. It'll help me figure out how to help you." Why couldn't he tell her that he wanted to know more for reasons he didn't want to explore? What was so hard about telling her he might be falling for her? Maybe it would break down some of that facade she so often wore.

Then again, move too fast and she might scurry up a tree like a frightened squirrel. She deserved to know how he felt about her. And he had every plan to tell her as soon as he figured it out himself. Right now, he didn't need the complication.

But that still didn't stop him from reaching out and touching her. He moved his finger across her swollen lip, lightly, so he wouldn't hurt her.

Those big hazel eyes of hers looked into his. "When my father left, my mother was devastated."

"Did he leave before or after he found out she was sick?" Reed's fists clenched. He knew exactly how it felt to have a father walk away. Except that Reed had had so much love in his life, it didn't affect him as much as it had his brothers.

"I wasn't completely honest with you before. I was too ashamed. She isn't sick in the traditional sense."

"Alcohol?" Lots of people turned to the bottle in hard times. Not everyone had the strength to battle their demons.

"No. Not exactly." She looked away.

"You can tell me anything. I won't judge you for it."

"How could you not? You have this big family around you, supporting you. I don't even know where to start."

He cupped her face and turned it until she was looking at him again. "Right here. Right now. This is where you start. Tell me what happened."

Tears fell and she released a sob that nearly broke Reed's heart. "It's okay. I'm right here."

She buried herself in his chest. "She drank at first. On a date with a man she barely knew, she was raped. After that, she just lost it. She joined a religious cult and moved us to California. Then she started popping out babies. She said that the men at the House cared about her, at least. Everything was up-front and honest. No one lied to her."

"At least there were people around to help. Your mother must've needed that."

"Except that they didn't. I did the best I could raising them. I'm used to living alone, being alone. Helping everyone else. But, it's not entirely her fault. I think she's sick or something. Underneath it all, my mother is very sweet. I mean, I know everything she did sounds bad, but she loved me. She kept me with her. Not like my father, who just walked away after pretending to care for us."

And Emily never wanted to be that vulnerable. It was starting to make sense why her work was so important to her. "It's okay to love your mother. Sounds like she was all you had growing up."

"It's screwed up, though, right?"

"Not really. I mean, all families are messed up in some way."

"She tried when I was little, but after all that, my mother was just…lost."

Also explained why Emily didn't want to be dependent on a man.

More sobs broke through, even though she was already struggling to contain them.

"It's okay to cry, sweetheart."

A few more tears fell that she quickly swiped away. "I just can't afford to let my guard down."

"Crying doesn't make you weak. But holding all that in for too long will break you down from the inside out one day. You don't have to put up a brave front all the time."

"I can't afford to fall apart. I'm all I've got."

"Right now, I'm here. Let me take some of the burden." Sure, Reed's father turned out to be a class-A disappointment, but he'd been one person. Reed couldn't imagine what it would feel like if everyone in his life had let him down.

"You are so lucky to have all this. To have such an amazing family…this beautiful ranch."

"We're a close-knit bunch. But then, we've always had to be. What about you and your father? He left your mother, but did he ever contact you?"

"I found him once. It was the week before college graduation. An internet search gave me his phone number, address. I thought I'd hit the jackpot. Guess as a child I'd convinced myself that even though he left Mom, he still loved me. I decided that he must not have known where I was after we moved. And that's why he never called on my birthday or had me to his house for Christmas."

"Kids make up fantasies when one of their parents is gone."

"Did you?"

"I didn't need a father. I had two older brothers constantly looking out for me. The whole situation was harder on them, and especially Nick being the oldest. He stepped inside a father's shoes and filled them out. I was damn lucky to have him."

"That must've been hard on your mother, too."

"She's an amazing woman for taking care of us the way she did."

"Did you ever look for your father?"

"Guess I never felt the need to find the man with all these jokers around trying to tell me what to do." He tried to lighten the mood, and was grateful when she smiled even though it didn't last.

"Some of my younger siblings were sent to live with other relatives when people found out about what went on at the House."

Reed had heard stories, too. Read reports about places like those, none specifically about the place where she grew up, but there were others. He'd had to raid a few since some on the border were known to harbor criminals. All kinds of marginalized people lived there. The thought Emily had endured a place like that made his heart fist in his chest.

Her bottom lip quivered.

He leaned forward and pressed a light kiss to her mouth. He kept his lips within an inch of hers. Her breath smelled like the peppermint toothpaste Gran kept on hand. "You're one of the bravest people I've ever met to go through all this alone and still be this normal."

She blinked. He imagined it was a defensive move to hold back more tears from flowing.

"Thank you, but—"

He pressed his lips to hers again to stop her from speaking. Her fingers came up and tunneled into his hair.

She pulled back and kept her gaze trained to his. "I'm not sure if throwing myself into my work or at you makes me brave, but I appreciate what you're saying."

"You survived. You carved out a normal life. You did that. And with no one there to support you. You are an amazing woman. And I'm one lucky bastard."

This time she pulled his lips to hers, deepening the kiss.

That moment was the second most intimate of his life. And both had to do with Emily. Both had similar effects on his body. He was growing rock hard again. No way would he risk hurting her. Both made him want to get lost in her.

She needed sleep, not complications.

"Think you can get some rest? I can come back to check on you in the morning."

She opened the covers. "Stay with me tonight?"

All his alarm bells warned him not to climb into those covers with this beautiful and strong woman. The more he learned about her, the more he respected her courage, her strength.

He thought about the women he'd dated in the past, and not one measured up. Not even the one he'd intended to marry.

Reed slipped under the sheets and took to his back.

Emily curled around his left side and he wrapped his arm around her. The perfect fit.

"Fair warning. You get any closer, and I can't be held responsible for my actions. Keep in mind the other bedrooms are at the opposite end of the house."

A laugh rolled up from her throat. It was low and sexy. "That makes two of us."

Getting stiff when Emily was around wasn't the problem. He had no doubt the sex would blow his mind. But then where would that leave them after?

Why should he risk getting closer to her when he knew the second he found Dueño's location and arrested him, their professional need to be together would be over?

With enough people working on the case, the information could take a little time to track down, but they'd find it…find him.

Emily deserved to have her life back. And, just maybe, she'd find a little room for him in her day-to-day life, too.

"GOOD MORNING," REED SAID as he brought a fresh cup of coffee to Emily. He'd made it a habit in the couple of weeks she'd been staying in Creek Bend.

She pushed up and then rubbed her eyes.

"You want me to come back later?"

"No. I'm awake. Besides, you brought coffee. That just about makes you my favorite person right now."

"Then I won't keep you waiting." He handed her the cup, smiling.

"You're up early. Any news?"

"We have three government agencies with men on this case and no new information. They've interviewed everyone linked to Knox and Phillips. Nothing there. All our hopes were riding on the summit, and that turned out to be a disappointment. Luke said one of his contacts in the FBI thinks he might be getting close to a breakthrough."

"It's only been two weeks."

Reed glanced at the clock. "Your boss will expect you online soon."

"Thanks for helping me figure out how to handle this whole mess with Jared. I'm still surprised he didn't want to come see me personally at the hospital to make sure I wasn't lying. But then, I've never heard him so worried."

Her boss was being a little too concerned, which didn't sit well.

"The part about you being in a wreck is true. We just fudged the rest." The only good news that had come out of the past couple of weeks was that Emily was up and moving. Her injuries were healing nicely. The bruises on her face were gone, and she was even more beautiful than before. Reed could see her light brown hair starting to show through, and he could only imagine how much more beautiful she'd look when it was restored to its natural color.

However, being landlocked was about to drive Reed to

drink. Plus, he was getting used to waking up to Emily every morning. A dangerous side effect.

"Caffeine and ibuprofen are my two best friends right now." She hesitated. "Aside from you."

"Good to know I rate right up there with your favorite drugs," he teased. "Speaking of which, I have a couple right here."

"I don't know if I've said this nearly enough, but thank you." Her playful expression turned serious as she took the pills from his outstretched hand. "Seriously, I don't know what I would've done without you."

The band that had been squeezing his chest for the past two weeks eased. Warmth and light flooded him. How had she become so important to him in such a short time? And maybe the better question was: what did he plan to do about it? "I have a feeling you would have figured out a way to get through this on your own."

And he already knew the answer to his question. He didn't plan to do anything about it. Their lives were in limbo until he found Dueño and put him behind bars.

"I'm not so sure." She tugged at his arm, pulling him toward her.

Happy to oblige, he leaned in for a kiss. The taste of coffee lingered on her lips. "Keep that up and I won't let you out of bed."

"Promises, promises."

"You let me know when I wouldn't be hurting you and I have every intention of living up to that promise."

They both knew sex wasn't an option while she was healing. They'd pushed it a time or two with bad results. He wouldn't take another risk of hurting her until he could be sure.

Reed chuckled. Restraint wasn't normally a problem

for him, but with Emily his normal rules of engagement had been obliterated. Holding back had become damn painful, especially when her warm body fit his so well.

"What? Why are you laughing?"

"No reason. You just focus on getting better. We'll take the rest one step at a time." Going slow would be better for the both of them. They both crashed into this—whatever *this* was—like a motorcycle into a barricade. They hit a brick wall wearing nothing but jeans and a T-shirt. No helmet. No protective gear. Being forced to cool their heels wasn't the worst thing that could happen as his heart careened out of control.

Reed Campbell didn't do out of control.

The pull toward Emily was stronger than anything he'd felt for Leslie, and he'd almost made the grave mistake of spending the rest of his life with her. Thinking back, had he even really wanted to marry Leslie? Or had the idea just seemed logical at the time?

They'd been dating for two years. She'd dropped every hint she possibly could they were ready. Even then, Reed had been cautious.

When she'd given him the ultimatum to move their relationship forward or she'd walk, he'd thought about it logically and decided to take the next step. She had a point. They'd been together long enough. She'd moved in, even though he hadn't remembered asking her to. Slowly, more and more of her stuff had ended up at his place. First, the toothbrush and makeup appeared in his bathroom. She'd been sleeping over a lot, so he figured it made sense. Then, she left a few clothes in his closet. Again, given the amount of time she spent at his place, a logical move.

When she'd approached him with the idea they could

both save money if she didn't renew her apartment lease, he'd thought about it and agreed. He'd gotten used to Leslie being there. Didn't especially want her to leave. So, he figured that was proof enough he must want her to be there. He didn't think much about it when she spent Saturdays watching shows about wedding dresses. Or when she'd started asking his opinion about what she'd called "way in the future" wedding locations. Bridal magazines had stacked fairly high on the bar between the living room and kitchen when she finally forced his hand.

Reed knew he wasn't ready for marriage. He figured most men who'd come from his background would have a hard time popping that question of their own free will.

When he'd really thought about it, he decided that he might never be ready. But it had made sense to marry the person he'd spent the past two years with, so he'd asked.

With Leslie, he didn't have to stress out about picking a ring because she'd already torn out a picture of what she wanted from one of those bridal magazines and left it in his work bag the day before.

She'd thought of everything.

Had he really ever been crazy in love with Leslie?

Being with Emily was totally different.

Sitting there now, enjoying a cup of coffee with her, gave him a contented feeling he'd never known. And made him want to jump in the water, feetfirst, consequences be damned.

And it was most likely because they couldn't, but he'd never wanted to have sex with a woman as badly as with her, either.

If absence made the heart grow fonder, then abstinence made a certain body part grow stiffer. Painfully stiff.

"I better hit the shower." And make it a very cold one at that.

"You sure I can't convince you to climb under the covers where it's warm?"

He stood and shook his head. The naked image of her just made him certain he'd need to dial the cold up even more.

Besides, he was going stir-crazy being holed up at the ranch for two solid weeks. He itched to get out today, figuring he'd be fine on a motorcycle.

Reed kissed Emily's forehead, ignoring the tug at his heart, and then strolled to the shower to cool his jets. And a few other body parts, too.

Drying afterward, he slipped on boxers, a pair of jeans and T-shirt. He didn't stop to eat breakfast, heading out the back door while everyone was busy instead.

He grabbed a helmet and pulled his motorcycle out of the barn. Anyone watching the house wouldn't know who was leaving since he and his brothers looked alike from a distance. Plus, he knew a back way off the land and onto the street.

The men watching were used to Reed checking the perimeter every morning by now, so he kept his helmet tied to the back so they could see it was him.

Before he hit the main road, he stopped long enough to slip on the helmet. A pair of shades would disguise him further.

On the road, he expected to feel free.

He slipped past the inconspicuous car parked behind an oak tree. There were two others he spotted and, most likely, one or two he didn't. The Feds were keeping an eye on movement outside the ranch. Since no laws were being broken, there wasn't much they could do about Dueño's men being there.

Getting out proved easier than he'd expected. Then again, they wanted her, not him. It would be clear to anyone that he was a man.

Winding around the roads, pushing the engine, should feed his need for adrenaline and feeling of being out of control while completely in control. The speed, the knowledge that he could go faster than anything on the road with him, made it almost feel as if he became one with the bike and was in total control. Gran had always said that Reed had a need for controlled chaos, which was a lot like how he felt with Emily. Instead, the more distance he put between himself and the ranch gave him an uneasy feeling in the pit of his stomach and an ache in his chest.

What if Dueño's men made a move while Reed was gone and they were one man down? Reed might have unwittingly just played right into their hands. Logic told him it didn't matter. The ranch had almost as much coverage as the president. Even so, being away from Emily left him with an unsettled feeling.

Reed needed to turn around and get back to the ranch. Except when he did, he noticed two cars heading toward him in the distance. They were coming fast, side by side on a two-lane road. Isolating him was the best way to get rid of him.

Run the other way and they'd chase him. The farther he got from the ranch, the more vulnerable he became.

Reed clenched his back teeth and opened the throttle. Looked as if he was about to be forced into a game of chicken.

Chapter Fifteen

Since Reed had left, Emily had a hard time concentrating. She'd eaten and logged on for work. An uneasy feeling had consumed her when she saw him take off on his motorcycle.

Being here with his family had brought a strange sense of rightness to her world.

Maybe it was just the thought of family that made her all warm and fuzzy on the inside. With a deserter for a dad and a sweet-but-lost mom, Emily had never known a life like this.

And how adorable was Gran?

No doubt, she was the one in charge of these grown men.

The house itself was well kept and had a feeling of ordered chaos. The rooms were cozy, and keepsakes were everywhere.

Emily dressed, ate and stepped outside. Life abounded. A small vegetable garden was next to the raised beds of planted herbs. Flowers grew in pots on the back porch complete with a couple of chairs around a fire pit. Birds nested in the trees.

But her favorite place was the barn and being with the horses.

No wonder the Campbell boys had grown up to be caring men. A place like this would do that.

After two weeks of big family meals, great conversation and being with people who genuinely cared about each other, Emily was surprised at how much this place felt like home to her.

And yet, it was like a home that had existed only in her imagination before. How many nights as a child had she fantasized her life could be more like this?

Hers had been filled with dry cereal and people who talked a whole lot about love without it ever feeling sincere.

Love, to Emily, was making a real breakfast for others. Love was kissing good-night and being tucked into bed. Love was being brought coffee in the morning.

Reed?

Did she love Reed?

Would she even know love if it smacked her in the forehead?

Emily hadn't known this kind of love existed. It was fairy tales and happily-ever-after. She had no idea it could happen in the real world. Even when she'd dated Jack, she hadn't felt like this. She had needed her space, and that's most likely why he'd been able to get away with being married while he told her she was the only one.

She cursed herself for not recognizing the signs. He hadn't worn a wedding ring. There was no tan line on his left hand.

But then, he hadn't had to be very deceiving when she let him come around only once a week and had insisted he go home every night.

Guess she was an easy target.

Then there was the guy she'd dated before him, who

after six months had told her three was a crowd in a relationship. She thought he was accusing her of seeing
someone else. When she told him she wasn't, he laughed
bitterly and said he knew she wasn't seeing another man.
He was talking about her job.

Being with Reed was different. It felt completely normal to wake up in his arms every day.

And that thought scared the hell out of her.

REED AIMED DEAD center at the car on his left. A split second before his wheel made contact with the bumper, he
swerved to the center line, narrowly avoiding both cars.

If that wasn't enough to kick his heart rate into full
speed, a near miss with a shell casing was. The blast had
come from behind.

Soon, the cars would turn around, but they'd have a
hell of a time trying to catch him. The curvy road would
make him a harder target to see and, therefore, shoot.

Getting back inside the ranch would be tricky. If he
could get a message to Luke, he could alert the men.

Reed had to take a chance and stop. He pulled over
and eased his motorcycle into the brush for cover.

The text that came back clued Reed in to just how
pissed off his brother was. In retrospect, his brother was
right. Going for a ride this morning was a boneheaded
move.

Not two minutes later, a pickup truck roared to a stop
followed by two unmarked vehicles.

Reed expected a lecture when Luke hopped out of
the driver's seat.

"You take the truck. I'll bring in the motorcycle." His
brother had been too focused on the mission of bringing
Reed home safely.

He understood. There was no room for feelings during an op.

Reed nodded and thanked Luke before taking a seat behind the wheel. Knowing that he came from a place of love humbled Reed. After spending time with Emily and hearing about her childhood and lack of family, he'd grown to appreciate his even more.

As he wound down the twisty road home, he thought about what it must've been like for her. To grow up surrounded by so many people in a communal house, but so very alone at the same time.

He hoped having her at the ranch had helped her see real families, though not perfect, existed. For his, Gran had provided the foundation. She'd given them a roof over their heads when their father had taken off.

Reed's mother was one of the strongest people he knew, but bringing up five kids alone was a lot for anyone. He wished Emily had had a mother who sacrificed for her the way his mother had for them. Her life wasn't about date nights or spa appointments. She'd given hers to her children. And yet, she didn't resent them. Loving them seemed to feed a place inside her soul and make her even stronger.

Emily was strong, too. And his chest puffed with pride every time he thought of her, of what she'd survived. Yeah, she had bruises. But hers were on the inside, and even with them she'd opened her heart a little to him.

Pulling up the drive, seeing her leave the barn stirred a deep place inside him. A spot deeply embedded in his heart that was normally reserved for people with the last name Campbell.

His circle might be small, but the relationships in it weren't. And they had a name. He needed to remind himself that Emily's last name was Baker. Leslie had pretty much destroyed the chance of anyone else finding their way inside permanently when he'd caught her in bed with Cal.

When he'd been shot later that day, she hadn't visited him in the hospital. For the week he'd been ordered on bed rest, she'd stopped by all of once.

The moment he'd broken consciousness, he'd waited for her. For an excuse. For an apology. Something.

She'd texted him that she was moving out of their apartment. Said that he wasn't there for her in the way Cal had been. Reed wondered if Cal was still there for her. If they were together somewhere in the hot, unforgiving jungle. It would serve her right.

Reed parked the truck as Emily came toward him.

"I thought you left on a motorcycle."

"That was a bad idea."

Luke didn't speak when he passed them. Reed understood why. They didn't need words to know his brother was frustrated. Inside the perimeter, the ranch had sufficient protection to keep out a militia. Reed was angry with himself. No one could punish him for his mistakes more than he could. Wasn't that exactly what he'd been doing since Leslie?

Not letting another woman get close to him?

Emily reached for his hand. "Come on. I want to show you something in the barn."

He had some explaining to do when Luke cooled off. In the meantime, staying out of his way wasn't such a bad idea. "What did you find in there?"

"Come on. You'll see." She tugged at his hand.

With her palm touching his, he could feel her pulse, her racing heartbeat. "Fine. But shouldn't you be working?"

"I'm on lunch break. Besides, Jared called. Said he didn't like me trying to work so much while I'm trying to heal."

Reed would bet her boss was concerned for more than just her general well-being. Was he just a little too worried? "I'll bet he is."

"Said he wanted to come see me."

A bolt of anger split through Reed's chest, spreading to his limbs. Logic said she wasn't interested in the guy. So, where was reasoning at a time like this? As it was, Reed's brain didn't seem to care a hill of beans about being rational with his body pulsing from anger and something else when she was this close—something far more primal.

He pushed those thoughts aside. "So what did you want to show me in the barn?" A few things came to mind. Her naked topped the list. So much for leaving those high-school-boy hormones behind. Her being vulnerable, with him putting her in that position, must be weighing on his mind and his body was trying to compensate. Otherwise, if those pink lips curled one more time he'd have no choice but to cover her mouth with his and show her just how much of a problem she was creating for his control.

Once again, his logical mind had failed.

Thinking back, didn't most of his ex-girlfriends accuse him of thinking too much in their relationships?

And now Emily had come along and seemed to be doing her darnedest to turn everything that made sense to him upside down.

And he didn't like one bit that her boss seemed to want more than nine-to-five from her. He'd ask Nick to run a background check on the guy just to see what

Reed was dealing with. "I don't think you ever told me Jared's last name."

"Why do you need it?" she teased.

"I like to know everything I can about my competition," he teased.

"Sanchez. His name is Jared Sanchez."

"Has he always kept such a tight leash on his employees? Or just you?"

"He's the worst. I can't go to the bathroom at work without him knowing my schedule."

Reed remembered his conversation with Jared. The man had acted as if he was guessing where she'd gone on vacation. A background check sounded like a better idea all the time. "So, what did you end up telling Mr. Sanchez?"

"That I was resting at a friend's place, and it was too far for him to drive."

Reed would've felt better if she'd said she was at her boyfriend's. "Feel free to use me as an excuse. I don't mind."

"What? And tell him we're in a relationship?" She snorted. "The only people you'll ever really trust have the last name Campbell."

It wasn't that funny.

She stopped at the closed barn doors and covered his eyes with her free hand. "No peeking."

In the dark with his eyes shut, he resigned himself to be surprised and let her lead him inside.

"Don't open yet." She closed the barn door.

Even at midday, it would be fairly dark inside unless she'd turned on the lights.

"Okay."

She hadn't. He glanced around. Nothing looked out

of place. No big surprises lurked anywhere. "Yep, it's a barn."

"Uh-huh."

"What did you want me to see exactly?"

She steeled herself with a deep breath, pushed up on her tiptoes and kissed him.

His arms around her waist felt like the most natural thing to him. He splayed his hand low on her back, springing to life more than a deep need to be inside her.

Her hands came around his neck, her body flush with his, and his body immediately took over—his hands moved down to her sweet bottom and caressed.

The little mewling sound that sprang from her lips heightened his anticipation.

The kiss ended far too fast for his liking. She looked him deep in the eye.

"You can't break me." She took his hand again, smiled a sexy little smile that caused his heart to stutter, and led him upstairs to the loft.

A thick blanket had been spread on the floor. There was a soft glow lighting the room by one of those battery-powered lamps.

Logic told him to turn around and walk out before he couldn't.

Practical thinking said he shouldn't let his relationship with a witness be muddied by sex. Even though he had no doubt it would be mind-blowing sex.

Reasoning said as soon as this case was over he'd be back in South Texas and her life would continue in Plano.

All of which made sense. Not to mention he'd be breaking agency rules.

Reed knew he should say something to stop her. If things ended badly between them, it could jeopardize his career, his future with the agency and his future employability.

"I wanted to show you this." Emily stopped in the center of the room, locked gazes and slowly unbuttoned her shirt.

One peek of that lacy pink bra did him in. To hell with logic.

He crossed to her before the blouse hit the floor.

This close, he could see hunger in her eyes that he was certain matched his own. His lips came down hard on hers, claiming her mouth, as his tongue thrust inside searching for her sweet honey.

The sound she released was pure pleasure.

He cupped her breast and then pressed his erection to her midsection, rocking his hips. "You sure about this?"

She nibbled his bottom lip. "I've never been more certain about anything in my life."

Emily took a step away from him and shimmied out of her jeans. He almost lost it right there when he saw her matching panties. Pink was his new favorite color.

Her hands went to the button fly of his jeans, but his made it there first. He toed off his boots, and his jeans hit the floor shortly after. She'd already made a move for his T-shirt, so he helped the rest of the way. "That's better. We've both had on way too many clothes."

Her musical laugh, a deep sexy note, urged him to continue.

Looking at her, her soft curves and full breasts, her gaze intent on his, was perfection. She was perfection. "You're beautiful."

That she blushed made her even sexier.

"Nothing hurts, right?" he asked, needing reassurance. This time he was already lost in her, and stopping would take heroic effort. He hoped like hell he'd be up to the challenge if he needed to be because looking at her in the low lamplight was the most erotic moment of his life.

"Fine. You first, then." He guided her onto the blanket, watching for any signs of pain.

There were none, so he made his next move. Her panties needed to go. If she could handle him pleasuring her with his tongue, he could think about filling her with something else.

He started at her feet and peppered kisses up the insides of her calves, her thighs.

Placing his hands gently on her silken thighs, he slowly opened her legs, checking to make sure she didn't grimace. Nope, he was good to go.

Her uneven breathing spiked as he bent down to roll his tongue on the inside of her thigh, moving closer to her sweet heat.

Using his finger, he delved inside her. A guttural groan released when he felt how hot and wet she was for him. His tongue couldn't get there fast enough. He needed to taste her. Now.

Her hands tunneled into his hair.

There were no signs of pain, just the low mewling of pleasure intensifying as he increased pressure, rubbing, pulsing his tongue inside her as she moved her hips with him.

Using his thumb, he moved in circles on her mound, and his tongue delved deeply, moving with her, tasting her, until her body quivered and she gasped and then fell apart around him.

He shouldn't be this satisfied with himself. He couldn't help it. Pleasuring her made another list he didn't know he had until meeting Emily. This one involved his favorite moments.

Taking a spot next to her, giving her a chance to catch her breath, he couldn't hold back a smile.

"That was… You are…amazing." She managed to get out in between breaths.

He turned on his side, needing to see her beautiful face. The compliment sure didn't hurt his ego. Truth was he wanted to hear her scream his name. And only his name.

Setting the thought aside when she rolled over to face him and gripped his straining erection, he took a second to really look at her. Perfection. She was that rare combination of beauty and strength. He wanted to bury himself inside her and get lost. Her mouth found his and he took the first step on the journey to bliss.

His heart hammered against his ribs, and for a split second he was nervous about his performance. He opened his eyes and chuckled against her lips. The vibration trailed down his neck, through his chest and arms.

Hers did the same. She smiled, too.

And his heart took a nosedive. He was in trouble, which had nothing to do with how great the sex was about to be.

Careful not to put too much weight on her, he rolled until he was on top of her. Her legs twined around his hips.

"Hold on." He tried not to move much while he wrangled a condom out of his wallet, grateful his jeans were within arm's reach. He ripped it open with his mouth, his hand shaking as he rolled it over the tip.

"Let me help with that." Her touch was firm but gentle

as she rolled the condom down his shaft, lighting a fire trail coursing through his body, electrifying him.

When she gripped him and guided him inside her, he nearly exploded. His body shook with anticipation as he eased deeper.

"You won't hurt me." Her gravelly voice was pure sex.

Reed needed to think about something else if he wanted this to last. And he did. Until her hips bucked, forcing him to let go of control and get lost in the moment, the sensation of her around him, her innermost muscles tightening around his erection.

Looking into those gorgeous hazel eyes, he thrust deeper, needing to reach her core.

There was no hint of pain, only need.

They moved in a rhythm that belonged only to them. He battled his own release until she shattered around him, begging him not to stop. She breathed his name as she exploded, her muscles tightening and contracting.

When her spasms slowed, he pumped faster and harder until his own sweet release pulsed through him.

Exhausted, he pulled out and disposed of the condom before collapsing beside her.

"That was amazing," she said.

"Yeah. We're pretty damn good together, aren't we?"

"Best sex of my life."

"I couldn't argue that." His, too. He hauled her close to him.

She settled into the crook of his arm.

"And you're okay?"

"Never felt better."

"You tired? You want to go back to bed and rest?"

"I want to go back to bed all right. But not to rest." Her smile lit up her eyes.

He could get used to looking into those eyes every day. His erection had already resurrected. "Good. Because I'm going to need to do that a lot more to you today."

She reached for his wallet, which was still splayed on the floor, and retrieved another condom.

He didn't need to worry about whether or not he would be able to accommodate her. He was already stiff again. "I want this, too. Believe me. But should we wait a little while?"

"Still worried about hurting me?" She opened the package and rolled the condom down his shaft.

"I'm always going to want to protect you. But, yeah, I don't want to cause you any pain. You've been through enough and you're just now healing."

"Then, cowboy, you better lie back and let me show you what I can and can't do." She mounted him, still wet, and he groaned as she eased onto him.

"Better watch out. I could get used to this."

The corners of her mouth tugged when she bent down to kiss him. "Good. Because I'm counting on it."

Chapter Sixteen

After taking a break from work to get fresh air, Emily walked into a house full of Campbells, and one very special little bundle in one of the women's arms. Reed introduced her to his sister Meg and her husband, Riley, the proud parents of baby Hitch.

"His name is Henry, but we call him Hitch for the way he 'hitched' a ride into our hearts," Reed explained.

Emily's heart skipped a beat at the proud twinkle in his eyes when he looked at the baby. And a place deep inside her stirred. She wanted a baby someday. But now? She'd kept herself so busy with work, it had been easy to avoid thinking about it. Maybe she'd been afraid to want something that seemed so far out of reach, something she had no idea how to attain given her screwed-up past. Seriously, her mom lived as if it were the sixties, probably a throwback to her youth. Although Emily could appreciate the Beatles, she believed the present was far more interesting than the past. And yet, hadn't she been stuck there in some ways, too?

Meg leaned toward Emily, who couldn't help but smile at the baby. "Do you want to hold him?"

"I would like that very much." Emily sat in a chair and

took the sweet boy, who was bundled in a blue blanket with a brown horse stitched on it. "I love this."

"Gran made it." Meg beamed and Emily figured the look of pride had more to do with Hitch than his wrap.

"It's beautiful. And he's a gorgeous baby."

Emily expected to be overwhelmed by the group, but everyone stood around and chatted easily. Their level of comfort with each other was contagious. Instead of wanting to blend in with the wallpaper, as she usually did in groups of people she barely knew, she enjoyed joining in conversation. Laughing. There was real laughter and connection, and love.

Reed stood next to her, smiling down during breaks in bantering with his brothers, and her heart skipped a beat every time.

When was the last time she was so at ease in a room full of strangers? Heck, in any room?

Emily couldn't remember if she'd ever felt this relaxed, normal, as if she belonged. She credited it to the Campbells' easy and inclusive nature. They had enough love for each other, and everyone else around them. Images of Christmas mornings spent huddled around a tree in this room came to mind. Warmth and happiness blanketed her like a summer sunrise.

Hot cocoa and a blazing fire in the fireplace would be more than enough heat to keep them warm as they exchanged gifts.

There'd be laughter and Reed by her side. The realization Emily wanted all those things startled her. Because she was a guest there. And no matter how comfortable they made her feel, she didn't belong. Had never belonged anywhere or to anyone.

The thought sat heavy on her chest as she cradled the baby closer, trying to edge out the pain.

She glanced at the clock. It was time to set her fantasies aside and retreat to her room to work.

Glancing down at the sweet, sleeping baby, the earth shifted underneath her feet. Good thing she was already sitting or she feared she'd lose her balance. Because holding this little Campbell was nice. Better than nice. Amazing. And Emily could only imagine how much more fantastic it would be to hold her own child someday. One created with the man she loved.

Realization hit her in a thunderclap, ringing in her ears. She did want to have a baby. *Someday.*

For now, she had more pressing needs. To stay alive, for one. To keep her job, for another. Maybe once she got back on her feet, she'd be in a position to open herself up to other possibilities, as well.

"I better get back to work." She stood and reluctantly handed the little bundle over to his mother. "Thank you for letting me hold him. He's a sweet baby, and it was gracious of him not to cry." The only babies she'd ever held before had wailed. Of course, she'd been stiff as a board when their mothers had placed them in her arms. The babies most likely picked up on her emotions. And now she realized she'd also been afraid—afraid that by holding them, she'd realize she wanted one of her own. Maybe, when her life was straight and she met the right man, she'd be ready to think about a future.

Meg rewarded Emily with a genuine smile. "He's especially good when he's sleeping, which isn't much these days since he started teething."

Reed followed her into her room, took off his shoes and made himself comfortable on top of the bedspread.

Seeing him there, fingers linked behind his head, made her almost wish she could start on her future now.

Silly idea.

But then great sex had a way of clouding judgment. And theirs had been beyond anything she'd ever experienced before. She couldn't help but crack a smile. Until reality dawned and she realized her time in paradise had a limit.

As soon as the right call came in, Reed would be out of there, tracking the most deadly man in Mexico. If this was anyone else other than Reed, she'd consider going into WitSec and asking him to come with her. She knew in her heart a man like him wouldn't give up his family or go into hiding for the rest of his life. He was honest, strong and capable. Injustice would hit him harder than a nail. And he wouldn't sleep until he'd made it right.

Her worry was probably written all over her face, but she couldn't help it. She'd grown to care for Reed in the past few weeks, and she didn't want to think about him leaving. She'd also overheard conversations where she knew they were getting close to pinpointing a location.

"What's wrong?" His dark brow lifted.

"Nothing. I was just thinking how cute Hitch is," she lied.

He patted the bed next to him. "Come here."

She sat on folded knees, facing him.

"I can't help if I don't know what's really bothering you. Is it my family? They can be a bit much for people when they're all together."

"Not at all. I like being with them very much."

He leaned forward and kissed her. "That's nice because they love you."

She couldn't hold back her smile. Love? Being near

Reed had a way of calming all her fears. But the last thing she needed to do was learn to depend on him. His family might love her, but did he?

"What is it really?" He kissed her again. "I hope you know you can tell me anything."

Except the part where she'd lost the battle against the slippery slope and was falling for him. Hard.

She had no doubt Reed could solve any problem, aside from that one.

"I'm just thinking about a work issue. It's nothing."

"WHY DON'T I believe that?" Reed surprised himself at just how important Emily had become to him in the past couple of weeks.

She leaned forward and kissed him.

"Keep that up and we're not leaving this room for a long time," he teased, but he was only half joking.

"Who said I'd mind?" She laughed against his lips.

Before she could get too comfortable with that thought, he flipped her onto her back and pressed his midsection into the open vee of her legs. "I have no problem rallying for that cause."

Reed cursed as he heard his name being called from down the hall. "Ignore it."

"Not happening, cowboy. Not in broad daylight with your family in the next room shouting for you."

"I was afraid you'd say that. Hold that thought. I'll get rid of them and be right back." He kissed her again and then hauled himself out of the bed. He sat on the edge for a long moment, needing to get control over his body before he headed out of the room. "This is your fault, you know."

"What did I do?"

"Made it where I can't get enough of you."

Luke shouted again.

With a sharp sigh, Reed pushed off the bed and headed down the hall. He followed the voice to the kitchen, where Nick and Luke were seated at the table. They were staring intently at someone's laptop.

"What did you guys find?"

"Turns out that name you wanted us to check out the other day is involved," Nick said.

"Jared Sanchez?"

"Yeah. His mother's maiden name is Ruiz."

Reed cursed and fisted his hands. So much of Jared's behavior made sense now. No wonder he'd been so forgiving. He was keeping tabs on Emily. "So, he's related to the guy at the town house."

"That's not all. He's up to his eyeballs involved," Luke said.

"I'll kill that SOB myself," Reed ground out. "What else did you find?"

"Sent in a couple of boys to 'talk' to him and once he started, they couldn't shut him up. Turns out his cousin— your friend from the town house—realized what a cash cow Jared could be with his job at SourceCon."

Reed's jaw twitched. He didn't like where this conversation was going. "Go on."

"Jared swears he didn't want Emily to get hurt. Says he made his cousin promise nothing would happen to her. Jared's the one who gave up her location at the resort. She was supposed to be returned once she gave the codes. No harm. No foul. Jared wouldn't be connected to the crime and he'd make sure she kept her job."

"Except she didn't have her passwords."

"With her access to accounts in major banking institutions, Dueño must've also realized the kind of money on the line because he doesn't normally get personally involved. When she wouldn't give him what he wanted... well...you know what happened next."

Anger burned a raging fire inside Reed. "Tell me Sanchez is in a cell."

"Of course," Nick said quickly. "And there's a silver lining. Ruiz feared for his life when the job went sour and turned state's evidence. He gave up the location of Dueño's compound. We had it checked out and our guys confirmed it. Dueño's compound is in Sierra Madre del Sur, midway between Acapulco and Santa Cruz."

"And they're sure it's him?"

"Ninety-six percent certainty." Luke repositioned his laptop so Reed could see the screen. "That's our guy."

"Dueño?"

"That's him."

Reed took a minute to study the dark features and black eyes. "I need a plane."

"You need to check your messages. Your boss wants you to stand down on this one," Luke said.

"No way. I'm not letting someone else risk their lives for this."

"That's exactly what we thought you'd say. We stalled your boss. A chopper's on its way to take us to the airport."

"What do you mean *us*?"

"We're going with you."

"It's too dangerous."

The look on both of his brothers' faces would've stopped anyone else dead in their tracks. But Reed was immune. "Look, I'm not saying you're not the best at what you do, but you have families now. I can't let you take that risk for me."

"What the hell is it with you and families?" Nick asked, disgusted. "I know how to do my job."

Reed wouldn't argue the point.

"And if my baby brother is going anywhere near that compound, I'm going with him. This isn't just your fight. They messed with a Campbell. We stand together."

"Goes without saying."

"Then stop being a jerk and let us help you," Nick said flatly.

Luke added, "I don't trust anyone else to watch your back."

Reed couldn't argue that point, either. He felt the exact same way. "Okay, then. Whose resources are we using for this? Because it doesn't sound like my boss is going to pony up."

Luke raised his hand. "FBI wants this guy, so they said they'd back the mission. However, anything goes wrong, and we're on our own to explain it. We can do whatever we want with the jerk who shot you if we find him. He's a bonus."

"Or collateral damage," Nick interjected.

"I'd like to see him spend a long time behind bars. Dying is too easy for him." Reed paused and then clapped his hands together. "Sounds like a party. So when do we leave?"

"About half an hour. We'll get close to the suspected location and then wait it out until the middle of the night."

"Sounds like you have it all figured out." Reed needed to tell Emily about the plan. He felt a lot better about his odds with his brothers backing him. "What coverage do we have here in Creek Bend?"

"Enough to ensure the safety of a dignitary in a red zone. When this is over, we have to talk about setting up our own company. Just us brothers," Luke said, but the deep set to his eyes said he wasn't joking around this time.

Reed glanced at Nick. "What do you think about the idea of us going into business together?"

"After what happened to me, heck, I'm the one who suggested it."

"Did not," Luke interrupted. "You know this was my original idea from way back."

Reed smiled. Working with his brothers wasn't a half-bad idea. His job at Border Patrol had gone sour the day he'd realized he couldn't trust some of his own. As it turned out, his shooting wasn't as uncommon as it should be. But then, one should be enough. "First things first. Let's go pick up a couple of hot tamales across the border, and then we'll talk business."

He couldn't ignore the possibility that forming an agency with his brothers would bring him back to North Texas and closer to Emily. Would she be open to exploring the idea of them as a couple when he returned? For now, he had to figure out a way to tell her he was about to leave. For a split second, he considered taking her with him. Having her by his side was the only way he could be certain she'd be safe. But bringing her to Dueño's door wasn't a bright idea. There were enough federal men crawling through Creek Bend and around the ranch to keep an eye on her and his family.

The right way to tell her he was leaving didn't come to him on his walk down the hall. He stopped at her doorway and asked if he could enter.

One look at his serious expression and her smile faded,

disappearing faster than a deer in the woods at the scent of man.

"What did your brother say?"

He kissed her, mostly to reassure himself, because he suddenly wasn't sure how she'd react to the news.

Tension bunched the muscles in his shoulders worse than a Dallas traffic jam as he prepared himself for the worst.

When she realized how dangerous his job was, she might not want to see him anymore. Especially once he gave her back her life, which he had every intention of doing by morning. He also had every intention of living to see it…but he couldn't make promises on that one.

The right words to tell her still eluded him, so he just came out with it. "We found him."

Reed studied her expression, surprised at how much he needed her reassurance. But she was completely unreadable. Should he tell her about her boss? On second thought, maybe he should wait. He could explain everything once this ordeal was over.

"When do you leave?"

"Soon. A chopper's on its way."

She drew in a deep breath. "And you're sure it's him?"

"You can never be one hundred percent, but this is about as close as it gets." He took her hand, relieved she didn't draw away from him.

Staring at the wall, as if she was reading a book, she took another deep breath. "Okay. We should get you ready to go."

She wasn't upset? No begging him to stay? "You're all right with this?"

"'This' is what you do, right?" Her honest hazel eyes were so clear he could almost see right through them.

"Yeah. It is." No way could she be okay.

"And 'this' is what you love. It's part of who you are, right?" There was no hesitation in her voice.

Was it possible she understood? "Yes."

"I'm falling hard for you, Reed Campbell. I wouldn't change a thing about you." She smiled, leaned forward and kissed him. "Who am I to complain about your job?"

Did she really mean that? He studied her for a long moment then squeezed her hand. He didn't like the idea of leaving her, especially since Dueño's men were never far. The best way to protect her was by putting Dueño in jail. "You are someone who has become very special to me."

"Good. Because I happen to like who you are, Mr. Campbell. You're kind of dangerous." She peppered a kiss on his lower lip. "And mysterious."

She captured his mouth this time then pulled back just enough to speak. "And I happen to think that's very hot."

Chapter Seventeen

Reed gathered his pack, loaded it onto the chopper and climbed aboard. The loud *whop, whop, whop* couldn't drown out the sweet sound of Emily's last words. It was still foreign to him that someone could become so special in such a short amount of time. His feelings defied logic, which confused the hell out of him. And he didn't need to be thinking about it when he should be focused on his mission.

To make this day more complicated, he didn't like being away from her, or not being there to protect her. Even though the ranch was under lockdown by the FBI.

Finding and arresting Dueño was the best way to keep his family safe. Throw in the bonus of possibly locating the man who'd betrayed Reed, and he'd be doubling down on this mission.

No matter what happened, Reed would be ready. He and his brothers had gone over the operation's details a half dozen times at the kitchen table. Reed had memorized the map. No one needed to be reminded that although the FBI funded the detail, it wasn't sanctioned by the US government. Meaning, if things went sour, they'd be on their own.

But he and his brothers would be in constant communication. Plus, they had the added bonus of knowing each other inside out. Most teams trained for years to get that kind of chemistry.

The chopper took them to DFW airport, where they climbed aboard a cargo plane that would take them to Oaxaca, Mexico.

All joking stopped during the three-hour flight the moment they crossed the border into Mexico. From there, they'd board a smaller aircraft headed to a military airstrip in the foothills of Sierra Madre del Sur, and it'd be a quick half-hour drive from there.

Flights had left on time and they were on schedule as the second plane landed. Every mission had its quiet time so that the men could gather their thoughts.

They were all business as they met the driver. He'd take them to the base of the mountains then leave. They'd be on foot for the rest of the journey.

From the airport to camp took another half hour. The camp had been set up at the base of the mountains. It wasn't much more than a tent and the makings for a fire. There was wood and a circle of rocks. Since both Nick and Reed had learned the hard way that not everyone could be trusted, Reed suggested they relocate as soon as the driver returned to his vehicle.

His brothers nodded.

As soon as the vintage Jeep disappeared, Reed pulled up the tent stakes. "I say we camp an hour from the compound at the most."

"Good idea," Nick said.

They'd walked a mile in silence when Luke finally spoke up. "She'll be all right, you know."

"I hope."

"They couldn't protect her any better than if she'd been placed in WitSec," Luke continued.

That Reed didn't know the men she was with personally didn't sit well on his chest. Especially after what Nick had gone through a year ago when a US marshal supervisor had gone bad. Reed knew all about working with the unpredictable as a Border Patrol agent. All it took for a dozen bad seeds to be planted was a piece of legislation mandating his agency double up on personnel in order to stem the flow of illegals. Reed didn't mind the legislation; the idea was in the right place. But mandating all the hires happen in a month wasn't realistic. Detailed background checks took longer than that to execute and return.

The current system made it way too easy for criminals to make it into the system as agents. His grip tightened around his pack. Phillips and Knox were prime examples.

But it was rare for a US marshal to turn.

"I hope you're right." Being separated made him jumpy. Fine if it kept him that much more alert while on his mission. Not so good if it distracted him. "How do you guys deal with it?"

"What?" Luke asked.

"The job. Having someone back home."

"I know what Leslie did, but it should never have been that way," Luke said. "Julie has never asked me to quit my job."

Nick rocked his head back and forth in agreement. "Sadie, either. Why? You think Leslie had a point?"

When Reed really thought about it, no. He didn't think she had a valid point. He'd been on the job when they met, so she knew what she was getting into from the get-go. "I can't blame her for not wanting to sign on to this."

"Then she shouldn't have from the beginning," Luke said emphatically as he eased through the brush.

"There should be a clearing with a water source over this next hill," Reed said, changing the subject. "We can camp there."

"I think I can speak for Nick when I say being in a relationship in this job is a good thing as long as it's with the right woman." Luke wasn't ready to let it go.

"How so?" Reed knew all about being in relationships with the wrong ones.

Luke didn't hesitate. "Training gives you the skill set to handle any mission. A family gives you the mental edge to make sure you make it out alive. I have so much more to come home to now. I can only imagine what it'll be like when we have kids."

There was something different about Luke's voice when he said the last word. If there was a pregnancy, his quickie wedding made more sense. "Do you have something else you want to tell us?"

"Yeah."

"And you waited until we were out in the jungle before giving us a hint?"

"If Gran freaked about the wedding, what will she say about this?"

"She'll be as happy for you as we are," Nick interjected.

The image of Emily holding Hitch edged into Reed's thoughts. Something deep and possessive overtook him at the memory. He shoved it away. Because it looked a little too right in his mind. And since he'd known her for all of two weeks, it didn't make any sense to start thinking about how beautiful she'd look pregnant with his child.

He climbed to the top of the hill and looked out at the lake in front of him. The ground was level enough to make a good campsite. "There it is. Let's settle down here for a few hours."

The climb to their new location had the added benefit of giving their bodies a chance to get used to the altitude. They would need to be at their absolute physical peak when they breached the compound later.

Every step closer to that complex and Reed's determination to put an end to all this craziness grew. Whether or not he spent another day with Emily, she deserved to have her life back. "Luke, you serious about starting an agency?"

His brother's surprised smile said it all. "Yeah. Why? You interested?"

"I might be." Options were a good thing, right?

Once this case was over and Cal was behind bars where he belonged, Reed could think about doing something else for a living.

"Then, let's talk about this tomorrow morning."

Reed knew what his brother was doing. It helped with nerves to start talking about the future. Knowing they'd have one gave the mind a mental boost. "Deal."

For the rest of this day, they'd settle around their camp and wait.

EMILY WRUNG HER hands as she paced. Focusing on work was a no-go. Reading a magazine didn't provide the distraction she needed. So, she resigned herself to worry.

What if something happened to Gran? It would be all Emily's fault.

And Reed? The thought of anything happening to him was worse than a knife through the chest.

With all the FBI crawling around, a cockroach couldn't slip past unseen. She wasn't worried about herself, anyway. Reed was the one running into danger, when most people ran the opposite direction.

He was brave and strong, and everything she admired in a man. It didn't hurt that he was drop-dead hotness under his Stetson.

The thought of anything happening to the man she loved seared her. *Love?*

Did she love Reed Campbell?

Oh, yeah, her heart said. And she figured there was no use arguing. The heart knew what it wanted, and hers wanted him.

Sleep was about as close as Christmas to the month of June. Hours had passed since her usual bedtime, but it didn't matter. Hot tea did little to calm her nerves. Warm milk had similar success.

She curled under the covers and tried to remember how she'd survived the many stresses of her childhood. Easy. She'd pictured her future exactly how she wanted it to be and then worked toward it with everything in her power. There was something incredibly powerful about making a decision and then holding it strong in her mind's eye.

Maybe she could use that same approach now.

It would be a heck of a lot better than wearing a hole in the carpet.

Determined to see his face again, she took a deep breath and pictured Reed holding Hitch at the family barbecue Gran had scheduled next month to celebrate Luke and Julie's marriage.

Closing her eyes tightly, she held that image in her mind as she drifted off to sleep.

THE AIR WAS still, the monkeys quiet.

Reed looked from one brother to another. "Give me a minute?"

They nodded and walked away, each in a separate direction. Apparently, he wasn't the only one with a ritual for when he intentionally put himself into harm's way.

This was the time he went into his private zone where he took a moment to think about his loved ones and re-committed himself to getting back to them safely. No way would he allow the only fathers he'd ever known, Nick and Luke, to be without their brother. Emily's face invaded his thoughts, too. He had every intention of seeing her again...the way her face flushed pink with desire when he kissed her. The feel of her soft skin underneath his rough hands. Her strength under adversity. And her smile. Those were things to get home to.

Reed moved back to the edge of the lake. Anything happened and they had a place to stay the night. They could carry an injured man this far without too much effort.

Every mission had to have a backup plan. With only three of them on an unsanctioned assignment, they had only each other to depend on. There'd be no Blackhawk if this thing went south.

First Luke returned, then Nick.

Reed performed a final check of their emergency supplies, shouldered his pack and put on his night-vision goggles. His cell was on vibrate, but communication back home was pretty much dead for now.

The compound was an hour's hike. They'd given themselves plenty of time to adjust to the altitude and hydrate for the trip. The mission had been timed to perfection. It was three o'clock in the morning. They'd reach the compound around four. They had roughly twenty minutes to locate the target and then drag his butt out of there.

A Jeep would pick them up at the original campsite at five thirty to take them to a waiting plane, which would be fueled and ready to go.

Dueño's actual place would be more difficult to reach. He'd built the small mansion in a valley that was flat, affording tall mountain views on all sides. Nature's perfect barrier. So, Reed would have to climb up and down to reach the place.

Based on intel, there were enough men with guns surrounding the nine-foot-high concrete fence to guard the president, all of whom were inside. Under the cover of night, Reed was confident they could make it down the side of the mountain undetected. Getting inside the gates would be a different story.

The hike was quiet, save for the soft steps behind him. Anyone else would have to strain to hear them. Reed could sense his brothers' movements. Years of playing in the trees long past dark on the ranch had honed their skills.

Luke was probably the most quiet of the trio. His military training had most likely kicked in at this point, and Reed hoped it didn't bring back bad memories.

At the peak of the last incline, a breeze carried voices from below. Reed made a mental note of how easily sounds traveled, and forged ahead.

The compound came into view as soon as he peaked. To say it was huge was an understatement. They'd seen it from a satellite picture, and yet the photo didn't do it justice.

Clearly, someone important lived here. A man like Dueño, someone with his power, would make his home in something like this. Crazy that a jerk like him made money hurting women.

The image of Emily when Reed had found her stamped his thoughts. She was beaten and vulnerable but not defeated. Dueño might have hurt her physically, but she'd made it clear that's all he could do.

From what Reed could see, coming in from the south, as they were, was still the best option. He'd wait for Luke's signal to continue.

Two thumbs-up, the sign to descend, came a minute later from Luke.

With each step down, Reed's temper flared. He'd become a master at controlling his emotions, and yet, getting closer to the man who'd hurt Emily, who had her running for her life, kept his mood just below boiling.

He'd enjoy hauling this guy's butt to the States, where he could be properly arrested.

Twenty more steps and they'd be at the concrete fence.

Luke popped over first. Then came the signal. Reed followed next, then Nick.

Crouched low, Reed moved behind the first guard.

With one quick jab, the guy was knocked unconscious. Reed pulled a rope from his bag and then tied and gagged the guy to his post just in case he woke before they'd finished.

They didn't have a lot of time.

It took another five minutes to locate the window of the room where the target was believed to be sleeping. A curtain blew in and out with the breeze. With all this security around, the guy didn't feel the need to close his windows. That was the first lucky thing Reed had encountered so far.

In his experience, a man got two, maybe three lucky

breaks on a mission. The op had to be planned to a T. Reed pulled on his face mask, giving the signal for the others to follow. When their masks were secure, he opened the tear gas canister and placed it on the sill. The gas wouldn't hurt anyone inside in case there were children, but it would disorient and confuse anyone who breathed it.

Reed pulled himself up and slipped inside. He rolled the canister toward the center of the room. Plumes of gray smoke expanded and filled the room. Before he could signal his brothers, a fist came out of nowhere. He took a hit to the face, dislodging his mask. He spun around and repositioned it. As soon as he got a visual on the guard, Reed kicked the guy. The blow was so hard, he took two steps back and began coughing as the gas shrouded him. He dropped to the floor and disappeared into the haze of smoke, giving Reed enough time to motion for his brothers to join him.

As they cleared the window, the light flipped on. The room was dense with smoke. Sounds of coughing were followed by footsteps.

Reed identified three distinct voices. Luckily, none belonged to children. He moved to the bed and handcuffed the biggest body. Luke had already dispatched the guard and Nick was subduing a screaming female.

When the guy spun around to face Reed, he got a good look at him. He released a string of curse words. This wasn't Dueño.

The door burst open and several men pushed through, choking and gagging as they breached the room. Reed studied their faces. Disappointment edged in when he realized neither Cal nor Knox was there.

Were they with Dueño? On their way to find Emily?

In fact, there wasn't nearly enough security at the compound. Had they mobilized most of their men to get to her?

Reed cleared the bed and yelled to Nick that the guy wasn't there. By the time they got to Luke, bullets were flying. Whoever was shooting couldn't see clearly, either. Not exactly the ideal scenario.

They needed to get out of there. Fast.

If Dueño wasn't here, he could be anywhere in Mexico, or Texas. And where was Cal? All hopes of finding him fizzled and died. An overwhelming urge to get back to Emily hit Reed faster than a car on the expressway.

"Abort!" he shouted, but his brothers were already to the window.

Fear gripped Reed. Had they just played right into Dueño's hands?

Chapter Eighteen

Emily jolted awake to the sound of glass being cut. Oh, God. She heard movement in the other room. She threw her covers off, hopped out of bed and grabbed the lamp on the bedside table. Her mind clicked through possibilities as she reached for her phone and shouted for help.

"Who's there? Somebody help." A shaky finger managed to touch the name of the supervisor she'd been given to call in an emergency on her phone.

Three men stormed her bedroom. Three guns pointed at her. Three voices shouted orders at her.

Adrenaline pumped through her. She could lie down and let them take her, or go out fighting. If she could stall long enough, maybe someone would hear her. She shouted again. Why wasn't he coming through that door?

Let the men with bandannas covering their faces take her and she might as well already be dead.

The first one rushed toward her, and the others followed suit. For a split second, she thought they looked like a bird formation. Emily reared back, grabbed the lamp and swung it toward the first man with everything inside her.

He took a hit hard enough for blood to spurt from his nose. Except the other two men were already there, grabbing her, before she could wind up and swing again. One jerked the lamp out of her hands.

The first man cursed bitterly, and she knew there'd be a consequence for her actions later. That didn't stop her from kicking another one in the groin. He bent forward but didn't loosen his grip.

With one man on each side of her and another behind, she was forced into the living room at the same time the front door burst open.

At least six men wearing vests marked SWAT surged inside the door, stopping the moment they saw the gun pointed at her temple.

"Stop or she's dead," one of the men said in broken English. "And we already took care of him."

The SWAT team didn't lower their weapons, but they didn't move, either.

A little piece of her heart wished it had been Reed storming through that door. Another broke for the officer they'd disposed of because of her. It would be too late because the men already had her. They'd torture and kill her once they got her to a secure location. But she wished she could see him one last time. She shut her eyes and tried to conjure up the details of his face, his intense and beautiful brown eyes. The sharp curve of his jaw. Hair so dark it was almost black.

If she concentrated, maybe his face would be the last thing she remembered.

Emily didn't open her eyes again until she was outside, being shoved toward a white van. By this time, officers were everywhere and she could imagine how helpless they felt. They'd sworn to protect, and the ones she'd met so far took that oath seriously.

It wasn't their fault. Not one had a shot with the way they'd used her as cover.

Dueño was powerful enough that if he got her to the border, it would be over. American law enforcement had no jurisdiction in Mexico. Without cooperation from the Mexican government, she'd be left defenseless.

Emily kicked the man in front of her. He spun around and smacked her so hard she thought her eyeball might pop out. Could she move out of the way enough for one of the SWAT officers to get a clean shot? It'd take more than that since one of the other two could shoot her.

No way would the officers risk her life.

Dread settled heavy on her shoulders as they forced her to move.

The van was only a few steps away, blocking the view of officers surrounding the ranch.

Let these men get her inside the vehicle… Game over. There'd be no cavalry.

She reared her right foot back again ready to deliver another blow, but it was caught this time. Twisting her body left to right like a washing machine, she struggled to break their grasps, to do anything that might give officers a line of sight to get off a shot and take down her captors.

The barrel of a gun pressed to her head. "Keep at it, bitch, and we'll shoot."

Why hadn't they already? Dueño must want her alive. She could only imagine the tortures he had planned for her. A shudder ran through her.

Even so, she'd pushed it as far as she could. Hopelessness pressed heavy on her chest as she was thrown into the back of the van. Her head slammed against the seat and something wet trickled down her forehead.

Pain roared through her body. Her injuries had been healing nicely until now. Being thrown around and kicked awakened her aches. But none of the physical pain was worse than the hole in her heart.

One of the men sat on top of her, his weight an anchor being tossed to the depths of the ocean.

"There. Now she won't move." His laugh was like fingers on a chalkboard, scraping down her spine.

He bounced, pressing her body against the seat so hard she thought her ribs might crack. She cried out in pain.

"Don't hurt her. Dueño wants her alive," the driver, a white man, said as he gunned the engine.

"I'm not killing her. But she deserves a little pain after breaking my nose." His words came out through gritted teeth, slow and laced with anger.

The emptiness of her life caused the first tears to roll down her cheeks as a stark realization hit her. She didn't fear death. She was only sorry for the life she'd led. Too many times she'd let her demons stop her from pushing herself out of her comfort zone. Her fear of ending up broke and needing some man to save her pushed her to spend too much time at work and too little with people she cared about. And whom did she really care about?

Of course, she loved her mom and siblings. But who else had she let inside her life?

Sobs racked her shoulders.

"Make her shut up," the driver said.

Chapter Nineteen

"What the hell do you mean they got her?" Reed fisted his hands as he glared at Luke. Their plane wouldn't land for another hour. "Have all airports and security check-points at the border been sealed?"

"Yes. And for what it's worth, I'm sorry, little bro." Anguish darkened Luke's eyes. "As you know, there are only a few places they can cross the border—"

"Legally. But this guy has more channels than cable TV." Whatever they'd done to Emily before would be nothing compared with the torture they'd dish out now. Reed cursed.

"I just spoke to the pilot. Our flight has been diverted to Laredo. There are only so many routes they can take to get to the border."

"That's true." Reed thought about it long and hard. Which highway in Texas would they take? Or was that too easy? "He expects everyone to be watching for him in Texas, so he won't risk it. Can you talk to the pilot, have him take us to El Paso instead?"

"I'm on it," Luke said as he made a move toward the cabin.

Reed leaned back in his seat and tried to stem the onset of a raging headache.

"We'll find her." The determination in Nick's eyes almost convinced Reed.

EMILY HAD NO idea how long they'd been driving when she heard a harsh word grunted and the screech of a hard brake. The van careened out of control and into a dangerous spin.

The next thing she knew, the van was in a death roll. The man who'd been sitting on top of her acted as a cushion, sparing her head from slamming against the ceiling now beneath them.

Emily braced herself as the van stopped. If she could get to the door while everyone was disoriented, maybe she could get away and make a run for it. She doubted there'd be anyone around to help since she hadn't heard a car pass by in hours.

She made a move to grab the handle. The Hispanic man caught her arm.

"Where do you think you're going?" he asked.

The door flew open, anyway, and there he stood. Reed. His gun was aimed at a spot on the Hispanic guy's head. Six other officers stood to each side of him.

"She's coming with me, Cal. And you're going to jail." Satisfaction lightened Reed's intense features.

Cal? The man who'd shot Reed?

Emily leaned toward him, unable to get her bearings enough to make her legs move. Or maybe they were broken because they didn't seem to want to move.

Dozens of officers moved on the men in the van, subduing them while Emily was being hauled into Reed's arms.

"I thought I lost you." The anguish in his voice nearly ripped out her heart.

"You can't get rid of me that easily, Campbell." She wrapped her arms around his neck.

He tightened his arms around her. "How badly are you hurt?"

"I'm shaken up, but I'll be okay." She tested her legs. Much to her relief, they worked fine. Adrenaline was fading, causing her to shake harder. Glancing around, all she could see was barren land. "Where am I?"

"In New Mexico. About five minutes from the Mexican border."

Reed held her so close she could hear his heart beat as wildly as her own. Relief flooded her.

"And that's the guy who shot you?" She motioned toward Cal.

"Yeah."

"I understand if you want to be the one to cuff him."

"I'm exactly where I want to be."

"And your brothers?"

"They're following a car we believe Dueño is in. We've been watching the caravan for an hour, waiting for it to split up so we could make a move. I knew Dueño wouldn't risk drawing too much attention so close to the border. He spread his men out and we made our move." His cell buzzed. He fished it from his pocket, keeping one arm secure around her waist, and then glanced from the screen to her. "It's Luke."

Reed said a few uh-huhs into the phone before ending the call. "Dueño got away. And they can't find him. Knox was driving. He's under arrest."

A helicopter roared toward them, hovering over him. If the officers shot it down, innocent lives would be lost. Reed tucked Emily behind him and moved to cover.

The chopper landed in a field, kicking up a tornado of dust.

"I have to distract him or he'll get away."

Reed caught Emily's elbow as she tried to pass him. His anger nearly scorched her skin. "I won't let you do this."

"It's the only way. If I can get him out in the open, maybe one of the guys can get a shot."

"A man who hides behind women and children won't risk being exposed." Reed stepped in between Emily and the chopper, weapon leveled and ready.

Movement to her left caught Emily's eye. She made a move to let Reed know, but his gun had already been redirected.

"Stop moving and put your hands where I can see them," Reed demanded.

"Put down your weapon and I'll consider it," Dueño said. The sound of his voice sent an icy chill down Emily's back.

"Always looking for the advantage, aren't you?"

"What would you do if you were in my position?"

"That's where you're wrong. I'm nothing like you. I'd never be in your position."

Dueño spun toward them, a flash of metal in his hand.

Fire exploded from Reed's gun first. Dueño took a few steps toward them, and then dropped to the ground. SWAT had already mobilized, taking down the pilot.

"We did it," Emily said. Relief and joy filled her soul as Reed's arms wrapped around her, pulling her body flush with his.

"You're safe now."

"When they abducted me, my worst fear wasn't dying. It was that I'd never see you again. I love you, Reed. I want to be with you, even though I know you'll never fully trust anyone who isn't a Campbell." She'd said it, and the heaviness on her chest released. Like a butterfly breaking free from its cocoon, flapping its wings for the very first time. He didn't have to say it back for happiness to engulf her. She loved him. And she wanted him to know.

His intense gaze pierced her for a long moment. "We can change that, you know."

"Change what?" she parroted.

"Your last name." Holding her gaze, right there, he bent down on one knee.

"I've always been a logical man, believing everything had a place and a time, and had to make sense. Until the day I met you. From that moment, I knew there was something different about you. I was in love. I love you. And the only thing that makes sense to me now is to grab hold with both hands, and hang on with everything I have. Will you do me the honor of becoming my wife?"

Tears of joy streamed down Emily's face as she said the one word she knew Reed needed to hear. "Yes."

"I've been talking about it with my brothers and we've decided to open a P.I. business together in Creek Bend. I want to be around for you. And I promise to love and protect you for the rest of my life." He rose to his feet, never breaking eye contact, and pulled her into a warm embrace.

In his arms, Emily had found her permanent family, she'd found exactly where she belonged. She'd found home.

* * * * *

MILLS & BOON®

First Time in Forever

Following the success of the Snow Crystal trilogy,
Sarah Morgan returns with the sensational
Puffin Island trilogy. Follow the life, loss and
love of Emily Armstrong in the first instalment,
as she looks for love on Puffin Island.

Pick up your copy today!

Visit
www.millsandboon.co.uk/Firsttime

MILLS & BOON®
INTRIGUE
Romantic Suspense

A SEDUCTIVE COMBINATION OF DANGER AND DESIRE

A sneak peek at next month's titles...

In stores from 20th February 2015:

- **The Deputy's Redemption** – Delores Fossen
  and **The Pregnant Witness** – Lisa Childs

- **Secrets** – Cynthia Eden
  and **The Ranger** – Angi Morgan

- **Seduced by the Sniper** – Elizabeth Heiter
  and **Deception Lake** – Paula Graves

Romantic Suspense

- **A Real Cowboy** – Carla Cassidy
- **The Marine's Temptation** – Jennifer Morey

Available at WHSmith, Tesco, Asda, Eason, Amazon and Apple

Just can't wait?
Buy our books online a month before they hit the shops!
visit www.millsandboon.co.uk

These books are also available in eBook format!